Advance Praise for *The Long Season*

"Michael Vance Gurley spins a tale full of stolen glances, lustful yearnings, and frozen pucks. Strap on your skates, pick up your stick, and get ready for the ride of a lifetime. There's never been a gay hockey love story like this!"
—David Henry Sterry, bestselling author of *Chicken*

"*The Long Season* is a fast-paced, interesting read, with layered, likable characters and a clever historical spin on the traditional gay coming-of-age novel. Well worth your time!"
—Bart Yates, author of *Leave Myself Behind* and *The Brothers Bishop*

Visit us at www.boldstrokesbooks.com

THE LONG SEASON

by

Michael Vance Gurley

A Division of Bold Strokes Books

2016

THE LONG SEASON

ISBN 13: 978-1-62639-655-5

This Trade Paperback Original Is Published By
Bold Strokes Books, Inc.
P.O. Box 249
Valley Falls, NY 12185

First Edition: June 2016

CREDITS
Editor: Jerry L. Wheeler
Production Design: Stacia Seaman
Cover Photos and Graphic Design by Jason Burian
Cover Design by Jeanine Henning

Acknowledgments

Thank you to all of my parents, biological, step, and in-law—Joe Gurley, Betty and Jim Green, and Bill and Kim Burian; my supportive brother Charles Gurley; my hockey brother Bageera Taylor; Arielle Eckstut and David Henry Sterry, because winning their Pitchapalooza contest thrust me extraordinarily forward; my editor, Jerry Wheeler, for his control of anachronism and timing, which are different things; all the incomparable folks at Bold Strokes Books, for taking a chance; Scott Smith, Vince Firpo, Kathryn Siddiqui, Sara Allen, and Kristin Bolf, for their hours in and out of critique group; authors Bart Yates, Robin Reardon, and JH Trumble, for advice; renowned children's author Andrea Beaty, whose support is priceless and because she's the only person I know whose book went to space; the hot jazz station that was my writing partner; Uncle James (JE) Gurley, horror writer and wisdom giver; Robert J Hudecek, whose belief in me and humanity humbles; and mostly Jason Burian for the cover and for saying yes.

There are countless people who have guided me, whether they meant to or not, and all of the mistakes and triumphs make me believe that I'm standing exactly where I'm supposed to be. I would be remiss not to thank the roster of the 1926–27 Chicago Black Hawks, all the other Chicagoans, and other teams whose lives inspired these pages. I borrowed them for a while, altered them or filled gaps that history created. I hope they are not unhappy with and won't haunt me for it.

PROLOGUE

Champagne splashed all over the walls of the dingy, electric-lamp-lined tunnel that snaked to the locker room. It kept getting in my eyes, burning them, causing me to blink and tear up as we made our way back to the relative safety our den provided. Everyone was screaming, grabbing and hugging each other as we crashed into the little room that had become our home away from home. This wasn't supposed to be in the cards for us. It wasn't supposed to happen. But none of that mattered to me, and all the bubbly in the world couldn't have distracted me from keeping steadfast vigil on the door, hoping against hope he wouldn't come.

The dank dressing area reeked like five-day-old salmon thanks to our sweat-drenched, woolen hockey sweaters, used socks, and spilled hooch. The stench, the closeness of the room, and the rapid drumbeat of the blood pumping in my ears made it hard to focus.

Each time the door opened and a new reveler entered, swinging his boater wildly about him, my heart dropped into my stomach and beads of sweat popped up across my forehead. The taste of bile nearly caused me to double over and vomit. What if they all knew what had really just happened? Or more importantly, what if they knew what we were told to do and why? My dirty little secret.

Percy, one of the big defensemen, grabbed me in a headlock and started laughing and throwing me around in a horrific parody of the Charleston. "Brett! We did it!" he shouted to me, to no one, maybe to all of us. I struggled wildly, my lungs pumping without catching breath, desperate to break free. I finally slipped away from his grasp to catch a panicked glimpse toward the doorway, but no one was there. If he had come, I would know.

Suddenly, the door opened again, and he appeared, shoulder pads filling the doorway, eliminating all thoughts of escape. He took giant steps into the room, the heavily padded legs of a goaltender swinging out widely in large semicircles as he charged forward. On the ice, he had been graceful and moved deftly. On cement, he lumbered across the floor, his skates clacking each step, but I still didn't have enough time.

The joyous locker room cheers fell silent in that single moment. Someone had let go of a foolish-looking beaded headband pulled off some woman in the stands, and it drifted to the floor in slow, sweeping arcs. Once the first person had seen him bolting into our sacred place wearing that rival bright maroon and white sweater in our locker room, an enemy behind the lines, I knew there would soon be horrible violence. One way or the other, things would never be the same.

Before words could form on anyone's lips, he had pointed his finger toward me and screamed. "You!"

The madness of the moment must have affected my hearing, because when he screamed, I swore his voice became a thunder-cracking chorus of angry angels ready to pass judgment. Sweat dripped off his fingers, taped from being broken this way and that during the many years he had stopped the puck with nothing but worn leather padding between his hand and the speeding rubber.

Jean-Paul leapt forward leading with a haymaker, clobbering the intruder hard across the side of the head, cutting his face. Blood splattered against the wall. Men sprang forward from every nook and cranny of the locker room to pull them apart, holding them relatively still.

Blood flowing from the nasty cut above his brow pooled at the bottom of his chin. His tight jaw shook with rage, the droplets of blood swaying back and forth, hanging for impossible seconds.

The roaring sound filling my ears, making it impossible to think, suddenly stopped. I could see and hear clearly. It all came into sharp focus. Our captain held up his long arms, the lone sheriff keeping the lynch mob at bay. The entire team had gathered in the center of our locker room, surrounding this stranger at the gates, hungry for a reason to explode. The intruder's face turned into a contorted, sickening version of itself, his finger pointed directly at me. It was almost over.

The intruder was about to destroy my entire universe with a single word. My breath caught in my throat. Would it be the next word he said out loud? Would I hear it as breaking glass or a shallow whimper? Tears had sprung from the corners of my reddened eyes, bile gurgled in the pit of my stomach. The captain put a hand up for everyone to be quiet, turned to the man, and said, "You'd better tell us what you're doing in here, right now!"

The man took a deep breath, caught the panic in my eyes, grinned, and began to speak.

CHAPTER ONE

September 7, 1926
Milwaukee, WI

The harsh ring of the wooden phone case hanging on the wall brought the room to attention. "Uh-huh. Yep. All right." The coach hung up the phone receiver, turning to us to see expectancy on our faces. "You're behind the eight ball today." The coach laughed, his ruddy face shining across the room, belly that was once hard bobbing up and down like an apple in a barrel on Halloween. "Betta look sharp and step lively or them scouts're gonna pass you by." The locker room sprang to life, noisy with nervous excitement.

Scouts. In a shrinking league, their all-powerful judgment meant everything. Life and death to us hopefuls, whether we languish here banging the boards for pennies, playing on one backwater team or another, or something more. I don't mean to disparage the Marauders. I don't know what I'd have done if my old coach hadn't called in a favor with an old pal.

"Boys, when it's me, I'm gonna get a shoeblack to pretty up my Oxfords every day!" Mickey MacKay, one of the boys who was nice to me, dreamed aloud.

"He's rollin' in it now!" Everyone roared.

"And how!" another boy exclaimed.

"I bet anyone here a fin I'll be the first to score today!" another fella boasted.

"They ain't gonna give you a second look after they give me the up and down!" Mickey continued. The boys were all jawing about who was going to score the most goals and who would block the most shots. All except for me. I couldn't even think about what it would mean to get picked up by a big team. Hell, I had just started here and was still trying to get used to hockey beginning in September. We didn't have indoor ice hockey back home in Delavan, Wisconsin, so we couldn't play until December most years.

When they came in, everybody paid heed. They wore shiny cap-toed shoes, their ankles covered in white spats that slapped the ground as they walked. With their dark fedoras shading their eyes and sharp, dark woolen suits contrasting those shoes, they resembled gangsters.

The scouts made a short stop in the locker room to see the coach, but none of them spoke to us at all. They were gone to their seats as quick as they had come, leaving a room full of anxious people worried about their futures. We should have been focusing on the game at hand.

When the scouts split, the team captain Billy added his two cents in his usual nice way. "You bums better be hard boiled today, playing with all you got if you want to make it to the big time, with the way things are."

"What do you mean?" I asked, instantly feeling stupid and regretting my words before they stopped reverberating off the walls like a horrible echo that wouldn't fade. He laughed at me, shooting me a glare that said he thought I had rocks banging around between my ears.

"What a chump, eh, fellas?" someone said, poking fun at my expense.

"You don't get it, do you, Blondie?" he scorned, swatting my head forward from behind, knocking my dirty blond hair—the hair that brought a bunch of girlie nicknames my way—over my eyes. It actually got my goat every time someone taunted me about it, but getting the captain's dander up wasn't the best choice for the new guy on a team, so I usually swallowed it. Hard.

"The chances of getting picked for a big team like Toronto or Montreal…slim to none, what with all them leagues collapsing," Billy continued in a belittling schoolmarm voice. "There are a lot of professional hockey leagues that didn't make it—"

"I know, lay off, I just forgot," I pled, trying to make him stop, feeling foolish.

Billy just looked at me with cold derision before continuing on, ignoring my interruption. "Like I was saying, up through last year several of them fell, like the Western Hockey League and the Western Canadian. Who else is gone?" he asked the crowd of followers like the teacher he was pretending to be, cocking his smile toward me the whole time.

"The Central Professional," someone answered, trying to impress Billy.

"Pacific Coast and the National Hockey Association." Each league mentioned stung like a slap in the face for having said anything in the first place.

"All right, I said lay off, would ya?" I whined.

All those players from those teams were flat busted and scrambling for work. It was frightening how the National League owned most of what was left, including the Stanley Cup, which represented the most prestigious, the most honored of all sports trophies. Scouts came around once a year to all the farm teams to look for prospects but contracts were scarce. I knew all this, yet the eighteen-year-old idiot inside me talked for me sometimes. I couldn't win.

Ever since I arrived in Milwaukee a week ago, big eyed and hopeful, things proved different than I expected. People were different. Back home, I had been the star of the team, the supposed golden boy with friends, even though I'm actually shy and never felt like I fit in, for my own reasons. Here, Billy had been beating his gums at me, razzing me, trying to get me to challenge him to a fight. He made sure I knew it would take more than playing skills to unseat him as the leader of the pack. He made me edgy whenever he was around, and he was always around. I loathed him.

I'm generally not the guy who asks for center stage, even when my involvement in sports drew people to me and got me whatever I wanted along with some things I didn't. Out there on the ice, out there things are different. Billy didn't really mean anything by it anyway. At least that's what I kept telling myself when he continued to give me the business about how I'd never make it.

He was wrong. I had to make it. Getting to the big leagues wasn't just my dream, after all. My mother wanted it badly, saying, "You could skate before you could even walk." It's like a tired cliché, and it wasn't true. As best as I could tell, it wasn't even possible. But my mother always said it. Sometimes I wondered if she was expressing pride or something else.

Once I scored my first goal, there was no turning back for my father, either. It was constantly drilled into my head—not in any way that could be mistaken as having a choice in the matter—that I was going to be the world's greatest hockey player. Some days, I even believed it.

Billy continued to rub salt in my wounds, and that's when it started.

While sitting in the locker room before the game, thinking about scouts, big leagues, and what my father would say if I didn't make it, my nerves started acting up like they sometimes did. I started counting things, eyes darting back and forth over whatever I was counting. It doesn't matter what it is that gets counted, or whether I count in single digits or escalating numbers. It just gets stuck in my head and I can't stop. One, two, three, four, as the count of the people sitting on benches went up. Then twenty-four, twenty-two, twenty as the skates were taken from the cubbies by each of the guys. There I was, staring into space unable to count to any conclusions, heart racing faster and faster, eyes welling in pain. This thing became an unstoppable monster in my head.

I started doing that as a little kid, and nobody seemed to know what it was or how to cure it. My face hurt from the jaw clenching I did while I counted things over and over, like a grinding and gnashing. Shit! I hated when it happened, and it happened way too often. Sometimes it was an endless circle, and I could never count my way to a stopping point, exhausting all my energy.

Even though the pills the doctor back home had prescribed for nerves made me groggy, I clasped the bottle in my pants pocket in the cubby. I started to bring it out, but the pills rattled in the bottle and I started counting pills in my head, reflecting on totals minus how many I took. Mickey pushed by Billy while I was in the middle of another run of numbers. He smacked me square on the back.

"Rate a game like you did against Madison the other day and, Brett, my friend…" He trailed off when he reached for his skates. A good whack on the back like that snapped me out of my head. I released my hold on the bottle and left the pills in my pants pocket where they continued to taunt me. I did not start counting again, however, using the movement to push myself up. I couldn't wait to get out on the ice, where that sort of thing never happened.

Coming out of the dark tunnel into the stadium, I heard the bustling sounds of the crowd. Hearing the people clapping and talking with excitement for their home team wound me up. Truth be told, it didn't matter if we were the home team or not. I just loved the feel of the game. The folks in the crowd in the big city were different than those back home, who all knew the players. These people were dressed in their Sunday best, big bright hats on the ladies, many of the men shouting out at each other in cheer or boast. They were businessmen, laborers, wives, rich and poor, all swirled together. More or less. The high cost of a ticket, five whole cents, kept most away.

I scanned the arena looking for the scouts. With all the faces in the crowd, it seemed silly to try to find them because the stadium was one of the biggest in Wisconsin. It held fifteen hundred people. After a tense minute or so looking, I finally spotted them behind our own players' bench, all sitting together, roster sheets in hand.

Stanley Garret, the owner of the Milwaukee Marauders, was sitting with them, smoking some giant Cuban cigar that smelled up the whole area. I knew it was a Cuban because he bragged about them to anyone who would listen. One of the scouts had these intense eyes that drilled each of us as we stepped onto the ice.

For a second, the idea of trying to do some fancy footwork to show off as soon as I took the ice popped into my head. But what if I tripped up and fell? That would definitely leave a lasting impression they could talk about on their train ride home. Finished before it even started. No thanks. I played it safe.

When my skates touched the ice, the wind brushed my face and ruffled my hair with each stride, and right then I could have cared less about scouts, coaches, Billy, or big league contracts. The world of ice swallowed up the shy, odd fellow I became when off it. Sometimes it grew so intoxicating, I had to force myself to remember to breathe out there. Swoosh, swoosh. That's all I could hear—the sound my skates made as they pushed through the water that formed on the ice surface.

Swoosh.

When the referee blew the whistle and dropped the puck, Billy won the face-off. He slid it right back to me as I moved up toward the middle of the ice. I didn't see any openings to skate into, so I passed it off to Mickey and headed to my spot. I called it my spot because everyone from Coach to my father had always taught me where each player should be when he has the puck and when he doesn't. As I moved past the front of the goalmouth, the boys were fighting against the boards for the puck until it popped out of the scrum. It seemed to slide right toward me as if I willed it to come to me. My stick reached out and grabbed the puck, pulling it back toward me as if it already knew what I wanted.

One of Toledo's big defensemen came charging at me. He lumbered, which made me believe that I could fake him out, deke him into moving as if I was going left when I was really going right. When the big guy committed to move with me, I quickly switched back to the other side so fast he couldn't follow, opening up a clear path to the goalie. A half step to my right, and I was alone. My eyes darted to the right as well, trying to get the goalie to think that I was going to shoot that way. When he took the bait, I shot to the left. The frozen rubber puck flew past the goalie as he reached across his body in vain.

A horn sounded somewhere high in the stadium to report the goal. I raised one hand up in celebration and let the momentum carry me forward, gliding toward my teammates. I was crushed as they skated into me without slowing, then into each other, cheering and hollering. It overjoyed me when a deke worked, which was far better than how I felt when it didn't.

I forgot the scouts were watching, and I focused on playing the game. In the second period, we were tied at one. With most of the guys heading one way toward our net, I noticed that someone had mishandled the puck. It was going to my teammate, Mickey. I pumped my feet, going down the ice, hoping he'd notice, which he did. Mickey saw me breaking away, headed for the goalie. He flipped the puck up in the air to me so that it came off the ice where no one could trap it, the pass landing flat and even. That puck slammed into my stick so hard I almost lost control of it. But I didn't. It went directly from the tape on the bottom of his hockey stick to the tape of mine just like we had practiced over and over.

I headed straight for the goalie with no other player anywhere in sight. It was a breakaway play. My heart pounded to the rhythm of my skates pushing forward. Their goalie had come out of his crease a few feet, past the painted square line around it, to challenge me for position. They almost never leave their safe zone, knowing we can't even cross their line unless we have the puck. I'd love to say I knew their goalie and had studied his style the way many of the guys did, but it'd be a lie. I just saw fear in his eyes. Having scored on him once, he knew I could do it again.

I pulled my stick back as if I was going to give it the old slammer. He dug deep to brace for it. That was when I saw what I needed to do. I flipped the puck to the backhand, causing him to move too fast across his own feet and stumble. I pushed the puck past him into the net while he sprawled out all over the ice. I would have laughed if I knew that would never be me on the ice looking like a sap. I actually felt a little bad for him. Not bad enough to stop, though.

In the next minute, I scored again when a smooth pass came from Billy and fooled the goalie. Billy might have been mean-spirited toward me almost every second of the day, but he played to win. I was able to tap it in nice and easy to bring the tally to three goals, the boys and the crowd screaming as if this game decided the Stanley Cup championships. In a way, it meant even more.

Walking to the locker room during the second intermission, I arrogantly looked up to see if the scouts were watching me. They weren't. They were talking in a tight little circle, two of them laughing like schoolkids, not even paying attention to us players. Some scouting! I hoped they had been watching us a few minutes before as I scored my third goal of the game.

Mickey slapped me on the back with an overenthusiastic heavy hand. He was short, stout, and strong. He had to be thirty, but he skated as fast as any man, his wavy blond hair flowing in the breeze. Mickey was a nice guy, if a bit boisterous and brash. He came from Canada, Quebec, I thought, which should have meant he was calmer and quieter like the rest of his countrymen were supposed to be. But he wasn't, not at all. He said it was because his people came from Scotland originally, but he sounded more like the modern city with all his slang.

"Man, that was the cat's pajamas! I practically gave you that goal, boy." He laughed real loud, and a couple of the other guys joined in, except Billy, who was scowling. Mickey's laugh was infectious, just like his personality. When he chuckled, his blue eyes would tear up, causing them to sparkle a little. The boys called him the Wee Scot, on account of his size and nationality, but his stature hid all of his raw power. I smirked a little at what he said.

Then it dawned on me. The scouts not looking at me, Billy's angry look, Mickey boasting about how he helped with my goal. The scouts thought I was being selfish with the puck. Although we were winning the game, and I had scored three goals, hockey only had so much room for showboating and grandstanding. I had to make sure that I played fairly with my teammates, so I made the decision to hand-feed them passes that were as close to perfect as possible. Sitting there thinking about it, I began to chuckle a little. If I ended up with some assist points for helping others score, it'd look good for me too, which might also make me look selfish. I had to stay away from the doubt building in my head and just play my way.

In the first few minutes of the third period, my chance came. When Mickey got the puck, we dished it back and forth to each other a few times until he finally took the shot and scored. The whole team flew over to hug him, the crowd waving its arms in the air in a giant blur. Just as we were separating, one of the enforcers from the other team clipped me in the back of the legs with the butt end of his stick. I went down like a sack of flour.

When I jumped back up, I took a swing at this big palooka. It shocked him a little. I would not claim my quick strike hurt him in any way. It simply took him by surprise, which wore off rather quickly. If we had a fight on even terms, it would be curtains for me. After all, it was his job to make players like me pay, mostly in pain, whenever he could. After the next swing at him missed, he connected with a few. Which hurt. Terribly.

Then half the Marauders' bench knocked him down and piled on his head. The mêlée allowed me to slip back away without getting murdered, which I'm sure looked real impressive to the scouts. A hockey player who skirts away from a fight? It had not been my greatest moment. The referee didn't seem to care who started it or who ran from it. He threw us both in the penalty box.

All told, I had three goals and two assists under my name on the score sheet in that game. Added to that, I also had two minutes in the penalty box for my semi-professional boxing debut. We won the game five to two. Mickey scored the other two goals, both off my passes. It was swell to help him out. Since showing up on the team, it hadn't been easy for me to make friends, friends that I actually wanted to be around. That was never my strong suit, but he was pretty good to me.

Back in the locker room, everyone seemed excited and happy the two of us had such a good showing. Surely they were worried that all of the stats had our names on them. I almost wet the front of my hockey pants in excitement when the door opened and the coach came into the locker room with the scouts. My pants were so wet from hitting the ice that no one would have noticed anyway.

"Boys, this here is Dick Irvin, Gordie Fraser, and Percy Traub," the coach said after clearing his throat. "They came all the way from Chicago to see the game today." We all just stared at them. Chicago. What team? They didn't even have a team. My brain spun around in circles, and the cogs couldn't seem to catch the gears. "I have to say they got one hell of a game at that!" The cheer went up at the high praise from our coach.

When the cheering died down, Dick, the more serious of the gangster-looking guys, said, "Fellas, you all played a good game. You know why we're here today, so I won't give you no bull." You could have heard a pin drop in the room as he drew some breath to continue.

"We have a new team down in Chicago. Most of you know that. We need some players who want to win games. We want to go all the way to the championship this year. Prove ourselves to our new city. The coach here has our list of people we want in Chicago, and it's also posted right outside on the wall. If you didn't make the list, keep playing hard and we'll see." We all looked at each other and back at him. "Well?"

The room became a stampede of bull elephants and rhinos giving Dick and Gordie and anyone else brave enough to be standing there the bum's rush. I stood in the back, waiting for the crowd to clear a little bit so I could see the list. The crowd stopped shoving each other and turned to face me.

"What?" They had me worried I had done something wrong, completely forgetting in all the rush what we were desperately trying to look at. Then I saw Billy's face, and I knew what had happened. He looked at me, his eyes a well of pain so profound it could stop your heart. For all the anger he spread around, I stayed my shock for a second to feel for him.

"Oh my God," I said finally.

Tacked on the wall, hanging at a slight angle, was a single crisp, off-white sheet of paper that read: *Brett Bennet. Mickey MacKay. Thank you.* My heart stopped working for a full minute. Then as quickly as it started, the silence ended with whoops and hollers from Mickey jumping up and down with me in his arms.

"Brett, I'm a man that pays his debts, and that's on the square." When he paused a second to collect himself, I thought he was going to cry. I started to tear up, either from the sentiment or the excitement. He continued, "We're pals now for sure! I know that some of those shots were yours to take, and you gave 'em up to me. I appreciate it something awful, and I'll be there whenever you need me. I don't skip out. Chicago, here we come!" It must have slipped my mind to tell him that passing the puck didn't exactly make me look bad either.

I thought the other boys would poke fun at me for crying, but I just couldn't help it. It had been too intense a day, such a great game, and now this. And it was happening for Mickey too? The other players didn't razz us at all, but they didn't congratulate us much either. They just disappeared into themselves, keeping busy with the tasks of putting away equipment and clothes. I'd like to think I understood them. I don't know how I'd deal with not seeing my name up on that wall. My tears weren't just little ones that were easy to wipe away, either.

CHAPTER TWO

September 8, 1926
Chicago, IL

Chicago was nothing like Milwaukee.

I didn't get to see any of its urban sprawl from the train's windows, asleep and drooling on myself. The nerve pill I had taken to deal with the unbearable counting of the railroad spars knocked me unconscious. I felt terribly small as I stepped out of the enormous Union Station train depot into the dirty streets with everything I owned shoved into my one bag. These giant metal monstrosities blotted out the sky above. They were immense but ornate, with scary stone gargoyles perched on their tops. Milwaukee had skyscrapers of its own, but Chicago stacked them one after another, stretching out as far as the eye could see. The sun poking through the clouds gleamed off the tall windows in the sky, going upward forever.

The city smelled too. Not bad, really. It just had this mixture that was hard to place, except for the train smoke. Judging by the construction workers and building materials all inside and around the station, the city was in a state of constant growth. The air was filled with the din of sledgehammers striking metal and workers yelling to be heard.

I must have looked like a country bumpkin, but back home we didn't have so many different motorcars and trucks. Milwaukee had some, but this was entirely different, this chaos in motion roaring by, its tires blasting water up from puddles and ruts over the sidewalks. People yelped as they jumped back out of the way of the splashing sludge, which seemed to be a mix of dirt, grime, coal dust, and rain.

"What'd I tell ya, pal?" Mickey said, slapping my back, which caused me to stumble forward toward the oncoming traffic. He smiled with this giant, toothy grin I found hard to ignore and even harder to resist as he reached his hand out to help me step back up on the curb. He had a ruggedly handsome way about him. This, along with his particular kind of charm, led some ladies to his side. His short body and solid muscles made him awfully strong, which I felt as he hoisted me up out of the street. I would hate to run into him when he was in a bad mood.

"It's…big."

"It's big. It's big? That's all you have to say?" Mickey looked up at one of the sky-eating buildings. "We are going to take this city by storm. All the rumble's gonna be 'bout us, buddy. Wait till the ladies get a load of my mug."

I grimaced. "Uh-huh."

"Oh, poor boy, don't be jealous. I'm sure the dames'll love you too," he said, ruffling my hair a little too aggressively for my taste.

"Let's go find the Coliseum offices," I said to change the subject. "I really want to get this squared away." I had been feeling this gnawing at the bottom of my belly since we left Milwaukee. I worried the guys in the main offices here were going to rescind the offer, if that's what it was. We weren't sure if we would have a tryout. They were going to take one look at this country boy and laugh me back to a bus because they weren't going to pay for a train ticket home.

"You worry way too much, Brett," Mickey said as he walked away from me toward the next corner, gesturing wildly at both sides of the street. "This is my city now. Everything is going to be just—"

"Jake. I heard," I finished for him. Mickey never seemed to run out of things to say. From what I could tell as I passed in and out of consciousness on the train, he talked all the way to Chicago. I recalled him saying that everything would be jake quite often. A skeptic, I protested. He waved away any concerns I had with the swat of one of his powerful hands.

"Yes sir, partner. It's gonna be just jake," he said, oblivious to my attempt at exposing his overuse of that word. "It will. You just wait and…hey, let's catch that hack!"

The cab ride to the Coliseum cost twenty whole cents, entirely too expensive considering the state of my affairs. The filthy yellow four-door taxi bumped and banged us around so much my ribs felt like they were going to pop right out of my shirt. Every time we hit a pothole, my window glass slammed down inside the door. I tried to roll it up and hold it in place until the next crash to no avail.

The cabbie was a heavyset man about fifty, with a bushy black beard. He was smoking a giant cigar that smelled awful. What is it with cigars? He kept blowing the smoke up over his shoulder so it wafted right into the backseat, and, of course, into my face. I coughed discreetly a few times, hoping he'd get the point. He didn't. Mickey didn't seem to notice, either.

"What are you two going to the Coliseum for? There ain't nothing going on there today," the cabbie yelled back at us through clouds of grey haze.

Mickey's face became a huge grin. "Mac, you are looking at the two newest stars in Chicago. In a month, you'll be asking for our autographs." This was embarrassing. Surely this cabbie was about to pull over to kick these two lunatics out right in the middle of who knows where. He looked us both over, scowled, and turned back to face the road, not even slowing down.

"You sure ain't dressed like no stars." We had to admit he was right. We looked so shabby compared to the wealthy with their shopping bags full from Marshall Field's or those other fancy places on State Street. Mickey continued to smile and gawk at the city moving by us at thirty bumpy miles an hour.

"Fourteenth and Wabash," the cabbie said with finality as he screeched up to the curb. Then he made some wisecrack about us being royalty or stars or something. He might have said other things to us, but I got caught off guard by the building and didn't quite hear him.

"The. Cat's. Pa-ja-mas!" Mickey exclaimed, accentuating each syllable.

We stood in front of quite possibly the most impressive building I'd ever seen. The Chicago Coliseum, a massive structure that spanned blocks on the south side of the city along Wabash Avenue, might not have been as tall as the downtown skyscrapers, but it outclassed them all. The first thing to grab my eye was the grand red roof cascading all across the building's many peaks and valleys. The building resembled an enormous medieval castle, like the kind I'd read about in history books.

The front of the building had this Big Ben–like clock tower on it. It was a red brick color, but lighter than the roof of the main building, which was a deeper, vibrant red tile. The white stones of the main building were rounded at the tops of the many turret-shaped towers, the kind you could imagine Rapunzel dropping her hair from for the prince to climb. The giant windows at the top looked bigger than our whole house back home.

A well-dressed businessman in a suit apologized after he bumped into me, waking me from my dreamlike daze. I had been walking around in circles with my head tilted up to see the whole of it. Mickey grabbed my arm and led me to the front doors where he knocked loudly. After a few minutes of uncomfortable silence, we heard this soft, faraway clomping noise that steadily grew louder. The whole thing made me think a butler was about to open a little hatch window above the door to ask us what business we had with the king.

The door swung open. An older, paunchy gentleman dressed in a blue security guard uniform stood there, looking as if we had interrupted something important. "How can I help you young men?" he asked in a formal tone.

"We're the newest stars for this here team, and—" Mickey began before I could shove him to make him stop acting like a horse's ass.

"Sir, we are here to see Mr. Muldoon. He sent for—"

"Not here," the security guard said, interrupting me. "The help gains entrance to the Coliseum through the service doors in the back."

"Listen, old-timer—"

I interrupted Mickey again and tried to tell the guard we were not the help. He ignored me, again instructing us to go around to the back. He pointed toward the right side of the building, then went back inside and closed the door with a reverberating clang.

CHAPTER THREE

The back of the building was just as huge as the front, but not nearly as ornate. It was covered with plain brick, as if they'd spent so much money on the front they didn't have enough left to do the back. We walked past the discarded wooden crates that cluttered the backside of the building, and we found the open service doors. We entered a small room with low ceilings and long hallways on either side.

Since we didn't see anyone around and no signs to speak of, we decided to go to the right. After a long walk, fruitlessly looking for the office or even the locker room area, we smelled it before we could see it: that familiar odor of the men's locker room, filled with ripe sweat and stale clothes desperately in need of a good washing.

Behind the door, people were laughing and hollering at each other. We went through to find the entire hockey team getting changed into their civilian clothes, obviously finishing up after a practice. None of the players paid any attention to us, acting like it was an everyday occurrence to have strangers traipse into their locker area while they were half-naked. It was a strange thing to even be in the locker room of a bona fide professional hockey team, and not some second-rate dopes. They remained unaffected. My biggest moment was just another Wednesday for these guys.

I didn't know any of their names. I'd never been to a professional hockey game. I had read about the games in the sports pages of the newspapers and occasionally listened to some on the radio down at Mr. Halston's drugstore. He was awful nice to us kids, letting us listen as long we bought penny candies to eat. If at least some of the faces and names were familiar, it might have gone a bit easier, I thought. Instead I came off sounding like a schoolkid looking for an autograph.

"Ex...excuse me." The meek will inherit the earth. "Can someone tell us where we can find Coach Muldoon's office?" No one bothered to look up. I asked again.

"Beat it!"

Undeterred, I was just about to tap someone on the shoulder to ask again when Mickey started bellowing. "What we have here, fellas, is a ground-floor opportunity to get in good with the newest stars of this here hockey club. It's gonna run on all eight now for sure." This ridiculousness stopped everyone in the room. Every single man stared at us. This was just how I didn't want to start. After a few seconds of silence, the room erupted with laughter and the wisecracks started. It was hard to tell how many comments were made because of how loud the room got. They had a real camaraderie, having played together in Portland before the move to Chicago.

I reached out my hand to shake with the man standing directly in front of me. He placed his dirty, wet towel over my arm instead. "When you stars get through washing the sweaters and mopping the floor, then you have our permission to go see the coach." Someone guffawed loudly.

Another man walked by me, threw his towel over my shoulder, and patted me on my head. "And not a moment before, Blondie." My ears grew hot as I clenched my fist.

Mickey and I both looked around the room at the others for someone to step in and set this straight. No one did. "House rules, rubes. Sorry." Someone patted my shoulder under a growing stack of towels and used sweaters.

By the time everyone left and the door closed behind us, we were both covered in mildewed hockey sweaters, towels, and a few pairs of socks and underwear. Mickey's face was bright red with anger, which probably matched mine. How he stood there the whole time and didn't fight anybody was beyond me. I wanted to, even knowing how that generally worked out. The clothes fell off us to the floor as we stood there dumbfounded, looking at it all. It was so ridiculous that even being mad over it seemed unthinkable. We stood there trying to decide if we should follow the apparent house rules or skip it and go look through the labyrinthine building for the coach. I reached down to start first.

Someone cleared his throat in the silence of the room, startling us. "You two ought not to believe everything you are told in this big city, eh?" I turned to the corner of the dressing room from where the voice had come. That's when I first saw him, sitting on the warped, wooden bench next to a stack of rugged goalie pads, pulling his black, polished, cap-toe shoes on over expensive silk socks.

He looked to be twenty-five, but could have been a little older. He had that kind of face, youthful but not. His lean body and lithe muscles protruded from under his shirt. Even though he looked shorter than me, he exuded a presence that made him seem tall. His short, black, wavy hair had been oiled up and slicked back until they outlined his chiseled jawline. His eyes were deep oceans of blue locked on mine. And the smooth, French accent that rolled as he spoke…I was instantly tongue-tied.

Mickey asked him who he was, but that gaze never left mine.

"I think the best thing you two can do right now is to either wash all of these filthy animals' clothes or…" He paused, and a sly, rakish grin formed across his full, puffy, red lips, "Maybe do something that they will not forget the next time they want to lead you around by the… un, how do you say…short hairs."

"Wha—what did you have in mind?"

We scooped up all of the clothes, following his energetic lead, and ran into the shower area to a big anteroom that held a bank of toilets. Mickey seemed to love this idea, like a kid who just found a whole apple pie cooling on a windowsill. Looking over at our new friend, he motioned to the toilets and said, "Your big chance, *mes amis.*"

Caught up in the frenzy, we wasted no time stuffing all of the clothing into the toilet bowls and even pulled a few of the handles for good measure. Laughing hysterically, we pushed the sweaters in one after another until they were all good and soaked. The last few remaining sweaters got tossed in the shower room after we turned several of the knobs, bringing water down across the whole lot. It happened so fast I hadn't even stopped to think about what we were doing.

"These guys are gonna murder us for sure," I spilled out. My legs started shaking, my jaw clenched up, and my eyes were glued to the wet floor tiles, preparing to count them all. I felt myself being drawn into it. My chest tightened up, my body preparing for the internal battle that was already edging its way to the forefront.

"You have made some impression now," said the mysterious goalie.

This crazy act would never have crossed my mind on my own. Something about him made me want to follow him, but that didn't save me from myself. When the goalie laid his hand on my shoulder, my legs fell still. At that moment, I stopped to take a deep breath, and my body slowly began to respond to commands.

"These guys deserve to be treated to a little special clothes washing from time to time," the Frenchman said. Mickey must have thought this was the funniest thing in the world because he started cackling. This was the first time in minutes I remembered Mickey was still in the room with us. "Now, let's go see if we can't find Angry Pete for you," he quipped. Did all the players call the coach that to his face?

We went down into a maze of halls and stairs and finally ended up in front of the coach's office, stopping to straighten up a bit. Before my nerves could grip me again, I felt a gentle hand on my shoulder that was clearly not Mickey's. "Everything will be all right. Dick will take care of you," which confused me. I didn't think I knew anyone named Dick. Almost as an afterthought he added, "Both of you. Trust him."

I turned to him and stuck my hand out to shake his. He looked down at it, smiling that same puckish smile.

"Your hands were just down in a toilet, so, *je crois que non*, er, I think not."

"What's your name? Who are you?"

He winked one of those blue eyes. "Ah, two interesting yet completely different questions." He reached up and straightened my shirt collar in both hands. Behind me, Mickey was straightening himself out rather than watching as this beautiful man fixed my shirt, for which I was thankful. "I am Jean-Paul. I'd say good luck in there, but you will not need it from what I hear. Remember to trust him." With that, he was gone with a few quick strides. The sound of Mickey knocking on the thick, wooden door put an end to the moment.

"Odd guy," Mickey said without apparent judgment.

Thoughts of the dark-haired, handsome man with the stormy blue eyes swirled around my head. "Yes. Odd."

CHAPTER FOUR

The door swung inward, opened by a large man a little rounded at the midsection smoking a fat stogie. Again with the cigars. He had a boxer's face, the kind that might have once been good looking but now had too many sharp angles and permanently swollen areas. He stuck his hand out, taking mine with a vise-like grip that almost had me asking for mercy. He held my hand a few moments too long before letting go and grabbing Mickey in the same manner.

This was simply a tactic to show he was the top dog and no young hillbillies would outdo him. If we made it out of the meeting, this was the man that would be our coach. When he stepped out of the doorway, his office came into view. His oversized desk was stacked with papers, and swirling grey smoke filled the room. Another man stood in the haze by the windows, looking out at the street below.

"We're awfully sorry we didn't get here in time for the, um, tryouts," I said. "We are really hoping that tomorrow we could—"

"Hah. Lucky you made it at all. And this *is* the tryout, son."

"Oh." It came out of my mouth, but I had no idea what he meant.

"You mean you don't know?" Muldoon asked. "The *Chicago Daily News* said fifty people died yesterday in a gigantic train wreck at the station. Why, I bet it'll be days before they get the schedules back on track. You boys must've seen the mess."

Fifty people? Right where we had just been? How did we not see the wreckage? My God, that must have been what all the construction workers and material was about. And I didn't even think. The people. Rail was supposed to be the safest way to travel these days. My heart started to thud, and sweat formed on the palms of my hands. "Well, that's awful."

"Come on in and sit down, boys," he said. He grabbed a couple of thick crystal glasses and a bottle of whiskey off a side table. "Have a drink. You must be thirsty after all that travel." The man by the window walked over to us. I instantly recognized him from the game in Milwaukee. He was one of the scouts, the serious-looking one. Great. "This here is Dick Irvin, captain of my team."

Dick was a tall, lean man of about thirty hard years. His brown eyes were intense, his face strong. I am not ashamed to say that Dick scared the hell out of me. This was the man Jean-Paul said would take care of us, to trust, but he was still downright scary. Something about Jean-Paul made me want to believe him. Dick did not put out his hand, but after the towel escapade and the vise grip from the coach, I was growing leery of handshakes anyway. Mr. Muldoon again directed us to some chairs opposite his desk and everyone except Dick sat down.

"I'm told that you scored two goals with two assists, Mr. Bennet. Is that right? Quite impressive." He had gotten the stats wrong, which made me wonder what he had been told about us.

"That was three goals, Mr. Muldoon, sir," I said while clearing my throat nervously. Correcting this man was a risky move. He just smiled and took a sip of his whiskey. I did not drink a drop of mine, although I put it up to my mouth several times. I figured I was better off drinking to look like I was an adult, rather than turn it down like a child still wearing short pants. But I couldn't stand the idea of that hot, bitter whiskey running down my parched throat.

"That's right, that's right. Three goals. And two for you, mister…"

"Mickey, everybody calls me Mickey," he finished.

"Ah, so I'm not wrong on that score as well?" He handled that with the ease of someone with lots of negotiating practice, subtly chiding me for correcting him. Now I was done for, having just pissed off the head coach of the team we left Milwaukee to join. Mickey seemed anxious by the whole event and had to stop sipping his drink long enough to agree. I envied the coach's level of confidence, real or not.

"Let's get down to some business," Mr. Muldoon said. "My team is going to go all the way. It's our first year in Chicago, and to say we need to prove ourselves to this fine metropolis is an understatement. I want only the best on my team. You had a good game back in Kenosha or wherever, but this is the big time here, boys." While Pete rambled on, Dick looked like the picture of calm.

"That's why you need us on your team, Mr. Muldoon," Mickey piped up. "We're a hell of a pair, Brett and I." This was the moment where the coach started to look like an angry Pete indeed. Jean-Paul had been right.

Muldoon took a swig of his whiskey and a long puff on his cigar before he cleared his throat and spoke directly to Dick. "What did you say to me about these boys, Dick?" Muldoon leaned back against his thick, creaky, wooden rolling chair and took another puff. This was clearly another tactic he used often.

Dick came over to us and sat down in one of the wooden chairs around the giant desk. He sat straight as an arrow, which caused me to straighten up a little as well. "All I know, Pete, is that the kid can play. Like I said, he might be a bit scrawny and needs some discipline, but with the right line behind him, he could really do something. The other one ain't too shabby, either."

Muldoon paused for what seemed like a year before taking in a deep, dramatic breath. "Big praise coming from you. Set them both up with the standard contract, Dick, one thousand dollars for the season. If you prove to be second-rate or just too damned difficult to deal with, we can dump you. And we will. If you get injured and can't play after our team doctor looks at you, you're out. If you refuse to play, you'll be fired and held legally responsible to pay us the remainder."

Mickey was already putting out his hand to shake on the deal, but over his shoulder I saw Dick subtly shake his head back and forth. Was he signaling no? I reached out and placed my hand on top of Mickey's, pushing it back. I took a swallow before speaking.

"I think that's a fine offer, sir, for a starter. But can I mention I blocked ten shots this season so far as well as scoring those goals?" My knees threatened to shake me out of the chair. We were not out on the ice. This was his territory. My heart ached, banging to escape my chest, worried that my boldness would ruin both our lives. "And Mickey here is part of the reason I'm able to get to those shots. You should see him clear out the ice."

Pete got up from his desk, and his face turned a deep, purple color. "I'll be damned if some snot-nosed nobody from Delavan tells me how to run my business!" Muldoon had made it seem like he didn't know much about us or didn't value my skills as a player, but when he mentioned my hometown, I knew he knew a lot more than he was letting on. He must have known about our playing.

All the way here, Mickey talked like he was going to carry us through with his powerhouse bravado, and he stood up for himself pretty well most of the time. Except for right now. He turned his head sideways with a terrified look, as if to ask if I had lost my marbles.

I just sat there for a minute in the uncomfortable silence. The tension was palpable, and I felt the familiar pull inside me to count things, pushing me to look at the ceiling tiles to figure out how many holes were in each square. My jaw muscles started to tighten up. Just as I began to count them, Muldoon slapped both of his big, veiny, lined hands on his desk and leaned forward. "Eleven hundred, but if you so much as have an off game—"

"Two thousand," I spat out before my brain could engage and scare me back into my shell.

"Son of a bitch!" Muldoon looked over to Dick, his sharp, exaggerated breathing blowing snot out of his nose like a mad bull. "You have got some nerve, kid," he raged as he looked back over to me. Just then he turned his gaze back to Mickey. "And *you*." Mickey's head shot straight up so fast, his hair would have flown off of his head if not for all the pomade. "Are you ready to leave this office and head back to the bus? Huh? Broke and flat on your ass?"

We sat in silence, not so much because Mickey had caught on to my shaky ploy, but because he was too scared to say anything. I was too. One thousand dollars was more money than anyone back home made in a year, including my father. Just the mere thought of walking out of that office with nothing but my hat in my hand terrified me. Especially because I was so flat busted, I didn't even own a hat. I looked over at Dick, catching his eyes just as he motioned them toward the door and back several times.

I cannot imagine what came over me at that particular moment. Sometimes we just have faith in something or someone, even if there seems to be no logical reasoning for it. "I'm sorry we couldn't reach an agreement, Mr. Muldoon. Best of luck to your team." I got up and headed for the door.

"Wait, you little son of a bitch," Pete said, just as I reached for the door handle. "I'll do sixteen for you, fourteen hundred for MacKay here. And that is it. Not one more goddamned nickel." Mickey had practically run back over to him, agreeing. Turning back toward the desk, my face hardened, I prepared to negotiate for more. I opened my mouth, but before I said anything, I looked at Dick for encouragement. What I saw was a stern look that said we'd won, and it was time to let it end or go too far and lose it all.

"Mr. Muldoon, you have a deal. You won't regret it, I promise you." I went back over to shake the hand of our new boss but was handed a pen instead. Muldoon did not look happy. Now Mickey, *he* looked happy. Contracts were signed. Dick was told to set us up in some boarding house until we got paid and could afford to rent an apartment.

"Bennet," Muldoon said as I was about to leave his office. "Remember, the road to victory is paved with gravel. Don't make me regret this and crush you beneath it. Now get out." When we left the office and headed back down the hallway, Mickey jumped all over me. He was boasting about how we took the team for a mint and about how we played the old man together. It was annoying, but he was so excited, it was hard to be mad at him.

We had been told to wait out back for Dick so he could take care of us. All I could think about was how I just made an enemy of my boss. Just maybe, I thought, there was a powerful ally to be had in the captain. The whole situation had left me shaky, my insides in knots.

Through the partially closed office door, we heard Pete threaten Dick. "If this kid isn't as good as you say he is, you'll be joining him on the train to Milwaukee, I swear to God. That's more than you're worth. Hear me?" Mickey's face fell as we stepped away from the door, maybe feeling bad for Dick, but more likely realizing they were not arguing about him or his skills, but about me and mine. I felt bad for both of them, even Dick, which was odd considering how frightening he seemed.

CHAPTER FIVE

B y the time we got out of our meeting with Dick and Coach
Muldoon, the sun had started its descent, and the streets around
the Coliseum were desolate. In the haze from the electric lamps lining
the front of the building, they looked like what I imagined when I
thought of England in those Jack the Ripper penny novels. Old and
creepy. My heart had been pounding out of my chest for at least twenty
solid minutes, and Mickey had been chattering like a child's wind-up
toy, clanging away nonstop.

So many feelings swirled around inside me, I couldn't describe
them all. We had barely listened when Dick told us where to go and
who to talk to for our lodgings, much less remembered when he said we
were supposed to be back in the morning for practice. Mickey smacked
my shoulder. "Let's grab this cab right here and go out to celebrate!"
All I could think about was sleeping. It was barely evening, but after
the train ride, the bumpy cab, and the battle in the coach's office, I was
exhausted. All I wanted was to slam my head into a pillow.

Then a new worry popped into my mind. What kind of flophouse
were we being set up in? And the bugs. Oh, there'd be bugs all over.
Fleas, lice, bed bugs, and roaches. My mother had beaten that fact
into my head before leaving for Milwaukee. "Make sure you tie up
your bags at night, Brett. Those things get in there and multiply!" The
thought nearly shut me down with repetitive counting for good the first
night at that last place.

"Look, Mickey, I don't want to be a bad sport, but I don't know."

"Nonsense. We'll drop off the bags and go somewhere close to the
apartment then. It's settled." Where did the quiet, scared Mickey, who
couldn't negotiate, go?

After a twenty-five-cent cab ride, we arrived at our boarding house.
Turns out it was a nice, two-flat brownstone home, not a giant building

full of homeless folks like my mother had warned. What a relief. The matron of the house, an elderly Irish lady named Moira Fleming, was waiting for us just inside.

Ms. Fleming stuck her hand out to shake mine, strong and straight like a man. I resisted the impulse to turn her hand upright like most women prefer. "I'm Moira Fleming, and this here is my place. Now it's yours too. Welcome, boys." She was cheery and happy. It was off-putting compared to the rest of the event-packed day, but nice. Her lilting brogue could have lulled me to sleep. It reminded me of home. Not mine, but what home is supposed to be like.

"Nice to meet you, Mrs. Fleming," Mickey offered.

"Nonsense, my mother is Mrs. Fleming. Now, call me Moira." Based on Moira's age, her mother must have been a hundred.

"Ma'am?" I said.

"Enough of that, young man." She grabbed our bags and started up the stairs with quickness surprising for her age, which appeared to be at least eighty. She called over her shoulder, "Come on now, boys, let us see to your lodgings."

The room we shared was more spacious than the building suggested from the outside. It had a big, full-sized bed with a nightstand on each side, a desk, and a small door leading to our own wash area and toilet. It was a better situation than the one we'd left the day before, bunking with a cavalcade of stinky, slovenly men. Mickey was the only person to put up with, which was no small task. After all, he held the snoring championship of Canada, which ensured I made it to the ice in the morning overtired.

"All right, Brett, my boy. It's past time we meet this city head-on."

We sat at the bar in a local saloon, listening to some men who looked like dockworkers, trying lines on dames, fishing for a pushover. I assumed they worked at the docks based on their navy blue pea coats, wool caps, and weather-worn faces. Mickey clamored about how we were going to show off some of our passing skills tomorrow at practice, until he got good and drunk. He had some money stashed away, and he seemed hell-bent on spending all of it in one night. We wouldn't get a payday for a week, and he was already acting like a big spender, buying beers served in paper bags. I was not. I was also tired from the few beers I had drunk. A questionable lady wearing a low-cut top and a skirt that was far too high came over and sat down next to Mickey.

"Buy a girl a drink, big fella?"

Mickey's rosy face lit up, although his eyes remained glassy and a bit droopy from drink. "Well, well, what do we have here? Pretty lady, let me buy youse a drank."

The barkeep barely had time to mix the lady the fancy drink, whose name I had never heard before—Moscow something or other—when three men approached us. "You messing with my girl, stupid?" one of them said.

"Did you just call this lady stupid, you big palooka?" Mickey said, poking fun at the way the dockworkers talked.

One of the men grabbed Mickey by the shirt and started to push him back and forth, accentuating his words with every push. "You big, fat...are you a moron?" Mickey started swinging his fists at this big fella. His fighting skills and his fists were feared on the ice, but these guys had never heard of the Wee Scot or his skills before. The other two men immediately jumped into the fray, grabbing at Mickey. Needing to defend my teammate, I threw a punch at one of the men. He went sprawling on the hardwood floor on his butt. The lady in question then balled up her fist, screamed some profanity I can't repeat, and punched me square in the eye.

What happened next was pandemonium. Fists, feet, punches, and a handbag went flying through the air. Some connected with their targets and others didn't. The barkeep yelled, "Break it up!" at the top of his lungs, to no avail. I grabbed Mickey by his belt loop and pulled him backward away from the pile toward the exit. In the insanity of the brawl, I didn't notice my eye had swollen enough to obscure my vision a little on the side. We made it outside, Mickey's lip bleeding a little bit.

"Woohoo, baby. Yeah! What a goddamned good time that was!" Mickey was a little mentally unstable. "Oh man, your eye." He reached up and touched the side of my face, which caused me to double over from the sharp pain. That's when I noticed it. My right eye had swollen up, and my vision was blurry.

"Ouch."

"Har-har." He was belly laughing at me now.

"I'm glad you're amused, you big ox," I said, gingerly testing the growing lump on my face.

"You are gonna make such a splash tomorrow with the fellas. Hit by a dame, no less."

"Oh God, Mick. You wouldn't?" But even before I said it, I knew he was going to tell everyone at the house, everyone on the bus, everyone in the locker room, and everyone in the stands if he could.

Mickey grabbed my arm and started to lead us away from the bar. "We'd better blow before some flatfoot comes by and throws us in the can."

I laughed at Mickey's street lingo and immediately winced in pain. "Ah shit, that smarts."

When we got back to the room, Moira handed me a cold piece of meat she had unwrapped from a crinkly piece of butcher paper. She placed it on my eye and said she'd add it to our bill. Bidding us good night, she pulled the door closed, but not before giving a wink and saying, "Don't you worry. I'm sure she was a big lass too." Mickey burst out laughing all over again. I laid back in the bed, a piece of meat draped across my face.

I wondered what Jean-Paul was doing right then.

CHAPTER SIX

September 9, 1926

The swelling went down a lot during the night, but the shiner still felt like it was throbbing along with my heartbeat. The meat smelled twice as bad when I peeled it off my face in the morning. Mickey made some wisecrack about it being wasteful to throw it out. Somehow I was still able to get myself ready to head to practice. Even though his face wasn't twice its normal size, Mickey looked worse for wear too.

We arrived at the Coliseum just in time to jump in the shower before practice. We missed our time at the bathtub back at the boarding house, so we smelled awfully ripe and needed it bad. The potent, rancid beef would not seem to wash off my face. I worried it would stay with me forever. Truth be told, Moira's bathtub probably wouldn't have helped make us smell much better either.

The few players in the locker room didn't even look up as we had come in. We undressed and went into the showers. The hot water felt wonderful against my back. My sore eye felt better, but the hot water hurt like hell when it hit my face directly. I ducked under the showerhead and was starting to relax when the sound of skates clacking against tiles resounded throughout the room. Before I was able to look up, a dozen hands grabbed me and hoisted me off my feet.

Mickey was cursing at the attackers, but I couldn't see much because soap had dripped into my stinging eye. Through my squinting, I saw about four or five people, but it sounded like a herd of elephants, so there could have been more. They were carrying me inches off the floor, my bare butt slapping against the ground every few steps.

"Careful now," said one.

"He's all slippery," said another.

Then I figured out where they were taking us. The guys started jogging with us in tow before they tossed us into a spin on our asses straight across the ice. Mickey thudded against the ice next to me, and I heard the sloshing of the thin sheen of icy water as we slid. Mickey made some kind of pained sound that wasn't quite a word. I started to make the same exact sound, but my teeth chattered, vibrating loudly inside my head.

My back instantly started to freeze as my body turned sideways. I tried to grab the ice to slow down the uncontrolled spin, which caused me to spin even more. After what seemed like a frozen forever, my pale, blue body slushed to a gradual stop, sprawled on the ice in front of the goal net. Jean-Paul, in full uniform, head and hands resting on his upside down goalie stick, smiled down at me.

"Hiya there, handsome."

Though shivering and chattering, my lips curved upward in what must have looked like a demented, demonic smile. Every spot of my body stung from the cold, and I couldn't think clearly. Then it dawned on me that I was laying spread-eagled across the ice in front of him, buck naked. *Oh my God, I am naked, and Jean-Paul is staring at me*, I thought. I tried to scramble to my feet, but training to get back up on skates goes out the window without skates. I floundered around, looking ridiculous and awkward as I pushed my feet along the freezing ice toward the bench area where the door to the lockers would be.

Mickey was doing the same thing a few feet away. The other players skated around us doing fast side stops so that the edges of their skates would scrape up the rink and shower us with a bunch of snow, ice, and water. You would think that having skidded on ice would make that snow shower less of an issue, but it didn't. Mickey managed to make it to the benches and scramble to his feet. I was about there when someone grabbed my ankle with a hockey stick and jerked it backward, causing me to lose my footing and crash knee first to the ice.

"Thanks for the wet sweaters, punk," said a very large man, who I mistook for two men through my blurry vision. My knee was screaming at me, but all I could do was hold it, writhing in pain as I did. When it settled down just a fraction, my vision cleared. I looked up again to make out who deserved the blame. I realized there were actually two men. They did not look as though they were joking. At that moment, Dick skated up between everybody and grabbed me by the arm to make sure I made it to the benches.

"Go get cleaned up and have doc take a look at that knee." He then turned to the big goons and raised his voice like he was giving them a dressing down. "Percy, Bob, you've gone too far." Then he said from over his shoulder as he skated away, "And you boys need to apologize to the kid for the cheap shot." Was this a dream? Did Dick just stand up for me again, against those big bruisers? The pain from my knee and frozen backside must have brought on delirium.

Less than twenty minutes later, with a bandage around my knee, I skated around the ice of the Coliseum for the first time, fully clothed. I made two full laps, testing my knee before having a chance to look up. Above, the ceiling looked like it was miles away. The sun shone through the giant windows, lighting up the ice like we were outside. The rink was situated in the middle of what looked like three football fields of seats. Six thousand people could file in to watch one game. That's five times bigger than the arena in Milwaukee. It was more than a little nerve-wracking.

The knee was holding up fine, so my mind turned to other things on my third pass around the ice. I looked at Jean-Paul as I skated past him. I had almost forgotten about him with all the pain and everything. Almost. He watched me as I moved around his net, still testing the angles and putting pressure on my knee by pushing over on my edges.

"Are you feeling all right?" His voice had a lilt. Well, it had more of a sway than a lilt, probably because his first language was French, which I don't speak. But I've heard a lot of it from the Canadians I've played with before. His had a melody.

"Yeah. I guess I deserved that."

He watched me as his body slowly pivoted to follow the motion, like I've seen a hundred goaltenders do before. This seemed different, somehow. "Well then, I guess I deserve a good whack as well." The guys obviously didn't think he had anything to do with shoving all the clothes in the toilets. "But don't you worry about mean old Percy Traub and Bob Trapp. Those boys have already moved on to something better, from what I hear."

"Who are they?" I asked, my grimace giving way to anger.

"Defensemen. They are here to keep your ass safe from other bruisers on the ice during games," Jean-Paul explained, "but during practice we are all targets." It looked more like I needed protection from them. "They get plenty of penalty minutes for it too."

Just then, one of the other skaters came close. He was a tall, slender man of about thirty-five. "So, Blondie, are you going to be able to punch men out here for us too, or do you only fight women?" He started to guffaw uproariously. A bunch of the fellas thought that was the funniest thing ever, joining in on the laughter. Now I knew what the "something better" was that they'd moved on to. And it was still me.

After a bit of being made fun of and taking a swat or two at Mickey, we started the morning skate. Mickey had fit right in with the rougher, more crass individuals on the team. He bought his way in at my expense, of course, but at least he was fitting in. I could take it. And Jean-Paul was right; getting in good with those guys was important or we wouldn't have any room to work out on the ice. Bigger players often fight any opponents who go out of their way to hit or hurt the scorers. Without them protecting and enforcing, I wouldn't score a single goal from all the beatings that'd be coming my way. I needed to think of a way to win them over. I also wanted to find a way to win over someone else.

After a few hours of drills, we broke up into two squads of eleven to start a practice game. When the puck dropped in front of me, everything on earth stopped for a moment. The puck bounced up off the ice in what looked like slow motion. My hands and stick moved so quickly, the puck was behind me before my opponent could react. It felt good.

Mickey was clearly trying to show the coach how well we worked together so we could end up on the same line. I wouldn't have minded if that happened, either. He sent several perfect passes my way. One of them connected while I was all alone on center ice. I exploded toward the goal and deked a few times around players as if they were stuck in quicksand. When I broke free, I glanced up and remembered that Jean-Paul would be in the goal. I skated up on him fast, dipped my shoulder, and when he moved to the side, I went to the backhand and let it fly. I looked up, hoping the puck went into the net, only to see that Jean-Paul had popped his free hand up like lightning to stop my shot.

"Woo-wee, that boy's fast," Mickey said as we skated around the corner together. He wasn't kidding. That was the fastest glove hand I'd ever seen. With the stick in the other hand, all the glove side had was reflexes. We practiced for about another hour, but I only beat Jean-Paul once. He winked at me when it happened, which made me wonder if I beat him or he let it go by for some reason. I couldn't imagine why he would do it other than to get in my head, but teammates don't need to do that. Maybe he was trying to make me look good. I managed to put a few goals past the other goaltender, Hugh, and wondered what would happen to Hugh when the season started. Teams usually carried only one goaltender.

"So, Brett. What say we celebrate your first day on the team, go get us a few steaks, and follow it up with some drinks?" Jean-Paul said as we got dressed. I looked over at him and paused to see if I'd really heard what I thought I'd heard or if I was imagining things. He repeated himself a little slower.

"Um, yeah. Sounds good."

"What sounds good?" Mickey had slid over to me on the bench.

"I simply asked if you both would like to go out on the town with a true expert to celebrate your arrival."

I smiled. "Expert?"

Jean-Paul started to glow at this invitation to boast. "Why, an expert in the skillful art of getting every drop of pleasure a town like this has to offer. Of course." Jean-Paul sounded like he was an official tour guide you get on the ferries or at the national parks.

"Every drop?" Mickey asked. "I like the sound of that."

Even though we agreed, Jean-Paul looked disappointed. If he didn't want us to go, I didn't get why he asked in the first place. It didn't make sense to be upset when he was the one who had asked us.

I pondered it for a bit before remembering. At first, he had only asked me.

CHAPTER SEVEN

Jean-Paul's car was fast. He had a brand new Chrysler Imperial, one of the fancier E80 models. Anybody who had enough money to buy an automobile back home could only afford a smoke spewing Model T, but this was a different class of machinery. This car was beautiful. It was painted such a potent maroon color, it sparkled in the light of the electric street lamps as if it had an inner fire daring to escape. The beige accents gave it a sharp contrast, and the solid black top made it look sleek and fast.

The big whitewall tires shined against the black rubber, matching the white spats Jean-Paul wore over his shiny black cap-toed shoes. His shoes were also inlaid with brown panels. I had never met anybody that dressed like Jean-Paul. He was a great dresser, no doubt, but in a way that made him look different than other folks. I mean, everyone that could afford it wore a suit coat and trousers. If they could, they'd also wear pressed cotton shirts, maybe even a vest with a nice pocket watch. Everyone but me had a fedora or boater hat as well. Men at the docks or in the factories wore newsboy hats. Jean-Paul seemed to exist on a wholly different plane of existence than the rest of us.

He wore a crisp black suit with thick white stripes running down it, a red scarf, and sharply pleated black trousers with the ankles cuffed up. His gold pocket watch chain sparkled in the lights the same way that his car did. To say I was jealous isn't strong enough. I didn't just envy the way he dressed. I wanted to be him.

"How do you afford all of these things?" I asked before realizing my blunder. "Um, sorry."

Jean-Paul pulled the choke out, turned the key, and stomped on the accelerator. His luxury car roared to life and jerked forward a little bit, which startled me. He shoved my shoulder as he laughed, ignoring my question. "Easy, easy. You ain't seen nothing yet." He popped the clutch, and the engine roared as we took off. When I say we took off, we were literally thrown back into our seats as Jean-Paul pushed it as fast as it would go. We sped away to the south, the Coliseum quickly becoming a tiny structure in the rear mirrors.

We whipped across the road to avoid holes in the street, slower cars, and people crossing. Mickey hollered out at the people on the streets to "gangway" and "heave to" like we were a runaway ship. He obviously enjoyed the breakneck speeds of this fancy hayride Jean-Paul was taking us on. I did not. I realized I had been clutching the door handle so tightly, my knuckles had gone pale white, worried that Wabash Avenue would open up and swallow us whole.

"Ease up there," Jean-Paul said, noticing my hands. When I didn't change my grip, he continued in his best American accent, "Hey, daredevil, lighten up on the fine appointments of this here automobile!"

"Maybe you want to consider easing up on the accelerator just a little bit before you kill us all," I protested, mostly pretending to be angry. His left hand lightly touched the steering wheel, his right hand resting loosely on the gearshift. He pushed the car up to a high enough speed where I knew he'd have to shift the gear selector close to my knee, but I didn't move out of the way. In fact, my leg tensed up, gluing itself into position during turns so I wouldn't miss the coming contact.

Then it happened, Jean-Paul slipped the car into gear and rubbed his hand against me. Tingles ran up my leg. I'm sure gooseflesh popped up all over my arms. I think I actually shivered. *Sissy boy.* I could hear my father's voice loud and clear in my head, and that's exactly what he would've called me. Well, that, and much, much more.

I bent my head down and turned it just a bit to see Jean-Paul's smirk. His head was turned toward me enough that he could clearly see his hand on the gear shifter, which was touching me. A voice inside my head screamed at me to move away, but what if I moved away too fast and he said something? Would I offend him?

My brain turned back on. I wondered what would happen if he had any idea how I felt. What kind of dangerous game was he playing here? With Mickey in the backseat, the thought of the two of them pulling me out of the car by my hair in a rage filled my head, and my mouth went dry.

The car suddenly swung around the corner at 35th Street, the tires squealing. My leg jerked away, and my knees knocked violently together. He shifted the car down twice in rapid succession. We came to an abrupt halt at State Street, brakes screeching with the sudden strain.

"We are here, boys. The world-famous Dreamland Café."

Mickey excitedly pushed me out of the way from his spot in the backseat in order to get out of the car first. "Watch out, you big lummox," I scolded, as his pile of stomach and shoulder slammed me face first into the dashboard.

"Can't stop me now. Chicago, here I come," he boasted.

I didn't want to burst poor Mickey's bubble with the fact that we were, in fact, poor. We probably weren't going to take anyplace by storm with what we had in our pockets. I'd heard that drinks in these places could be pricey, sometimes fifty cents all the way up to two dollars. Apiece. We hadn't even gotten paid yet. I wondered what the night would end up costing us.

People lined up waiting to get into the club, its neon sign lighting up the street. Apparently, we were in the midst of jazz heaven. Lit up like Christmas trees, it was a wonder why they hadn't been shut down. Jean-Paul said that within a few blocks were a dozen joints with names like Fiume, De Luxe, and the Phoenix Theatre. Back home all we had was the occasional still.

We walked right past the line straight up to the front door, several angry people shaking their fists at us. Right in front of the door, a large bald man sat on a stool, stopping people from going inside. I noticed he had a small wad of money in his hands. I immediately felt a sense of panic and dread. When Jean-Paul saw how broke I was...

My worries were quickly assuaged. Jean-Paul stuck his hand out to shake the doorman's, and I caught the faintest edge of green paper poking out of his palm as he withdrew his hand. The doorman got up, pulled the door open for us to enter, and chuckled. "You and your friends go right on in, Mr. Moreau. Miss Clara will be happy to see you back so soon."

Jean-Paul grinned. "I bet she will, Mack, I just bet."

"You just remember what I said to you last time." The big man laid a giant, sweaty hand on Jean-Paul's shoulder, causing him to spin around. The doorman's hand was now empty, so he must have pocketed the money.

As we walked in, Jean-Paul stopped to pull back the curtains separating the two rooms. I bumped against his back and put my hand on his shoulder to stop from falling farther. "What was that about?" I asked him. "What did he tell you last time?"

Jean-Paul grinned deviously at me over his shoulder and shouted with glee, "I have no idea!"

The main room of the Dreamland Café was large, with a lot of little tables spread out in a half circle around a big stage elevated a few feet off the ground. I looked around the room with wide-eyed amazement at its size and at the goings-on. The people wore nice clothes, but not as nice as Jean-Paul. They drank out of fancy glasses and smoked cigarettes from long holders like in newspaper ads. Waiters hustled back and forth with big, round silver trays of food.

I stopped for a waiter carrying a full tray of drinks and Mickey, who had been gazing around the room in amazement or awe, stumbled hard into my back. "Cut it out, rube," I told him. "Stop gawking. You look like some dumb hillbilly that's never seen the city."

"I have never seen anything as exciting, as grand as this place. It's a fine joint," he replied. His voice had a twinge of wonderment mixed with a hint of mischievousness.

"Enjoy it, but be cool as a cucumber like me," Jean-Paul told both of us. This brought a smile to my lips, and my shoulders loosened a little. I felt them slowly dropping as we reached our table. One of the waiters pulled out my chair as I sat down, which made me feel uncomfortable. No one had ever pulled out a chair for me before. Another waiter came by and handed me a linen napkin. Yet another came by and poured some water from a pitcher into the glasses on the table.

"Mr. Moreau. Boy, Miss Clara gone just spit when she sees you here," said an elderly black waiter who was dressed a mite better than I was. Then he smiled and walked away.

I leaned in to Jean-Paul, smelling his aftershave. "All right, everybody knows you here? Who's Miss Clara and—"

He cut me off. "Relax, I said, it's nothing. Waiter. Three rare steaks, and some martinis."

I panicked. I couldn't afford a steak, at least not yet. I hadn't been paid and could barely afford the drink, whatever a martini was. I started to protest, "Wait, I—" Jean-Paul waved me off and would hear nothing about it. Mickey could care less. He was caught up in looking around the great room at all the flappers and high society ladies moving about.

Jean-Paul watched Mickey for a few seconds. "So, Mickey, tell me, how good a time are you looking to have tonight?" Then he started to chuckle, and Mickey loudly joined him.

The waiter returned carrying a tray with three large-rimmed glasses filled with clear liquid. When I took my first swig of the crystal-clear martini—too big of a swig at that—I started to choke, nearly drowning myself in it.

"Whoa, there. You have to sip one of these, at least until you're an expert like me," Jean-Paul said as he patted me on the middle of the back. As if to accentuate the point, he tilted his drink back. He slurped down the second half of it as he raised his other hand to signal the waiter for a refill.

After we had a few drinks and ate our steaks, the lights dimmed. Several men, some black and some white, walked onstage and picked up their instruments. The lights went way down low in the club as the music started. The room was instantly lost in the clarinets and the rhythmic thumping of the standing bass. That sweet jazz music filled my ears and heart as it swelled with jovial tempos and wild, rushed collections of notes. I was in love.

I didn't know much about music and don't recall ever listening to jazz or anything like it before. My family never owned a radio receiver of our own. During the war, the family would load into the wagon on Saturday to head into town to listen to the news reports from the radio they had at Casey's General Store. It was never a happy day for us, waiting for an hour to hear the fates of the local boys, including my brother, overseas. This was different. At that moment, I was converted. I loved jazz.

I looked over to Jean-Paul. His slicked-back black hair was coming loose a little bit here and there as he moved his head back and forth and up and down with the beat. I took a risk by watching him, his eyes closed as he enjoyed the rhythms. I must have been looking at him too long, because I didn't notice him turn his head quickly, catching me. I hastily snapped my head back to the front, hoping he didn't think I was staring.

I looked at the band while they played for a few moments, my attention one hundred percent directed to Jean-Paul, wondering if he was still looking. I finally ventured a glance back toward him to find him staring directly at me. His bright, blue eyes illuminated the room, catching every glint of light from each candle on every table. I knew I had looked at him longer than I should have.

When I finally forced myself to snap my head away, Mickey was eyeballing me. His face contorted as he searched for his words. "What the hell you looking at?"

Reaching for my drink, I pulled it up to my mouth and sipped at it two or three times, not getting any liquid. Mickey chuckled.

"It's empty," he said.

"Uh, yeah, yes it is. Empty." Stupid.

Jean-Paul waved his hand in the air with a debonair flip, catching a waiter who stooped low to take his order, as if he had planned the whole thing in order to look good. It worked. The waiter rushed off after nodding vigorously. Jean-Paul winked at me, then turned his whole body back to the band, which was ending its song.

After the clapping died down, my drink was delivered. A spotlight cut through the crowd, aimed at the center of the curtains at the back of the stage. They slowly parted as a beautiful, light brown-skinned woman slid between them. Jean-Paul smiled widely at her. She was in character and acted as if she didn't notice anyone as she glided across the floor to a large microphone set up in the middle of the stage. Her soft breath sounded across the room as she inhaled slowly. Then she sang.

When she sang about finding that perfect love, the room held its collective breath. Her voice was silky smooth and lovely, expressing her desire from head to toe, her breaths filling every pained silence. Her song affected me deeply, making me long for something I couldn't put my finger on. I caught myself sniffing and raised a napkin to discreetly wipe the tears from my eyes. Jean-Paul noticed but said nothing, because his eyes were wet as well.

During the next song, she walked around the stage making humorous comments about people's clothes or, worse, insinuating sexual things about people's relationships. When she reached our table, she locked eyes with Jean-Paul. She smiled a sideways grin, like the one a mother would give a boy that she caught in the cookie jar. Most mothers, I mean. Not mine. Mine never smiled.

She made her way down the side stairs while she sang as if she had intended to end up at our table. She was singing about a lover that had been done wrong, and at just the right moment she grinned again. When the song mentioned a jilted lover, she slapped Jean-Paul in the face without missing a note. To his credit, he took the slap well and even wagged a finger at her in an overly dramatic way, like they had planned it. I wondered what I had gotten myself into.

After her set, this beautiful singer came over to our table. "I can't believe they let you in here again," she said. Her speaking voice was as hypnotically melodious as her singing one.

"Clara!" he said pleadingly, with humor.

"Boy, don't you Clara me in here. Not after what you and that little redheaded rich girl did to the place," she replied, her hand hanging in the air between them.

"It was a small misunderstanding."

"Small? That window cost me twenty-five dollars to fix." She looked angry. "And I had to buy a round of drinks for a whole table cause they was covered in glass!"

Jean-Paul grinned, and it looked to me like she was starting to grin a little too. "We paid for the window," he said. "Have a seat, and I'll buy you a drink for your troubles." He put a hand out for hers. "Miss Clara?"

She put one hand out, palm first in his face, as she sat down. "Mmm-hmm. Tell me who this fine young gentleman is," she said, looking at me. I felt extremely nervous.

"This is Mr. Bennet and Mr. MacKay. They also like to play with ice," Jean-Paul said playfully.

Miss Clara put her hand out, fingers pointing down, like a lady would. So I gently kissed the top of it. "A true gentleman. Honey, please tell me you won't go out on the town with this scoundrel again," she implored me.

Mickey leaned over and interrupted. "We might just be the scoundrels that you're worried about." I had almost forgotten that he was there.

"Wait, I'm not a...what exactly did you do?" I said, looking at Jean-Paul. "Who are you?"

"Scoundrel is such a dirty word for such pretty lips," he said, looking at Miss Clara.

She winked at me as she walked away. A third drink appeared in front of Jean-Paul and Mickey while I nursed my second. The martinis tasted like gasoline on ice, but the ice didn't help the burning at all. We had hooch back home when we were sneaking around with the girls, but this was worse by far. My throat felt like it was on fire, and I could melt glass with my breath. They were both taking large gulps at a time before their fourths showed up. I didn't even see either one of them wave or order them.

Mickey stood up. "Well, boys, I hope you can make it home without me. I'm gonna go get me one of these fine fillies over here. Show her the town." At least it sounded like he said town. I couldn't tell over the burp that ended his sentence. And then he was gone.

I was worried about him being drunk and alone in a strange town. "I...hey, Mickey!" I turned to Jean-Paul, annoyed. "I think we should go after him." He pulled me back down, and I sat heavily from the effects of the drinks. When I looked into his eyes, the entire room went dark and fuzzy and I didn't see any other person in the room but him. His attention was so focused on me, I felt like he wasn't interested in anyone else or looking at anybody but me. It made me sweat.

"He's a big boy and a grown man, Brett. Besides, we can have our own fun." More sweat. I wasn't sure what he meant, but I figured he didn't mean what I wanted him to. Could I be wrong? I must have been. *He's not...like me. Is he?*

I definitely got the sense he didn't like Mickey all that much. Mickey had a habit of being a little center stage in the big top when out in public. In private too, I guess. He's a good guy, though. Someone I wanted on my side. I felt like he needed to be corralled before he did any real damage to himself or to the town he wanted to impress so much.

"We'd better go," I said to Jean-Paul in defeat. "Mickey's a mess."

Jean-Paul stared at me for a minute, then replied, "If we must. If we must." He slammed down the rest of his drink and set it down next to mine, which I had barely touched.

"How do we want to do the bill?" I asked, wondering how I was going to pay my portion without any money.

"Don't let it trouble you for a second."

"But..."

"It's done. My treat. Let's just say I'm the official welcome wagon of the big city. Whenever you take me to Milwaukee, you can treat me to whatever it is they have out there in the sticks."

I couldn't tell whether he meant to be insulting or wisecracking. "Delavan. I'm not actually from Milwaukee. I'm from Delavan."

He laughed. "Everything outside the major cities is a wasteland I do not want to know about."

"Do you like the circus? Delavan is the nation's capital city of circuses. Most summers we have—"

He grabbed my arm and pulled us both up and away from the table. He did it to cut me off. I was sounding like a hick from the sticks. I knew it as I was saying it. The circus? What the hell was I getting at? He could care less about my stupid town. He had pretty much said so.

"Let's go. Your friend is about to get me barred for life." Mickey looked angry with his chest puffed out, and he leaned against two large, black men as if about to fight.

Shit, I thought.

"Shit," Jean-Paul said.

"You uppity coloreds need to back the hell away from me before..."

boy, I'll..." Mickey was in a full red-faced string of swear words, swaying a little as he ranted. "You jigaboo!"

Jean-Paul stepped between them all with an effortlessness I envied. Mickey instantly took an off-kilter step backward. To their credit, none took a swing at Mickey. They looked angry, but they looked scared too. I couldn't figure out why. They were large men. They couldn't have thought they were in too much danger from Mickey.

Just then, a skinny man with a pencil-thin moustache strode smoothly across the dining area and arrived in front of the mob scene we had created. I took him for the manager or owner. "What is the problem here?" he said, shooting the cuffs on his tuxedo jacket, his tone sharp and judgmental. "Are these colored gentlemen causing a scene in my club?"

Behind all of them, Miss Clara clenched her fists, and tears streamed out of the corners of her eyes in rage. That was when I got it. They weren't afraid of Mickey. Their jobs were on the line. They play in a whites-only club. How could I have been so stupid?

Jean-Paul was calm and smooth. "No sir, not at all. These fine men were helping me get my friend here to the car when he tripped. That's all. Too much strong coffee." He winked as he mentioned the nickname bootleggers used for liquor. He had been convincing at first, but the longer the charade went on, the flimsier it sounded. Luckily, the penguin manager believed his lie.

"Very well, then. Please leave the club once you've collected your friend." We scooped up a swaying Mickey and walked through the curtains out onto the street. The big doorman asked if we were leaving already, but he was laughing at us at the same time. We dumped Mickey, who by now had passed out, into the backseat of the Imperial.

Clara leaned in close to my ear, her flawless, ageless skin glistening in the electric glow of the Dreamland sign. Her creamed-coffee-colored eyes were moist and intense. "Think on what I said, white boy. Stay far away from this one. He's a bad alley cat. A wolf in sheep's clothing, you follow?" She directed a severe stare at Jean-Paul and turned sharply, her short hair bouncing before snapping back into place. Jean-Paul had his hands up in a "what, me?" gesture, but Clara ignored it and stormed back into the club. Behind her, the two musicians said something to the doorman, and all three of them glared at us for a moment.

We were all sucked into the back of the car's seats again, Jean-Paul racing through the city streets at top, inebriated speed. "Why do you have to go so damned fast all the time?" I pleaded. Jean-Paul just howled out to the night through his side window, like the wolf Clara accused him of being, before slapping my knee roughly.

Mickey started snoring in the car and didn't stop even when we picked him up to drag him into Moira's. The cacophony grew louder as we ascended each step in the narrow staircase, carrying him between us, one of his big arms over each of our shoulders.

Jean-Paul looked around the place. "We'll have to do something about these environs when you get your first paycheck." I liked the boardinghouse and said as much. I even grew to like the snoring, but I didn't add that to my protest for fear of sounding queer. It's the little things that make a place a home, even if the little things are annoying.

When I had finished taking Mickey's shoes off, Jean-Paul was gone, not having made a sound as he left or as he went down the stairs. It was all very mysterious. He was a mystery I wanted to solve, like why he hadn't asked me anything about myself all night. Or why he seemed to be annoyed with Mickey. As usual, Mickey had invited himself, but it still didn't make sense. Why ask me and then not talk to me?

I lay down to sleep wondering how we were going to get up in five hours to get to practice. Mostly, I was thinking about Jean-Paul's hand on my knee, those blue eyes piercing mine, his hand on my arm. I grew embarrassed as my underwear became a little tighter around me as I thought more about him. I looked over at Mickey, ashamed that he might have seen my excitement. When I was sure he hadn't, I rolled over to sleep.

"Ugh!" I exclaimed in frustration.

"Whah happun?" he managed to ask from his slumber, his face smashed by the pillows.

"It's nothing. Go to sleep."

Damn.

Chapter Eight

September 10, 1926

My head felt like Jack Dempsey had used it as a practice bag all night. The pounding was awful, and the smell from both of us in the locker room overwhelming. Mickey looked like a few miles of bad road himself, which gave me a little sense of satisfaction, having had to literally carry the moose all over town. I wondered how our third for dinner felt when he awoke. I didn't see Jean-Paul anywhere in the locker room. What if he missed practice, too drunk to play?

Dick walked into the locker room, took one look at us in our sorry state, and exclaimed, "Oh Jesus, Mary, and Joseph at the likes of you." How I didn't vomit was beyond me. We both managed to get our uniforms on and head out to the ice. The closer we got to the large cold slab, the better I felt. The frigid, wet air filled my lungs, taking just enough of the funk away to allow me to feel somewhat normal.

Jean-Paul was out in the goal crease, fully dressed, geared up, and practicing. He must have gone early. He took shots from the boys, jumping and sliding back and forth across his net mouth as if he had never touched a drop just a few scant hours previously. I couldn't believe it. Getting up close to take a shot at the net, I looked in his face, but he appeared fine. Shaved, bathed, and hair greased back like always. I hated him at that moment and felt miserable again.

"Ah, cheer up, *mon ami*. It will get better after we have some breakfast. Eggs. Some bacon. Nice and greasy. Strong coffee."

"Ulp." That's all it took to send me scurrying for the walls, bent over the half boards, butt aimed straight up in the air, puking my guts out. Not being able to eat anything, all I could upchuck was water. I could barely stand to think of food after the night we had. Drinking had never been a favorite pastime of mine. I'd have an occasional bootleg beer here or there, maybe, but never the hard stuff.

Someone skated behind me and swatted me on the backside with his hockey stick saying, "They ain't payin' ya to lay on the boards. Let's go!" Death was coming from deep down in my gullet, but I stood back up on shaky legs and started skating. I felt like lying down, but a million hours of training and practice kept me on my feet.

The culprit behind the stick swat was Charley McVeigh, a little guy they all called the Rabbit. Charley was a short left-handed shooter who barely weighed a buck fifty soaking wet. Boy, could he ever skate fast. When he got pumping, his little legs churned some real butter, leaving scrapes in the ice. When he skated by me and tapped me on the ass, he was going at a good clip. It didn't hurt half as much as my head, but it did sting a bit. It was nerve-wracking as hell to have anyone on the team thinking I was some lazy, drunken slacker.

We scrimmaged a little that afternoon, everybody trying their hardest to not just earn a spot on the team, but a spot on the starting line up. We all wanted to prove we deserved to be starters so we could get ice time in games. Rabbit, Mickey, Dick, and I took turns scoring on alternating shots that morning, and I could see we might become either great teammates or bitter rivals for that coveted first line spot. Dick was a sure thing since he was the captain, but the rest of us had to fight. We raced up the ice, weaving in and out of traffic, avoiding the big checks coming our way from Percy and Bob.

I accidently made up a nickname for them that stuck amongst the guys when I called them the peanut butter sandwich line. All the great teams had nicknames for the top scoring line-ups, but the great defensive pairings rarely got any consideration.

Charley had just slipped between Bob and Percy, who were skating hard toward him on either side. To slip through untouched, he put on a burst of speed so fast they had to jump aside to keep from delivering terrible smashes on each other. I said to Mickey as he skated by, "You better do whatever you can to avoid getting caught in a peanut butter sandwich if you know what's good for you."

It took him a minute to understand what I meant. "P is for Percy, B for Bob. It's clever," he said. After that, the phrase got repeated a lot by the guys. This did not make me popular with Bob and Percy, but later in the day, I added the jelly portion, saying that no one wanted to be made into jelly by the Peanut Butter and Jelly Sandwich line. The big boys liked that better, and they started heartily smacking me on the back each time I scored.

By the time the afternoon skate rolled around, the coach had seen how well Dick and I had been partnering up on the ice. It felt really good to be skating for the day with someone who knew exactly where I was going to be on the ice, sometimes even before I did. His passes would come between my legs from behind and appear exactly where they needed to be, or they'd come bouncing over an opponent's stick and land right on the fat part of mine. All of his passes were hand-delivered and marked for scoring, and I found the twine in the back of the net several times.

Getting any of the pucks past Jean-Paul was tricky. You couldn't just skate up and throw a simple wrister at the net. Dick did some fancy stick handling when he'd try, and he scored a little too. This meant a few goals went past Jean-Paul, which didn't seem to bother him. More were scored on poor Hugh at the other end of the ice.

Fitting in with all the players was going to be difficult. I had to be careful what I said and did around them. Most of them came from small towns like I did, but the majority of them had played together the previous season in Portland. None of them were taking away a spot on the roster from anyone, like Mickey and I might. These guys knew some of the players laid off in the closing of the other pro leagues. They knew guys with experience who were now left out in the cold. This painted a big bull's-eye on my back. At least playing well was a good start.

I didn't get to play much with Mickey, but he was doing just fine playing alongside two other guys named Georgie and Cully. I watched him skate hard at Jean-Paul and stop suddenly, showering him with ice and water several times. This didn't shake Jean-Paul out of his zone. He was able to shut Mickey down more often than not, his goaltending job remaining safe. After an excessively nasty snow shower, Jean-Paul clipped Mickey on the ear with the edge of his goal stick, which sent him to the ice. Mickey clutched the side of his head as he lay there writhing in pain.

"Son of a bitch!" Mickey shouted angrily. I knew he would start throwing some fists before too long. To his credit, Mickey got up and skated by the goalie without saying a word to him. I didn't know how this would end, or if it was worse that they didn't just fight. The next pass Mickey made by Jean-Paul ended with another snow shower. That time the puck ended up in Jean-Paul's glove.

"Were you trying to give me this thing, eh?" Jean-Paul taunted him, pointing toward the back of the goal net. "It is supposed to go in there, no?" That's when the fight broke loose. Jean-Paul and Mickey were going at it. I started to jump off the bench, but Coach Muldoon grabbed a handful of sweater and jerked me back.

"Let them work this out on their own, kid." He said it like it was part of some plan. I was worried Mickey was going to murder our goalkeeper. Mickey swung a haymaker that Jean-Paul ducked safely out of the way of. After a few wild punches, neither of them able to connect with more than a glancing blow, the P, B, and J boys broke it up. Mickey skated away, huffing and puffing while Jean-Paul grinned, looking as calm as could be.

CHAPTER NINE

The locker room buzzed with stories of what everyone had done that day in practice. Each player recounted his goal like it was the greatest achievement in sports to date. The prospect of getting placed on a top line was palpable for everyone. The coach walked in to make an announcement as we were getting dressed.

"I hope you know today was just garbage out there, boys. You were all too slow, shot too weak, and skated like a bunch of sissy girls and goaltenders. You're all way too tender, if you know what I mean." It was a typical coach speech, no matter how well practice or games went. I looked at Jean-Paul's face when Pete made the last jibe, but his face was expressionless. "We'll be changing the lines tomorrow until I get some proper production out of you clowns." As if he had forgotten something unimportant, he added, "Be here thirty minutes early tomorrow."

"How come, Coach?" someone in the locker room asked.

Pete looked around the room as if to catch the culprit before saying, "'Cuz I says so, you bunch of pansies." He started to walk out of the room, thought better of it, then turned back. "There's going to be some reporters here to interview some of you, and we're taking a team photo. For the likes of me, I can't imagine why, but be here!" He stormed out of the locker room.

Dick walked over to me after the door closed behind the coach. "You did well out there today, Bennet."

"Th-thanks."

"You are a natural scorer," he continued, "just like I saw in Milwaukee." I started to interrupt him to say thanks again, but his face was stern, so I didn't. "I watched you learn a few things today."

He paused long enough for me to respond. "Thanks, I'm really trying to do a good job."

"Yeah, that's great," he replied quickly. "Now we need to talk about why you can't seem to score on him." Dick pointed to Jean-Paul, sitting on the bench tying up his shoelaces. I had grown uncomfortable and nervous, so I focused in on how many times Jean-Paul was wrapping his laces around themselves to make a bow. He seemed to have some ritual about it that reminded me of my own issue. That was just the sort of thing I found in people, and everyone had something odd about how they acted.

"I don't know what you mean."

"What I mean is that you go hard on Hugh's end of the ice, and you barely make an effort on the other." I wasn't sure where this was coming from since I had scored on Jean-Paul, maybe not as well as on Hugh, but some. Was I taking it easy on him? I didn't think so.

Dick got up to leave.

"Um, Dick, I wanted to thank you for what you did in the office with—"

"I don't know what you're talking about. Focus on playing both ways tomorrow, or I'll have you skating till you puke." He pulled his coat on and walked out of the locker room, leaving me sitting on the bench, confused. I looked over to see what Jean-Paul was doing. He had already left while I was talking to Dick. He hadn't said anything to me all day, and he hadn't asked to go out that evening.

CHAPTER TEN

September 11, 1926

A good night's rest cleared my head. I hadn't even been bothered by Mickey's snoring, which I assumed he did all night as usual. We had both gone back to Moira's and flopped into our beds for the remainder of the evening. We were exhausted from our first real big league practice. Waking up bright and early on a Saturday morning after the hard practices over the last few days wasn't going to be easy. Unfortunately, the coach always called the shots.

Mickey paid the cabbie after he dropped us off behind the Coliseum. I was getting sick of everyone around me paying for everything. The crowd had already gathered, waiting for the doors to open. We pushed through the crowd to get to the players' entrance. Reporters in straw boaters shouted questions at us. "What does it feel like to play for Chicago?" "Can we get a quote about why you chose an Indian mascot?" I had no idea what they were talking about. As far as I knew, no one had even seen the real bona fide team sweaters.

Mickey leaned into me and said, "Guess one of these scoops snuck a peak at the new sweater design. Indian, huh?" All the while, several of them shouted at Dick, trying to get him to turn around to talk to them after he reached the door. He opened it as Mickey and I met up with him. That's when Mickey turned to the reporters.

"Do you want to take a photo of me from my good side?" he joked, showing the crowd his left profile. He then turned his right side to them, pointing at his cheek. "Or my good side?" Both of my eyes rolled all the way into the back of my head. Photos snapped, puffs of smoke from the flash trays blinding people. I blinked several times, seeing green circles floating in front of everything. Dick grabbed me around the waist and pulled me inside, Mickey following us in while waving to the crowd.

We had been told to dress in our game gear and report to some hallway area in the main concourse to be interviewed. Getting dressed was going to be an absolutely fantastic treat, because we were going to see our official sweaters for the first time. Until then, we had been playing in our practice ones.

The major's wife, who was well known in the fashion world, designed our emblem herself. So whether it was up to par or not, he had little choice but to decide it was the best one. The crest was the head of a real Indian chief from Illinois who lived there a long time ago, and was allegedly a scary man. Indians always seemed to carry an ancient power, so if our opponents see one coming at them, they should quake a little in their boots. That was the idea, at any rate. I hate to admit it, but even though I'm no judge of art, the drawing left a lot to be desired.

"Hot off the presses. Come and get 'em." The trainers carried the large boxes into the locker room and set them on the floor. They started pulling out our sweaters by the numbers, but soon realized that most of us didn't know which number was assigned to us. They grabbed a roster sheet to start calling us by name. This was almost as exciting as playing in my first big league game. Almost.

The sweater they handed me was grand looking. Its crisp black and white stripes with the giant Indian face on the front gave me gooseflesh. I hurriedly flipped it over to read my number. The number nine was in ten-inch tall writing over the back. "Hey, dummy. Don't forget your stockings and your pants," one of the trainers said as he threw them to me. The stockings had black and white stripes that matched the sweater, and the black pants had a white stripe on the bottom. They were really short pants since they only went down to the knee area, but grown men would never allow them to be called that.

I looked around the room at all of the guys putting on their uniforms for the first time. Some just slipped them on as if it meant nothing new to them, and it probably didn't at that. Most of them had worn at least two other pro sweaters. This was my first. Mickey was grinning ear to ear when he caught my eye. He clutched his sweater in his fist, shaking it in a triumphant gesture. He was absolutely right. This meant something and needed to always mean something. I decided then and there I'd have a new tradition that would happen no matter which team I played for. With both arms stuck inside the sweater, I paused and kissed the number on the back before slipping it over my head. The number nine is as good a number as any. Maybe it'll be a lucky hockey number.

The boys complained about clacking through the concrete halls on our skates because it would dull or chip the blades. No one had thought this through very well.

The whole team gathered to take photos for the press in the main hall, which was just off of the front entrance to the Coliseum. We heard that the coach and the owner hoped the pictures would be in the Sunday papers. The chances of that happening seemed pretty high, since the owner of the team was a true to life war hero. I had been too young for the Great War, but my older brother wasn't so lucky. When he left for France, I started to read everything available about the war. I loved to, needed to, learn about the big battles, planes, tanks, and the like. Being in a plane high above the ground with the wind in your hair must be the closest thing to the free feeling I got when ice-skating. I wondered if my brother had gotten a chance to feel that.

Major Fredric McLaughlin, the team owner, commanded the entire room to circle around him as if he was about to give a speech, which he, in fact, was. He was a striking figure, tall and well built, dressed in fine military regalia, medals and all. He must have seen a lot of action to win that many medals. Is it "win," or do they "get" them? Or are they awarded? Regardless, he looked dashing, not scared, like the boys back home did as they boarded the train that would take them off to war.

As powerful as the major looked, the woman standing next to him really drew everyone's attention. He was the third or fourth husband of the extremely beautiful Mrs. Irene Castle, who carried herself with this straight-backed, yet relaxed demeanor. She appeared proud and professional, yet had a playfulness about her. I may never have seen the major before, but I'd seen her. Her pictures were in advertisements in just about all the papers and catalogues. She was a fashion model with short, brown hair and wispy clothing that flowed like I'd imagined an angel's would. She looked like the classiest flapper I've ever seen.

She was standing next to the major. However, she was not clinging to his arm like most of the wives of rich husbands I'd seen. She was off on her own, talking to different people, yet remained close enough to be supportive. Every time someone asked for her photo, she stepped close to her husband, making sure he was in the shot. She did it with such ease and carelessness it seemed rehearsed, as if people clamored for her often.

The fellas had seen her too. They jostled each other for position like they were in front of the goalmouth waiting for an opportunity to make a great shot. Mickey had made his way over to me. "Wow, did you get a load of the dame? That broad's got gams!" He draped his arm over my shoulder, and I could smell the acrid coffee Moira always made clinging to his breath.

She had that certain something, although her appeal to me was more in line with the awe I felt for, well, Jean-Paul's fine automobile. Wait. That's insulting. She's not a car, and I didn't want to drive her. I appreciated her beauty. I said to Mickey, "Ease up there, Romeo. She's married."

"To your boss," said Percy, the big lummox of a defenseman. "To your boss's boss, technically. So don't jerk around and get your newly hired ass fired." He must have decided he liked us now if he was going out of his way to protect us from doing something stupid, even off the ice. From the wide-eyed look Mickey was aiming toward Mrs. Castle, he was about to get us into all sorts of trouble.

"Good point, Percy," I said, thanking him for his help.

"Agh, I wasn't gonna do anything. Just window shopping. I mean, I would like to try on the merchandise." Mickey couldn't help himself from being crass.

Jean-Paul interrupted from behind us. "Do you mean that you'd like to try on her clothing? I have to say, I'm not sure it'd fit around that belly." He finished by poking a finger at Mickey's belly. Mickey's upper chest and neck turned splotchy red.

Percy guffawed at Jean-Paul's remark. He added, "I don't think Mickey here'd make a purty woman, neither!" Everyone around chuckled and snorted.

We were making a scene with our loud banter. The coach cast warning glances our way. I grabbed Mickey by the arm just as his thermometer had reached a nice cherry red boiling point. "Ease up, buddy. The coach." I nodded my head in his direction. This seemed to settle Mickey down, although his beef with Jean-Paul was starting to concern me. Mickey had grown into a truly good friend, so I had to keep these two men from hating each other. But I didn't know how.

An unfamiliar elderly gentleman walked up to a microphone on a stand in the middle of the room. "May I have your attention? Ladies and gentlemen, on behalf of your new team, I'd like to introduce you to the mayor of this fine city, the honorable Mr. William E. Dever!"

This entire event was surely one of the grandest I've ever

witnessed. The mayor of Chicago might have been the most famous person in America, except for President Coolidge. He had started many building and road projects that defied logic and gravity, like the double-decker Wacker Drive, but somehow they all worked. He was also known to be above reproach, whereas the last mayor was as crooked as a witch's nose.

Mayor Dever, a portly man, waddled up to the microphone amid uproarious applause. He had a distinguished look, white hair and full beard. His three-piece suit was immaculately pressed, and his long gold pocket watch chain swung from one side of his vest to the other. Classy. He cleared his throat to speak.

"Thank you all so much for coming out to this grand building, the Chicago Coliseum!" This brought on another round of cheering. Frankly, we were all so enraptured with him, anything he said would have had the same effect. "It is in this fine architectural marvel that we formally announce the first of many seasons of this brand-new professional hockey team!" More applause ensued.

Jean-Paul had moved away from our little group to walk toward the back of the crowd. I wondered where he was going and craned my neck around the people to see. Percy poked me in the ribs. "Quit your rubber-necking and pay attention."

The mayor continued. "This city has a fine tradition of success, growth, and building champions. We have some amazing teams here in the city of big shoulders. Let's hope you boys have as much success as our football and baseball teams did this year. Just don't do what the Cubs did last year." People laughed. Percy leaned forward to tell me that the Cubs had finished in last place last year. They had apparently turned it around and done well this season. I needed to learn more about this city, fast.

"We are very proud to add another winner to this city!" he added. When the applause died down, he continued. "At this time, ladies and gentlemen, I'd like to introduce you to the coach of Chicago's very own ice hockey team, Mr. Peter Muldoon." More clapping and blinding photographer flashes.

I slipped away from my little group and headed to the back to see where Jean-Paul had gone. I pushed through the thick crowd of reporters, and then I saw him, or should I say *them*. He stood near the back of the crowd with a woman, talking closely into her ear. She tilted her head back several times to laugh, but she was quiet about it.

Giant motion picture cameras were set up around the main

concourse to capture the event on film. I circled around and hid behind one of the cameramen so I could spy on Jean-Paul and the woman. I couldn't hear much with the noise of the film fluttering directly into my ears. Not knowing what was going on started to make me angry. Not sure why. Jealousy maybe?

From this closer vantage point, I could see the woman was quite gorgeous. She, like Mrs. Castle, had short-cropped hair that flipped out and back toward her neck in a little curl. It was a deep red color that would have been vivacious had her hair been longer. Even short, it still drew your eyes right to her face. Her skin was pale and smooth, dotted with tiny brown freckles. She was young, maybe in her early twenties. Her dress came down to her knees and seemed to be light and airy, even though the hall was a little chilly. This woman had a kind of magnetism that drew you in and made you want to talk to her, be around her. Not just beauty, something else. I felt the same thing when I was around Jean-Paul.

They turned abruptly and walked right toward me in my hiding spot behind the cameras. Jean-Paul's face was lit up from ear to ear in a sly grin. He had caught me spying on them, although he didn't seem mad. It probably wasn't hard at all to spot one of us in the crowd, what with the ice skates putting us head and shoulders above everyone else. He made a sweeping gesture toward me with his palm open as he spoke to her. "This, my dear, is one Mr. Brett Bennet of Wisconsin. He is going places."

Jean-Paul continued his introduction, "Brett, this is the lovely and enchanting Miss Margret Field-Madison." Did she not take her husband's name? But miss? Was she widowed? Or divorced like Mrs. Castle? But she was so young. It was unbelievable to think either was true. He had surely said her maiden name was Field. That was familiar for some reason. I knew I'd heard that name somewhere before.

"A pleasure to meet you," I offered. She put her pale hand in mine. I pulled it up to my lips to kiss it gently. "How do you two know each other?"

She turned to Jean-Paul with a wry smile. "You are so right, darling." So right about what, I didn't know. What I did know was that he had been talking about me to her. That must mean something. "We have quite the sordid history, he and I," she said to me. "We've known one another since the gutters of—"

"We are old friends, let's leave it at that." Jean-Paul cut her off in mid-jibe. "We saw you standing over here, so we thought—"

"We thought what an ideal opportunity to meet the new star attraction that has this one so…" She paused to think of the right words, but Jean-Paul interrupted her before she finished.

"We really should be paying attention to the proceedings, darling," he implored. The fact that he was having thoughts about me and sharing them with her made me feel warm inside.

"Maybe you can finally tell me some of his secrets," I said to her.

The coach called the team over to the center of the hall for photos. "We'll see you later tonight," he promised her over his shoulder as we walked away.

We?

"It was very nice meeting you, Miss—"

"Margret, honey. Call me Margret." Her poise gave way to her youth as she exuberantly shouted after us, "And you'd better come by tonight too!" Tonight?

After a few photographs had been made in front of the giant oak doors that led to the seating area, Pete swung them open and motioned everyone to follow him in. The crowd followed the players, who had to scrape down the wooden stairs in our ice skates. It wasn't just dangerous to walk down stairs in them, it was a little painful. But the moment we stepped out onto the ice, just like always, I forgot about them all and started to fly.

A few minutes into our skate, photographers set up their cameras on the ice. Some of the boys nearly collided with the big, cumbersome wooden tripods. Dick wrangled us all to the center of the ice for the team photograph. I wondered if we'd each get a print of the photo they were making, or if it'd be too expensive. Did being in the official team photograph mean that each of us was now officially on the team? People get cut from teams, but this had to make the odds higher that we'd all stay.

We were quickly put into rows, mostly by height. I was in the middle row behind Mickey. Jean-Paul, in all his goalie gear, sat on the ice in the front row a little to my right. The photographer kept telling us to move before insisting that we hold still. Staying in position for minutes at a time while they got it right got boring for some of the boys. They started goofing around and got yelled at by Dick and Pete to cut it out.

When the photograph was developed later, each of us did not get one. A big print was pinned up in the locker room for all to see. I was embarrassed by how I looked. The still captured my face flawlessly.

I had the scrunched-up grimace I get when overly nervous about something, with serious forehead lines. But my eyes aren't facing forward. They're focused on someone in the front row to my right.

CHAPTER ELEVEN

Practice ended right after the press left the stadium. The coach said the rest of the day was ours to do with as we pleased. Seeing the sights of the city was at the top of the list, since I hadn't gotten to do much of that so far. All my time had been divided between body-bruising practices and dwelling on a certain someone, so I was glad to get away on a Saturday night to have some fun without fear of early practice in the morning.

It took some walking, a bus, and two different streetcar rides before I finally made it to the north side of the city. I didn't think we were going to survive some of the turns those things made. The crisscross patchwork pattern of cables hanging overhead often gets stretched and pulled taut as the streetcars rock side to side under their own weight and speed. At a few places, they came dangerously close to coming off the rails as I hung on for dear life.

The conductor pointed to the enormous stadium where he said the football team and one of the baseball teams played. He called it Cubs Park but the sign read Wrigley Field. Plenty of businesses along Clark Street sold everything from fruit to men's ties. I bought a banana for twenty cents and its freshness amazed me. It was worth the money, even though it was borrowed money from Mickey. I felt a little guilty he wasn't with me, but he seemed excited to go out with the other players. They were heading to a burlesque show, which didn't quite hold the same appeal for me as it did for them. Besides, I knew he didn't like Jean-Paul very much. I wanted to change that, but I didn't know how.

Loads of people were moving to and fro no matter where you went in this city. Every street had construction. Buildings were going up or being repaired on every block. I could have wandered around investigating the city all day, but it was getting near time to meet Jean-Paul at Margret's apartment. Two more dangerous streetcar rides, and I was downtown, close to the address Jean-Paul had given me.

None of the buildings had addresses on their doors, and I got confused and more lost by the minute. Finally, a doorman dressed nicer than me approached and asked if he could help me. One look at the piece of paper with her address, and he opened the hotel doors. "Welcome to the Palmer, sir," he said. "The front desk will help you. You have a good night now, sir." Two sirs. I thanked him as I slowly entered the hotel lobby.

The Palmer House was opulent. The high, curved ceilings had been painted with ornate frescoes. Fancy lights hung every few feet. It must have cost a fortune to light the place, let alone heat it. Bellboys buzzed around carrying bags and leading guests around, but that didn't stop several of them from offering to help me all the same. The man at the front desk watched me silently as I looked around from expensive paintings to the couch to a piano. "How may I help you this evening, sir?"

"Um, I'm…looking for someone. Margret, um…" What was her last name? "Field something."

The moment I had said her name, he brightened and stood straighter. "Ah, Ms. Field-Madison, yes. She would be on the twentieth floor." Noticing my glassy-eyed look, he directed a bellboy to help me find the elevator. The bellboy walked to the elevator bank and pressed the button. When the doors clanged open, the bellboy put his hand out for a tip. A nickel later, the elevator operator was speeding us up hundreds of feet. I readied another nickel.

The bang of the carved brass doorknocker reverberated throughout the hallway. It felt rude to make that much noise in such a fancy place. Margret appeared at the door a moment later by herself, dressed in a knee-length red silk gown that clung to her in several places. Her hair was wrapped in a towel, and she had clearly come from a bathtub in the last few minutes. The robe stuck to her back, causing the bottom to come up over her thighs, exposing some of her backside.

"Oh." I tried to look up over her head, but she just swatted me on the arm.

"Hiya, Brett. Come on in, don't be shy." Margret turned and walked into the foyer.

"Am I early? I can come back if it's a bad time."

She stopped and turned to me. "Nonsense, it'll give me time to get to know you." She leaned forward and gave me a full, wraparound hug with both arms. It was terribly off-putting to be embraced by practically a total stranger.

"So, Jean-Paul isn't here yet?" I asked.

"I wouldn't expect that boy to be on time for his own funeral, and if he doesn't get here soon, that'll happen even quicker than he thinks." She giggled at her own joke as the door swung open to the rest of her apartment.

It was lavishly appointed and expansive, with a living room, sitting room, two bedrooms, a kitchen, and its own bath. The hotel room was bigger than most full-sized houses. The main area doubled as a sitting room with oversized, stuffed couches and high-backed, red cloth chairs. The throw carpets looked like Persian rugs that surely weren't real, just meant to look that way. A fluffy white cat sat on top of the chair.

I hated cats.

"Make yourself comfortable and get a drink," she yelled from the bedroom.

A dark, wooden bar angled off the edge of the couch, containing several bottles of expensive vodka, rum and whiskey. The whole place smacked of high prices. Wonder how she afforded it without a husband.

While I made two drinks with rum in them like I had seen done before, Margret changed into her evening clothes. She didn't bother to close the bedroom door. I turned and glanced just in time to see her slip out of her robe into a silky undergarment.

"Where are you from again?" she asked, catching me off guard. I had been looking at her beautiful curves in the mirror. Seeing nude women was not a daily occurrence where I was from. I had to admit I was curious enough to catch a few more glimpses, but I started to worry that she'd seen me and would think me a fiend.

"Wisconsin. Delavan, you know, home of the circus?" I said it on the slim chance that she had heard of my town. "How about you?"

"I adore the circus. You must take me when it comes to town again," she said, sounding more genuine than simply polite. "I bet you must know all the—what are they called—roost abouts?"

"Roustabouts," I corrected. "Not really."

She walked out and spun around, exposing her bare back with the zipper of her dress down. I assumed she meant for me to zip her up the back, so I did. "Yes, yes. Do you have my drink, darling?"

"Right here," I said, reaching back to the bar.

"Tell me all there is to know about you, you handsome devil, you.

Everything." She sat down on the chaise, held the drink to her lips, and stared at me over the edge of the glass.

"Well, there really isn't much to say. I'm from a small town, play hockey, got signed in Chicago, and now I'm here."

She took a deep breath, smiled and exhaled. "What do you think of Jean-Paul?"

Wow. That was abrupt and unexpected. Was it a trap? I wasn't sure what to say without incriminating myself. "He's…interesting." The drink was sour and made my throat raw as I slurped too much of it to avoid the rest of this conversation. My face burned from the heat of the drink.

"He is, isn't he?"

Curiosity took over. "How is it you know him, exactly?" It was bold, but she acted nothing but bold in every move she'd made so far.

Margret slid down the chaise toward me. "Jean-Paul is, shall we say, my closest friend in life and death."

This did not make sense to me. "Are you two, well, together?" I asked nervously, not really wanting the answer.

Margret spilled a little of her drink back into the glass from her mouth. "No, honey. It depends on whom you ask, but we are not together. I've known Jean-Paul for a few years now, long enough to know better."

"Didn't he just come to Chicago to play for the team?" My own question made me realize I didn't know anything about him other than how he made me feel when he was around.

"Yes, he did, although he's been playing his game for a long time now. He's been coming to the scene here for years." It was like a secret code she was talking, and I did not have the cipher to crack it. The question I most wanted answered was when Jean-Paul would get there.

"So you met him while he was on a hockey trip," I declared more than asked.

She took a slow drink, crossed her legs, and set the glass against the top of her knee. "Hockey, of course. We met out and about on the town a few years ago, while he was in for a game. You know there's been a hockey team here for many years?"

I actually did. It made the whole day's events at the press conference seem like a stunt to sell tickets since having a team here wasn't exactly news, and I said as much. She said I was very astute.

"So did you and he ever…"

"Date?" she interrupted. "No. Well, there was a moment when I… anyway, he and I are both quite free, so don't worry."

What? What had she just said? What did she mean? We sat on the couch in silence for an eternity. Jealousy had given way to panic. I didn't want to be there with her anymore. It was not really her fault. She must be a fine person, but something was off.

"This is a nice place. How long have you lived here?" The conversation had grown awkward enough. It was time to move on.

"I've lived here for about two years now." Looking around at the blouses and dresses strewn against chairs and laid on the floor, she had obviously been there a while. Her face grew sullen and blue, her silence inflicting guilt on me for having asked, although I had no idea why. Almost to herself, she quietly added, "Has it been that long?"

"It's a nice place. Better than nice, actually. It's bigger than any house I've seen." This was not making her feel any better. "I'm sorry if I've upset you in any way. I didn't think we'd…I'd…be here alone for so long, imposing on you."

She snapped out of her mood with a suddenness that frightened me. "Oh, don't you worry about it. We are going to go have a lot of fun tonight," she boasted loudly.

The knocker banged on the outside door, startling both of us. Margret bolted upright and rushed to answer it, squealing like a little girl.

CHAPTER TWELVE

Jean-Paul stormed into the room, hugging us both, all the while talking nonstop about traffic in town and crazy autoists, without ever once offering an apology for being late. Although Margret seemed annoyed not two minutes ago, she beamed from ear to ear, talking about which waiters she liked best, and the clubs we were going to visit. After the fourth or fifth place she mentioned, I started to worry I'd never make it home.

"Have you been treating my best girl with the proper respect?" he asked me with a fake look of concern as he walked by me to grab her scarf from a coat rack. He was, of course, dressed to the nines again. He wore a white suit coat and pants, with shiny, pointed black shoes. His own scarf choice was black, his hat white. He looked dashing, like a young nightclub owner.

"Of course he has," Margret said, leaning in to kiss me on the cheek when she returned. "He knows how to treat a lady with respect, after all. He's from Wisconsin!" She proclaimed it as fact, as if everyone back home knew how to treat women. I intimately knew it wasn't true because of my father.

"Good. He'd better, eh?" Jean-Paul said as he grabbed my coat sleeve for a second. Shivers went up my arm; surely my whole body quivered. He noticed. "Are you cold? We need to get you some new clothes with your first check," he said, slowly fingering the fabric of my coat lapel.

Margret stared at me as I reached for the drink that had been neglected on the coffee table. I wasn't sure what thoughts lay behind her look, but it seemed more like jealousy than anything else.

Having generously tipped the doorman, we roared away from the hotel and sped down State Street toward the north end of the city. Jean-Paul made sure to drive exactly the same as he had before, regardless of a lady being in the car. He weaved in and out of traffic, coming much closer to streetcars, cabs, and people than I felt comfortable with. Judging by Margret's screeches, she felt none too comfortable either. He ignored the brand-new traffic signal at Division, sharply turned left, and screeched the tires while turning right on LaSalle. He was either guessing, or he sure knew the city streets well.

"Where are we going in such a hurry?" I wondered aloud.

The car slammed to a halt on Broadway after several hairpin turns. We were in front of the glowing, twinkling sign that read *The Green Mill*. There must have been over a hundred light bulbs that covered the whole thing. Jean-Paul handed the keys to the valet, and we headed toward the door. He let Margret get a few feet in front of us before pulling me back to his side.

"Don't make me look bad by reaching for your billfold. Tonight is on me." Then he let me go to catch up with Margret before I could protest.

The Mill, as everyone called it, was a long, narrow room with a big wooden bar in the front half. Round booths with high backs covered in gold sat along the sides of the bar, with smaller, rickety tables filling in the rest of the open floor. The juice joint was jammed with people sitting in every seat at the bar, in the booths, and also wall to wall along the front entrance, waiting for seats. There was a piano behind the bar. The doorman, a short portly fellow, had handlebar mustachios waxed to stick straight out to the sides. Jean-Paul greased his palm and we got inside, walking to a table with a "Reserved" note card on it.

To get to our table, we had to walk toward the back where the musicians played on an elevated stage. The bartender appeared to be slowly sinking behind the bar, his head disappearing with each step. It was curious. I popped my head over the edge of the wooden bar rails to see where he went. A trap door behind the bar swung open, with narrow wooden stairs leading to a basement. Having a cellar entrance in the middle of the room was quite odd.

"Jean-Paul, where does that lead?" I asked.

"Let's hope you don't find out tonight," he answered without answering, leaving me with a mystery.

Live jazz music filled the room with peppy syncopation. Occasionally, if the crowd started to talk too much over the music, the doorman or the barkeep would hold his finger to his lips and shush the crowd.

Martinis showed up at our table without being ordered. Did

everyone in town know these two? How much money did he make to be so well known at every speakeasy in town? They both seemed to have money, and I had none to speak of. Jean-Paul wanted me to ride on his good graces or suffer him some insult, which was a new concept for me. Back home, that was simply called freeloading.

Margret and Jean-Paul drank several stiff drinks, whereas I sipped mine slowly. I sat between them, so they had to lean into and over me to talk. Jean-Paul placed his arm around my shoulders and with his dangling hand, pointed to a booth to the right of the bar, across from the exit door where a well-dressed, chubby man was sitting.

"Do you have any idea who that is?" he asked, sounding impressed and excited.

I had no idea, although the man looked important. He had been sitting on the end of the bar, being tended to by just about every waiter that passed. Margret grew giddy with a little, kid-sized smile. "Oh wow, is that him?" She leaned her head in close so the three of our faces were practically touching.

"Who?"

"That's Big Al."

Even I knew who he was. He was the biggest gangster in town, maybe in America. He pretty much ran all the rackets and bootlegging in the city. He was famous for being a nice guy and being well liked. He was also famous for killing people. All my instincts screamed at me to get up out of the booth, even if I had to slink down between their legs to get the hell out of that place. That's when Big Al noticed us looking, which froze me to my seat. Margret waved. He smiled our way and raised one of his fingers back, and that concluded our brush with crime. Jean-Paul paid the bill, and we all got up to leave.

We strolled a little ways until we arrived at a place with a sign out front that read *Mann's Million Dollar Rainbo Room*. Margret cracked a joke about how they had misspelled the name, but Jean-Paul ignored her, pushing us under the awning and into the front doors. The place was a palace, with lush wall-to-wall carpet, fine furnishings in the hallways, and doormen at each entry. Jean-Paul said we were going to a restaurant close by. He had not mentioned the place was a giant, arena-sized dance hall. Inside, a band played swing music for about two thousand people who were eating their dinners.

Once again, we had steaks and baked potatoes smothered in sour cream and bacon. They served fresh corn on the cob with sweet iced tea, which was spiked with some variety of bathtub gin. The food tasted so good, it had to be out of my price range. Margret had ordered a filet mignon and moaned with delight at every bite she took. It was very unladylike, but she didn't seem to care what we, or anyone around us, thought about it.

Margret played by her own rules. She did not follow the accepted standards for women. She didn't cover her mouth, she talked while she ate, and she drank alcohol. She even burped during dinner and giggled instead of apologizing. My mother would have thought her a beast. When she did these things, she did them in such a way that I couldn't help liking her more. She wasn't boorish or crass, just freer than most.

After the band finished, a comedian told jokes and sang wildly funny songs about his first driving experience. It reminded me of getting in the car with Jean-Paul. Some were a little off color, and I foolishly worried Margret would be offended. After a while, the comedian left the stage, our sides still hurting from laughing. As another band started to play on the revolving stage, Jean-Paul asked us if we felt up to a little dancing.

The ballroom at the nightclub had a large, wooden dance floor, where a few older couples were slowly making the rounds. That got Margret excited. It made me feel a little queasy. We had drunk a lot already, and I had hardly eaten enough to soak up the alcohol. My stomach churned at the idea of dancing in front of them, no matter how much we had imbibed. I didn't think I'd vomit, but I thought about making a hasty retreat to the bathroom just the same.

To our surprise, instead of leading us to the dance floor, Jean-Paul led us both away from the massive stages and dance areas of the Rainbo Room. He pulled us along until we were outside, where he cajoled us down the block.

"What was wrong with the last place, if you don't mind me asking?" I inquired as to the seemingly unnecessary change of venue. We had walked to another large building with a long marquee, called the Aragon Ballroom.

"Nothing," he said. "Why nothing wrong with it at all, if you want to dance with the ancient and decrepit to that boring drivel." He gestured at the Aragon sign that read *Live Jazz Tonight*. "Now, this place will be really wailing."

His excitement raged like a fever. Margret squealed, grabbed my arm tight, and ushered me forward. "Easy, don't break my arm."

"Is the poor little hockey player getting hurt by little old me?" she said through giggles.

We walked inside to the sounds of a live jazz band. The long hallway was wide and made of beautiful flecked marble. The music bounced off the walls and came at us from all angles. Entering the main hall, we saw hundreds of people dancing under the football field–sized ceiling. People were drinking booze out of coffee cups, which I passed on. The band must have had ten or more players in it, most of whom were black.

Jean-Paul and Margret danced every dance for an hour or so before I felt bold enough to give it a try. They prodded me to dance over and over, but I'd steadily refused. Finally, Margret and I swung around the floor for a while, having a grand time. Dancing to the odd beats of jazz was tough, but we had fun trying.

"You're wondering about him, aren't you?" Margret surmised.

"I have to admit he doesn't quite fit the bill. Most of the players I know are farm boys, ruffians, and he's so…"

"Refined? Well, he's quite practiced. You know his parents made him leave home very early when they…" Her eyes clouded with the edge of tears.

Jean-Paul cut in and swung Margret around a few twirls before spinning her back to me. "His parents were cold people," she continued as if never having been interrupted. "No one deserves being cut out. Even though he didn't come from big money, they weren't poor by any means. He had grown accustomed to certain things, things he had to give up for a while, which is why he didn't end up on Montreal's team, where he wanted. He had to leave and has been floundering to get noticed again, until now. But we've been doing okay, he and I."

Jean-Paul cut in again and pushed Margret out of the way to make a show of dancing with me. She put on like the interruption offended her, but moved aside to let us dance. The people around us laughed at this as well. He smiled and smoothly swayed his hips around, but my body stiffened when he put his hand on the small of my back to lead.

That's when the police whistles started blowing. The crowd erupted into madness in a split second. People dashed everywhere, coffee cups crashing to the ground across the hall. Sweat popped up on my forehead, breath catching in my throat. I was going to prison for lewd indecent behavior, dancing with a man. The team wouldn't have anything to do with me. I'd have to move, never work again.

"God damn Mayor Dever and his private little war!" Jean-Paul yelled to no one in particular. The mayor was tough on crime. Sometimes the police do the proper rounds, regardless of who has paid for a blind eye. I wondered if these places ever asked for some of their bribe money back after a shakedown. Margret laughed, an incredibly excited look on her face, like we were riding rides at the state fair. Sometimes she looked as sweet as an angel, at others like a mischievous child.

Jean-Paul grabbed us by the hands and led us to the side of the room. "Come on, quick, down, down." We rushed down the stairs together. We went through a small door into a crowded tunnel below the hall. The crowd had the same escape route in mind, the tunnels already crammed with around a hundred people, more streaming in behind us every second.

We ran down the tunnel with all these strangers, some having a grand time, others crying and panicking. Up ahead of us, the crowd split into two groups, heading in opposite directions. Jean-Paul shouted more instructions to us. "Left, go to the left. It comes up under the Riviera Theatre. We'll be safe there."

How did he know so much about these tunnels? They looked to go on for miles and miles. My jaw clenched and unclenched as we ran. Several minutes passed in near darkness, my heart pounding, and my forehead wet with sweat. We could get lost forever under the city. The dim lights bobbed and swayed overhead as we ran down the cramped aisle. It started. One light swinging left, one light swinging right, two lights swinging left…

Jean-Paul must have noticed when I slowed to count. He grabbed me harshly by the jacket, jerking me forward. "Don't crack up now, mon petit."

"Dying in the catacombs was not my idea of a fun evening," I said, sounding like a petulant child.

Margret swatted me on the shoulder. "Lighten up, you little wet blanket. Don't be such a daisy. Keep moving before we get pinched by some flatfoot." She stopped talking for a second, took a few more steps, and then thought better of remaining silent. "The last thing either of you need is to spend a night in the cooler. What would the team say then?"

I stopped dead in my tracks, petrified. About ten people slammed into my back, almost pitching me over on my face. She burst out in hysterics. "You should see the look on your face. JP, honey, did you see his face? Come on, babe. Don't be such a chump." She pushed people off me and wrapped around my arm to pull me in close. Somehow, this absurdity turned my growing rage into laughter, which spread like wildfire amongst the crowd of drunken partygoers.

About forty or so of us climbed the stairs at the other end of the tunnel, emerging into another dance hall. It was amazing so many nightclubs could exist so close to one another and make enough money without being able to properly sell booze. Prohibition was not alive and well in Chicago. Jean-Paul led us through the club, out the side doors, and into the alleyway to our freedom. The rotten food and rats accentuated the fine point on the end of the evening.

"Ha-ha! What a grand time that was, no?" Jean-Paul shouted.

Margret shushed him as we walked quickly and quietly through the alleyway back to the main street. My entire body shook with the terrible excitement. The night had been a mixture of absolute fear and wonderful thrills. To be caught in a gin joint might mean getting kicked off the team, career over before it had begun. Either way, we broke out of there, safe and sound, thanks to Jean-Paul.

CHAPTER THIRTEEN

September 17, 1926

One week passed by with hardly a word between Jean-Paul and myself. He wasn't mean or angry looking; he just focused on hockey during the workweek. Immediately after practice, he would light out of the locker room with all speed. The other fellas made comments about the fact that he wouldn't go carousing with them. They thought him snooty, palling around with rich folk, acting too good for them. I don't know if I enjoyed the team's company either, but if I didn't make a show of letting them buy me horrible tasting drinks occasionally, they might not back me up in a scrape.

In a way, it was nice to be able to build those relationships and forget the fact that I felt over my head in a world I may have had no business in. After all, this underweight, under-muscled kid from the sticks played in the big city with some full-grown, giant bruisers. Percy, one of those bruisers, had arranged for a bunch of us to go out after practice. He was secretive about where we were going. Word around the locker room was that most of them had been going to the burlesque shows, so we'd probably be seeing the Can Can. I had never seen it, so was looking forward to that part, at least.

We had gotten paid that afternoon, and it felt good to be able to square away with Mickey. He joked with me when I paid him, asking, "Where's the vig?" He then had to explain it meant interest on a loan. I told him I'd treat him to some drinks that night, and he could count that as the "vig."

As far as pay goes, it wasn't much. I thought it would be a lot more, but the coach said taxes and medical expenses got taken out of everybody's pay. I made a note to talk to Mr. Irvin about that first chance I had. That'd have to wait, because it was well known in the locker room that Dick never drank a drop, and he wouldn't be going out with the boys to houses of ill repute of any kind. He wasn't the only force out there against drinking either.

The Women's Christian Temperance Union had made lots of inroads in Chicago, stopping people from imbibing spirits. Since we stepped off the train that first night, we'd seen bills posted at the station, along construction fences, and even around the Coliseum. We had run into a group of women in long frumpy dresses, trying to talk to us on the streets about the evils of drinking and the sin of gluttony. They sounded sure that if a man were to give in to the temptations of drink, he would feel the fires of hell. Being raised Christian and not being much of a lush, I saw their point. I hadn't known a lot of good to come from drinking. Some of the other boys just poked fun at them, even to their faces.

We all piled into Percy and Bob's beaters, made our way to a mostly deserted avenue, and parked. We walked down the avenue, a rowdy, belligerent crew, and stopped in front of a row of houses. Percy opened the chain link gate between the houses to step through.

"Shit, Perce, do you know the folks that live here?" Gordie asked. I think getting pinched for trespassing made it on my list of concerns too.

Percy playfully pushed Gordie into the fence. "Lay off, ya crazy futz. Trust me. I know what I'm doing." This did not inspire confidence in me. As we walked down the gangway between the two-flat houses, the sound of music wafted toward us. We walked down the stairs of one of the houses. At the bottom stood a large, bald doorman. Should I worry that every place I seemed to go had a big guy outside as a bouncer?

We each paid a dollar to get in. I paid two to cover Mickey's entrance fee. He clapped me hard on the back and exclaimed, "Yes! This is what I've been talking about, Bennet. Time to stop being pals with the queer goalie and time to get in the big leagues." I stared at the back of his head when he walked by me, wondering what he meant by calling Jean-Paul queer. Why did he think him odd? Aren't all goaltenders strange people with strange rituals? That must have been it.

The basement cabaret was not too spectacular. They had removed everything that made it a proper basement, adding ragged, red velvet drapes from floor to ceiling, solid, hardwood floors, two bar areas, and a stage against the back brick wall. It was a small, intimate club. Off to the side of the stage, a five-piece band played some lively, swing dance music in a roped-off area. No one was dancing.

On the stage, a beautiful, scantily clad woman with two oversized white feathers did a routine called the Fan Dance. She moved around the stage, waving those fans in front of her whole body, quickly exchanging one fan for the other. She made sure to cover most of her exposed body, often showing large areas of bare skin beneath the fans. It looked very much like she was naked under the feathers.

"Marry me!" Bob shouted at the top of his lungs. The club was loud, so she probably didn't hear him.

"Are you serious?" I asked stupidly.

"Of course! Might as well give my money to someone pretty for a change," he answered, to many guffaws.

We sat down at a couple of tables in the middle of the floor and ordered drinks. What we got served, in the expected brown paper bags, was nothing more than poisonous swill. After one sip, I put mine on the table where it stayed for the rest of the night. The boys didn't seem to mind the horrific taste, chugging copious amounts of liquor. They were quickly, terribly lit.

Once the fan dancer had shown enough of her backside to whip the crowd up into a proper frenzy, she left the stage. After a brief interlude, three dancers wearing elaborate costumes replaced her. They wore see-through mesh leggings, dresses that ended in multiple layers of frill at the top of their thighs, and small bonnets on their heads. Each of them had their breasts smashed into their bustiers, pulled tight with white laces. The look appealed to the men in the room, who removed their hats to wave them in circles in the air over their heads while whooping.

The girls leaped into their rendition of the Can Can and did a kick line that showed off most, if not all, of their wares. I have to admit it was exciting and intoxicating to watch them move around the stage in synchronized steps they clearly practiced often. I even whooped and hollered along with the rest of the fellas, but for a very different reason.

A ballad singer came on stage as several of the girls made their way through the crowd to work the men into giving them tips. All of the men turned to each other and began carrying on loud conversations, rudely drowning the singer out. Every so often, one of the men in the crowd would shout to her to get off the stage or to bring back the girls. This must have been a scheduled break in the act to allow the men to drink more of the vicious swill and spend their money on the girls.

Percy leaned over and asked me if I wanted to go upstairs to have a smoke. I don't smoke and never have but agreed to go just the same.

We walked up the back staircase and sat down in what appeared to be someone's living room. A cigarette girl carrying a tray strapped around her neck came by to ask if we wanted anything. Percy bought us a couple of thick cigars, one of which he handed to me. I had no idea what to do with it, so I watched him cut the end off, lick the side, then light the other end. He puffed inward, held his breath for a moment, and then released the smoke. What an intricate ritual to do something so nasty.

I did what he had done. After inhaling a ridiculous amount of noxious smoke, I started to choke. Percy laughed at me. I slowly regained composure. I had a sip of a Coca-Cola, which drew the eyes of more than one person in the room for the crime of not being a boozehound.

After Percy's instruction to take smaller puffs, it not only became a little easier, but maybe even the slightest bit enjoyable. The horrible smell did not seem to bother me when I smoked one too. I got too busy with the act of smoking, full of the strong tastes, that the smell eluded me. Percy congratulated me. "Now you're gettin' it."

"Thanks for asking me to come out with you guys," I said.

Percy took a long drag of his stogie, let the smoke swirl around in his opened mouth for a second, then puffed it out in small white circles that expanded as they drifted away. It was a neat trick. I tried it. I failed miserably, coughing a little more.

"So a lot of the fellas is wondering about you," he started. Wondering about me? Oh God, what did he mean? "We don't know much about you."

"Not much to tell."

"I doubt that," he said, maybe a little tipsy. "Well anyway, we're real glad you came out with us tonight. Mickey seems to be enjoying himself here in Chicago. You?"

I wasn't sure where this was going. "Oh yeah, it's a great place. Big. And the guys have been real welcoming." I paused to shoot him a look before adding, "For the most part."

He chuckled before taking another drag. "Yeah, we're a bunch of ruffians and scoundrels, all right. Most of us have known each other for years. Playing on different teams, different leagues even, like your pal, Jean-Paul."

"You mean you knew him from before?" I ventured nervously.

"Yeah, played against him for a few years on different teams. Hell of a net jockey, damned hard to beat."

"Yep, having the hardest time getting it by him."

"He's a very odd fella." His eyes narrowed. "Hard to read on and off the ice. Lots of rumors about that guy."

The nerves in my legs started twitching, causing my knees to bounce up and down on their own. My hands searched for something to do, found the edge of the table and started fiddling with it. I didn't ask what rumors he meant, but it was certainly on my mind. Doing my best to deflect, I answered, "Well, he is a goalie."

Percy stared at me a moment. It was almost a glare. Then he followed my lead away from rumors to the subject of hockey. "He is one of the strangest, though. You know he can't step on a blue line on his way to the crease?" I had noticed that during practice.

"He just hops over it on his way to the net. He also had to have a brand-new pair of socks before each practice, morning and afternoon," Percy added. "And before each game for sure!" We were bonding over how goofy our friend was. It felt wrong, but it was also sort of a wicked fun. He grew serious. "You ought to stick to some of the other skaters and learn something from 'em. Like Rabbit or the Silver Fox."

"You don't mean Lester Patrick, right?" Charley's nickname was the Rabbit. That I knew. The Silver Fox was hockey legend Lester Patrick, who had just lost his Pacific Coast hockey league. He had already landed on his feet with a new hockey job. Percy couldn't have been referring to Lester, so I asked. He laughed about that.

"Old Lester could teach you a thing or two, that old coot. I meant Dick. His hair started to turn silver at the ripe old age of thirty-four. So we all call him the silver fox too." Hockey folk make up the oddest nicknames that were apparently just reused and shared. There's no telling how many guys had "little" or "rocket" before their names. Wonder what they'll call me?

He was steering me clear of Jean-Paul. I wanted to know why, but I figured I ought to move off the topic. Adjusting my worn cotton overcoat, I said, "Well, I don't think Mr. Irvin likes me all too much. He's always criticizing everything I do. He wouldn't even let me thank him for his help negotiating my contract with coach. I bet he thinks I'm a total rube."

Percy dismissed this with an exaggerated wave of his cigar. "Nah, he's just mighty competitive, you know. He wants us to be the best team we can be. In case you hadn't noticed, you're pretty jake out there, scoring goals, making passes. We work like a well-oiled engine with him working the wrenches." This felt good to hear. "He's also a bit of a top dog. You know he scored thirty goals in thirty games last year? Can you imagine it?"

"Wow. It's amazing to be able to learn from him," I said.

Percy leaned forward. "Oh Lord, don't be telling that to him, or his head'll never get through the doorways!" He leaned in close. "And don't ever talk about the negotiations out loud again. With anyone." After a few minutes of quiet, he finished. "Yeah, old Dick's a real stand-up guy." We sat in silence the rest of the time, smoking our fifty-cent cigars, me laughing at him as he blew smoke rings across the table.

CHAPTER FOURTEEN

September 25, 1926

I spent Saturday afternoon at the public library on Washington Street, right off Michigan Avenue. No matter where I went, I always seemed to end up back on Michigan Avenue. The library took up an entire square city block. The façade consisted of giant twenty-foot-tall windows so big my knees started shaking just thinking about who had to clean them. The beige color and the gothic look stood in stark contrast to the newer buildings surrounding it.

The gothic outside gave way to an interior of deep, rich woods and hundreds of rows of bookcases. The stale odor of paper filling the rooms grew thicker the farther I walked through the stacks. The librarians were helpful, finding information for me on Chicago history. Living in this metropolis would be easier once some of the streets, places, and people became less of a mystery. I was determined to learn as much as I could.

I've always read a lot, much to my father's chagrin. If he had his way, I would have lived either on the ice or behind a plow. Reading all the time and getting good grades would have severely damaged my reputation at school, if not for being on the hockey team. Most of the sports players at school were not into book learning. They were too busy trying to get girls to pay attention to them. Some occupied themselves by tormenting the weaker boys. Books or hockey: one of those two was going to be my way out of that town.

The newspapers the librarians brought over to the table weren't helpful. They reported the city was exploding with new construction, and crime and bootlegging had been stamped out since the new mayor had taken over from the last, corrupt one. From what I had seen in the last two weeks, this was not the case at all. I switched to looking at books on the history of the city and maps. Lots of maps.

I learned about the "L" trains, frustrated to find out how much of my money had been wasted so far on cabs and streetcar exchanges. The train did the same job cheaper. Chicago already had a vast system of streetcars and elevated trains I could have taken to within a block of the baseball field.

I worked my way through the stack of books by my side, slowly flipping through them and placing them in a discard pile. The librarians seemed to enjoy my quest, coming by every few minutes with another interesting book. The problem with all this quiet study was that I kept thinking about him every few minutes.

Even though I developed a mental picture of the overall grid system of the city with each book I devoured, spending the afternoon in the library became taxing. I left with my head swimming in street names and architects like Burnham. But bounding alone around the city was an excellent distraction from all the stress of the team. It also provided some much needed time to decide what I wanted to do next.

Back at Moira's, I called Jean-Paul's telephone. He didn't answer, but his next-door neighbor did. They had a party line. Not knowing what to say or what I was going to say if he'd answered, I just said my name and disconnected. I walked down the hallway to go back up to my room before turning back, picking up the receiver, and phoning Margret's hotel. They connected me to her room right away, and when she answered, we made plans to have dinner.

CHAPTER FIFTEEN

Chicago is not a walking city by far, but with a few coins in my pocket and my newly acquired knowledge, I could make it all over town without an automobile. I met Margret about six in the evening in the lobby of the grand Palmer House Hotel. She looked amazing, and I still did not. With only one paltry paycheck under my belt, I wasn't even sure I could pay for the meal.

"I hope you'll please forgive me for being so forward and calling on you tonight," I said, worrying she would think me a nuisance or clingy child.

She giggled and said, "Nonsense. Once you get to know me better, you wouldn't even think to ask such a thing."

When we stepped out of the hotel, the same well-dressed doorman that greeted me before motioned us toward the street. "Oh, we don't need a cab," I told him. "We are going to take the streetcars." He laughed a little before he quickly covered his mouth with his white-gloved hand.

"I'm very sorry, sir, my apologies."

Margret stepped in to save the man from some blunder I did not understand yet. "You do drive, honey, don't you? I mean you do have your motorist license? I hope so, because I abhor being behind the wheel in that thing." At that last cryptic statement, she pointed to an automobile pulling up in the hotel's circle drive in front of us. It rivaled Jean-Paul's Imperial in style. Mickey would call it the cat's meow.

The valet hopped out of the blue Bugatti Torpedo and left it running for us. She meant for me to drive us to dinner in her car. It was nothing less than a racecar—I have no other words to describe it. The Torpedo's top was down and stored away, the black leather seats sparkling under the hotel's marquee lights. To offset the vast curving metal of the hood, the automakers had inlaid smooth, light-colored wooden finishes in front of the glass and surrounding the seating area. I might never use the streetcars again. The strangest thing was that the steering column was on the wrong side.

At that moment, I was filled with joy I had gone to driving lessons in town with some boys from the team. My mother was scared about it, telling me that I'd end up breaking my neck. She was only worried about me ending my hockey career, rather than showing actual concern for my well-being. My father was all for it, knowing that having another driver would help around the farm.

My tongue tripped over itself in excitement. "Yes, I do have—can drive—car." She laughed. When the doorman opened the left side door, she slid in and sat down. "I've only driven farm trucks really. I've never driven on the right side either. Are you sure?"

"Get in. You look like a kid in a penny candy store, I swear." She faked an annoyed frump at first, then she laughed at herself. "Come on. I'm hungry."

The Torpedo's hefty engine roared to life as I pressed the accelerator pedal down and let out the clutch. Sitting on the wrong side of the car felt strange. Thankfully, the gear selector wasn't backward. I worked it with my left hand instead of the right, but the pattern was the same as on American cars. It took a few rough stops and starts to get used to, and even though I made sure to be careful at first, soon we were charging down the streets at real breakneck speeds.

"I swear you drive just like Jean-Paul."

"I'm sorry, I'll slow down," I said, sounding disappointed.

"No, go on. Boys must have their fun with their toys." She looked out the window for a few seconds before turning back to me with a pained expression on her face.

"Margret, what's wrong? Am I scaring you?" I asked, as if she were a frail thing in need of protecting. I regretted it the second the words came out. She had proven the other night she was far from weak. Outwardly, she was a free, independent flapper. A new breed of woman. And nothing about her made me think her interior was any different.

She ignored the unintended insult, saying, "It's been a long time since I've been in this car."

"How come? It's such a fine auto."

She smiled briefly. "Yes, I'm sure it's wonderful. I just can't bring myself to drive it anymore. It was my husband's, you see."

I didn't see. "What happened, if you don't mind the intrusion?" I ventured.

"My husband and I met while he attended law school. My family, as you know, has money." I wouldn't have known what she was referring to until today at the library, when I discovered the name Field in just about every book about Chicago. "Well, his did too. When he finished law school, he was placed—through connections of course, as these kinds of things always are—with one of the biggest, wealthiest law firms in Chicago. He was so smart, so funny. He could wake up a sleepy room with his smile. We knew everyone back then. He loved cars. This was one of his. He had a few. I sold the others, but this was his favorite. Anyway…"

She stopped and grew still. Quiet. The only sound between us the roar of the Torpedo's engine. She listened for a few minutes before continuing. "One night, he was running late for a dinner date we were having with the mayor and some of his cronies. They were working on some public land share agreement with one of the parks. He was coming to fetch me at our house, you see, and lost control. He died in his car, dressed in a tuxedo, all alone on the side of the road."

We had passed the turn for the restaurant, but I wasn't going to interrupt her story. I kept on driving past the address she had given me and looped around the area. For the rest of the time, we drove noticeably slower. Margret had wiped her face a few times. I couldn't decide if I should say anything or let her have the memory to herself.

She made the decision to break the sadness. "Well, I don't know why I am telling all of this to a stranger."

"I am very sorry."

"Oh, Brett, listen to me," she exclaimed, as if suddenly coming back to life. "I'm very sorry for calling you a stranger. You are a wonderful person who is spoken highly of by a certain someone. I have treated you dreadfully." I tried to protest as she interrupted me. "Well, let's go eat. You can turn around and head back to the restaurant." She put her hand over mine on the gear shifter, giving it a little squeeze. Her vulnerability had not drawn compassion or pity from me, but it had made us closer. Inner strength radiated from her in perceptible waves.

We made small talk at dinner, which started with her telling me to order anything off of the menu since it was her treat. Being cared for financially really started to become an issue for me. I had been taught that when a man asks a lady out to dinner, he pays for her. That had been before she recommended this place, with its fresh seafood tank and all. It really had to be her treat after that.

"So tell me, how do you really know a hockey player like Jean-

Paul?" I ventured, dying to bring it up since she'd evaded me before. She sipped her club soda and smiled at me, playfully bobbing her head around the flower centerpiece.

"My husband worked with Jean-Paul's team's manager for a few years. See, Jean-Paul was on a few teams that traveled through Chicago pretty often, and boy, did he ever enjoy this city. Well, that's a different story. Those teams needed someone to manage their legal affairs. James, my husband, became interested in the game—sorry, the *sport*—of hockey. So they arranged for him to go to the matches. Wait, that's not right, is it?"

"It's games usually. It's okay," I confirmed, being the expert on hockey grammar.

"Well, they took me along once or twice. It was all so dreadfully barbaric. All that bashing each other on the head with sticks stuff is not for me. I'm not a proper lady now, but even then I couldn't go in for all that sort. After the, um, game, James wanted to meet the winning goaltender and that, of course, was Jean-Paul.

"He was so charming and debonair that it was only a matter of minutes before we had invited him out to dinner, then for cruises on the lake and the like," she said. Margret's face lit up talking about her husband this time. When she had spoken of the automobile accident earlier, I thought the night was soon to come to a close. Now she was alive again.

The dinner salad arrived. She continued to talk while we ate, which was very unladylike. "Very soon, every time his team came to town, Jean-Paul would be at our house to take meals with us that were anything but quiet affairs. He would lavish James with stories of battles on the ice and of famous people he had met. James would try his best at oneupsmanship.

"Jean-Paul would come to take me out on the town whenever James was too busy with late nights at the office. It was quite scandalous, a high society woman out with a dashing young hockey player. Everyone was talking about how we were flaunting our..." She paused to giggle. "Our two-timing ways in the public eye. It simply wasn't so."

What a relief to hear her say they were not intimate, at least not back then. They certainly were a hot ticket that must have gotten all the society ladies' tongues wagging. She hadn't alluded to them being involved now, though. "Wasn't your husband worried?" I asked.

Margret rocked her head back and laughed. Several dinner guests turned to face her, looking annoyed. She either didn't notice or pretended not to. "Heavens, no." Then she thought harder for a moment. "Well, maybe at first there were a few private conversations, but it was a laugh really. Besides, we financed the whole affair then. Well, I suppose still do." She gave no explanation as to why it was more funny than dangerous, which I wanted to know. It didn't feel like the moment to press her, though. She was like a faucet that had been rusted shut for a long time and was now spewing years of backwater after being wrenched open. She had confirmed my suspicions about one of Jean-Paul's secrets, the money.

She continued to talk with her mouth full. "James insisted Jean-Paul stay with us when he was in town for his games, and he did so. At least he dropped off his bags with us each time. If he wasn't out with us, he would...well you know he's something of a night owl. He'd leave for an entire night, some lucky person the beneficiary of his affections for the evening. There were, there are, a lot of those. None of them last. Nothing ever does."

She grew a little more somber just as the steaks arrived. From the looks of the delicious-smelling porterhouses, her mood had little to do with them and more to do with her last comment. Jean-Paul going out sleeping with many women bothered me. But she didn't say women, did she? What was the word she used?

Person.

Margret continued. "He was such a good friend to James, who was always under so much pressure. He was pulled at all angles all the time. By the end, it was all he could do to keep up. We hadn't taken a vacation in a year. Jean-Paul would breeze into town and, like I said, fill us with stories. He was the life of the party. Did you know he was from Montreal? His parents only spoke French at work and at home. Like I said earlier, they weren't wealthy but had money, not that you'd know from Jean-Paul's situation."

This was all making sense. He always pays for everything, and what about that car of his? A hockey player could never afford such things. She went on. "Well, they didn't really pay attention to him as a child. The poor thing says they didn't like him, although I don't think it's even possible for a mother or father to dislike their child. But he claimed it so."

I agreed that parents were supposed to love their children no matter what. My own situation seemed to be proof that a parent could provide for a child, yet make them feel unloved or worthless. My own father was no shining example of proper parenting. And my mother?

"He told me then that his parents abandoned him to an au pair and never looked back," she said before stopping to chew some steak. I was beginning to wonder how her story had turned into Jean-Paul's. "Well, you know him. He did every outlandish thing he could think of to shock them into paying attention to him. It didn't work. They gave him very little love. Instead, they smothered his younger brother and two sisters with attention. He said they paid for hockey lessons and arranged for him to go away to school just to be rid of him. I think it's where he gets his distaste for being tied down, and maybe why he ruins things. I really don't know if that man even believes in love. Maybe they rejected him because they knew who he really was at an early age."

"What do you mean?" I interjected before thinking.

She turned pink, which must have been how someone with her fair, freckled complexion showed embarrassment. She quickly tried to undo what she had said. "I mean he just mustn't have fit into their quaint little lifestyles, with his brashness and yearning for excitement. Anyway, he...I went through an extraordinarily difficult time when James passed. If it hadn't been for him..."

We ate our food and finished off another round of drinks, without alcohol for a change. I didn't say anything, not because I didn't care about her pain, but because I didn't know what to say. She had said so much to me, about her life, about Jean-Paul. Finally the silence became overbearingly heavy, and I had to chop through it.

"I'm so glad that you agreed to go out with me this evening. I really don't know anyone in this city that doesn't play hockey. And I spend all day long, all week, with those fellas."

"I hope I'm a little better company?"

"I didn't mean..."

She cut me off with a wave of her hand. "Brett, you simply must stop worrying about offending me. I'm no vexing young thing that can't handle herself."

I laughed a little at this. "No. No you most certainly are not."

"My, whatever do you mean?" she said, pretending to be offended. "Are you saying that I'm not a young thing, or that I can't handle myself?"

Now it was my turn to blush. "I was...I only...gee, I put my foot in it that time."

She slapped me on the leg and said, "Oh! Ha!" She was kidding, which didn't make the moment any less uncomfortable.

She paid the check and left the tip. We gave the valet the ticket to retrieve the car, then watched him bolt down the street to some secret hideaway where they stored autos. While we waited, I started to feel awkward, having been told so much personal information about Jean-Paul behind his back. I felt guilty, somehow. Like a gossip. Margret was quiet, so maybe she felt it too. She shivered in the evening breeze, so I took off my jacket and placed it around her shoulders. She gripped my hands and held me there a moment as I slipped the jacket on her.

The late September air filled the open top of the car on the way back to her hotel, forcing us to lean forward and hide behind the glass to keep out of the wind. She giggled as we turned corners, the cold breeze hitting our faces and pushing the longer hair on the top of my head straight back, which urged me to edge a bit faster. Between shifting gears, she grabbed my hand and gave it a squeeze. I hoped she hadn't gotten the wrong idea. Turning to her to explain, I noticed she was leaning forward into the wind, holding the dash for dear life with her other hand. I looked to her for permission. Her eyes gleamed as she nodded. I sped up and screamed up over the glass. She looked at me for a moment before the corners of her mouth turned up. Then we were both taking turns yelling to the world at the top of our lungs as we raced through the dark city, both of us in stitches.

When we arrived at the hotel, she kissed me good night and jumped out of the car before I could open her door. She told me it was late, and I should take the car home. I tried to protest, but she waved me off as she entered the building. I watched her until she was inside. The car's engine was humming in front of me, shaking my body with its vibrations. It felt amazing being in control of something so powerful. I thought of poor James alone in the wreckage, popped the clutch and slowly eased down the street.

CHAPTER SIXTEEN

October 2, 1926

Another week had gone by. Mickey and I had gone from parties and excitement to flopping into bed after long practices that seemed to last all day. We were off on weekends, but we still spent a lot of that time with the other players. Going out drinking with the boys from the team was fun. Bonding with them off the ice was nice, but carrying Mickey back up Moira's narrow stairwell at night, or having to stand over his snoring, drunken mass curled around the toilet in order to piss in the morning, got old fast.

Jean-Paul had all but disappeared after practices. We barely said two words to each other in two weeks. I tried to make plans with him. He seemed preoccupied, making unbelievable excuses each time until I stopped trying. I felt guilty knowing so much about someone that didn't know anything about me. On Friday after practice, I decided to try again. I told him Margret and I had a fun time last weekend going out on the town, throwing in that we had a few laughs talking about him. This seemed to pique his interest a little. Nevertheless, he left in his car just as soon as he finished getting dressed.

Then Saturday at seven in the evening, Moira called up the stairs in her lilting Irish brogue, "Brett, darling, you have a telephone caller down here now."

Payday had come by twice now, and we each had some money in our pocket. Some of the boys tried to get us to spend a little to move out into a decent place in a better neighborhood. Mickey had actually been thinking about bunking with one of the guys from the team. Me, I liked living at Moira's. The area wasn't the greatest, but Moira cooked some great food, and she minded her own business. That was an important quality in a landlord for a guy like me. The last thing I needed was her asking why I never went out with the ladies, or worse, why I never asked her to chaperone me on a date.

The telephone was on the wall in the hallway downstairs. The brass dialing circle on the bottom of the candlestick-shaped device was shiny and new looking, but the black handle of the receiver had faded from people holding it. You could even see the whiter colors beneath the black on the Bakelite earpiece. More people must answer the phone here than make calls. "Hello?" Talking on the telephone was such a foreign concept, and I hated to do it. Most everyone and every business had one. I'd still rather talk to the person face-to-face. It's more personal.

"Hey there, handsome," Jean-Paul said from the other end of the line. Panic struck again. This was a party line, and any number of people could be on the other end listening in. And what did he mean calling me handsome anyway? "I'm swinging by there in a few minutes. Get dolled up. We're going out on the town."

"Jean-Paul, I don't know if I feel up to a big night." I looked over my shoulder down the hall to see if anyone was listening, "Besides, where've you been for the last two weeks? Jean-Paul? Hello?" The line had gone dead, and I was talking to myself.

An hour went by after I got cleaned up and dressed, but he still hadn't shown up yet. Mickey was going out to the burlesque shows with some teammates. Over the last two weeks, whenever we didn't simply fall asleep standing up, he and the other players had been going to girlie shows or one gin joint or another.

"Why you all dolled up for if you ain't going to go out on the town with us?" he asked. When I continued to pretend to straighten my clothes, he added, "You better not be going out with that goaltender again. I tell you, that guy rubs me—"

"If you must know, I am going to dinner with a girl," I said, maybe a little too boastingly. His wisecrack about Jean-Paul bothered me, but I let it go. "She's coming to pick me up now."

"Har-har! You ain't got nothing but class, boy, having her pick your sorry ass up. Wait, what dame you going out with? What happened to that hot automobile you had the other night? Now, that's the girl you need to stick with, my boy. And what kinda girl picks up a gentleman for a date anyway?" He guffawed all the way out the door and out to the car he'd bought the other day. It wasn't much of a car, but it ran, and on what Mickey was making, he wasn't going to get much more. Neither of us were.

A car horn bleated out front where Mickey was talking to someone. Jean-Paul had pulled up next to Mickey's jalopy in his shiny new Imperial. Oh boy. How was I going to explain this? I had told Mickey I couldn't go out with them because of a date.

"Brett?" Jean-Paul called out. "Look who's got some snazzy new glad rags." I was definitely tired of looking like a ragamuffin every day. I had spent my second check not on a car or fancy dinners, but on a new suit and a brand-new fedora. They were purchased, at ridiculous prices I might add, for the sole purpose of getting this reaction. Even though he said I looked good in my new clothes, he looked fantastic as always. He was wearing a grey suit without a vest this time, a black cotton button-up shirt with a striking, slim red tie, which led my gaze from his chest and drew them toward his eyes. Between the grey of the suit and the fedora he balanced cockeyed on his head, the tint turned his usually deep blue eyes a shiny silver I wanted to get lost in. I couldn't help but stare.

Jean-Paul had blocked Mickey's car in, so he couldn't pull away. "Thought you were going out on a date?" he yelled up at me with a curious gaze on his face.

"Eh?" Jean-Paul asked.

"Um, yeah, it's a double," I responded, thinking fast on my feet, hoping Jean-Paul wouldn't futz it up. It would help if he actually hadn't heard any of it.

"Oh. Well, get that piece of shit jalopy out of my way, wouldja?" He was obviously angry about something and not thinking clearly, because Jean-Paul's car was not even close to being a jalopy.

Speeding away from the curb, Mickey's old car sputtered away far behind us. Jean-Paul looked over at me. "What was that all about, eh?"

"Where are we going?" I responded, knowing that sometimes ignoring a question and moving on is the safest response.

The car sped up. "You might want to hang on tight." We poured through a tight turn and when the car straightened out, we faced a giant gothic stone tower surrounded by an expansive white stone castle right in the heart of the city. It was not nearly as massive as the Coliseum but impressive nonetheless. Across the road from the tower was another castle building.

It was magnificent.

In the dim light of the electric streetlights, crowds of people wandered about, slipping in and out of unmarked storefronts. Music swirled in the air all around us, an ungainly mixture of musical styles, speeds, and instruments. Much of it was a sweet sound of the jazz I had grown to love. Some of it had fiddles and instrumentation I was unfamiliar with. It sounded like a blend of different foreign lands.

"What is this place?"

"It's called Tower Town because—"

"Because it's around this big tower?" I finished sarcastically.

He thought it was funny, letting me know with a smack on the arm. "Yes, all these places around the Water Tower are part of it. It's a Bohemian community of sorts. All kinds of people gather here to exchange ideas and share thoughts."

"You mean the Bolsheviks?" I asked, referring to our country being at risk of being infiltrated by the Reds. This was true even in Chicago, where the gangsters ruled the streets, saying they wouldn't stand for any Communists disparaging their country. This was kind of funny considering all of the mobs were Irishmen, Jews, or Italians who had just gotten to this country.

We parked the car on the side streets. "No. Well, some of them. Listen, don't tell me you bought into all that Red malarkey?" Jean-Paul waved a hand in the air to dismiss the whole idea. "That's this government yet again telling you what to think. These people down here are free thinkers. Have I steered you wrong yet?" I opened my mouth to answer him, but he raised his voice and finished his own sentence. "Come on, I bet you'll love it." I was definitely leery now.

Yes. He *had* steered me wrong. Nearly getting killed every time we got in a car together, almost being pinched in a hooch house, and, and…well, all those things would count. Now we were about to go mingle with the mad Reds on Michigan Avenue. Great. For whatever reason, I got out of the car and followed him down the street.

"Hey, how is Margret? I haven't heard from her since the other night," I wondered aloud.

"Why don't you ask her yourself tonight? She'll probably be here. She loves the poetry nights." Poetry? We were on our way to a poetry reading? I love to read books on all types of subjects and consider myself to be a fairly intelligent person. I even earned an "A" in English class when we covered poetry, but I can't really say as it ever took my fancy. Thinking about it now, though, jazz seemed very much like poetry. The music made it different.

We turned right on Tooker Place, a dark, seedy-looking block that might as well be a hundred miles from the bright lights of Michigan Avenue. He led me to a brick building with an orange door. Above the old wooden door, a pale green light allowed me to see the word "Danger" and two arrows that led to what was painted on the door. In sloppy black marking, the words read *Step High, Stoop Low, Leave Your Dignity Outside*, and I knew that this place was probably going to get me arrested and end my hockey career.

My nerves acted up, my brain planning out the mode of attack for counting all the bricks up and then across, when Jean-Paul grabbed my arm and led me up to the door. This snapped me out of it or at least drew my focus onto something else. He is getting quite good at that. He rapped on the door and waited for an answer. The door cracked open, and a black man stuck his head out.

"Password, please."

Jean-Paul tried to hand the man some cash. "Man, that ain't the password." Finally, somewhere they didn't know him by name. We all stared at each other for a moment and then he started to shut the door on us.

"Margret is waiting for us," I exclaimed just before the door pushed closed. He opened the door back up and smiled a big toothy grin.

"Well, why didn't you just say so? Come on in. We've got to be careful, honey. Can't let just anyone in here, now can we?"

I cast a questioning look at Jean-Paul, who shrugged. "I forgot it." We both chuckled then. Everywhere we went and everything we did happened like it had been custom tailored to Jean-Paul's size. Until now. This time I got us in, and it felt good.

We followed the slender man through a crowd of people waiting for a table. He walked with a sway to each step as if he were a woman. It was definitely a sashay. No man had ever acted that way around me that I could remember. Something felt odd about the whole place, and I couldn't immediately put my finger on why.

We came to a clearing and saw Margret. "Darlings!" Several people turned our way and one older gentleman shushed us. In his defense, a poet was on the stage reading, albeit overdramatically. She grew a little quieter, although that enormously joyous face of hers kept on beaming. "I am so glad to see you two. Come, sit." Two short chairs sat around a barrel used as a table. Paper bags were on most of the tables or in people's hands, and every so often people would take a swig of whatever liquid they poorly hid. Two more showed up in front of us before long, and we sipped from our "strong coffees," which consisted basically of bathtub gin.

Margret looked amazing in a rose-pattered billowing dress that ended just above the knee. Her hair was done up in a matching rose scarf, leaving tufts of her short red locks poking out the sides. All the red brought out her natural fiery hair, and she glowed in the candlelight emanating from the tables.

The poet left the little stage area to some calm applause. He couldn't compete with the performance at our table. The stage was a loose term anyway, being a tiny raised platform shoved off to the side of the tables as an afterthought. With its barrels and draping cloths made into curtains, the room looked more like it was part of a textile factory than a performance hall.

The lights suddenly dimmed, and the slender black man who had let us in pranced through the crowd and hopped up on the stage. Someone threw a feather boa to him. Having caught it in midair, he draped it over his shoulders. He made a big show of flipping one end of it at a couple sitting close to the edge of the stage. He spoke with a feminine voice that still held traces of his deeper male one.

"Ladies and gentlemen, flappers and flaming youth, and you know who you are, welcome to the Dil Pickle," he paused to look down at a man sitting near the front, "and I do mean one hell of a pickle, club." The man in the front waved him away, and the crowd chuckled. I did not. What did he mean, flaming youth? I'd never heard that before. At this point, the fear about what this place was consumed me, and I felt an almost imperceptible pull toward the door.

To run.

To hide safely away like I had done all my life.

He continued. "Well, let's give a very warm Dil Pickle welcome to Madam Jugsy Malone!" He left the stage and was replaced by a tall, full-bodied woman in a bright blond wig, her face painted with bright red and blue makeup no lady would be caught dead wearing. As she passed us, I saw she wasn't a woman at all. Everyone clapped except me. Several people whistled. My body stiffened, and I didn't dare look at my friends. My mind raced. *Why did they bring me here?* I wondered. *I am not like these people.*

Several men around us were holding hands below the tables. Some even above. Two women who looked like men, with suit jackets, slicked-back hair, thin moustaches and all, fawned over each other in the corner. This wasn't the first time in my life I'd heard of places like this. Several of the boys back home joked about men acting like girls. They weren't really joshing about what it meant. Whenever a boy got hurt and cried, he was laughed at and called a sissy. Boys who didn't gloat about doing some heavy petting with the chicks at school were tormented for being virgins and nancy boys. They'd call you weak and tell you to stop acting like a girl. "A girl could hit better than that" and crap like that. They'd even make comments about a guy needing a handbag or lipstick if he did anything that wasn't manly. Violence usually followed in all of these cases, which was why my instinct said to get up and light out of there.

The performer started to talk to the crowd in the voice of a woman, or at least an obvious man trying to sound like a woman. It didn't fool me. He told jokes everyone appeared to enjoy but, again, I was not laughing. He must have noticed my nervous fidgeting.

"What do we have over here?" Malone said, walking over to our table and leaning close to my side. "You're just the most gorgeous little thing, aren't you?" Then his voice changed to an exaggerated deep version of what it must normally be and he continued, "What's the matter, honey, ain't never seen a lady before?" This brought about a roar from the crowd, and I froze into a block of ice.

I became dizzy and could feel my forehead getting hot enough to cook eggs on. In panic I looked over to Margret, who was already looking at me and laughing. Jean-Paul was laughing at me too. At *me*. They were *all* laughing at me. I had overreacted with my stiffness and shocked expression, I just knew it. I was too nervous and they knew. They knew about me. They all thought I was like these people. I was ruined. I stood abruptly, the table rattling and wobbling as I bumped into it. The chair skidded backward across the knotty wood floor, bounced off someone's foot, and spilled noisily over. Jean-Paul made a grab for me, and I jerked back a little too far. Head feeling light, I nearly fell over backward, but he took me by the shoulders and steadied me.

"Whoa, whoa, it's all right," he pleaded.

But it wasn't all right. That's when I hastily made for the door. Faces crashed in on my vision as I rushed through the throng of people who pushed forward to see what the commotion was about. If they didn't know who I was and what I was, seeing me here confirmed it. I was sure camera flashes were going off all around, filling the room with powdery smoke. The headlines in the paper tomorrow were going to be all about this moment. My life, my career was over before it began.

"Oh heavens, I even shaved today!" the performer shouted behind me, now in his feminine voice again. The crowd laughed as it turned away from me and back to the stage again. But it was too late.

Out. I needed to get out, just out. The door gave way easily, and the slight doorman stumbled backward as I began running down the street. Someone was calling my name from behind, out of breath from chasing me, but I didn't stop. Tears poured out of me now. I slowed down and bent over, putting my hands on my shaky knees, breathing deeply. The pounding sound of leather soles on the street behind me grew louder. I stood up and stiffened, not sure what to expect.

A gentle hand touched my shoulder. Instantly my body was a solid pillar, its well-toned muscles taut as bridge cables, ready to snap. "Brett, it's okay. It's just a bit of fun, *mon ami*. She wasn't trying to razz you." Jean-Paul had run into the streets after me. He remained still, letting me make the next move.

The sounds of our panting filled the streets until our breaths slowed, and we listened to the silence. *He has to know now after that panic, that scene. Why else would he bring me to this kind of place if he didn't know I'm...that I'm falling for him?* I felt absolutely terrified to turn around and look at him right now. He gently tried to spin me to him with his hand on my shoulder, and I resisted at first.

Giving in, I turned toward him in the darkened side street and let him see my face wet with tears like some little girl. This causes more tears and sobbing. "I...oh God, why? Why did you bring me there around those people!" I shouted through horrible sounding snivels. He paused, calmly gazing into my eyes at my pain.

"You think I'm like those—" I began to scream. Then looking around, with a hushed voice, "Those faggots? Huh?" His blue eyes grew deep, and he grinned rakishly. "This isn't fucking funny. Maybe back in Montreal it's just fine to push people into—argh!" I was too full of rage and pain to finish.

Jean-Paul leaned forward, pulled me closer to him, and kissed me. His lips were soft and supple. He pressed them just firm enough against mine that our faces touched. I could feel the curves of his cheeks. His fingers gently wiped away the wetness from my cheeks with a delicacy that set my body to quivering.

I snapped away from him in shock. It felt amazing, but my old friend panic returned in force. "I—"

He put both of his hands on my face, pulled me in deeply, and kissed me again. This time he slipped his hands from my face around my back and pulled me up against his body. He had to hold me up when my legs gave out. This wasn't just necking like some simple schoolchildren. I had no words to do it justice. I had read a million words and none described my heart now. There was Shakespeare. And then there was this.

"Now dry your beautiful face and come back inside. With me."

I moved away from him, slowly pulling my hand out of his, not knowing how our hands had ended up like that. I needed to get away. "No, I need to…need to go home."

He smiled as he always seemed to. "No, come on, we'll go back inside and have a drink, then maybe…"

That sentence could not be finished. We were out in the middle of the street in Chicago. What the hell were we doing? "No. I'm going home, I'll take the train," I said. I thrust my hands into my pockets and found nothing. I turned back to him, holding away more tears. "I don't have any money." I had forgotten to take any with me. I hadn't really been spending any going out since Jean-Paul and Margret always insisted on paying everywhere we went. He walked over to me, reached into his pocket, and retrieved a fin. Handing it over, he reached for me, insisting on driving me home. I turned and walked away.

CHAPTER SEVENTEEN

October 4, 1926

Yesterday, Mickey caught me counting down the ceiling tiles in Moira's house and made me go to church with him. The Catholic church we went to was huge. A swirling rainbow mixture of colors came from the enormous stained glass windows. Inside, it smelled of incense and candle wax. Not being Catholic and never having gone to one of their churches, I was at first enthralled with all the ritual until it turned into something else to count. Mickey asked me when he'd get to meet the girl that's got me so twisted up. When we got back to the boarding house, I swallowed some Nervine pills and slept.

The morning was no better. I usually relished practice. Getting out on the ice, having a good time showing off. This morning, all I wanted to do was bury my head in the sand like an ostrich. That's hard to do when you are getting paid to be around the one person you want to be close to and avoid at the same time.

The coach broke the team up into two squads. Of course I was placed on the squad facing off against Jean-Paul. This meant that I'd have to shoot on him all day. To his credit, he did not approach me to talk about what had happened. We just glanced at each other across the dressing room, and it was enough.

We started to play our scrimmage game. The coach had put me on the line with Dick and Charley, trying him out on right wing, and the PB and J line backed us on defense. Hughie was in goal. I got the call to do the opening face-off against Mickey, which he won cleanly and raced off. My heart wasn't in it, which was odd for me. Usually all the cares in the world faded away once I got on the ice, but I was distracted. It's not like I had to worry about Jean-Paul telling anybody about me since he's the one that took us to that club in the first place. He's the one that kissed me, after all.

He kissed me. That fact hadn't left my mind in two days. Luckily for me, Dick bopped me on the head with his gloved hand on his way by to chase after Mickey. "Get your head in the game, kid. Now," he ordered. So I did.

Bob blocked Mickey's shot, and the puck rebounded back to Dick, who rushed it up the ice. Once in the offensive zone, training took over. Dick fooled Gordie and left him in the dust as he burst forward to the net. Jean-Paul quickly slid over side to side to face off square against the shooter, leaving the other side of the net wide open. I saw it and took off to the net like a banshee. Dick saw it too. Instead of taking the shot himself, he passed it to me as I was skidding to a stop in front of the net. The sudden skate stop covered Jean-Paul in a wall of snow. My stick made a slapping noise when it hit the puck, redirecting it into the back of the net.

Jean-Paul looked chilled and unfazed, but it had to bother him at least a little bit. His face was dripping with little specks of ice from the spray off my skates. The boys circled up and commented on the play. We must have spent too much time celebrating, because just then the whistle blew a few feet behind us.

"What the hell are you nancy boys doing? Get back to center and let's go again," the coach hollered as he skated around the ice.

We set up again, and this time I won the face-off. It went on like that all day. I felt a lot better getting back on the skates and pushing my body to its limits. The team ate lunch together before quickly getting back to skating. At the end of practice, the coach blew the whistle and yelled at us to hit the showers, saying what he said every day, "You're smelling up the place." We didn't laugh. Exhausted, all of us headed for the door to the locker room by the benches so we could go home.

I was careful not to look at Jean-Paul as we all were taking showers. I never took quick peeks at the other boys. It was way too dangerous a prospect and wasn't worth the risk. Not to say there weren't a lot of great-looking men on our team, one of course in particular. It was rude to look. Really the only person I'd seen in a state of undress in a long time was Margret the other night.

On my way out, Jean-Paul stopped me. "It was a nice day out there today, eh? I particularly liked the ice shower you gave me. Did I need cooling off?"

I looked around hastily. "Take it easy. Someone will hear you."

His head cocked to the side, he whispered, "No, they won't. Come to my place tonight, pick up where we—"

My desire to be with him was outmatched by this terrible gut feeling we were going to be found out. It was like the panic when I feared my father had seen me looking at my tutor Jordan, but so much worse. I wasn't some kid anymore. The stakes were so much higher. If anyone on the team even suspected something like this was going on between two teammates, we'd be beaten to death by our supposed friends. I'd heard horror stories back home. As much as I didn't want to say it, I had to say no. "I don't think that's a good—"

He interrupted me before I could turn him down. "Dinner then?"

I remembered all the times I wanted to go out with him after practice, but he had just disappeared. "Don't you have somewhere to go, like all the other times you ignored me?" It came out sounding a little too hurt, but I pressed on anyway. "Where do you go all the time?"

And the moment was ruined.

The thought that he was leaving practice, leaving me, to go spend time with some other man filled me with jealousy and anger. I had no idea what I wanted to happen here, so I said the next thing that popped into my head. "And with who?"

He fixed his tie and paused at the exit door, trying not to look annoyed with me. "I guess there is somewhere I can be. Just thought you'd want to, well…"

No, don't go, I wanted to say. I'd tried so hard to get him to pay attention to me in this way. His last question was filled with hidden innuendo, which set my heart to skipping beats. He was so smooth and carefree, but I wanted him to be upset I was playing hard to get. There was no real plan behind it. I didn't want to be playing these games with him. But if we went out again, I'd have to face what I am. I was also worried he would surely learn how inexperienced I am at this.

He leaned in a bit too close, which made me shiver. Before walking away, he said, "Some other time maybe, *mon ami*." Pieces of my broken heart clattered on the wooden floor. He let the door close behind him as he disappeared into the night.

CHAPTER EIGHTEEN

October 15, 1926

The train steamed away from the station in the early morning hours heading to the great white north. At least it was the only part of the great white north that I had ever seen. We were going to Canada—Toronto, to be exact—on our way to our first game against another team. We had grown pretty tired of smashing into each other by now, getting anxious to test our skills against different people. Their club was already established, but they weren't exactly at the top of their game, having gone from a Cup victory a few years ago to a sixth place finish last year. They still had a bunch of serious heavy hitters and fast skaters. The boys on the train were excited about the game and the chance to show what we had.

The real excitement at least for me was a chance to meet the Babe Ruth of hockey. His real name was Cecil Dye, but he went by and liked to be called the Babe. The papers had mentioned him by name many times, talking about how he was an all-around athlete. He had been offered money to play football and baseball but had turned them down to play hockey. None of that made any sense since those other sports paid a whole lot more money. When asked, he'd say, "Baseball already has its Babe Ruth."

The train rolled north, and the scenery changed from the concrete and steel skyscrapers of Chicago to the vast green rolling hills of Michigan. Lots of fields had been harvested already and were now barren. It was America the beautiful, just like in the song. I wondered what the nicer cars looked like up front where the major and the coach were. I was surprised to see that Dick had chosen, or was assigned, to sit in the players' car with the rest of us.

Jean-Paul had been sitting alone in one of the booths, staring out the window. I wondered what he was thinking about, whether he wanted me to go over by him, or if like most goalies, he wanted to be left alone. They are, of course, a weird lot. On the other end of the train car, Hughie was also sitting by himself. All of the guys just knew to leave them alone. It was not going to look good for me to walk over and sit down, so I didn't. My heart wanted to. Ever since the other night, I wondered about nothing but where he went off to when he left practice. I wanted to go with him, wherever it was.

Worrying about another man's comings and goings isn't really appropriate. I knew what people would think. Worse, I knew what they'd do about it if they ever thought I was this different than everybody else on the inside. Feeling this way about another man was wrong. I knew it, but I just couldn't help it no matter what. I've tried to be normal. Maybe my father was right about me.

My nerves kicked in, and I started counting. This time it was the heads of my teammates sticking up over the backs of their seats. I had to count how many there were and then double-check to make sure everyone was there. If the count was wrong, we were going to lose the game. I recounted and recounted to make sure we were all there. Bob put his head down on the armrest and disappeared behind the seat in the middle of the fourth count, which threw the number off by one. He was there. I had just seen him and counted him three times before. But it wasn't right. I looked up and down the aisles. Sweat dripped from my forehead. The count was wrong, and the train was going to derail. It wasn't, but it was—or it could if I was wrong. Trapped in counting, I frantically searched for a way to make the count work. I was so preoccupied and terrified, I hadn't noticed someone sit down next to me.

"Are you okay, *mon ami*?" Jean-Paul said, his body pushing up against mine in the small bench seat, forcing me to move over. My heart wanted me to stop the senseless counting to talk to him. All I wanted for weeks was to be with him, and now he had come to me. My mind, on the other hand, had its own plan. The terrible urge to count consumed me. The counting began again until Jean-Paul grabbed my chin and pulled my face to his.

"What!" I shouted a little too loudly, my body electric with the need to finish.

Concern washed over his face. "Are you all right, Brett?" he quietly inquired in his soothing accent.

My racing thoughts of train derailment and loss of the game slowed. His warmth brought peace and eased the need. It's a strong need. As a matter of fact, when my mother found me in my room one night, locked in a cycle like this one, it was so severe that she wanted to take me to town to see the doctor. My father was afraid of what the folks in town would think of him, so they took me all the way to Janesville for a doctor. No one would know us there. No shame to the family, no loss for the farm. No one would worry about the young hockey star's skills that way.

The thumping in my chest eased. Embarrassment quickly took the place of any other feeling. This beautiful man whom I wanted with all my heart had seen me do my freakish thing. I was ruined with him. I felt a shame as vast as the empty fields disappearing in the darkening of twilight outside the windows of the train.

Just then, Jean-Paul placed his hand on my knee. "It is going to be fine. Do you want to tell me about it?"

I did. I wanted to tell him. Everything about me. I moved my leg so he got the idea and removed his hand. "I'm…I'm fine. I sometimes…" I reached into my left trouser pocket and fished out the bottle of nerve pills.

"What's that? No. *Mon dieu.*" He pulled the bottle out of my grip faster than I could follow. Damn goalie hands.

"I need…" I began much too loudly, then after controlling myself, quietly said, "I need one to calm down."

He slid the bottle into his trousers and tried to comfort me. "No, no. If you take these you will be unable to play tonight. This is your biggest night, *mon ami.* Tonight you will shine like the shooting star you are." I forgot about the pills as my heart returned to normal. The evil thoughts of death and loss faded away until nothing was left but him. Well, him and every other player on the team.

He laid his hand over the back of the seat we shared, and he shifted his body so that most of him was facing me. He continued softly, looking into my eyes. "Please tell me what happened there. Why were your eyes jerking back and forth so violently?"

I had always been ashamed and never answered that question even for the few who asked. But now sitting here with him, I did not feel that at all, so I told him my second darkest secret. "Ever since high school sophomore year I have had these…episodes. I know it sounds crazy, probably because I am crazy to think this way and to do these things, but I feel the urge, the need really, to…well, to *count* things."

"What kinds of things?" he whispered, eyes intently watching me, being with me.

"What do I count? It can be anything." I swallowed. "Just now, it was a need to know if we were all on the train. I mean, of course nobody jumped off a moving train, but it doesn't stop my need to know. So I counted heads, but it can be anything."

I had never told a living soul about this before. My mother had talked with the doctor after he did his physical on me that night, but I never told him a thing about what had happened. I never even told Jordan. He had seen me have a fit before, but was too troubled by it to help and certainly must have been too scared to ask. Saying it now felt liberating and right. A small part of me worried what he'd think. Would he get up and walk away, telling the others they had hired a crazy person? I doubted that. Somehow I felt safe with him.

He smiled. Well, really only half of his face smiled his grin, as usual. He always looked like he knew something others didn't, or he was up to no good. "I'm sure the other boys have talked about the crazy goaltender?" I tried to shake my head to deny it, but he waved me off and continued. "'Stay away from him,' 'his elevator does not go all the way to the top,' things of that nature? I suppose it is true, some of the things I do can be seen as strange.

"It's very, very hard for me to cross the blue lines on the rink during a game, or a practice for that matter. I cross them but can't, you know, *touch* them. I don't have a feeling that something bad will happen like you do. Its just that one day I hopped over the line on a whim and I had a shutout game then. So ever since I just know that if I am to win, I cannot cut that line with a skate. Does that make me insane?"

A grin spread across my face. "Yeah, a little." We both laughed.

Percy and Bob slid into the bench across from us. Bob asked, "How on earth did you get Jeany out of his crease?" Percy chuckled, but Jean-Paul did not.

"It's Jean-Paul."

"All right, all right, relax. Just havin' a little fun. Haven't seen you socialize on a road trip before is all," Bob finished. Having all four of us crammed in such a small space felt tense and close. I was nervous again. All the calmness Jean-Paul had brought to me moments ago was slipping away.

"What are you boys busy runnin' yer yaps about?" Percy tossed out.

"Nothing really. Just wondering what it was going to be like playing against the Pats," I lied, referring to the St. Patricks, the team we were going to play in a few hours.

"You mean, what is it going to be like to play against those guys after this long, smoky, miserable train ride, tired and ready for bed? Yeah, that's a good question." Percy filled in the blanks on what we were all thinking. Then he yelled up to the front of the car, "Why couldn't we play in the morning, Dickie?"

Someone nudged Dick on the arm and woke him up. "I'm sorry, I couldn't hear you complaining, I was too busy sleeping. Like all a you lot ought ta be." All the boys who were already awake roared at this, waking everyone else up.

"Where we at?" someone asked.

"Outskirts of Toronto," Charley threw over his shoulder. "Almost there, fellas."

"Don't worry, Rabbit. You'll get your chance soon enough, soon enough," Gordie added sleepily. A bunch of laughs joined mine and filled the train car. Jean-Paul's leg had fallen against mine in the bench and lay there, pressing into me. None of the fellas thought anything of it. Don't know what he thought, but to me, it was fantastic.

CHAPTER NINETEEN

First Preseason Game against Toronto

The Arena Gardens building, home of the Pats, was nothing compared to the grandeur of the Coliseum. Maybe that's a biased viewpoint, but the Arena, as it was called, was just a big, regular-looking building with a rounded, black top. Nothing special. It even held about a thousand less people.

As the team approached the Arena, we saw how fully this city had embraced the sport of hockey. Automobiles jammed the streets around the building while people crowded the sidewalks. The ticket lines were easily fifty people deep, the front doors clogged with ticketholders trying to get in. Gordie said all of them had paid fifteen cents to see us play. He started to count the people in an exaggerated manner, loudly proclaiming dollar amounts far too high to be accurate.

Charley corrected him. "I don't think they came to see us play. And I don't think there's a hundred thousand people out there." We all knew that we were not the big draw tonight, but we wanted badly to change people's minds.

The game was set to start in an hour. The train had been late into the station. We all transferred to the bus to make our way to the arena, but the crowds slowed the bus down. By the time we got into our locker room, we only had twenty minutes to get ready and to warm up.

With all of us dressed and lined up, Dick stood next to me in the tunnel. He was waiting for one of the officials to give the high sign for our team to enter the rink. The players chattered back and forth amongst themselves. Some of it was jittery-type yapping, like you do to keep from talking about what's really on your mind. Some of it was just the boys making plans for what to do on the ice.

"You nervous, kid?"

The steel in the captain's voice exuded pure strength and poise. Although the coach knew his stuff, he could be something of a hothead, all of us turning more to Dick as our leader. Playing high-pressure games had never affected me much. Not because I was cocky or ignored the seriousness, but because I shined out there in a way I couldn't anywhere else. I knew what I was going to do before I really even figured what the options were. It was like a sixth sense, knowing the limits of my physical body and then how to push it past that point.

"Nervous? Not really. I'm ready." I tried to exude confidence.

He just laughed at me as the usher waved at him to bring us on through. "You ought to be, boy. You're in the soup now. All right, boys, let's go!" Did he mean I ought to be nervous or ready?

Swoosh. Swoosh. The sounds of the skates cutting through the playing surface filled my ears even more than the barrage of boos and jeers of the hometown crowd. Being hated for no other reason than coming from a different city was nothing new, but the sheer volume of the cries took some getting used to. A couple of the guys didn't do so well at keeping their feelings to themselves.

Percy yelled at some fan leaning over the tunnel entryway, telling him where he could get off. This made the man pretty angry, and he threw his soda cup at Percy. I caught a glimpse at Percy as we skated in circles for the warm-up, and I saw him smiling.

"What's so funny?" I asked him.

"Always just love giving the people a hard time and a good show," he replied.

"Good show?" It was relatively common for some of the players to yell at fans and occasionally go after one of them, but never have any of them said it was part of the show.

"Eh, they pay their hard-earned fifteen cents and expect a good time, so what's the harm in giving 'em one?" I guessed it was so. The fans never factored into my play. As a matter of fact, even when we scored I don't remember hearing or at least caring about the crowd.

Right then, Charley skated by. "What pretty boy here means is that these cretins pay your salary. So whatever you do, don't ignore them too much." It had never been explained to me that way, but being in the big time league is a different world.

"Love me or hate me," Percy said, "just don't ignore me!" He skated off around the rink.

As we were all going back around for another circle, Jean-Paul, who was last in the line, came out onto the rink and made his way to his end. He hopped over the blue line that marked our side of the rink, just like he had said he would. We all have our little peccadilloes, it seems. With his dark curls bouncing a little each step, he struck a handsome figure. Instead of exemplifying how weird he was, it actually made him adorable. I looked away from him and toward the other end of the ice, worried about whether anyone saw my glances. I shouldn't get distracted.

Coming from the other player bench was number four. After asking around, I found out that it was the Babe himself. Never having seen him play, of course, all I had to go on were the reports in the papers, which described him as the greatest player of all time. They said he was so tricky with the stick that watching him was like watching a magician doing close-up magic. I was excited to watch him play, but on the other hand I wanted to be better, to win. To do that tonight, we'd have to shut Babe down in front of his home crowd. Easier said than done.

The coach had put me on the starting line in my usual position on the left wing, along with Dick and Cully. A second or two before the referee was to drop the puck, the players all circled around to their starting positions. At this point, I made the mistake of looking up and around the arena to see how big it was. The Coliseum was about the same size, but this building already had a history with this team, whereas ours didn't.

Dick saw me just before the opening face-off and yelled at me. "Get your head out of the clouds, moron. Or should we wait for you?" Bill Carson, their center man, who was waiting for the face-off too, chuckled and looked back at his teammates, who all joined in. Dick had embarrassed me in front of everybody. At that moment, putting my head down into the coming action, I decided I was going to blow everyone out of the water tonight. Then there'd be no laughing.

Dick won the face-off cleanly. Bob caught the puck, and we all started moving forward in attack mode. The puck got passed to Cully, who skated forward with it into their end. I had made my way to the left of the net where I was waiting for a pass. Cully snapped a quick wrister at JR Roach, their goalie, who chopped at it with his left toe. The puck spilled out to center into the waiting stick of the man himself, Babe Dye.

Babe flew like the wind up the center. With a quick side step, he passed Bob and Percy, who had skated backward to block him. No one was in front of him or in place to catch up before he could take his shot. Jean-Paul looked cool in the net. I shifted focus from Babe's back to the front of the net while skating like hell to make it back in time to stop a goal.

Babe wound up, reaching behind and up level with his head before he swung with all his might at the gliding puck. It zinged through the air toward the net at about a hundred miles an hour. Jean-Paul caught it in his glove with an unbelievably fast motion. He held up his hand to Babe as if to show him where the puck had gone. It was like spiking the football after a running back makes a touchdown. It added insult to injury.

"Son of a—" Babe exclaimed as he skated past the net. The referee had blown the whistle because Jean-Paul held on to the puck too long. Babe kept skating on by and headed to where the face-off would be. Jean-Paul hefted the puck out of his glove and tossed it lightly to the passing linesman. The whole thing was so impressive it made me want to go to him and hug him.

After the next face-off, the puck came to me. This was the golden opportunity I had been waiting for all night. I was going to show them all. After deking around a few forwards, I made it all the way to the center into the attacking zone. Without looking up to the net, since I had my bearings, I wound up to take my shot. In one swift motion, Hap, their defenseman, poked the puck away with his stick before slamming into me so hard that both of my feet came off the ice. I heard a sick, squishy sound as I landed flat on my back and slid.

"Welcome to Toronto, punk," Hap yelled at me. That particular word was getting really old, really quick. Just then, Percy and Bob grabbed him from either side and started punching and slapping at him. In seconds, most of the players on the ice were smacking at each other or trying to pull each other's sweaters over their heads. If you can get someone's sweater over his head, it makes for a nice arm lock, leaving his face open as an easy target. Luckily for everyone involved, the referees restored order pretty quickly.

The check knocked the wind out of me. The worst part about the whole affair was that when I got up to look down the rink, Jean-Paul was skating back and forth in front of his net, not even looking toward the mêlée. Didn't he care that I had gotten pummeled? Wasn't he worried about me at all? During the first intermission in the locker room, I wanted so badly to ask him, but I didn't. He was having his pads looked at in the back of the room again; his face was a thousand miles away. I was being ridiculous anyway. Everyone knows that a goalie can't skate across the rink, not even to fight.

Dick sat down beside me and leaned over to adjust his skates. "Now that that's over and your feet are wet, how about remembering those fancy moves and throwing the puck at their net a little bit?" I hadn't had a good scoring opportunity during the entire first period.

"Yeah. I'm trying," was all I could say. It was weak.

"Pete is making line decisions based off today's play. I know you have more in you than this." He stood up and walked back to his bench. I shook my head. Now he wanted to help again?

I was ready to score a goal. That was for sure.

Two minutes into the second period, Babe got another lucky, bouncing puck. In a split second, he was off to the races toward Jean-Paul again. I bolted up the sideboards after him. Babe had avoided Percy's check with a fancy dipsy-do move, giving him another clean shot at the net. He pumped faster with his feet, and he bobbed the puck from left to right. I pushed against the ice with all my might, hoping to get there in time. As Babe's arm came back to shoot the puck, I leapt forward and slid across the ice behind him. I positioned my hockey stick in front of my sliding body, using the tip of it to poke the puck away from him. This caused him to over-skate it.

I popped up off the ice and found the puck. I pushed it off in front of me and started to skate. Behind me Jean-Paul yelled, "Go, Brett, go!" which was invigorating. Each of the opposing players took a run at me. I easily avoided them, heading for the net. The last player that stood in my way fell for my fake moves to the left, but I didn't get away clean. He ended up draped across my back, one hand grabbing at my stick. I kept up the pace and pumped forward to the net, single-minded. I snapped both of my wrists over. The puck flipped up and over the goaltender's outstretched leg just under his flailing arm, going in.

The red light went off over the back of the cage behind the goalie, and the scorekeeper rang the bell to mark the goal. The other player and I fell onto the ice like a sack of potatoes and rolled. Once he had gotten off my back, I popped up into the arms of my teammates. They were whooping and hollering about the goal, my first goal in the big leagues. Dick reached into the net and grabbed the puck. I looked down the ice to see our net minder just standing there, still as a statue.

Back at the bench, Dick handed my puck to one of the trainers to hold on to. Mickey joked about getting it bronzed. Pete congratulated me for the goal. Percy came over and sat next to me on the bench when the second line went out on the ice. We needed the breather.

"Good job. Good job. You know, the best play you made today

wasn't the goal. It was the poke check, knocking the puck away from Babe. Defense wins games. Remember that," Percy lectured. He was right, but the joy of lighting the lamp had filled me up with confidence, and I couldn't wait to add to the tally sheet today.

Back on the ice, Dick took a shot at their goalie, who stuck his goal stick out and knocked the puck away from the net, right into my stick. I handled it once to the left and once to the right before snapping it into the twine of the net, bringing my goal tally to two. Dick didn't reach in to get that one. Only the first one is special. The rest is just my job, as some of the old timers thought. The boys circled up, slapped me on the head with their gloves, and smacked my shins with their sticks to congratulate me. It felt amazing. I couldn't wait for another.

During the third period, I was rushing up the left side with the puck when Babe skated by, easily took the puck away from me and took off toward our end. He was determined, and we couldn't do anything to stop him this time. He took a check from Mickey but kept going. Bob smacked him in the ribs with his stick and still Babe kept going. Jean-Paul looked intense, ready. Babe's stick dragged the rubber along with it, not faking, deking, or doing any fancy moves.

At the last possible second, Babe jerked his head to the right and his hands to the left, as he flung the rubber up and over Jean-Paul's outstretched glove into the net for the goal. The red light went on, accompanied by a screaming, steam-powered horn that blared throughout the arena, touting the goal for the home team. When we had all caught up with him a second after the goal, Babe leaned toward Jean-Paul. "If you're looking for the puck, it's behind you." Jean-Paul didn't seem to be bothered by this, but it had to get into his attic a little bit.

With a minute to go in the game, we were up by a score of two to one. Both of our goals had come from me, theirs from Babe. Dick won the next face-off, and the puck popped over to me. I skated it into their zone and passed it to Bob, who passed it to Dick. Dick took a few steps forward to their net. Their defensemen tried to swat at the puck, but Dick leaned in with his body to protect it. He was able to skate backward a few more feet to the net before unleashing a wrist shot that would break a man's hand. It went into the net, drawing the red light again. No horns sounded for the visitors, but our whole team cheered for the captain.

After the game, we celebrated in the locker room. Some of the boys boasted our team was good enough to make it to the Cup this year and about what a coup it'd be for a first-year team to win it. It was probably a little early for talk like that, but Dick let everyone carry on like idiots just the same. He walked over to me to hand me the puck from earlier, my first goal.

"Put this in your bag and never lose it. Never forget it, either. Let it be a reminder that hockey's a two-way game, not just offense." His words were like having the golden goose in your hands.

Coach Muldoon walked through the door and said, "Okay, okay, boys. You did okay. We were tough on the boards and fast up the middle. We need to remember that if we want to win, we have to play tougher hockey than what I saw tonight." This guy would not give a pat on the back for anything. "Pack up your stuff. We're heading to the train in thirty."

"I thought we were staying the night out here?" I asked Percy.

"Naw. Cheaper to send us back on the red-eye train than pay for hotel rooms. Next game's at home."

Someone shouted in the hallway. The voices came into focus after a second or two, and we could tell that it was the major yelling at Pete. "Firepower. I told you we need more firepower!"

"Those boys scored three damned goals tonight," Pete yelled back. "That's a great night for hockey. I don't know about polo but—" A few of the guys in the locker room started to snicker at that last comment and drowned out whatever he said next. The owner was a world renowned competitor in the sport of polo. Most of the guys also knew he didn't know a lot about hockey. At least not yet.

We couldn't hear a few of the exchanges because of the snickers, but we quieted down some to hear more. "...gonna have to just buy some. I didn't spend two hundred thousand dollars to lose, Muldoon! Not to lose. A man can lose for free."

"You can't just buy a winning team. We have a tight squad right now. They just need time." Why didn't Pete talk to us like this? Instead he complained and told us how mediocre we are.

"Well we will just have to see about that, won't we?" After that, we couldn't hear much more than the stomping sounds of feet heading down the hallway.

"All right, boys, that's enough eavesdropping for one night. Let's get to the train, you bunch of ladies," Percy instructed, although he was one of the people at the edge of the door when the yelling was happening.

The major was rumored not to be on the train ride back to

Chicago. Some of the stories were that he stayed back to put in an offer on the entire Toronto team, others that he was buying Babe's contract. Someone even said they might trade Jean-Paul since he had let in a goal. Surely they wouldn't do that. It was just a preseason game, and he had played marvelously. Just the thought of him leaving the team made my brow sweat. Some had him trading half of our team for theirs, but if that were true, he wouldn't have sent us all on the train. We had won the game, but the train ride back was pretty somber.

CHAPTER TWENTY

October 19, 1926

Bunches of people walked toward the back entrance of the Coliseum as Mickey and I arrived for practice. We wondered what the crowd was about. We couldn't remember if anything special was going on that day. Dozens of newspapermen were by the back door with their cameramen flashing their cameras toward the entrance.

The major stood in the entryway in full military regalia. Next to him was a sullen-looking Coach Muldoon. The major held up his hands and the crowd quieted down. "I'd like to make a statement, if you'd please." The reporters hushed each other as they jostled with one another to get closer.

"At this time, it is with great pleasure to announce that we have acquired the rights to one of the greatest hockey players of all time. A player with whom I'm sure you are acquainted and will most definitely be by the end of the season, Mr. Babe Dye!" He stepped aside, and out from behind him, Babe stepped into his first interview in our uniform.

Babe waved to the crowd. "How do ya like my new sweater? Ain't it grand?" Photographers' flash powder lit up the back alley. The crowd laughed and clapped, eating up his humor, but it had a biting sharpness to it.

"What do you think of the team's chances now?" a reporter shouted.

Babe winked at the cameras. "Much better now that I'm here." The crowd ate it up, roaring. It sounded kind of rude to the rest of the team he was joining, considering he had just lost a game to us.

"What about leaving the mighty Pats and coming to the Windy City? Are you upset?"

"Ah, boys, you should know me. I'm gonna light this town's lamps the same way as always."

"What about those who say the team is destined to fail? What about being headed by a coffee magnate businessman?" This reporter was going for the major's jugular, since he did actually make his money selling and distributing coffee around the world.

Babe was not taken aback by these questions. "Aw, now you know we all won't fall asleep during the games with all this coffee around." They ate that up too. The coach stepped in front of Babe and waved his hands to the crowd to distract their attention from the man who was just criticizing his new owner.

"Time for practice now. Sorry, folks, but the Babe needs time to get to know his new team." Mickey and I went through the doorway as security men held back the reporters.

At least one of the rumors about the team had come true. I hoped that none of the others were true. At least one of them, anyway.

Still being a little starstruck by him, I stuck out my hand to greet him. "It sure is nice to have you on the team, Mr. Dye."

Babe shook my hand but looked annoyed by the whole event. "Hope someone back home sees those pictures, remembers that the best player in the league is here in this hockey gutter, and gets me outta this burg," he snapped before turning away toward the locker room. He sure was angry to be in Chicago, which was unbelievable. How could anyone who wanted to be a pro be angry about being signed to a team in such a huge city? I didn't understand it at all. And that's when I started to see the Babe in a whole different light.

Chapter Twenty-one

Practice was horrible. Babe was horrible. At least he was to me. I wasn't sure what he seemed to hate more, Chicago, the team, or me. He certainly went out of his way all day to show me how easy it was to take the puck off the end of my stick whenever it pleased him. All I wanted was a mentor, a seasoned pro I looked up to who could show me a few tricks. I found none of that in him, at least not verbally.

I had always been a quick study in hockey, noticing the way people move, the strides of their skates, or the way they shift their weight from right to left. When my teams played new towns or clubs, it only took me a short while before I could instinctually know which way a player would go. It wasn't just reading people's patterns either. Lots of folks could do that if they looked hard enough. We all have them. This was something different I could never put my finger on.

Watching Babe play was like being in school again. He showed me things no other player had. He faked left and shot left at the same time when everyone knows you fake one way and shoot the other. That's why it's called a fake. Not him, though. He'd make it look like a fake and then follow through. He geared up to shoot hard, then stopped short before he knuckled under it to lift it slowly past you. His eyes never gave away what he was doing. That was the hard part. It was like playing poker with an old cowboy.

After a few hours of watching him, all of the moves Babe had been showing and fooling everyone with, just clicked. A steel trap closed around him in my mind, and I knew how to meet him. I knew how to beat him. That didn't mean that each tactic I chose to defend against him worked, because they didn't. He had an elusive, thoughtless side to his play that kept him fluid and unpredictable. It felt much like I imagined my play to be.

Babe had just scored on Jean-Paul again, and we could all see that his mission today was to make his place by showing how much better he was than everyone else. What he didn't know, and what I didn't know, was that I wasn't the only one watching him and taking notes. After the lunch break, things started to heat up.

I scooped up the face-off and headed straight for Babe's area. He charged at me. His arms went out to his sides, and his stick found its way to the puck. This time instead of having this end with the puck on his stick, it would end differently. I moved a little toward his stick side and flipped the puck up and over his stick at the same time I dipped my head down and slid under his arm. I zipped down the ice and scored on Hughie. When I circled back around, arms raised in victory, Babe stood still, glaring at me.

The next play ended the same way, my stealing the puck away from him or getting it by him as he tried one of his fancy moves on me. It took about an hour of trying before he adjusted his style to mine. He eventually started matching me again. That's when his cockiness came out.

"Hey, young buck. How long you been going to the school of the Babe? You can't beat me by simply copying my style. See, I have no single set of rules to follow like these other clowns."

The next time the puck landed on my stick, he tried to charge it away from me. I pulled a dipsy little turn, protecting the puck with my body. Babe tried to lift my stick with his. I kicked the puck away from him with one skate, using the other to execute a spin move so that I ended up against his back with the puck. I skated away to the net and scored on poor Hughie again.

Percy had taken a distinct dislike to Babe from the start, and when he started getting snotty to me, Percy rubbed it in. "I sure hope the boys back in Toronto don't see this in the paper, or you'll be stuck in this backwater burg for a long time." He had thrown Babe's own words back in his face. All the boys burst out in hysterics. At that moment it became a Brett versus Babe world, and I hoped I'd survive long enough to keep learning from him.

CHAPTER TWENTY-TWO

October 21, 1926

I pretended to tie my shoes for a ridiculously long period of time so I could start the secret spy mission. Jean-Paul had been slipping off right after practice every day. I didn't know where he had been going, but he had not been going home. Margret, on one of our many tiny adventures over the last few weeks, had spilled the beans about his comings and goings.

At first, she resisted every attempt to discuss it, but finally she said he didn't like to associate with the other players unless he was required. This was not a secret to them or to anyone. This behavior was tolerated due to the fact that anyone choosing to have a hundred-mile-an-hour puck screaming toward their own face was probably too crazy to associate with. But he had told her what happened between us, which allowed her to share certain parts of his private life she would not have shared with anyone else.

Places like the Dil Pickle club—and Tower Town had many—opened quite late and stayed open even later. To frequent those particular establishments during the weeknights and still function at practice each day, he rushed home to sleep for a few hours before going out. That was all I needed to hear to hash out the master plan.

First, I'd need Margret's Bugatti, which was no problem. She'd been loaning it to me every time I wanted it. All she ever asked in return was for me to drive her out in the country at fast speeds with the top down from time to time. After what happened to James, one would think risky driving would be the last thing she wanted, but that was wrong. She would have no problem loaning me the car for the evening's adventure.

Second, I'd follow Jean-Paul home after practice. I should have asked Margret where he lived, but that didn't occur to me until I was following him during phase two of my master plan. Jean-Paul had driven north from the Coliseum. We crossed the river and kept going until the neighborhoods started to become familiar to me. He turned down a side street very close to the baseball park and pulled into a small driveway.

The house he had pulled into was a mansion. The three-story Victorian home looked grand and fantastic. The bright yellow color of the front of the house was offset by the shiny black shutters and trim around the eaves. All of the houses in the area were larger, older homes, obviously built before or right after the great fire. This house was absolutely gorgeous. No hockey player could afford it on his own. I was going to find out his secret.

He had gotten out to open the gate before driving around to the back of the house. The Torpedo was loud, which made me fear getting caught before this game of cat and mouse could begin. So I quickly cut the engines and coasted past the house to find a place to pull in, rolling to a stop. After positioning myself in a comfortable spot, I hunkered down to wait for him to come back out.

Third, I would stay awake and follow him to wherever it was he went at night. This part of the plan required me to stay awake after a long practice, my body beaten and exhausted. It worked for about fifteen minutes before I dozed off. Luckily the sound of the wrought iron gate closing woke me up with a start. He got back in his car and drove right past the Bugatti, me shoving my almost six-foot frame down below the steering wheel.

Fourth, he would lead me to one of his usual late-night haunts. Once there, I would spring phase five on him. I hadn't really developed this part so well. I wasn't sure what I'd do. Maybe if I had more money and had gone to the pictures and seen more of the serials all the boys talked about, I would have learned how to do this spy thing a little better. I learned about it mostly from reading Poirot novels, and they didn't exactly cover this.

I followed him down a dark side street and clicked off the Torpedo's headlamps. Keeping the car back and well away, I waited to see what he'd do next. He parked, got out and walked away from my position. I whipped the racecar into a spot and quietly closed the door. He walked up the street for a block before turning. Not wanting to lose him after all this effort, my stride turned into an all-out run.

I peeked around the edge of the building just in time to see him enter a place on 19th and Halsted Street. Several men tumbled out the front door of the establishment, arm in arm and soused, singing at the top of their lungs. I pushed myself as far into the brick wall of the buildings as I could. The idea of drawing attention to yourself out in public, or anywhere for that matter, while holding hands with another man was ghastly. I was sure these men would not take kindly to being spied on. The door that they had fallen out from had a sign hanging over it that read *The Bally Hoo Café. Come as you are or as someone else.*

That didn't make sense until the door opened and I caught a glimpse of what was inside. Whereas the Dil Pickle had a single performer, this place was filled with dozens of men wearing ladies' clothing of all sorts. Some men wore full Victorian dresses with petticoats. Some women, if you could call them that, wore tuxedos and tails. One man looked like Little Bo Peep! At this place, a normally dressed fella stuck out like a sore thumb.

A woman, or a man, I wasn't sure which, sat me down at a small round table off to the back of the club. When I told her all I wanted to drink was a club soda, she practically bowled me over by walking away so fast. Some boozehound with a pencil-thin moustache sat down at my table, trying to distract me from my mission with small talk.

"You are such a gorgeous boy. How about you come over and sit on my lap for a while and keep me company?" he said. My God, no one ever said anything even close to that to me before. How direct. Trying to ignore him so that he would go away, I glanced over his shoulders to see where Jean-Paul had gone.

The creep did not take the hint. He grabbed my wrist and tried to pull me close to him for a kiss. He was very strong. I was afraid I'd have to make a scene to get away from him, but then a stocky man, er, woman, stepped between us and pushed him off his seat. "Lay off, ya big Ethel. Beat it." The moustache looked cross at her a moment, then sized her up. When he picked himself off the floor to start his retreat, she added, "Scram."

"I...what the hell was wrong with that guy?" I immediately felt bad for what I had thought about these ladies dressed as men a moment earlier. She had saved me and, most likely, my mission.

She winked at me before following the beeline I was making with my eyes across the room to where Jean-Paul was standing and talking with another man. She nodded her head the direction Mr. Moustache had exited. "Looks like Ethel there ain't the only one who knows what he wants in this place." Then she motioned over her shoulder with her thumb at Jean-Paul. "Now he is quite the cat's meow, there. Tell you what, go on over there and get him. You could probably have any man in this place, darlin.' Hell, if I was interested in men, I'd try to woo you myself tonight. With that blond hair, those cute little blue eyes, and those muscles? And your little tush ain't half bad either."

This brought about some ruby red, blindingly bright blush on my cheeks, I'm sure. I chuckled, dropping my eyes to look at her. "Brett," I proclaimed, extending my hand over the table to make the introduction. "Thank you so much for your help with, what did you call him?"

"Ethel."

"Why?"

"You want to know what it stands for?" When I nodded, she obliged. "An Ethel is what we call any overly effeminate man. It ain't nice to say to someone unless you mean it, darlin'."

My face must have betrayed my innocence, because she just smiled as she got up to walk away. She again pointed toward Jean-Paul. "Oh, be extra careful with that one. He's a real heartbreaker." She stared into my face for a second. "But I see my warning is too late." She had saved me from the letch and helped me keep focus on…wait, where was Jean-Paul?

In all the commotion, he had slipped out of view. So had the man he had been talking to. I swiveled around the room looking for them. All of a sudden, they emerged from between the throng of patrons right in front of the table. They were both two feet in front of me now, with no way for me to hide, so I didn't even try. I relaxed all of my muscles like right before a face-off and prepared for whatever was about to happen.

Phase five was a tremendous failure.

CHAPTER TWENTY-THREE

His face lit up the second his eyes fell on me. He was holding hands with the slender man he had pulled through the crowd. The man was maybe in his mid-twenties like Jean-Paul, blond curly hair bouncing on top of his head. He was attractive enough to make me jealous. I tried not to show how excited I was. When the man saw the look on Jean-Paul's face, his own look turned to a scowl aimed directly at me.

"*Mon ami,*" Jean-Paul exclaimed in a tidbit of French-Canadian I was growing very fond of. He let go of the scowl's hand and placed his on his hips. "What are you doing here?"

My mind froze into a solid block of ice. My legs had a mind of their own, jiggling and bouncing like mad under the table. "Looking for you," was all I could think of on the spot, so that's what came out of my mouth.

"Looking for...Ha-ha. *Fantastique.* How about we get a drink?" He had completely forgotten about the scowl, who was still standing behind him. "I knew we'd get another chance."

The blond man grabbed Jean-Paul by the arm and tugged him sharply backward. "Hey, let's get outta here now. I'm ready to go to your place."

"Say, maybe next time, darling. Eh?" He had turned his whole body back to me, completely disregarding the man. He stood behind Jean-Paul for a minute before harrumphing and stomping away.

"What's say we get that drink now?" Jean-Paul asked.

To hell with the mission, I thought. *He* is *the mission, and I make for a terrible spy.* Before losing the moment, I invited myself before I even knew what I was going to say. "How's about we go to your place right now?"

He grinned that mischievous sideways grin like he was a gangster.

He grabbed me by the hand, leading me toward the door. Once we were outside, he started to walk toward his automobile. "Wait," I said. "We'd better take my car."

"You bought a car already?" he said, looking surprised.

"Not exactly," I said with my best rakish grin. When we reached the Torpedo, he slapped his knee and exclaimed that he had always wanted to drive this monster, but Margret wouldn't let him. "She probably doesn't let you drive it for the same reason I'm not going to now." He swayed for a second, shrugged his shoulders, and hopped over the door into the passenger seat.

"Home, James," he commanded. I paused at the mention of the car's previous owner, and the serious look that crossed his face told me he had reminded himself of it as well. "Oh, she must have told you about him. Whoops." James had been his best friend, and all he could say was "whoops"?

The engine once again roared to life, and we went down the block out onto Halsted north to his house. He gestured with his hands to tell me the directions, but a few times he forgot to tell me which way to go. We still found our way right to his door. I realized the mistake a little too late.

"Say, why do you know where I live?"

Panic again started to make its way up my throat. With a throaty swallow, my poise returned. Calmly I told him Margret must have told me on one of our many outings together. He didn't look like he believed me, but he didn't say anything. We opened the gate and drove the car into the back of the house. After he unlocked the door, we went in.

After he latched the door behind us, he took my face into his hands and kissed me deeply. My legs, solid with corded muscles from thousands of hours of training, failed me once again. He had to hold me up. He dropped his jacket on the dining room table and led me to the staircase without ever breaking his lip lock on me. We climbed up the stairs in one long kiss, him dropping one article of clothing on the stairs and one in the hall on the way to what I assumed would be his bedroom.

At the foot of his four-poster antique bed, he stepped away from me so he could gaze into my eyes. When his eyes traveled down my body, I finally allowed myself to look at his. He had taken off everything except his underwear, which were high quality and not the stodgy union suit variety. His chest had a patch of hair in the middle, and his stomach was flat and taut, each muscle rippling beneath the skin. He was beautiful.

The only distraction was the large, horrifying purple-black bruises from pucks that had hit him around the ribs and shoulders in practice.

He unbuttoned my shirt and pulled it up over my head, laying it carefully on the nightstand. Even in the dim light of the bedroom, I could see he was hard under his remaining clothes. Mine was straining painfully against my pants. He bent over to undo my trouser buttons. I automatically touched one of the shoulder bruises. He winced.

"Sorry. These are awful. Do they hurt badly? Isn't there some kind of…padding you could use?"

He playfully slapped my butt. "This is all the padding I need."

He gently pushed me backward onto the bed before he leaned over and slid my pants down past my ankles. When he climbed into bed to lay down next to me, my stupid brain started to throw one worry after another at me: *Are you really ready for this? What will this mean? Does he truly love you if he was about to leave with someone else tonight? Why didn't he chase you before? I'm afraid. I'm afraid. I'm afraid.*

"Wait." I placed my hand against his chest, pushing him back as he kissed my neck. His lips felt so hot and so unbelievably good there, like the summer afternoon sun on your face. "Wait, I don't think I'm ready for this, Jean-Paul."

My brain was ruining this.

"What do you mean?" He leaned back and caressed my face as he continued to look into my eyes. I was drowning in him, my resolve drowning too. Then it dawned on him. "Wait, have you…have you never…"

I rolled onto my back and counted the shadows on the ceiling. He leaned close to kiss me on the neck, which ended the counting. "We can take it as slow as you need."

"I…" A few tears rolled past my cheeks to land in small circles on the fluffy down pillows. He wiped them away from my cheeks. With incredible gentleness he slid close against me, wrapped his arms around me, and pulled me to him.

"The moment has to be right." He was so smooth and genuine, I almost gave in to wild abandon, swooning. We lay there holding each other for minutes before I could say another word.

"Jean-Paul?"

"Mon petit?" His nickname for me. I asked him about it, and he'd said it was only half of a little nothing that didn't even make sense. It meant my little, but little what? He said to say it in full was something else. Regardless of how it might have sounded to others, it was warm rain to me.

"Can you just hold me like this all night?"

"Of course, *mon petit garcon amoureux*. Of course."

Wait. I think... My little lover boy? Oh my. I squeezed his arms tight as we drifted off to sleep.

CHAPTER TWENTY-FOUR

October 23, 1926

Since the first day I set foot in this city I'd had nothing on my mind except hockey and Jean-Paul. With the way the practice schedule had been lately, all I had time to do was hockey regardless of what I was thinking about. Frankly, it made things simpler. Hockey always does.

During practice, Jean-Paul told me Margret was planning a big Saturday for the three of us. The weather had been extremely nice for this time of year, so Margret suggested we all go to Riverview Park. She said we'd enjoy a day of rides and eating candied popcorn before staying to see the fireworks over the parkway at night.

Growing up around circuses, I got used to the thrills of action and adventure people. Carnies were always in town, showing off with a magic trick or riding an elephant on Main Street without fanfare as if it were a daily occurrence. And it sometimes was. When the circuses were in town, you'd always see entertaining rides, funhouse mirrors, and small attractions. I had read at the library about the gargantuan roller coasters at Riverview and was desperate to go on them. So when they said that we were going there, I was excited and giddy like a schoolgirl. I would just make certain not to mention the giddy schoolgirl thing around Margret or face the wrath of the suffragettes.

At breakfast that morning, Mickey had already been down at the table for a while chatting with Moira as she served food to him. When I walked down the stairs, they both stopped and looked at me.

Moira smiled. "Who is the lucky young lady, Brett? Don't be shy, I can tell it, that ye've been bitten by the love bug."

I had no idea what to say to that. How on earth did she figure that out? Mickey was staring. Did he wonder if I was in love too? If he did, he surely must be curious as to whom, since the only person he'd seen me with was Jean-Paul.

"Are you two gonna sit here all day clucking like old hens about me or what?" I deflected.

"I knew it!" Mickey exclaimed.

Moira beamed from ear to ear. "Ah, you have the look about you. When are you going to bring her around here?"

"For your information, we are going out tonight." I completely lied to them. I scraped some jelly onto toast and tried to make my way out of the kitchen in haste.

They clattered on behind me. I sure wasn't going to miss Mickey being all over my comings and goings when he moved out. He had decided to move into a proper apartment with a couple of the other guys. Mickey was a good guy, a close friend, and I knew I'd miss his company even if it would make things easier between Jean-Paul and me. Moira was sure and true. She'd keep her nose out of your business when it counted.

The streetcar clacked against the tracks, swaying its way north toward the Palmer Hotel where I was supposed to pick up Margret. She kept trying to get me to keep the Torpedo all the time, but Moira's neighborhood wasn't as safe for it as leaving it at the Palmer. I was sure I'd end up bringing it home tonight anyway, though. It's not like anyone would miss the opportunity to travel by streetcar.

I walked the few blocks to the hotel from where the streetcar dropped me off. Sure enough, the Bugatti was waiting out front for me. I was beginning to love that woman and that car. I went up the elevator and knocked with the doorknocker. Behind the door, I could hear a couple of women talking.

A young lady in her mid-twenties opened the door. She was dressed very much like Margret always dressed, flapper chic. She was a pretty, blond-haired, blue-eyed masterpiece any man would love to date. I knew Margret knew about my feelings for Jean-Paul and wondered why she had invited a fourth wheel along.

"I'm Alistaire, Margret's favorite friend," she said, sticking out her right hand. I shook it gently. "I hope you don't mind my tagging along today?" She laughed. "I just adore roller coasters."

Mind? Of course I minded. All day now I'd have to be self-conscious and careful about everything I said or did where Jean-Paul was concerned. I was starting to get peeved by the intrusion. Who did this little blond floozy think she was?

"How do you know Margret?" she continued to intrude.

"We met through Jean-Paul. Do you know him?"

Her tone was polite and inquisitive, but her question was accusatory. Like I couldn't possibly know Margret through social means. Alistaire and I were getting off to a terrible start. Margret walked in from the bedroom fixing her hair wrap. She wore a beautiful white dress that came to her knees, with a brown wool coat draped across her shoulders. The coat dulled her hair, but her eyes shone brighter against the dark color.

"Brett, my darling. I see you two have already met. Fantastic. Well, let's get going."

When we got to the car, I realized we had both forgotten it was a two-seater. "We'll just have to squeeze in tight then, won't we?" Margret practically squealed. The two of them crushed in next to me as we headed to the park. Jean-Paul was, of course, going to meet us there. Far be it for him to spend too much time with me.

Riverview Park was on the north side of the city surrounded by luscious green fields on two sides. It was quite odd having this sprawling amusement park here smack dab in the city. You'd think they'd never allow this much land to go without a tall building. The entrance was a plain old set of pillars, but then again, they weren't the main attraction.

Towering over any of the structures around it was the enormous Bobs roller coaster. It was a long, high wooden coaster with so many white painted tracks even Tom Sawyer couldn't get this thing whitewashed. The loud gears clacked and banged across the parkway, pulling tons of train cars filled with people up and over the giant hill. Then there were the screams. Every time a full load of people arched over the top, the girls would scream and the men would whoop and holler with joy. I couldn't wait to ride it.

Jean-Paul waited for us under the main archway. He was leaning against the pillar, eating some popcorn from a red and yellow striped box, looking as if he didn't have a care in the world. Like Margret, he was wearing white except for the black overcoat. He was dashingly handsome. Their outfits contrasted starkly with the dingy grey of the brewing storm in the sky.

As we approached, I stuck my hand out to shake his. He just walked past me straight into Margret's outstretched arms for a hug. He picked her up off her feet and twirled her around. She let out a "Wheeee" before he set her back down to turn his attention to us.

"*Mon ami*," he directed at me with a subtle wink before turning to

Margret's friend. "Alistaire." The way he said it was like broken glass against the pavement. These two had some history, probably bad.

"I was surprised to hear you were joining us today, Frenchie," she sneered back at him. "It's very early in the morning for the captain of the night owls, isn't it?"

Frenchie?

"You know I wouldn't miss out on an opportunity to make the society papers with you once again, *mon cher.*"

"All right, you two lovebirds. That's enough," Margret chided. "Besides, the clouds look like they're going to rain pitchforks any minute, and we don't need to get an early jump on that."

The four of us turned toward the park and strolled in. Jean-Paul, despite his obvious hatred of Alistaire, had already purchased all four tickets along with some tickets to ride the coasters. He stepped back to walk with me and let the two girls step ahead of us. He faked a stumble so he could bump into my shoulder. I kicked him softly on the backside with a sideways foot just like Charlie Chaplin in his silent films.

We both laughed, the awkwardness over. Jean-Paul had taken me to the Biograph Theater once to see a Chaplin film. He couldn't believe it was my first time at a motion picture. The glimmer of the hundreds of lights in the marquee was amazing to look at, but the enormous theater and the flickering movies took my breath away. Chaplin was a dashing man underneath all that makeup and tomfoolery. And was he ever funny. I had never laughed so hard in all my life. I tried to slip away to see more movies whenever I could.

Back away from the girls, I leaned in to talk to Jean-Paul quietly. "What's the deal between you two?" He shrugged his shoulders at me as if to reply that he didn't know. I was sure there was more to that story. I was also sure I could pry it out of Margret at some point, but thought I'd give Jean-Paul another try.

"Give over, what happened between you? She upset that you only have eyes for me?"

"Not likely, ours was a one-time affair," he said a little too harshly before he collected himself. He placed his finger on my chest. When I looked down, he flipped his finger up and popped me in the nose. The oldest gag in the book. He ran ahead a few steps before turning around to see that I had stopped. He ran back to me, which was where I wanted him to always be. Throwing an arm sideways around me, he squeezed me and pulled me forward. "Aw, don't be sore. To ride the rides you need even numbers. Come on." I wasn't sure if he was explaining why she was there or why I was there. Either way, having his arm around me felt good if only for a brief time.

It was closing day for the season at the park. Today felt extra special since it was the last day for them and the first day for me. I wanted to ride everything. Looking out across the park, I could see the giant Roman-style pillars that surrounded part of the Bobs roller coaster, which rose to over eighty feet high. I grabbed Margret by the hand and started heading that way when Jean-Paul grabbed us both by the shoulders.

"Take it easy now, children."

"Come on, let's go ride the Bobs," I said, sounding just a little too much like an overexcited child.

Jean-Paul grinned rakishly before he talked to us like we were, in fact, children. "You must be patient. If you ride the biggest and best ride of them all first, you might as well go home. How can the rest of them compare?" My shoulders slumped a little, but I could see the logic behind what he had said. I also wanted to recover from having just sounded ridiculous.

We walked over to stand in line for a parachute ride. The tower that took riders up and down looked to be a hundred feet high. It was breathtaking. I couldn't wait to get all the way up there. I was sure we would be able to see the Coliseum from the top.

"This is your plan to start smaller?" Alistaire complained.

"How about the merry-go-round instead?" he said.

We got strapped into the parachutes, two to a ride. Jean-Paul had hastily gotten in with Margret, pushing me out of the way with his butt. I was fine riding with Alistaire, although she couldn't seem to wipe the scowl off her face. The ride's chains clattered as they pulled us all the way to the top. I could see over the tops of most of the trees, but not all the way across town to the arena.

We chuted down, though the drop was slow and controlled and not quite as thrilling as I thought. Alistaire made little girl noises of joy as we swooped around. When the chains caught for a second, the parachute we were in jolted hard to the left. She reached out and put my hand in a death lock. I let her squeeze my hand for the rest of the ride down.

The park smelled so good almost everywhere. The wafting aromas of hot dogs, popcorn, and cotton candy filled my nostrils like unearthly delights. I hadn't eaten much that morning before going to the park. "Time for a hot dog!" I announced before rushing over to the stand.

After a few seconds, I returned with four that we sat on a bench and ate. They were barely finished eating when I had jumped up to start to pull them to the next ride.

"I can't keep up with him," Alistaire said. "Do you think you could find a younger one, Jean-Paul?" I chafed at that comment. So did Jean-Paul, but you'd never know it by his calm demeanor.

Margret bolted up and started running down the parkway with me. She held my hand while she made big circles out to her left with the other as we ran like she was holding it against the wind. When we arrived at the Flying Turns, we saw it was a tandem ride with one rider practically sitting in the lap of the person behind them. Alistaire grabbed Margret and got into a car, leaving Jean-Paul and me to do the same. He was a little heavier than me, but I was taller, so I got in the car behind them first. He sat down in front of me. Even though he was trying to hold himself up, he felt good against me.

With a loud bang, the ride jerked forward and started its ascent to the big drop. As the cars shifted backward, going upright at a sixty degree angle, Jean-Paul had no choice but to fall back into my chest. My hands had been resting on the edge of the car, but I eased them around his waist. He didn't protest.

During some of the turns, his head rested against my neck. It felt so good I never wanted the ride to stop. But it did. I never wanted the mood to stop, but it did too. Alistaire began vomiting up her hot dog before she was even unstrapped from the car. Somehow, she managed to miss Margret's dress. I helped her out of the car and held her coat back away from her as she let loose another volley of red and green liquids. We had not eaten anything green. The thought of what it could be made me ill. I had to raise my head up and away from her as she grasped the edges of the garbage cans, going again.

"I guess we shouldn't have eaten right before a ride," Margret concluded.

Jean-Paul leaned his back against the fence, close to Alistaire, and crossed his arms. "I don't know about you guys, but I could really go for some fried dough!" If Alistaire could have shot daggers from her eyes, Jean-Paul would have been skewered.

She leaned back against the garbage can as she sat on the ground, her dress getting crumpled beneath her. "Whose wise idea was it to get food before a ride anyway?"

"Ah, blame. There it is. No one made you eat it," Jean-Paul said.

"All right, you boys go on ahead and ride something while I help

Alistaire get cleaned up. There's a restroom over there," Margret said, gently guiding the sickly girl away.

We walked down the parkway toward the games area and saw the shooting gallery. "Hey, I'm good at this game. Let's win a doll or something for the girls. It'll make them feel better."

Jean-Paul frowned at me. "Winning prizes at the fair for your best girl, are you? You are such the romantic."

"What's wrong with being a romantic?"

"Eh, nothing. I guess."

I pushed like I always do. "Don't you ever feel like being the romantic with someone you really care about?"

He walked past me toward the shooting gallery. "It's all right for some people, I guess. If they need that." He handed the worker the money, picked up the rifle, and proceeded to miss more than he hit.

"Give me a gun, please," I said to the worker. This game was easy. If you just lead your target, you can hit all the ducks as they swim by. I let out a series of shots and knocked all the ducks and a bull's-eye down. The worker handed me a large teddy bear, which I gloatingly showed to Jean-Paul. He frowned at me before walking over to the ring toss.

It must be the great hand-eye coordination with goalies but Jean-Paul could not be beat at the ring toss. In a matter of minutes, he had two large bears and a small yellow duck. I was more excited about his prowess than he was.

"Why, Jean-Paul, who did you win the duckie for? Could it be for me?" I taunted. He looked to the ground, sighed, and shook his head.

As we walked through the park to our next ride, we came across a crying little girl, her mother trying to console her. Jean-Paul bent down to hand her one of the giant bears he had won. The girl stopped crying and hugged the bear tightly, smiling. I was enamored with his generosity and caring at that moment. He hadn't given her the duckie. I wanted to hold his hand more than anything in the world.

But I knew I couldn't.

"That was—"

He cut me off in mid sentence. "Come on, Aladdin's Castle awaits." He ran off toward the giant façade of Aladdin's upper body and dashed up the stairs, bear in tow. I was beaming and not sure why.

Inside, we had to walk through a giant mouth to get into the funhouse. The mirrors confused me, and I kept bumping into them. He grabbed my arm and led me out of the mirrors into the rolling drum bridge. The spinning barrel threw everyone off balance so that we all started to lean to the right. Everyone, that is, except Jean-Paul. The man had supernatural balance.

When we got to a staircase, it looked like we had reached the end of the funhouse until the staircase collapsed beneath us, sending us tumbling out onto a mat. I was laughing like a schoolboy for sure. I laughed until I realized the bear I had won had gotten his leg ripped off in the fall. Jean-Paul inspected the tear for a second and said, "We still at least have one. They can share." The duck was for me.

We rode all the rides that afternoon: The Comet, The Jetstream, The Rotor, The Big Dipper, and The Pippin. Some of the names didn't make any sense, but they were amazingly fast and thrilling. By the time we got back to the girls, they were doing much better. They were at the Fool the Guesser attraction, the man trying to guess their weights.

Jean-Paul held up a coin behind the girls and raised his finger up to the sky as the man started in on Margret's turn. He winked at the man and waved the coin. The man got the idea and started to guess her weight. "I think something tells me I might be wrong on this one. You're a tricky lass. I wanna say…" He shut his eyes and wrinkled his forehead, thinking hard before continuing. "Easy, four hundred pounds and not a pound more!"

People laughed and cheered as Margret stepped up on the platform and playfully swatted the man on the arm. She turned to see Jean-Paul and me laughing hysterically and charged us. When she finished, Jean-Paul tossed the coin to the worker, who tipped his hat graciously. He called out as we started away. We turned back to him as he guessed her weight exactly, which, when she said he was right, caused us to have fits and starts all over again.

We presented the girls with their bears and told them how we'd won them. Jean-Paul gave his to Alistaire, telling her he hoped it made her feel better. I gave my torn stuffed animal to Margret, who got a real laugh out of the fact that it was broken. Jean-Paul was really showing his playful side like usual, but this caring side, giving the toy to the little girl and now this, threw me for a loop.

I looked longingly off to the towering monstrosity that was the Bobs roller coaster. Margret caught my gaze and gave in. "Let's go ride that thing before Brett pees his pants from excitement." She was joshing me but was also being completely truthful. The other rides were exciting and thrilling, but none of them looked as if they could hold a candle to the Bobs.

As we approached the ride, we all caught each other looking at the Roman columns that surrounded one side. The massive structure looped back and forth through itself, the tracks bobbing up and down and curving around, looking as if no car could possibly stay on them.

We sat next to each other, girls in front and boys in back. Once again, when the track curved almost straight up to the drop, our bodies slammed into the back of the seats. My hand found Jean-Paul's and held it tight, but not out of fear. At the top, we could see the towers of the city off in the distance set against the vast expanse of Lake Michigan beyond. I looked for the Coliseum, but couldn't see it.

We were sitting off to the back of the train. The front of it slipped over the abyss of the eighty-seven-foot drop and for a moment, the entire train car came to a stop. Then gravity kicked back in and pulled us all screaming over the edge. We plunged down at a rickety breakneck speed. When the train hit the curve at the bottom, we were thrown against the side of the car, our hair flapping in the breeze, faces chilled in the cold air rushing around us. Margret was clutching her head wrap in her hand, her hair a red flame in the winds.

Jean-Paul and I grabbed the handrail with our outer hands, steadying ourselves against the constant shimmy and bounce of the ride, but our inner hands remained clasped tightly. After the last dip and weave, the ride smoothed out as we sailed into the station again. Just before we entered the deck area, Jean-Paul let loose of my hand. When we had gotten out, my body was abuzz with the electricity of the ride.

"You were so right! There is nothing out there that compares to that ride!" I said a little too loudly. "I want to go again."

"Again?" Alistaire said with exasperation. "I can't believe we made it that time. Again?"

I frowned.

"We will come again next season, I'm sure," Jean-Paul said as if to a small child threatening a pout or a temper tantrum. But I took it.

"It's a date," I proclaimed. Margret laughed.

As we walked to the front of the park, we passed a tent with a crowd of people inside. We stopped to see what the hubbub was about. A carnival-style barker was out front with a sign over his shoulder that read: *Freak Show Five Cents*. I had never been much of a fan of the freak show. Not that there's a thing wrong with the people in them, or even those that paid to see it. It's more that paying to see someone for what made them different, special, seemed wrong somehow.

I tried to get them to leave, but they all wanted to stay. Inside was a room of curiosities and cabinets filled with odd-shaped skulls and bones. We passed through a tent flap to enter a room with a caged boy who had his back to the crowd. A different barker stood in front.

"Step right up, step right up, ladies and gentlemen. What you are about to see will astound and amaze you. It might even horrify you. If there are young children or women faint of heart in the audience, I encourage them to step on through or avert your eyes. May I present to you, found in the deepest depths of darkest Africa, the one and only Lion Boy!"

Shrouded in darkness, a shirtless boy lay on the dirt floor, chained by the leg with a shackle to the wall, leapt up and started toward the crowd, roaring. A ball of fur feathered out around his head like the mane of a lion. Dark lines raked his cheeks, and he was dirty from head to toe. The entire crowd jumped backward, startled, except me. The boy landed on all fours, threw his head back, and roared as loud as he could, only the roar was mixed with a real lion's roar played on a phonograph off to the side of the room.

He lunged forward again. "Out!" the barker exclaimed. "Let's get out before he breaks those chains!" And he started pushing people toward the flap to the next room.

Outside we headed to the parking lot. They had all been excited by the show, but I was disturbed. "Do you think the boy has parents that care he's chained to a wall for people's enjoyment?"

"I'm sure his parents work here, Brett," Alistaire said. I wasn't so sure. I could see my parents turning their backs and walking away as the train took me to Milwaukee.

"It's just a show, for giggles," Margret added.

Jean-Paul looked at me with compassionate eyes.

"I grew up around circus people," I continued, "and you never know. They always said small sideshows were brutal to their workers. It's usually the bottom of the barrel talent-wise, so they put up with... well, anything. He was just a little boy. Doesn't anyone care?"

I must have started to shake with rage because I didn't realize Jean-Paul had placed his hands on my shoulders from behind as we walked to the car. Alistaire looked horrified by my outburst. She asked if Jean-Paul could take her home. I looked longingly at him, wanting nothing more than to be with him now. We separated, and I went off to the Palmer with Margret, the sun going down over the hulking coasters.

CHAPTER TWENTY-FIVE

I calmed down pretty quickly, feeling like a complete imbecile for my outburst. Whenever I put the car in gear, Margret let her hand rest on my hand over the selector. She held my hand and let it stay there just long enough to be comforting without feeling awkward or condescending. It felt good. Even with the top up for colder weather, she still enjoyed the fast turns and showed it by the occasional squeal. She didn't say anything for a long while.

Finally the silence grew too much, and I opened up. "I don't know why I got so upset seeing the Lion Boy. I just couldn't stand seeing him like that."

She put her hand on my shoulder, waiting a while before speaking. "It's only just for show, right?"

"You know I grew up surrounded by circus people, right?"

Margret giggled and patted my hand. "Yeah, you might have mentioned it once or twice." We both chuckled.

"I guess it's a sense of pride for me. It does probably get mentioned from time to time." Now we both laughed at my understatement. When things settled down, I continued. "I got to know lots of the people who worked there."

The engine's roar quieted to a hum as we slowed for a curve, then grew loud again as I throttled up the Torpedo. She moved her hand deftly off my shoulder and back onto my hand as all the movement of the shifter smoothed out. "The thing about them most people never learn is they are just regular people. For the most part, like you and me. Well, maybe more like me.

"They worked so hard, but always had time to show the local kids a few tricks or let us ride some of the animals. Some of them even tricked us into working around their farms in the hopes we'd get a chance to fly on the trapeze or ride an elephant. Whatever we could get away with.

The carnies, that's what people called them, they had an uneasy peace with the adults in town, but the kids, that was a different story.

"My dad, he was no different than the others. He hated them, but he didn't have a problem with hiring some of their hands to help on the farm in their off times. The ones that stayed back were often injured, and they worked cheaply. They worked out at our place and instead of working at home for my father, I was always taking care of a camel or something."

Margret had been listening carefully and attentively. "Brett, honey," she asked in a strained voice, "why do you know so much about them? Did all the boys back home spend so much time with them, or was it something else?" She had cut right to the quick of the matter.

I stiffened noticeably in the driver's seat, biting my lip a little, choking back the coming tears. "Let's just say that the carnies weren't the only thing my father hated."

"What happened?"

I focused on the steady thrum of the engine to keep moving my story forward. "I skipped hockey practice one day when I was about thirteen, going instead to one of the road farms, where one of the bigger tent shows had set up for the coming winter. It was a beautiful autumn day, and one of the other boys was helping me hammer tent spikes on one of the side tents. His name was Jake, Jacob really, pronounced with a Y instead of a J. They were Jewish gypsies. We had begun to spend a lot of time together, working and not.

"He had black curly hair and this olive complexion that was unlike anyone in town. I didn't realize it at the time, but I was falling for him. He was a Jew and…well…my father would have killed me for both reasons. After work, we slipped off to the pond at the edge of their farm. We had been working in short pants but didn't want to get them wet, so Jake convinced me to go in naked."

"Oh my, how tantalizing," she interjected.

The words almost caught in my throat, not being used to speaking like this out loud to another living soul. "Tell me about it. Well, of course, just as he had swum up and edged close to plant a kiss on me, his father caught us!"

"No!" she exclaimed. "What did you do?"

"What did I do? I froze solid. I was petrified. Jake acted like it was no big deal. His father yelled at us in Hebrew I think, and Jake said I had to go home. I was so worried about his father telling mine. I asked Jake what would happen, and he frowned and said they weren't supposed to fraternize with townies like that. Fraternize. That's what he said. I didn't even know what it was then, but I did know that I felt in love with him. We never even kissed."

"Did you keep seeing him?"

"No, that was the end of that. I only saw him one more time. His father wouldn't let me work there anymore after that. Besides, my father nearly killed me when he found out about the missed practices. He trapped me in my bedroom with a leather strop, like the kind barbers have for sharpening razors. He caught me in my underwear and wore me out. I had welts on my legs and ass and back. My father is a farmer and has strong workman muscles and could really swing a scythe or a strop. One of the licks caught me in the cheek and drew blood."

She leaned her head against my shoulder. It felt nice and comforting. I continued, "My mother must have heard the whole thing and never said a word. When I felt I could finally get up off the floor, I pulled clothes on over the open wounds and crawled out the window and left. I decided it was time to run away to where people loved me. Jake's parents would let me join their circus and live with them as one of them. His dad hadn't beaten him when he found us naked together. He was only upset because I wasn't a carnie. I'd rectify that."

"What happened then?" I glanced over at her and saw that she had started to cry.

"Are you sure you want me to tell you this story?"

"I need to hear it."

I didn't think anybody needed to hear this mess of a life. "I walked through miles of brush and brambles to get through the woods to their house. I knocked on the door. It was a few minutes before Jake answered. He took one look at me with all the cuts, swelling, and bruises that had already started to form, and started to cry for his mother. She quickly came to the door, took one look at me, and carried me in to the bed. Carnie people never turn their backs on people in need, I thought then. I was so naïve.

"She dressed my wounds with some salve and made me drink some awful-tasting tea. I must have passed out because when I woke up, I was bandaged, and Jake's father was standing over me with a blanket telling me it was time to go home. I pleaded with him to let me stay. I don't know if he spoke English. Jake was translating feverishly, but his father finally pushed him aside and said in English so that I could hear, 'We want no trouble.' And I understood.

"He drove me home that night. I never saw Jake again. My mother was at the door and let me in. She didn't make a fuss over my bruising or wounds. She already knew what had happened. She told me to get back to bed before my father knew I'd run away from home with 'those Jews.' The punishment for that would be more of the same."

"How awful," she whispered.

"I wanted to run away to the circus. Instead, the circus delivered me back home. Even they didn't want me. At least they were motivated by worries about what the town would do to them if they harbored a local rather than because they hated my guts. I wanted out and had no place to go. After that, my father pushed me to play hockey even harder, carrying me back and forth from practice, checking with the coaches, showing up unannounced. He made sure I didn't shirk or slip away.

"So I guess I know a little about how the carnies take care of their own, and that *lion* boy would never be treated like that if he was in a real troupe. He should never be treated like that."

"You mean he should never be chained like you were chained, hurt like you were hurt by the same people who were supposed to love you." She said it very quietly, not a question or a challenge. She spoke directly with calm tenderness in her voice. I pulled the car over to the side of the road just as the violent shaking threatened to break me apart at the seams. Margret hugged me tightly through my convulsive sobs while I cried.

When I stopped, she let me go and scooted back to her seat. "It seems that Sigmund Freud should have used this car for therapy, as much as we talk in it." We both smiled at that. I felt closer to her than any friend I had ever had. She asked me up to her rooms, where I spent the night in her bed, talking, laughing and dreaming of Jean-Paul.

CHAPTER TWENTY-SIX

October 27, 1926

The train trip from Chicago to Detroit was longer than the seven hours it would have taken us to drive there. We stopped in every little town, taking on passengers. The boys said the one we'd take for longer trips had sleeping cars on it and didn't stop so much. Either way, getting off of a long train ride was quickly beginning to be one of my least favorite pastimes.

Playing in Detroit meant going through the city on the train all the way across the Canadian border into Windsor, Ontario, to their home away from home. Like us, they were a new team, but they didn't have a permanent home. At least not yet. Through the window, Detroit looked a lot like Chicago with its grand buildings touching the clouds, its clogged streets choked with automobiles, and the people bustling to who knows where.

When the train stopped in Windsor, the air looked cleaner and the sky bluer. The buildings weren't as tall as the ones we could still see across the river in Detroit. It was strange. I could see two countries at the same time standing on the train platform. The people in Windsor were extremely nice to us. Usually when people found out who we were, they turned cold. But it was different here. They didn't seem to care for Detroit much, which made me wonder why they even had a team.

The stadium, Border Cities Arena, was a pretty small place. Not too many people knew about our two teams, because the stands were only half-full. That didn't matter so much to me. The air was crisp and cool, and the breeze from skating ran its fingers though my hair as I circled during warm-ups.

When the game started, I won the face-off cleanly to pitch the puck back to Babe. He avoided some defenders with a little puck handling before we both crossed the blue line into the attack zone at the same time. I cocked my head sideways watching his stick to see what he was going to do. One of their bigger defensemen stood up right in the way, and it looked like Babe's little run was over.

Babe started to go to the right, but then as quickly as he and the defender started to move, Babe flipped the puck across the center of the ice. The pass fooled the defense and slapped into place on the flat of my stick. The goalie had slid over toward the right side to be able to stop any shot coming from Babe on that side. When he saw that the shot would now be coming from the left side where I was at, he raised his right leg and slid over to stop me.

I looked for the best possible scenario. He swept his leg over to the side of the net. I could have thrown the puck several places and had a good chance of making a goal. His leg hadn't made it all the way to the post yet so I could have gotten it in there. He was leaving the right of the net, and maybe I could have gotten it past him over there at the rough angle.

I watched as he slid across, dragging his sharp skates and pulling up peel after peel of ice chunks. I flashed on the area where his legs were going to be apart and slapped the rubber with a fast wrist shot. The black disc sailed across the floor about an inch over the ice, finding its home a split second before the goalie could snap his feet together. Goal!

The fellas, minus Babe, piled over on top of me as we all spilled to the ice in an embarrassing display of joy. It was one to nothing, not exactly winning the championship cup, but it was a great feeling. Babe skated by me after I had gotten up from the dog pile and slapped me on the shins with the flat of his stick.

"That's all the celebratin' ya need for a goal this early in the game."

You know what? To hell with him. If he didn't want me to score, he should stop throwing the perfect biscuit my way. He had been peeved at me since the day we met. It wasn't my fault he made an ass out of himself to the newspapers. It also wasn't my fault he told us he didn't even want to be here. I was trying my best to like the guy, being he was a hockey legend and all, but it was taking some work. What didn't take any effort at all was playing in games with him. He was an ideal player, so despite all of his asinine comments, he could really send home the mail.

Mickey missed his line change during the second period, being too far from our visitor bench, but he made the Cougars pay for it. I had blocked a shot and sent the puck back toward Percy purely by accident. I wished I had the ability to block a shot and angle it to where I wanted it to go at the same time. I was just happy if it didn't go in the net. No, I left that to the goaltenders. After the puck had gone off my leg to Percy, he passed it back to me where I had carried it up the ice to the left circle area. The traffic over there was too much as they had been double-teaming me since the first goal I made. I saw no way out, so I passed it through the ankles of a group of players, while Mickey was waiting for it by the goalmouth to backhand it right in.

He was so excited that he skated across the ice, got up a head of steam, put his stick between his legs, sat on it and started to ride it as he slid. It was the greatest goal celebration I had ever witnessed. He looked like he was riding a horse or a train. We all cheered at him or gave him hugs when he circled back to us. I thought about making up some kind of celebration that I could do to top that. I'd done a few moves as a high schooler that I thought looked good at the time, but nothing like that. Mostly, I liked the camaraderie of the group hugs after a goal too much to skate off by myself.

In the third period, I was backing up to stop a rush of three forwards in an unfortunate three-on-one attack. Dick was charging hard up the center to catch up with us. I could feel Jean-Paul steel himself behind us, waiting for the coming shot. At least that's all I could imagine he'd do in a situation where a shot was an inevitability. I had very little hope of stopping all of them. I decided to go down to the ice in front of one, sliding to the left toward center, splayed out my arms and legs and poked my stick at the puck.

It was no use. The player with the puck popped it across and over my back to one of his waiting partners. He jumped over my arm with all his rushing momentum and kept on to the net. I rolled back over to see him receive the pass back and knock the puck into our net. His forward motion also kept him careening into our net, knocking Jean-Paul backward into the posts, hard. His head snapped back as he went down to the ice with one of the other Cougars crashing down on top of his back.

"No!" I screamed.

I got up immediately and raced over to them, seeing only red. When the first red sweater had gotten up, I met him with a sweeping haymaker that knocked him down flat. One of the other Cougars grabbed my sweater to yank me into his clenched fist, bashing my face back hard. It didn't faze me like it probably should have, but through all my rage my arms kept flailing and striking out at anyone in a red shirt. The rest of my team skated over to the mêlée, fists and elbows becoming the norm of the day.

Someone pulled me down flat to the ice and sat on my back, ending my battle, but not my rage. I screamed for them to let me up and at them, clawing at the ice in front of me, desperate to get up, desperate to protect him. The referee, a large, sturdy older man, manhandled me by the collar while he jerked me toward my bench. He was yelling at Muldoon to control his men and to get rid of me. He didn't call me by my name but used some colorful language that was actually pretty demeaning. By the time they dragged me away, everyone had pretty much stopped fighting. Jean-Paul was skating in circles by his net, using his skates to scratch away the blood that was splattered all around the goal crease. He turned his head and found me staring at him, but the look on his face was not gratitude at all.

Back in the locker room, I waited fifteen minutes until the end of the game. I sat on the empty, lonely bench, my head in my hands. I was worried about the game. Would they fire me for causing such a ruckus? I doubted it. Why had Jean-Paul looked at me with such anger?

The silence of the locker room was destroyed in a second when the boys crashed through the door, cheering in victory. I had just stood up when Percy threw his sweaty, bloodstained arm around me.

"What a right hand on this guy," he shouted. "We need to get you on defense, boy."

The other guys mostly tousled my hair and told me that it was a good thing what I had done. Mickey didn't. He looked at me with confusion and concern.

"What the hell did you do that for?" he asked me quietly. "That kind of shit's for the enforcers. You let them protect the goalie, friend or not. You hear me? Huh?"

I shook my head, worried that he suspected something. He was right. We all protect, but we leave it to the real enforcers to bum rush people. I could've, might've broken a hand. Then I'd more than likely be off the team. And for what? For whom? The entire team had entered the room before Jean-Paul did. When I tried to get his attention, he simply ignored me and went to his corner to start undressing.

Some of the guys took advantage of the few hours we had before the train was to leave and went to one of the wineries where drinking was permitted. Jean-Paul was sitting alone on a station bench, so I walked over to him and sat down. He didn't welcome me or give me room. My hand was throbbing. The bag of ice taped to my hand looked silly outside in the cold air.

"Are you all right?" I asked him.

He broke his silence after a few minutes. "What's eating you, eh?"

"Nothing. I'm sorry."

"You are sorry?"

I playfully bumped his knee with mine. He pulled his away. I continued to chip away at the ice. "Yes, but I was worried about you. It looked so…bad. I—"

"I'm fine." He sat in silence a moment. "How's your hand?"

"It hurts. It was worth it."

"No. You can't do that again, Brett. You just can't. You have to leave us off the ice. Out there we are hockey players."

"Us?" I smiled. My heart lightened considerably. "You said us. You do care." I felt that this admission was the first crack in the *Titanic*, caused by the relentless iceberg. My hard work was paying off.

He stood up to look around for anyone, but we were alone on the train platform. "Damn it, *mon pe*—" He cut himself off before continuing. "You have to—If you can't—" He walked away after searching several times for the right words. I understood what he meant, but I didn't care. He thought of our relationship as an "us."

CHAPTER TWENTY-SEVEN

October 31, 1926
Halloween

Jean-Paul and I hadn't gone out together or to his house again since the unfortunate incident at the game in Detroit, although I wanted to. We had eaten lunch together a few times only because I forced myself on him. He was punishing me by giving me the cold shoulder. For someone who rarely talked to the rest of the guys on the team, he made a point of doing it when I was around. He talked to them as a way to avoid talking to me.

Someone mentioned that Halloween was only a few days away and asked what everyone was doing. With all the commotion going on, Halloween had completely slipped my mind. Halloween was on a Sunday, which meant we'd have to make an early night of it or pay the price during practice on Monday.

"Aren't you going to a costume party with your girl?" Jean-Paul said.

I hadn't forgotten Margret was planning what she referred to as the "Festivities," although I didn't know what the real festivities were going to be. Jean-Paul mentioning Margret as my girl had become a thing since Detroit as well.

I arrived at Margret's hotel a few hours early as she had commanded, although I did not know why. Margret had the hotel's tailor come up to her rooms to fit me for a suit. They were both waiting for me when I banged on the door. "We'll get you a nice suit for the evening's festivities," she exclaimed. She had been so excited that I agreed to let her buy me a new suit. Only money like hers could get a tailor to alter a suit in the few hours we had before going out, on a Sunday no less.

"What festivities are you referring to?"

She waved me in as she walked into her apartment. "You'll see," she said, grinning like Puck.

I had never been fitted by a professional tailor before. He and his assistant brought up a rack of suits to choose from. None of them had the swagger of a Jean-Paul suit, but they were all of better quality than the one I had purchased after my second check. I picked out a black suit with a black cotton long-sleeved shirt. It came with a black tie and fedora.

Margret wrinkled up her nose. "It's dark. Don't you think it's morbid?"

"It is Halloween. What do you think?" I asked the tailor.

"Whatever the gentleman wants. I have it done for you before you leave. Guaranteed," said the elderly Italian man.

"Adolpho," Margret asked, "can you please get my friend a few pairs of underwear suitable for a sports star such as himself?"

Adolpho looked me up and down. "Baseball? My grandsons all love the baseball." I corrected him. He looked me up and down again. "Too skinny. Needs some of my wife's cooking, no?" He patted himself on the belly as he walked out the door.

Margret grabbed my hand and led me to the door. "Wait, where are we going? I'm not wearing any clothes." I had on underwear and a robe for the fitting. We headed to the elevator and went up to the floor marked "P." I assumed it meant penthouse, but she had the biggest apartment I could imagine. When the doors opened, I got a whiff of swimming pool chlorine. "I don't have a swimsuit! What are you doing?"

She was taking off her clothes. "Don't worry. While you were in the fitting, I called ahead. No one will be coming in. It's all ours." She slipped out of her dress, kicked off her shoes, and stood there naked. From behind, her beautiful form was a perfect hourglass. I realized that I hadn't seen a completely nude woman before other than in art books. She waved for me to go into the pool with her. I instinctively turned away, but not before noticing that she had red pubic hair that was thin and smartly trimmed. She also had some brown freckles across her flat stomach. I was ashamed to show the tangled, matted mess hidden underneath my robe.

I undressed after she jumped into the pool. I walked up to the edge of the pool, covering my genitals with my hand. I dipped my toes into the water, which was cool despite the pool being heated.

"Come in, chicken."

I took a deep breath, swung my arms back, and dove in. The feel of the cool water enveloping me completely was intense. All I wanted to do was stay underwater and feel the bliss of weightlessness forever. Eventually the need for oxygen took over and forced me to the surface. "Wow!"

"I'll say. Now we know that our hair colors are both natural." I was embarrassed for some reason and started to blush until she laughed, letting me know that it was all right.

SPLASH!!!

Someone had jumped into the pool between us, causing a massive splash. It also stopped my heart. I thought for a second I would drown with all the water I had gulped in surprise. The waves lapped over my shoulders as I ducked my head to see under the water, looking for whoever had jumped into the pool. Jean-Paul popped up next to us, laughing hysterically at the looks on our faces.

"Damn you," I shouted, but I barely finished the protest before I succumbed to the hilarity of the moment. Jean-Paul said something about us jumping off the diving board, so we started to swim to the edge. After a moment or two, modesty caught up with me. "Oh, wait, I'm not wearing a bathing suit." I wasn't ashamed or anything. In fact, the fresh water rushing between my bare legs felt fantastic. It just wasn't done.

"Me neither," he said as he popped his bare backside out of the water to execute a dive.

Jean-Paul swam up close to me, looked into the water at my body, and said, "So this is what you do when I leave you alone for a few minutes? Swim naked with my best girl?"

Margret splashed water at him. "Don't forget, darling. I'm not your girl anymore," she said. Now I was confused and wanted to press them about what they mean, but I'd had enough of him ignoring me lately and let it go. "Wait," she finished. "I'm sorry. Did you mean me or him?" That was one more thing to add to the list of things I was letting go.

We swam for about an hour, only Jean-Paul getting in and out of the water to cannonball back in each time. And each time he got out of the pool, both Margret and I made no bones about staring at his wet, naked body emerging from the deep. After several big splashes, Margret got out of the pool while I averted my eyes. Jean-Paul not only looked, he commented. "I swear you need to eat something, my darling." I had looked then, but didn't see a thing wrong with her curvy body.

"Do you know how hard I work to keep this figure? All the martinis and steaks we eat? And have you looked at that black-and-blue mess you call a body lately?" Margret opened the door to the natatorium as she closed her robe. "I'll see you boys in half an hour. Don't be late. Adolpho will be waiting."

"Adolpho? You need to let me send you to my tailor. Really." He dove under the water and appeared right in front of me, his fingers caressing my legs and stomach on his way to the surface. He barely grazed my penis, but his touch sent my entire body into convulsions. He had placed his arms around my neck and clasped his fingers together behind my head, resting himself on me.

"The old girl sure knows when to make an exit," he said.

I stared at the curves of his mouth. I wanted to feel his tongue, to taste him so badly. He leaned in closer and closer, so slowly that the water barely moved between us. He kissed me deeply, our wet lips collapsing in on each other with the pull of gravity. He pushed us apart before he went in from the other side to kiss me again. This time he had drawn our bodies together until every inch of him touched every inch of me, pushing all the water out of the way. We slipped away from the wall and went underwater where we continued to kiss until I had to come up for air.

My mind was on fire and I was erect, wanting him now more than ever. I could see under the water that he was erect too as he had glided toward me. He gathered me to him again, rubbing his body against me. His hands curved around my butt, and when his fingers had made it to the middle, I panicked, pushing him away and diving into the water. I reached the other end of the pool, got out and wrapped the robe around me. I just stared back at him from across the divide the water formed between us.

He was confused; he had to be. He still managed to remain calm and collected. "Don't you want me?" he asked, barely audible above the pounding in my chest.

"Of—of course I do," I almost cried. "Do you really want me? Or am I just another boy to you?"

"*Mon petit garcon amoureux*, surely it does not have to mean all of that," he said, adding a little French-Canadian accent into his voice.

Under any other circumstances, it would have been downright

sexy. I guess I had a thing for accents. "All of what?" I said. "Yes, it does. It does to me."

He smiled his normally rakish smile at me, his face turning from seduction to disappointment. The blue depths of the pool still brought out the dazzle in his eyes, which made what I was about to do even tougher. With a deep breath, I steeled my nerve and left the room.

CHAPTER TWENTY-EIGHT

Halloween Night

We would have sat in Jean-Paul's Imperial in uncomfortable silence if not for Margret's refusal to let that happen. When she was nervous, she filled the air with chatter. It was endearing. It wasn't long before we reached the giant Allerton Hotel, one of the newer skyscrapers in town. It was a fat, tall brown brick building that seemed to stick out of the city center like a sore thumb. It had a gothic feel, with tall pillars or turrets that jutted off the four edges of the monstrosity like an afterthought.

I focused back on the interior of the car to catch the tail end of her oratory. "We are going to have so much fun tonight, I guarantee it. And Brett, don't you look dashing in your new suit? I don't care what Jean-Paul says. Adolpho makes the best suits for men. James always used him." She went on and on. This was a new thing I learned about her.

Jean-Paul kept giving me sideways glances and rolling his eyes at her. He was being so disarmingly cute, I stopped being mad at him at some point and started relaxing a little. The last thing I wanted was to be the killjoy of the evening. I couldn't stay mad at him for long.

The guests in the lobby were all dressed in costumes and looked inebriated. It dawned on me that although I had spent almost the entire day with Jean-Paul and Margret, none of us had even drunk a drop yet. The elevator opened and spilled out more drunken revelers.

"Margret, are we going to a costume party?" I asked, pointing to my clothes.

"Unless your plan is to get all of us naked again, because if that's the case we are terribly overdressed," Jean-Paul joked.

"You two detectives will just have to wait for more clues," she replied. At the top floor, the elevator bell dinged our arrival. When the doors opened, several young women and men were waiting for us with party favors in their hands. They placed a face mask with straps on Jean-Paul and then one on me. Margret was adorned with a feather boa that matched her dress and a Mardi Gras mask on a stick, which she held in front of her eyes as she spoke to us.

"Do I look...mysterious?" She giggled and waved the end of her mask at us.

We all looked at each other for a moment. Jean-Paul's mask was a fiery red with orange and yellow flames and tiny jewels around the eyes. If I didn't know better, I'd say that they were diamonds and rubies, but since that would make the mask worth thousands of dollars, I assumed they were colored glass. Either way, he looked dashing.

"You look—the mask is great," I stammered. I held up my mask before my eyes. "How do I look in mine?"

Jean-Paul fiddled with his mask and finally had to get a little closer to see me. "Can't see a damned thing through these little eye holes. There, that's better. Why, green is your color, *mon petit*."

I bent to look in the mirror by the elevators. My mask was dark green with yellow streaks and green feathers sprayed across the top. Against my black shirt and tie, I have to admit, it was the cat's meow.

Hundreds of people were in the parlor, which was the size of a ballroom. Some of the guests were in masks and fancy dress. Scattered throughout the room, men and women were outfitted in full eighteenth-century French costumes. Some had big white powdered wigs, flashy, billowing skirts, and faces painted a pasty cream. They were magnificent looking. I wondered for a minute if they were actors or guests until I saw several of them abruptly break into a choreographed old-style dance.

A jazz band, all dressed in white for some reason, played in the back of the room. People were dancing and twirling and drinking. Waiters who thankfully didn't look more dressed up than me swirled around the room delivering champagne and gin to anyone who held up their glass. When a slow song started, Margret grabbed my hand and pulled me to the dance floor. Jean-Paul slipped away into the crowd, and I hoped I would be able to find him again in all of this madness.

Margret leaned in close enough to brush her lips against my neck. "Tell me what happened in the pool," she said. "Why were you two so glum on the way over here?" She took no time at all to ask the tough questions. She really should be a newspaperman.

"It's nothing, nothing at all."

"Hmph."

"What?"

She stretched up to my cheek and kissed me. "Now what is it?"

"I just don't understand why he is so…so…"

"Jean-Paul like?"

I started our slow move across the floor again. "Yes! I tried to tell him that this…this…whatever it is, is a big deal for me. I don't understand why it isn't for him."

We twirled around a bit more. "You know, you shouldn't be convinced of what people mean by what they say, or what people mean by what they do."

I was confused. "What does that even mean?"

She put her head back and laughed.

Someone cut in on us and asked Margret to dance. Before being pulled away, she handed me two embossed black tickets. "Midnight. Find Jean-Paul and give him a ticket, please." She shouted the last words as the man in a mask whirled her away out of sight into the crowd.

The problem with a masquerade ball is that every guest has a mask. It makes finding people you want to find tough. It also made it equally hard to know whom you were with when you were with them. I scoured the room for the fire red mask Jean-Paul had been wearing. Not finding him, I grabbed a candle to read the card by. It was black and the words were in dark grey, which made it next to impossible to read. The embossing was professionally done and the card stock was quite thick. I finally found a dim table lamp at a good angle to read the card, which had a picture of a ghostly character hovering over a table with a woman bent in concentration:

YOU ARE CORDIALLY INVITED TO A NIGHT OF
SPIRITUAL CONJURING AND JOURNEYING
INTO THE GREATEST OF UNKNOWNS
ON THE EVENING OF ALL HALLOWS
12:00 AM IN THE PALM ROOM
DON'T BE ALARMED BY WHAT YOU SEE
WE WILL RAISE THE SPIRITS
NON-BELIEVERS BEWARE
MADAM HELENA KNOWS ALL

Across the bar in the middle of the room, I saw Jean-Paul's bright red mask. He was standing still, watching me. I stopped moving and watched him watch me for a minute. His gaze filled me with hope. I turned to walk around to meet him and ran into Margret. When I looked up to catch a glimpse of him, the red mask had slipped into the crowd again.

Margret grabbed me by the sleeve and spoke as if she was absolutely sure I was behind the mask. "Brett, I'd like you to meet my brother, Marshall. Marsh, this is Mr. Brett Bennet, Chicago's best hockey player."

I blushed at that. "It's a pleasure to meet any family of Margret's," I said. Marshall was a tall slender man with dark set eyes, but they did not cause him to look severe, foreboding, or mean-spirited. He looked good. He seemed to be memorizing every feature of everything and everyone around him. He was dressed in a grey three-piece suit and held his colorful Mardi Gras mask in his hands instead of over his face.

Marshall extended his hand and gave a solid shake. "So you're the dashing young man whose been wearing out my Bugatti? Margret speaks so highly of you, she is quite smitten."

Margret swatted him on the arm. "It's not your car, brother. I'm leaving it to Mr. Bennet here," she exclaimed.

"Wait, no one is dying any time soon, I hope," I said. He laughed, but his demeanor was calm and controlled. He was likeable but serious. He began to ask me about a hundred questions.

"Lighten up a little, brother of mine. You're going to make Brett nervous. My brother envisions himself a budding newspaperman," she said to me.

I am out with a newsman? Oh my God. No wonder he asked so many questions. If he found out my secrets... My dear friend panic put its hand on my back and started to add weight to the moment. It would only be moments before I had to excuse myself.

"Sorry. I tend to get away from myself," Marshall explained. "I'm just interested in the boy."

The three of us were tense when a portly man of about fifty with salt-and-pepper mustachios stepped into our circle. "Excuse me, Margret, I was coming by to ask how you are enjoying your evening."

"Robert!" she exclaimed, reaching over and wrapping both arms around the man to embrace him in a full hug. When she let him go, he shook hands and exchanged nods with Marshall as if they knew one another already.

"And who is this?" he asked, looking at me.

"Robert, may I introduce Mr. Brett Bennet? Brett, this is Mr. Robert Allerton."

We shook, but I was a little tongue-tied. "Aller...Allerton? As in the owner of this hotel, Allerton?"

His belly shook up and down with mirth, and he placed a hand on my shoulder. "Just plain old Robert. What brings you to Chicago?"

He instinctively knew that I was not from here? "I play here. Um, hockey, that is. I play hockey with the new team."

"Well, we all play here as often as we can, right John?" He brought the young man he was with to the forefront. "Brett, this is J.W., my close friend. J.W., this is Margret's friend Brett."

J.W. was slender and very attractive, if a little effeminate. He was well dressed and stood tall and straight. Appearing to glide forward, he extended his hand gracefully, as if through water. His handshake was soft, but his hands were rough like a man who had worked hard. "So very pleased to meet you," he said, although the look on his face said he was anything but.

"Good to meet you too."

The fiery red mask bobbed through the crowd a few feet away from us. Jean-Paul was about to approach our little group when he caught sight of J.W. and turned away. I called after him. "Jean-Paul! Come join us."

Everyone in our circle watched him approach. The air filled with tension, and it seemed to be emanating between him and J.W. My curiosity filled the spaces. He shook hands with Robert and Marsh, and nodded to J.W. "Robert, Marshy, John."

J.W. nodded back. "Jean-Paul." The group was silent for about thirty seconds.

Robert leaned forward and smacked J.W. on the arm. "Down, boy. These two." He said it with a smile as if they were brothers who tussled all the time, but his face held just a slight nervous edge to it. "Tell us what you have planned this evening, Margret. I received the card invites. Quality!"

"Well, thank you for letting us do it, but you'll just have to wait and see, Robert. It will be loads of fun, though. Don't fret."

"I just hope it's good. They've turned my private cigar room into some kind of Clara Bow movie set back there." He jerked his thumb over his shoulder at an entrance off the main room. Two doormen in the entryway kept out the partygoers. "We'll see at midnight, I imagine."

"Oh, Jean-Paul, I forgot to give you…" We all turned around to look for him, but he had slipped away once again. He was getting quite good at disappearing. He would probably make a much better spy than I would, judging by my performance the other night.

Robert smiled. "I had better mingle around the room a little bit. I think the mayor is here somewhere, and he is probably none too happy about the beverages. I heard that the editors in chief of the *Daily* and the *Tribune* are here as well. I'd better make sure they don't kill each other and make it into their own papers, or worse, write something awful about me."

"Oh, Robert, you donate far too much to them for them to write a single contrary word about you," Margret said. Everyone expressed amusement at that, Robert included.

"That's true, but better safe than sorry. Say, Marshall, I heard you are still thinking about buying a paper, or doing some writing? You'd better come with me and meet some people. Excuse us."

After they had walked away, Margret leaned into my shoulder before I could say a word. "Jean-Paul and J.W. used to…you know."

"I guessed." I hated hearing that anyone…you know'd with Jean-Paul but me. Well, maybe not with me yet, but I was thinking about it. I knew he had a past, but all I wanted was for him to see only me.

"That was a long time ago. He's moved on now, full-time it seems. They're pretty dedicated these days."

The full weight of her words took several beats before they fully clicked into gear in my head. "Wait, Robert? He's—"

"Oh, Brett, honey. We need to work on that."

"Work on what?" Before I could get an answer, she slipped off into the crowd.

I saw the fiery mask across the room but lost him in the crowd again. I ran the last few steps to his last location, spinning around, looking up and down from the staircases to the bar before I saw him leaning over one of the balconies, apparently watching while I searched for him. Hockey was not the only game he excelled at. Whatever he was playing at, it was clearly working on me. I may have never wanted anything so much in my life.

I ran up to the balconies but couldn't find which one he was in. As I was about to give up, someone grabbed me from behind, pulled me between the curtains, placed his strong hands on my neck, and kissed me. His lips were passionate, warm and wet with gin. I closed my eyes and gave my body over completely to him. He held me up next to him. He leaned back and lightly traced the curves of my lips with his fingertips. Each soft touch sent electric sparks up and down my entire body. He spun me around and hugged my back against his solidly muscled chest. He pressed his head against mine. His breathing became hypnotic. My head rolled back against his, and we swayed.

Then he slipped through the curtains and was gone.

"Jean-Paul? Where did you go?" I pulled the curtains apart, and I poked my head into the hall, looking right then left. No Jean-Paul to be seen anywhere. Sinking against the plush wall, a smile drew up and across my mouth. I traced my lips with my finger, relishing the memory of his lips, his fingers.

My smile turned to a frown when I looked across the room to the other balcony and saw a figure in the shadows watching me. I was able to make out that it was J.W. who had been across the room, watching us kissing from another balcony. Was he as over Jean-Paul and in love with Robert as Margret thought? I hoped so.

CHAPTER TWENTY-NINE

S tanding in front of the Palm room, I looked around for Jean-Paul. The doorman was watching to see if I was going to enter. That reminded me I never gave Jean-Paul his ticket, which had his name on it. Even though I hadn't been looking forward to some phony spiritual thing, I was interested to see what would happen.

I didn't want to be rude or late to the show Margret had so painstakingly prepared, so I reached into my pocket and pulled out my ticket. I realized that Jean-Paul's ticket was gone. Sneaky devil.

Up a few stairs, the room was mostly dark except for areas that had been thrown into a reddish-hued light by lamps covered with brightly colored scarves. It had a spooky ambience, a nice Halloween touch. In the center of the room was a circular wooden table surrounded by several curved-back chairs. Robert, J.W., and Marshall were already there along with a few other people I did not know. Marshall saw me and motioned me over to them.

"Brett, so glad you could make it to my sister's little gathering. I think we are in for a night of some serious spook hunting," he said. "Or some serious debunking."

J.W. sneered at me. "I think Brett has already seen some bunk tonight, am I right?" he said. If daggers shot from my eyes at that point, I'd surely be on trial for murder.

"Actually, I've found everything at this party magical." Okay, I admit I was trying to get under his skin.

Marshall must have felt awkward about our interchange. He directed all of our attentions to a man of about fifty and introduced us. "Brett, I don't know if you have ever heard of Harry Houdini—"

I cut him off with an exaggerated handshake. "Mr.—Wow, Mr. Houdini, it's such an honor," I gushed. He stood erect, maintaining his stoic face. He was short and stocky but muscular under his suit coat.

Marshall leapt forward, put his hand on my back and corrected me. "No, sorry. I simply meant to say, meet Mr. Franz Kukol. He was Houdini's right-hand man for years."

Franz smiled as he interjected, "I much appreciate your enthusiasm, young man, but I am no longer with Houdini. However, I still enjoy debunking charlatans." His face was hard and sharp, even though he had the rounded jowls of most men his age. Most people probably assumed he was mad all the time.

"Ah, I see you have met Franz." Robert clapped the man loudly on the back. "All that time with Houdini, I wish you'd reconsider doing some magic for my guests tonight."

"I am content to watch tonight, I'm afraid." Franz smiled and nodded his head curtly before he walked away. He had taken a step away when Robert asked what time it was getting to be. When he said this, Franz turned back toward us. He opened his coat to produce a shiny gold pocket watch, the chain firmly secured through his vest's buttonhole. Robert patted his own empty vest pocket.

This caused Robert to shout in excitement. "Why, you devil you! May I have my watch back now, good sir?" We all broke out into cheers and claps after that.

A gong rang, the sound reverberating around the room. Margret spread her arms open with a grand gesture, inviting everyone in the room to the table. "Take your seats, please. We are about to begin."

I looked around one last time for Jean-Paul. To my amused surprise, he was standing right behind me. I had no idea when he had arrived. I was simply glad he'd made it, and hopefully he'd be with me for the rest of the evening. I wasn't too fond of the idea of us being here longer than we had to with that J.W. lurking about like he owned the place. I guessed in a way, he kind of did.

The table had place cards with our names on them, so I found mine and sat down. Unfortunately, Jean-Paul sat across the table from me. Margret was on my right and Franz on my left. Even if he was a little odd, it was exciting to be sitting next to a world-famous person.

J.W. sat next to Jean-Paul, entirely too close for my comfort. Robert did not seem to mind it, but it was making my skin crawl. J.W. wore a triumphant smirk that made me wonder if he had somehow switched the place cards. If Margret arranged this whole event down to the very last detail, surely she would not have made this seating arrangement.

The red lights dimmed all the way down, leaving nothing but

ambient candlelight shining over the circular table. The curtains parted one more time, and Madam Helena entered the room. She wore jangling, oversized jewelry in her ears and around her wrists. A multitude of necklaces fell down into her abundant cleavage. She looked too overdone to be honest. Despite all the eccentric clothing, jewelry, and rigmarole of the event, she was quite beautiful. Her long black hair framed her thin face, which was adorned with slight hints of rouge.

She waved her hands over our heads when she walked around the circle. She paused over each of us, closing her eyes and breathing in deeply. Franz shifted uncomfortably in his chair when she stopped behind him and made great circles above him with her arms. She had started to walk to the next person when she grimaced, stopped, thought for a second, and then moved on. He rolled his eyes toward me before shaking his head.

"The spirits ask of us, speak the truth," she blurted out. I sat with my eyes glued to her.

She continued, looking at each of us again before stopping on Franz. "Cleanse yourself of doubt, of negative emotions, pain, suffering, hate." He stared at her like a competitor in a poker game.

She turned her head to J.W. "Please remove from your heart your agenda. We must purify each of us for the journey ahead." She looked at me, then at Jean-Paul, and paused without saying a word to us. Her gaze stopped on Margret for a moment and then she tilted her head back. "Think not of your pains and darkness tonight, for we have one another to strengthen and support us." Back at Margret she said, "There are people in this room that love you beyond words. Yes, love, not sorrow."

I was getting the willies something awful. She seemed to know things about each of us as her eyes traveled the room. "Join hands now!" All of us placed our hands on the tabletop and clasped them with the person to our side. I glared at J.W., who seemed to take great delight in holding Jean-Paul's hand.

"We let go of our inner selves, or desires and claims, to invite you spirits to move amongst us," she said before going on to give directions. "No matter what extravagances that you may see, hear, or even smell, do not break the chain, do not let go of the hand with whom you are now joined. I may release your hands. I may leave the table and move about the room. Please remain seated, remain joined."

Madam Helena spoke louder to cover our whispering. "If I open my vessel and offer it to the spirits, you may commune with them directly through me." This was all very spooky. What good could come from this? And on Halloween night no less.

One of the candles suddenly blew out. Margret squealed in delight, and I shivered from head to toe. I looked around the room at each of the guests, all of whom were wide-eyed and looking back and forth amongst us, except for Franz. He was holding Madam Helena in his intense gaze.

CHAPTER THIRTY

B am!
    Her head and hands slammed against the table. We all jumped a little. Margret reminded us all to keep holding hands. Her command was wasted on me, as I held my neighbors' hands in a solid death grip. Madam Helena's upper body slowly straightened back up. She looked around the room at each of us until she paused on Robert.

"Robert, is that you? Robert? My son, look at you, all grown up," Madam Helena said using a deep, gravelly voice.

Robert's face opened up and he responded. "Father? Is that you?"

"If you are truly the spirit of Mr. Allerton's father, tell us something that only he would know," Franz commanded in a loud voice.

Madam Helena had turned eerily to face Franz as he spoke, and then back to Robert. "Do you still have my gold pocket watch?" The voice coming from this women wasn't just eerie, it was downright frightening.

Robert, with Margret's hand still clenched in his, used both of their hands to pull out the watch from his vest pocket. "I—I do have it. It will always be in the family, as I promised."

Madam Helena's focus shifted to J.W., and then to Robert before she leaned back groaning. This exchange clearly shook Robert. In the dim light, I saw a tear fall from his face. J.W. looked like he was in pain as well, his body vibrating, bent as far forward as the table would allow.

"You could have seen the watch a few minutes ago when I took it from Mr. Allerton," Franz said with a condescending tone, "and the odds are in favor of a gold watch being a family heirloom."

Madam Helena ignored him and turned to me. My entire body was racked in fear of what she was about to say. Her face changed from the cold, stiff expression she wore as Robert's father to a scared, youthful looking one. "Does anyone else smell that?" Margret asked.

"It...smells like gunpowder," Marshall said.

"Brett, is that you, brother? You look so much older now. How did you get so big so fast?" Madam Helena said, sounding a little like a young man.

My heart raced and tears instantly sprung from me. "No, it can't be."

Madam Helena's face turned serious. "I wanted to get home so badly but the damned Hun, they keep overrunning our trenches. We win 'em back the next day and then they keep right on again. It's pointless. I know I am expected to be brave for Father, but I want to come home. I am so scared."

My face was a wet mess now. Margret squeezed my hand as tight as she could, but it did not help. "Michael? Is that really you?" I managed to eke out through sobs.

"Mother wrote to me, says you're nothing but trouble, but you won your first hockey game. You must be so small in those pads. I wish I could have been there to see it." Madam Helena started to cry at that point.

Franz gave my hand a strong squeeze. His voice this time was swelling with emotions. "You could have researched this young man. For that matter, most families sent brothers and sons off to the war. How dare you, madam?"

"Brett, who is that talking? Is that Father? Don't let him beat you down. Oh, this godforsaken place. I want to come home."

"Michael, why didn't you come home?!" I shouted, but it was too late. He was gone, and Madam Helena was blankly staring again.

"I would swear that I smelled gunpowder, like we were in the war. Brett, was your brother killed in action?" Marshall asked. "Is that why we smelled gunpowder?"

"A simple trick. I see nothing to prove otherwise," Franz explained. But at this point, I don't know if we believed his explanations. J.W. barely held hands now, his focus on a blank and sullen Robert, Franz was angry, and I was a blubbering wreck.

"Magpie?" Madam Helena cried out.

"James?" Margret replied softly as if she didn't want to believe it. "James. Is...that you?"

"Margret, are you all right?" Marshall called from across the table.

"Who is Magpie?" Franz asked.

"It is what her husband called her," Jean-Paul answered.

"Well, if you knew that…" Franz once again tried to explain away the events unfolding before our eyes when Helena turned to him.

"Frank Kukol, my boy? Is that you?" Madam Helena took on a slightly male version with a thick European accent. "Are you copying my act now too?"

Franz's face grew stern. "What insult is this? Do you dare? You charlatan. No one calls me that but Houdini himself, and he is not dead! You were better off playing these other games." He sounded shaken.

"No, it is truly I. It isn't what I thought it to be. But we were wrong, I needed to tell you that. Some things cannot be escaped. Tell my brother, Deshi."

"Liar! Fraud!" Franz shouted, visibly disturbed. With that proclamation, he retrieved his coat and hat, and left, knocking over the red-covered lamp, throwing the room into bright light.

Madam Helena slumped back into her chair. Half of us were still seated and the other half standing, all of us stunned. With Franz's departure, the circle was broken and most of us had let go of one another's hand.

"How did she know about my brother?" I asked as if she wasn't still in the room.

"The only person with any idea about how just walked out of here in a huff," Marshall said. "But I would swear on a stack of Bibles that I smelled gunpowder."

Robert sat back down in his chair and set a quivering hand upon the table. "I would say, Marshall, that I didn't."

"And what of your own experience?" Marshall continued.

"Well, I am afraid Franz may be right about that. Everyone around me knows about the watch," Robert conceded.

Margret spoke up. "Brett, I swear I didn't even know anything about your brother. I am sorry." Jean-Paul was standing beside me then. My exhausted body threatened to betray me. I felt his strength steady me.

We all turned to Madam Helena, who was slumped in her chair, snoring. This brought about a few giggles. "I guess talking to the dead is quite taxing," Marshall joked.

I had had about enough of the evening. The mixture of the booze and the stress from the festivities had gotten the better of me. My head ached, and my eyes were afire. I wasn't quite sure if I believed what I had witnessed. Could it be an elaborate ruse? I guess Franz knew a lot more about it than any of us, and he seemed absolutely convinced of fraud.

The grandfather clock struck one. Jean-Paul put his arm around my shoulders to prop me up as we walked back to the elevator. "Let's get him back to your place, Margret, dear. Looks like he could use a little sleep." They were talking about me like I was a child, but at this point I didn't care. My body was drained.

Jean-Paul drove. I sat in the backseat, my head pregnant with things to say. Thoughts of Michael swam in and out of my consciousness, threatening to drag me down into the abyss with them as they passed. Margret scooted in next to me, leaving Jean-Paul alone up in the front. He didn't protest. I caught him looking back at me several times with a worried expression. I wanted to say I was not a child. I could handle it. The reality was that I wanted to forget the whole night. I wanted to forget what Madam Helena had said about my brother.

To lift this unbearable weight, I tried to tell them about my brother several times, but the words wouldn't come out right. All of a sudden, I collapsed into Margret's arms, exploding into desperate tears. She hushed me as she pulled me in tight to match the turns of the Imperial. I started to ramble incoherently. "My brother was not a goddamned coward. She is a liar. He was never afraid to do his duty. He never cried to come home. Never!" My shouts were punctuated with heaving sobs.

When my sobbing eased, Margret quietly asked me about my brother. I was lying in her lap, staring blankly at the rearview mirror where Jean-Paul's face bounced in and out of view. What had begun as a trickle became a full flowing fountain. "He went to France. He volunteered. Or rather my father pushed him into it. He was older than I was then. I was only nine or ten when he left, barely old enough to even understand what was going on.

"My father, God, he was so proud of Michael, like he never was of me. Never. He could do no wrong. And when he signed up for the Army, I—I stopped existing. Not all at once, but I was never good enough in his eyes. And my mother never once stood up for me. Not once. She curled up and died when the letters stopped coming. Waiting for an answer from the War Department was hell. My father didn't even cry when the soldiers drove down the long dirt road that connected our farm to the highway. We saw them coming the whole way. We knew.

"My mother hit her knees, covered her heart and never uncovered it again. My father didn't cry. He saluted the soldiers, who saluted him back. He left my mother on her knees and walked back into the house to finish dinner. He acted like nothing had happened. Any time anyone mentioned the war, he puffed out his stupid chest in pride, boasting about his little hero soldier. The son that should have…"

Margret brushed my hair with her fingers. Jean-Paul kept sneaking glances at me while he drove on. "You were only a kid. What could you do?"

"I hated him for it."

"Oh, Brett. Your father—"

"Not him. My brother. I hate him for leaving me with them, alone. He was the one they loved, the one they were proud of. No matter what I did, no matter how many goals I scored, I was nothing in their eyes. Not compared to him. And I keep trying and trying. I hated him for that. For being allowed to fail. For getting out." My last words hung there in the backseat of the car, filling my own ears with their power. And I hated myself. Margret sniffed back her own tears.

"Oh Brett. Brett. You beautiful boy."

The next morning, Margret brought the newspaper into the room she had put me and Jean-Paul into last night. My head was thrumming with a hangover from emotion and alcohol. Jean-Paul was lying next to me, his arms folded behind his head, his bare chest rising gently up and down with each breath, a big smile on his face. I didn't remember how last night ended, but we were clearly sleeping together. I noticed the horrified look on Margret's face.

"What is it, darling?" Jean-Paul asked, charming even at this early hour.

"Look." She pointed to the headline announcing that yesterday afternoon in Detroit, the greatest magician the world had ever known, Harry Houdini, had died.

CHAPTER THIRTY-ONE

November 17, 1926
Game 1

We spent a few days on a road trip for our preseason games in Montreal and Pittsburgh. It kept me pretty busy, but when not playing hockey, I was focused on what to do about him. Jean-Paul went back to ignoring me again. That was a relief, since I was incredibly embarrassed and ashamed about acting like a sissy on Halloween night. We hadn't done anything together since that night. Margret called after me, but I asked Moira to tell her that I wasn't feeling well. Moira had given me some serious sideways glances about that but did as I asked without a lot of prying questions. I appreciated her for it.

I ate lunch by myself a few times before Percy found me and made me eat with the guys. To be honest, I didn't put up much of a fight. What would I tell him anyway? He didn't ask about why I was isolating myself or why I wasn't sitting with Jean-Paul like I normally would. He wasn't really the type to ask a lot of questions, so I was glad for the easy company. Luckily for me, I threw all my inner turmoil into my playing and was catching on fire on the ice.

A few days later on the train ride back, I had all but forgotten about my moment on Halloween night and sat down for lunch with Jean-Paul. To his credit he picked up right where we had left off. Of course, when I asked where he had gone at night and if there were places like the Dil Pickle in Montreal, he became obviously evasive. This made me wonder who he had been with. I knew he was meeting men while still pursuing me. I hated it, but I couldn't really hold it against him since I hadn't even made it clear to myself what we were. Could we be anything?

These things cluttered my mind as I walked into the Coliseum toward the locker room. This game would actually be my first professional hockey game for the regular season. It meant a lot considering that this was to be the first real big league game in Chicago, in the Coliseum, and for this team. What would it mean to all of us if we lost, or worse, lost badly? I was glad to think about my problems with Jean-Paul in a way, because concentrating on losing could interfere with my game.

My inner pains have always provided fuel for the fire I brought to the ice. On the bench in the locker room, dragging the tape around my calves to hold up my stockings, it burned in my belly. I felt hungry with a deep wanting that had so often filled my body with energy. I had been keeping my head down and focusing on my own process, but I couldn't help looking over at Jean-Paul getting ready.

He sat on the floor in full gear minus socks and skates, one leg pulled close under him with the other out to the side, stretching. His body moved unnaturally, and the pregame warm-up stretches he did pushed his legs and arms into positions that people had only ever seen in circus performers. His eyes were closed. He made small subtle movements with his head as if he was quietly going through some routine. It was beautiful to watch, like seeing poetry.

And then he opened his eyes and screamed. "Oh my God! I don't have any clean socks! I can't play."

"Someone give Jean-Paul a pair of socks," Dick commanded.

The boys started rifling through their lockers but no one was coming up with a pair. Jean-Paul paced around his little area, talking to himself. I couldn't quite hear what he was saying, but I understood the word *disaster* and then a bunch of things in French. After watching everyone frantically looking for socks, I snapped out of it, reached into my bag, and found the pair I had brought for him.

"Oh, I forgot these, here you go," I said when I tossed him the pair. The relief on his and everyone's faces was palpable. He was a strange bird all right. He slid them on, his determination returning. I was ready. Even feeling better now that I had played the savior to Jean-Paul in need. So I promised myself to always bring a new pair of socks.

We were playing Babe's old team, but now they had gone through as many changes as we had. We had beaten them that night, but beating a team once to me only meant you beat them once. Each game was a new adventure. Any team can beat any team on any given night. You just never knew. We had Babe now, but they knew all of his moves. He was making a big deal out of what this game meant to him.

"Now you remember what I told you," he pointed out to Percy, who looked disinterested. Percy wasn't much of a fan. "When they come up the middle hard like, you need to stand them up so they will pass to the right. They always pass to the right." I wondered why they always passed to the right. That didn't make sense, but he should know the moves of the team he played with for years so I made a mental note, as did the rest of the fellas, I'm sure.

The Coliseum was half-full with men, women, and children who weren't quite sure what to expect from us. We weren't a hundred percent sure what to expect either. As we skated out onto the ice, the broom men were making their way off at the other end of the rink after smoothing out the ice. I knocked a bunch of pucks off the railing onto the ice for us to practice with for a few minutes. I scooped up a couple of them on my stick and shot them both into the net. Hitting the back of the net was so much easier without a goaltender. They sure got in the way.

Jean-Paul hopped over the blue line and slid into place in his crease, looking grimly across the ice at the other goalie. It was his way of making a bet against the other man. The pucks had all been gathered up and removed except the one in the referee's hand. I slid into place in my spot on the left, waiting. Sweat dripped off of my chin and landed on the ice. I watched it quickly freeze into the massive plain that extended for two hundred feet. The whistle blew, which alerted the players, the crowd, and the timekeeper that the puck was about to drop.

Everything went silent except for the sound of the heartbeat in my chest and the slow grind of my opponent's skates as he slowly moved his feet back and forth in anticipation. Then I heard the sound of the puck being slapped hard against the ice. It bounced up over both of the centers' sticks. Dick swatted at it in the air, sending it careening into the boards. And we were off.

The puck made its way up and down the ice several times, each of us trying to catch on to the rhythms of the other players as well as our own. After about five minutes of play, the Pats started a good rush up the middle. It looked exactly like Babe had described it. Percy and Bob skated into the middle and stood the player up, forcing him to pass. We all cheated over to the right side, where Babe said they'd pass the puck.

Only they didn't pass it right; they passed it to the left to a man that was wide open. Everyone had crowded to my side, including Babe. His man caught the puck nice and even on his stick. We started tripping over ourselves to regroup to catch up with him, but it was too late. They had a two-on-one situation against Jean-Paul. After they passed it back and forth a few times, the shooter tricked him to the left and shot it easily in on the right. Then it dawned on me.

They had always passed the puck to the right side before because that was where the Babe had always been. He was their main guy until he came to our team. I pulled the guys into a quick huddle to tell them what I had figured out. Dick shook his head and laughed.

"Well no shit," Percy said. "Now you tell us."

Dick lightly grabbed Percy by the sweater. "Listen, next time do the same play. Make it look like we are cheating again, but when you guys press the middle, Brett will fall back and wait for it." It was a good plan but put me against two men. I was ready.

After a few back and forth attempts, the Pats broke up the middle in formation and we were on. The P, B, and J line pressed inward at the middle and the pass popped out to the left instead of the right side. They didn't see me racing full speed ahead toward them. When the puck arrived on his stick, I was there too, slapping at it. My blade knocked the puck out in front of all of us and I kept skating right on by them both. I had gotten the puck back pretty easily, leaving me a one-on-one with their goalie.

I skated up the middle much too fast to do many fancy moves. I thought of a hundred different kinds that I'd used before. The goaltender came out of his net a few feet to challenge me, blocking off most of the good angle shots, forcing me to shoot right at him or try something risky. My mind was alive with the geometric shapes that each move and shot would take. I had decided on a play when I saw his back right leg move just a smidge behind him, showing me the five hole between his legs. I slapped my stick on the ice, making a sharp cracking sound. My stick angled over the puck, hiding it a little as I dragged it behind me. When the goalie's leg moved again, I sent a clean, fast wrist shot straight at the tiny space between his legs.

The net popped backward when the rubber found its way to the back of the net. The sound of the stadium went from anticipation to uproarious cheering. My momentum sent me into the board behind the goal, crashing into the cage. The fans behind the net were screaming and slapping at the cage, congratulating me. The rest of the team encircled me, celebrating the tie score. Dick pulled the puck out of the referee's hand as he skated by him. I saw him hand it to one of our trainers behind the bench like he had done for my first preseason goal.

Dick pointed to me with a big smile on his face. My heart filled with glee and pride. Back at the center of the ice, waiting for the next face-off, I caught a glimpse of Babe. He was staring me down with hate in his eyes. We won the next face-off, and the puck went to me. I skated like hell to their end to try my luck again, but it was easily blocked aside. The next few rushes I tried to pass to Dick or to Babe but without luck. We went to the locker room after the first period in a tie. After a scoreless second period, we hit the locker room wondering what it would take to edge them out.

Percy sat down next to me at the benches leaning in to talk. "Look, I know what you're trying to do here." I looked at him quizzically. "But you beat this goalie today. You're the only one, and believe me, we have been trying like the dickens. Stop passing and start shooting, boy. Stop trying to help out Babe. Help out the team." With that he stood, went back to his seat and began taping up his stick. I was left with his words swirling between my ears. In my zeal to provide opportunities to my teammates, I was forgetting the simplest rule of hockey: when you should, shoot.

Back on the ice, we won the puck, which got sent my way. I remembered what Percy had said, and I took off with it down the ice. I slid sideways a little to avoid a check from one of their enforcers and cut back across center toward the net. I faked a shot when I got close, pulled the puck across to my backhand, swung around to the other side of the net and then shot it behind the goalie. The buzzer and light went off, and the hometown crowd went wild. I had broken the stalemate. Percy shot a knowing look my way.

I did not bother to look at the Babe.

Taking a breather on the bench, I got to see Mickey make a great cross-ice pass back to the line where Gordie slapped a hard, fast shot straight up the middle. It bounced off of one of their own player's legs and went into the net. Sometimes hard work pays off with lucky bounces. Gordie was excited and hollering. He skated by the bench slapping hands with each of us.

With a minute to go in the game, I found the puck once again on my stick. I couldn't get into the middle to be in front of the net due to all the defense they had built around the goalie. So I passed it sharply over to Babe, who took his shot. The goalie saw it at the last minute and swatted at it with his goalie stick, barely catching it, sending it the other way. Unfortunately for him, he sent it directly onto my stick, where I made an easy tap in to bring our total to four, and mine to three in one game.

Our bench erupted. All of the team came screaming across the ice to celebrate with me. The referee and linesman finally restored order, clearing everyone off the ice. I watched the other guys finish out the game from the bench. My chest swelled with pride. I wanted to get back out there and score again. Dick must have sensed it.

He placed his glove on my arm. "Take it easy. We're done for today. Save it for Boston." I had gotten caught up in all of the excitement of my first real game that I forgot it wasn't a championship but only a first game. We would play against Boston in three days, then Detroit, then Pittsburgh and on and on.

CHAPTER THIRTY-TWO

Back in the locker room, the boys were jubilant, slapping each other on their backs, on their heads, on their asses. Basically anywhere we could show happiness, we hit. Coach gave us an uplifting speech that included us trying harder and showing more initiative considering the whole town was watching. The usual.

The shower room was big but not really big enough for all of us at once, even though we crammed in. I had a head full of shampoo running down in my eyes, and that's when Babe attacked me. He grabbed me by the shoulders and slammed me up against the slick, tile shower wall. He pressed his forearm into my throat. It was so unexpected he knocked the wind out of me. His eyes, an inch away from mine, were afire with rage. His face was shaking. I looked over his shoulder to see the other boys watching us in disbelief, it had happened so fast.

I pushed back against him, but he used his strong, stouter frame to hold me up. I tried to speak. "Guh, ah, what—"

"Fucking show-off!" he spat directly into my face. "That was my game. Mine! This ain't the rookie show, whelp." With his last word, he shoved his arm into my throat one more time for emphasis before someone pulled him off me.

Babe was a raging bull of anger. That's when I saw who was holding him back by the throat. It was Jean-Paul. "What were you going to do, Cecil? Kiss the boy?" he quipped. "We can leave you two alone if you'd like." The other guys laughed at this, which caused Babe's already red face to start to glow. He tried to shove Jean-Paul off him, but Jean-Paul kept him in place for one more second. "That's enough. Understand me?" he said, quieter now and closer to Babe's face.

I wanted to reach out to kiss him for that. It was the most heroic, brave, loving thing I thought anyone had ever done for me. I almost cried from the sheer weight of the day, but I held myself back from it somehow. The locker room remained quiet for a few minutes after the fight, then it slipped back into revelry. You'd think we'd already won the big Cup.

Dick passed me on his way to the shower. He stopped for just a second. "Well, that didn't take too long now, did it?" I assumed he was referring to Babe's anger at me for stealing his thunder.

"Yeah, I'll keep my distance."

"Good idea," he said before heading off into the steam of the shower room.

I kept eyeballing Jean-Paul while I got dressed. I was going to try to leave with him. I hoped I could convey that to him without everyone else suspecting. Jean-Paul started toward the door. I had one shoe on and my shirttail was half-tucked, but that didn't stop me from bolting out the door to catch up with him.

"Jean-Paul, wait up for me," I called out.

He turned around and gave me that boyish, crooked smile. When I caught up to him in the hallway, he threw a playful arm around my neck and squeezed it several times before letting me go.

"You played a great game tonight, *mon petit*. Dazzling even." I blushed.

We walked in silence to his car together. I could feel the heat coming off him from either the steam of the shower, the excitement of the game, or from something else. Or was that me? He opened his car door. When he looked back to say good-bye to me, I was not there anymore. He swiveled his head around and caught me as I opened the passenger door of his Imperial.

"Are we going or what?" I asked. His head cocked to the side a little bit. I threw him my best rakish Jean-Paul impression, slipped into the seat, and closed the door behind me. He paused outside the car a moment before getting in.

"Are you not worried the others will suspect something?" he asked.

"Come on, let's go."

He cranked up the car and it roared to life. "Where are we going?"

"I just played the first professional hockey game of my life. I scored a goal! A professional goal!"

"Three goals, *mon petit*," he reminded me.

In all the crazy excitement of the night, the game had become a blur. My neck still throbbed a little from the thrashing I had just taken. None of that mattered right now. "That's right, and I want to celebrate."

"Where to?" he asked again.

I turned to him to look him directly in those eyes, those beautiful blue circles. "Take me home."

Jean-Paul stared at me, into a face full of expectation and desire. My heart was thundering away. I dropped my head slightly down to look at him with my best puppy dog eyes. An eternity of silences passed. Eventually, he smiled so wide it lit me through to my toes.

The Imperial pulled out onto Wabash, turned right, and headed north. Mickey waved at me as we passed him, and I stuck my head out the window and yelled, "Woohoo!" He returned the holler even though we weren't exactly hollering about the same thing.

CHAPTER THIRTY-THREE

His house was cold. Jean-Paul told me to go outside in the back and gather up some firewood to light a fire downstairs. This sounded incredibly romantic, so I sped off through the house and out the back door. I found a woodpile in the backyard, but the wood had not been split yet. Most of the logs would be too big to put in the fireplace. I saw an axe off to the edge of the pile, and I groaned. I didn't mind the labor, but I didn't want to take the time. My desire was elsewhere.

The wood stood up straight on the chopping block, just like so many times back home. I didn't like it then and I didn't like it now, but not for the same reasons. After only five minutes of chopping, my hands were on fire, my back covered in cold sweat. When I labored through a short stack, enough to make about eight good-sized pieces, I rushed back into the house.

The drinks that Jean-Paul had poured us dripped with moisture as he waited for me to return. When he saw my sweaty face, he exclaimed, "Where have you been? I didn't know you'd have to chop down a tree." He laughed at his own joke until he noticed my angry red, swollen hands.

I set the wood down, and he joined me by the fireplace. He squeezed my hand as he knelt down to build the fire, evaporating my anger. He grabbed some wood, placed it in the pit so their ends supported one another, then he put broken bits of kindling between the larger pieces. He slowly wiped sweat from my face and arms with a towel. In a few minutes, the fire roared as we sat on the couch sipping our vodka. Like usual, his glass slipped below the halfway mark before I even took my second drink. My resolve shook as I sat there on the couch, our bodies too far apart and the air filled with pregnant pauses.

A knot in the wood exploded violently in the fireplace, and the woodpile shifted, sending sparks up the chimney, and I jumped. Jean-Paul slid over to me, setting down his empty glass. "Oh, let me protect you, *mon petit*." I laughed, but it must have sounded like a machine gun through my heaving chest. My heart pounded. I was as nervous as a schoolgirl on prom night.

I was staring into the hypnotic flicker of the fire when I felt him caress my shoulders and peck playfully at my neck. All the fears that had been building in my stomach smoothed away. I leaned back into him. His eyelashes brushed against mine when I turned my face toward his. Our lips were so close, swaying slightly back and forth, awaiting the inevitable. Then the distance became unbearable, and we kissed. The kiss I had waited weeks for, my whole life for. The kiss that meant something, that would become something. And it did.

He encircled me with his arms, drawing me into his body, hot with expectations. I leaned forward, letting him remove my shirt. He slid off his shirt and undershirt, letting the light of the fire dance across the bruises and muscles of his chest and stomach. He stayed like that for a moment, looking at my body with desire until his eyes rose to meet mine. His look was so full of emotion that for the second time, I almost started to cry. He pulled me to him. We sat in the glow of the fire, kissing and exploring our bodies until we had undressed each other completely.

He gently pushed me back until I was lying down. He slipped himself up over my hips, spat in his hand, reached back and grabbed me with his hand, and gently guided me up and into him. Even like this, he was in complete control of us. Every fear that ever troubled me in the past disappeared in that moment, and all there was in my life were the red flames dancing across his eyes, and my thrusts matching his rocking. His sighs, which grew and grew, expanded to fill every part of me until we collapsed into each other, spent and exhausted.

We lay there on his couch in the warm embrace of our bodies mixed with that of the fire. Our heaving breaths slowed into one, relaxed and steady. I kissed him deeply. Suddenly overcome with the possibility of losing this joy, I once again held myself back from the tears that formed at the bottom of my eyelids. He wiped one away with his thumb and kissed me gently across the cheek.

I had finally done what I had feared for so long. So many painful years of worry and self-loathing had all been for nothing. This was what I wanted, who I was. I loved Jean-Paul Moreau with all of my heart, which broke a tiny fraction as I thought about how I would not be able to hold his hand in public tomorrow, or ever. *How we will never be able to show people how much we are in love?*

Jean-Paul's face changed from relaxed to puzzled. "What are you thinking about now?" When I didn't say anything, he continued. "Your face just squished all up. It's not a good look for you, *mon petit*." Then he laughed. The funny way he had said *squished* must have tickled him as much as it had me. His body shook against mine, and soon I joined in his fit of laughter.

He grabbed a blanket off the back of the couch and led me by the hand directly in front of the fireplace, where he spread the blanket over the hot slate tiles. He began to kiss me again, and I knew we were not finished making love. His penis had grown stiff again, his chest rising and falling more forcefully. I quickly matched his erection.

He gently guided me up to my knees. He pulled me close to his lips as if to kiss me before spinning me around, my face turned away from his. I knew what would happen next. My body immediately tensed up in fear.

"I've never—" I began to tell him before he cut me off by pulling my body close. The heat from his chest sent my brain spinning. The rhythmic pounding of his heart against my back changed my mind. He had given himself to me, and I was going to be able to do the same for him. My pulse raced in anticipation of giving in and in fear of the pain.

Jean-Paul caressed my back as he leaned over me to kiss my neck. He wet his hand before gently probing his fingers into me while he drew my head backward to him, angling my lips over my shoulder so he could kiss me passionately. At the same time, he eased himself into me gently. The shocking fear of it still sent a wave of panic through me, and I shouted out. My face wrenched up, and I tensed, wanting to run. He paused his entry while he kissed me, leaving his penis pressed against me. I felt myself relax in a wave that started at my head and worked all the way down to the floor.

He gently pushed himself forward into me, and although it hurt, my body exploded in ecstasy like nothing before. "Jean-Paul. Jean-Paul," I moaned. We made love in front of the fireplace, exploring every inch of each other. When we collapsed to the floor, he spread the blanket over us. I put my head on his chest and promptly fell asleep.

CHAPTER THIRTY-FOUR

November 18, 1926

When I woke up, the house was cold again. The roaring fire from last night had gone out. Jean-Paul had gotten up at some point, because he was gone. I wrapped the blanket tightly around me before walking through the house looking for him.

"Jean-Paul?"

A steaming cup of hot chocolate waited for me on the kitchen table. I wrapped my hands around the warmth of the mug. Jean-Paul had put extra sugar in it. The heat refilled my freezing body some. Jean-Paul emerged from the upstairs bathroom fully dressed. He bounded down the staircase, full of energy.

"Good morning, sleepyhead," he said with a wink as he grabbed his own mug of cocoa. I stepped over to hug him. He continued to drink his cocoa, ignoring my attentions. After a few seconds, he pulled away from me.

"I have to run, but feel free to take a shower. I laid out fresh linens up there for you."

I was confused. "Where are you going? Don't you want to, I don't know, stay?"

He put a piece of toast in his mouth before heading for the back door. "Sorry to take the car, but the train is just up the block."

"Wait, where are you going? After last night I thought we'd—"

"Brett—"

Not wanting to hear any of the words that could possibly come after his change of posture and tone, I cut him off before he could speak. "Brett? Since when do you call me by my damn name? What do you mean sending me off on the train? Don't you want to be here with me?" It came out sounding much more pathetic than it had been in my head.

"Brett, please don't make this into more than it is. We had a wonderful time. Hopefully one of many, but don't take this the wrong way. That's all it can be. All right?"

I didn't understand what he was saying to me. We had made love last night. We slept together. I wasn't an idiot. I knew people had sex without love all the time. But I didn't. I just needed to tell him, to make him understand.

"No," I exclaimed, a little too loudly before taking a deep breath to regain any semblance of my composure. Calmer, I stepped closer to him. "No, that's not all right. I love—"

"Just wait." Visibly coming off his calm and collected game, Jean-Paul raised both hands as if to put up an invisible barrier between us. "Don't say what I think you are about to say. Don't ever say it. We can't."

"Can't what?"

"People like us? We don't love each other. It's just not possible. Love is for them, the normal people."

"Normal?" Tears formed around the corners of my eye, threatening to enter the conversation.

"You know what the hell I mean. Don't play the child." His words hurt me deeply. "We live in dark bars, parks, and alleys. Getting sex where we can find it. They despise us, each other, and we despise ourselves."

I couldn't decide if I should rage at him full tilt or squeeze him tight and never let him go. My mind made up, I grabbed handfuls of his shirt, drawing him to me, begging for him to touch me too. "Why can't we be together? I don't expect us to be together in public. But that doesn't mean we can't be together. There are those places you've shown me. You took me there!"

"Argh, you are such a kid, full of foolish notions. Listen, you need to learn, to grow up. I've been there. You need to know something it took me too long to learn." He gently grabbed my hands, pried them off his shirt and stood me upright.

"What is that? That you're a bastard?"

"That glimmers of normalcy are not the same as normalcy. If you can't accept this, it's because…you are so young. Give it a few more years. You'll see. Take a shower. I have to go." He turned and walked to the door.

"Son of a bitch!" I yelled, not so much at him but about this whole mess. The door clicked closed behind him, and I was left wrapped naked in a blanket, standing in the middle of his kitchen. Alone.

After standing there counting the tiles on the floor for an hour, front to back and across the width of the kitchen, I finally moved my feet. My head was exploding with pain. It was all I could do to pull on my clothes and walk out the front door of his house into the cold void of empty streets.

CHAPTER THIRTY-FIVE

The knocker on the door clanged against the metal backing plate, sending the familiar gongs down the hallway. I continued to rap it against the door, harder and harder, until Margret answered. She took one look at me, and her face switched from anger to concern. She instantly registered my pain in such a knowing way, I wondered if I was the first to come to her this way. She ushered me into her apartment.

"What did he do, honey?" She cut right to the heart of my life.

I plopped down on the chaise lounge at the edge of the living room and let out a tremendous sigh, which didn't help. I still felt like my heart had been ripped out of my chest. Margret poured me a glass of gin and put it up to my lips. I drank a few swigs of it, letting the coldness drip. She reached across with a handkerchief and wiped my mouth off. I couldn't find the words to talk quite yet.

We sat there like that, her arm around me, her head on my shoulder, waiting for me to speak. Finally, I couldn't stand it any longer. All the anger I was feeling at him, at the world, came crashing out. My voice was a whisper at first, growing louder like a coming storm. "He said he doesn't want me. Not the way I want him. It was all about sex to that… he's a bastard. I hate him!"

Margret just held me closely, her body gently rocking.

I quickly lost all steam. "He doesn't even think I'm worth the risk. I guess I'm not."

Margret shushed me as she brushed my hair down with her palm. "I tried to tell you, honey. I wanted to tell you that man wouldn't be good for you. I hoped that he'd…" She trailed off and started to cry softly as she held me tightly.

"I don't deserve it anyway. I don't know what I was thinking. I just wanted it, him, so badly."

Margret leaned back a little so that she could make eye contact.

"Brett, were you a virgin?" She wasn't making fun of me at all. She looked concerned.

I took a deep breath. "Yes" dribbled out of my mouth past the sorrow and the tears. She squeezed me tighter.

"Oh, Jean-Paul, you incorrigible lout."

My jaw stiffened. "This is what I get. I turned my back on love once before. I was a horrible, evil person then." She tried to stop me, but I shrugged off her kind words. "No, I did something to someone who loved me, and I'm just not worth loving anymore. Do you believe that a person can do something so bad it clings to their soul forever, making them untouchable? Like Cain?"

"Well, that was quite dramatic. Cain?" she asked. I sniffled back snot. She kept herself entwined with me even as I straightened up a little. "If you're asking me if I think your soul is black, then the answer is no. I've never met someone as true as you."

I bristled at her compliment. She was just trying to make me feel better. But what I was to say would cause her to smarten up and kick me out on my ear. "True? Hardly.

"Delavan, my home town, we made it to the state finals. In hockey."

"I figured, but what does—"

"Well, it was a big deal since the only thing we were famous for was being the home of the circus." Margret rolled her eyes, and I pushed myself to go ahead with it. "We won the game but I missed the penalty shot. You know, that's—"

"I get it, Brett, go on."

"I missed it. We won anyway, but my father was furious. As people were leaving, I noticed my father. He had an angry scowl on his face as he motioned for me to wait for him. I obeyed.

"My father reached out and grabbed my collar, and pulled me close to his face. I started to beg, but it didn't matter. He screamed at me about wasting his hard work, how I let them down, and then...Then with Mother watching, he smacked me across the face. I fell. Before I could react, he grabbed my sweater and pulled me closer, beating me in front of all those people. I wanted desperately for Mother to finally care enough to make him stop, but she didn't. He kept punching me and punching me. Finally, Coach must have seen and ordered me to the locker room and stood there so I could escape."

"Oh, darling, my darling boy," Margret called out, trying to comfort me.

"It gets worse. In the doorway to the locker room, Jordan stood there with this tortured, pained look on his face…"

After a moment of silence, Margret quietly prodded me to go on. "Honey, who is Jordan?"

"Jordan was an upperclassman. When I almost got benched for failing math, he became my tutor. We spent a lot of time together. He pushed me hard and wouldn't let me give up, and I started passing. I pushed past him to get into the showers, to clean my bloody face. He must have waited outside until all the players had left me in the locker room, crying like a sissy, my face bloody. They knew about my father and how he was.

"Jordan walked over, sat down next to me, and began to clean off my face. I threw myself against him, and he held me there until I stopped shaking. He…then he kissed me. I was so confused I didn't know what to think. Behind us, we hadn't heard Jimmy, the team tough guy, come back into the locker room. After seeing us siting so close, he yelled at Jordan, calling him a fairy, and lunged forward to grab Jordan. I-I didn't know what to do. He must have thought Jordan was forcing me…

"My chest welled up with panic and rage against my father. Jimmy would tell everyone I was a sissy. My father would kill me. I told Jimmy that Jordan had surprised me, had forced himself on me. Jimmy yelled something about teaching the fag a lesson. He started smacking Jordan's head into a locker. Jordan cried out in such pain, it broke my heart. I was so afraid of being found out. Jimmy yelled at me to hit 'the little faggot,' and God help me, Margret, I did. I did. I hit him. I hit him so hard. God, he was so beautiful to me, and I broke it all. Oh God. Oh God." My voice weakened, all the strength within me used. The whole truth laid bare.

I pushed at her, Margret only held tighter, her face a smear of running makeup and pain. "You were a scared kid. It doesn't make you unworthy of love. Oh Brett, you can't go around the rest of your life feeling that you don't deserve love. If anyone doesn't deserve love—"

Bolting upright, grabbing her by both arms, I shook her once. "No. Don't say it. He didn't do anything wrong. I don't know what I was thinking trying to make him fall for me."

"Listen, I've never seen Jean-Paul say one person's name as much as he has said yours these past few months. Yes, he's still a scoundrel, but how many times now has he stayed with you when he could have gone out? Yes, that's it. Let's dry it up. Both of us. Don't cry anymore.

And to hell with him. Don't give up, either. You just keep on until you win that boy. As a matter of fact, I'm not going to give up until he accepts the fact that you're the best thing that's ever happened to that man."

"Even after what I just told you? You still think anyone could love me?"

"You big idiot, I love you. He loves you. He's just too damned stupid to admit it," she declared. She picked up the phone to dial the concierge of her hotel. While she waited for an answer she said, "Now, after I clean off my face, lets go skinny dippin'. I need a swim, and we need a plan."

I looked at her, confused and not feeling up for a swim. "What plan?"

"How we're going to win that man for you."

CHAPTER THIRTY-SIX

November 30, 1926

Since the beginning of the long road trip, which would take the team from Detroit to New York City and back through Montreal, I made it impossible for Jean-Paul to ignore me. He wasn't rude to me per se, but he sure was uncomfortable with how much time I was spending around him. He hadn't been making his usual passes or sly innuendos toward me. Since I had made my plan with Margret, it was easy for me to disregard his comments and snub routines. Margret had told me all about his games, giving me the unfair advantage. I was bound and determined to win that man over.

New York City. The Big Apple. I had never been to New York, but the stories about its grandiosity were all understatements. It was alive, the streets from the train station to the hotel clogged with people. Cars choked the streets. The giant flashing lights down every street made them as bright as daytime. I found Jean-Paul in the small sitting room of our hotel, sipping coffee and reading the paper as he waited for the bus to take us to the game. I sat down beside him. He pretended not to notice.

I crossed my legs as I sat in the chair. Every so often, I slipped my foot forward a bit and tapped the center of his paper. Jean-Paul pulled it back, readjusted, and flared it out in an obvious attempt to tell me to leave it alone. I kept right on kicking the paper until he put it down to stare at me.

"Yes?" he said, sounding exasperated.

I leaned forward so only he could hear me. "We are in New York City, Jean-Paul. The big city. I'm sure you know of some places we could go to. I want to dance."

"So, go dance."

"I want to dance with you," I said quietly, my eye contact unwavering.

He darted his head around to see if anyone was listening. "All right, but if I find someone, don't get cheesed at me."

I knew he was just trying to back me off him. Margret had said he'd do this. I wasn't buying it, and I didn't want him to slip away quickly after the game. "Let's go tonight right after the game."

Madison Square Garden was hot. I don't mean happening kind of hot, like a jazz club, but hot like Africa. Tex Rickard, their team's owner, demanded the arena be heated enough that the fans attending the game would be comfortable. I wasn't aware that fans weren't comfortable at hockey games in other places. But the temperature in the Garden along with the heavy sweaters we all wore on the ice nearly made us pass out.

Between every shift, I gulped water trying to keep myself standing upright. What made things worse was that they were whipping us something awful. Nearing the end of the second period, we were getting stomped four to one, and that was only because Percy knocked one in. When we rely on the defensemen to win our games, we are in deep trouble. I needed to pour it on but couldn't find the muster to do it.

That's when I saw it happen. One of the niftiest moves invented. New York had this brother team, Bill and Bun. Bun is a strange name, but hockey is full of them. We couldn't wisecrack since most people think Mickey being called the Wee Scot, or Cecil going by the Babe, was strange. Well, Bill came screaming across the blue line toward our goal, hauled off like he was going to smack the puck and purposely whiffed on it. At first, it looked like he missed the puck completely. Missed that puck and kept right on skating as if he didn't see he'd missed it.

What we didn't see was his brother Bun trailing behind him moving like a bullet. Bun slapped that puck hard. It whizzed through the air and past Jean-Paul's right side. It was so unexpected. I thought we'd tried everything, every trick pass and spin maneuver imaginable, but we hadn't. I was determined to do it. When I got back out on the ice, I pulled Babe aside. He tried to skate away from me, mumbling something about me not touching him, but I skated into him and grabbed a hold.

"Come on, let's give that fake drop pass thing a shot. What've we got to lose?" I asked. Babe nodded. The next time we entered enemy territory, I raised back my stick and took a shot that missed by a few inches. I aimed too high off the ice on purpose before going right on skating by. I heard the whack sound of Babe's stick cracking into the ice and lifting the puck toward the net. Their goalie, like ours, didn't see the trick shot coming and missed it completely.

I raised both my arms in the air when I skated over to congratulate Babe. He accepted the praise, grumbling something about me not being as stupid as I looked. He might have said useless instead of stupid, which were his two most common love notes for me. When I headed back to center ice for the puck drop, Frank Boucher from their team, who normally plays with the Cook brother line, slapped my shin with his stick.

"Picked that up awful fast, punk," he said. "Try our move again, and I'll brain you."

I was actually a little worried he'd take a shot at my head. But not worried enough. I had to try that again. The opportunity didn't present itself again that night. I was able to score on a little redirected shot. I was standing in front of the net, taking awful whacks from the goalie's stick, hitting me in the small of the back and on the unpadded backs of my knees. He was trying to clear me out of his area, but I was bound and determined to block his line of sight so someone could get one past him.

Mickey took a shot from the point, which flew through the air a little to my right. I swatted at the puck like a baseball player going for a bunt at a ball that was thrown a little too fast. I stabbed at it, catching the top of the rubber and sending it bounding down between the goalie's knees and into the net. For this move, their defensemen plowed me over, and I got a swift skate kicked into a rib. It didn't crack, but I got the wind knocked out of me for a second or two.

In the end it wasn't enough, and we extended our losing streak to three games. It was depressing. The boys in the locker room were down in the dumps, most of them talking about going back to the hotel and getting some sleep before tomorrow's game. We were playing across town with the other New York team, which played for the Canadian division. I have no idea why since they weren't from Canada.

I persuaded Jean-Paul to follow through with his agreement to go out, even though he suggested that we just go back to his room. My face lit up broad and wide at his invitation to join him in his room. "We need to get some sleep," he added. He was usually given his own room by management so he could brood, or whatever goaltenders usually do before and after games. I remembered what Margret had said about his game playing and insisted that we head out on the town.

"Besides," I said, "I've never been to New York City."

CHAPTER THIRTY-SEVEN

Jean-Paul didn't pull his knee away as I rested mine against it during the cab ride to Harlem. The cabbie tried to talk us out of going up to Harlem, claiming that all the "blacks up there" would mug us and leave us for dead. We have had lots of experience visiting the black neighborhoods back in Chicago. It's usually where the best jazz was. The cab let us out at 133rd and 7th.

"You two sure this is where youse wanna go? Them shines can be awful dangerous. 'Sides, wouldn't youse be more, I don't know, better off in the Village?"

Jean-Paul gave the man his money and leaned away from the car, ignoring the comment. I was not feeling that generous. "You wanna crack wise wit me like you're hard boiled? Got some beef? Scram before I change my mind." The driver screeched his tires as he sped away from us. When I stood back up, Jean-Paul was gaping at me wide eyed.

"Since when did you start talking like a gangster?" he asked.

I straightened up to puff out my chest a little. "I've been around."

His rakish grin returned. "I kinda like it." His protected, distant veneer stripped away a little. Maybe, I thought, we could move forward tonight. "But you're not good at it, so don't try it again."

The Clam House was a dingy little place, not like the grand Chicago jazz halls. This place was a real dive, with seedy-looking characters. "Stick close to me, *mon petit*, the cabbie was right about this place." I could have been stabbed and shot at that point, having gotten him back on track, calling me by his little nickname again.

We sat down at a small round table. After a couple of drinks, I finally relaxed enough to look around the room. I noticed it was mixed with not only scary-looking gangster types as well as blacks and whites sitting together, but I saw some homosexuals throughout the crowd. I saw Jean-Paul scanning around, his eyes stopping on each hot young man in the room. I knew just what to do about that now, thanks to Margret.

The lights dimmed even more. A spotlight hit the center of the stage. When the curtain parted, a large black woman stood there, dressed from head to toe in a bright white tuxedo with top hat and gloves. She was even carrying a white cane in one hand. The crowd came to its feet and roared with applause.

"Gladys Bentley. She's remarkable," Jean-Paul said, leaning in close enough that I could smell the aftershave on his face. He clapped and cheered along with the crowd. Gladys bowed a few times for the crowd before beginning a fast-paced, raucous song that got the crowd back on its feet. That was my cue. Before I could even think my way out of it, I grabbed the hand of the best-looking dandy of a man I saw and started to dance. He was attractive, but I barely even noticed him. When I turned my head toward our table in between spins and dips, I saw Jean-Paul glaring our way.

Halfway through the song, another man came over to cut into our dance, dragging me all around the room. When she finished singing, the people clapped like mad again. Gladys took a drink before she breathed deeply into the microphone. She was a big woman, out of breath. She looked over at Jean-Paul. "Honey, you best keep dibs on yo man fore he get swept on down the road. Go on, Jean-Paul, go on," she said. She knew him too? Was there any club in America he didn't frequent?

Jean-Paul frowned, waving her away. I was beaming from ear to ear. Jean-Paul got up from his seat. He swaggered across to me, pushed aside the man I had been dancing with, and grabbed my hips with both hands, making me face him. "It seems I'm to dance with you now."

"Don't be so coy. You know you've been staring at my backside for the last ten minutes." He reached down and squeezed my butt hard. I yelped, leaning into his swaying body. And we danced.

"And a fine one it is."

After a few more hours in the club and a few more in his room, Jean-Paul convinced me it would be awkward at the least if anyone saw me leaving in the morning. He thought I'd better go on back to my room. It was probably a good idea to give him some space. I'd proven my point tonight, and he'd also gotten what he'd wanted. Everybody won. So why push him too hard all at once? And it was already very risky, what we'd done right here in our hotel with all the guys on the same floor.

I paused at his door, wearing a towel, carrying my clothes in my hand. If anyone saw me, I had simply taken a shower, which was where I was actually going to go next. "When are you going to admit you're crazy about me, handsome?" I asked. He leaned in, planted a quick kiss on my cheek, opened the door, and pushed me out. He swiftly grabbed the towel and said it was his before closing the door behind me.

"Hey!" I said a bit too loudly. I chuckled as quietly as I could for a hallway in the middle of the night, excited about Jean-Paul's playfulness.

Mickey woke when I clicked our room door shut. "What? What time is it? You just come in?"

"Its late, I'm drunk, go on back to sleep. Time for Mr. Sandman."

"Why you carrying your clothes?"

I panicked for a second before replying. "Why do you think?"

Mickey chuckled, rolled over, and fell asleep about thirty seconds before I did.

CHAPTER THIRTY-EIGHT

December 4, 1926
Montreal

We tied the Americans, who played for the Canadian Division, strange as that sounds, then we won a game in Montreal. Jean-Paul had let four goals in. Although the boys were excited about the win, they were more anxious to get back home. We sat on the train in the station, waiting for it to take us back home, but I couldn't find Jean-Paul anywhere. I searched through the cars until I found him sitting alone, moping his way through a glass of hooch. I slid in next to him and asked him what was wrong.

"There are things you don't know." He paused to pull out a flask from his coat pocket and took a few swigs. He offered it to me, but I declined. "I told you I just wanted a fling. And it was wonderful, *mon petit*. But I am a bad man. You need to stay away from me." He paused, I guess expecting that I'd get up and walk out on him, but I didn't.

"*Was* wonderful?" For the longest time we sat listening to the train as it clambered away down the track, gaining speed. I finally asked, "Why are you a bad man?"

"Margret was married to my friend, James. You know this much." I did, although I was confused about where he was headed. "Well, James was really just some rich fan that, to be frank, I was taking advantage of."

"What do you mean?"

He took another swig of his flask before he continued his story. "Do not get the wrong idea. I liked him, and I'd like to think I would have been friends with him even if he had not been wealthy. His status and money are what got him a meeting with me in the first place. He wanted to meet the winning goalie. Many people want to meet a sports figure, but you either wait outside the arenas, or you use your influence to gain a meeting. This is what he did. At first I wanted to shake his hand, make with the smiles, and then light out of there as fast as I could.

"But I didn't. He was an interesting man, and I liked his wife very much. They were fresh and alive. I was not. I used them to live, mostly to live a life that I could not afford. Nice clothes, nice cars, big dinners. All the things, by the way, that you are enjoying now." His little barb stung me just as he intended. "Then James died. We didn't realize it at the time, but his logic, his organized life, was keeping us all afloat. When he died, Margret and I both fell apart."

We sat surrounded by the clacking of the tracks until he was ready to go on. "Oh, you know our friendship benefited me greatly. She came around to the games to show everyone that we were an item, so they'd leave me alone. That's when she cut her hair short. But her society friends shunned her. Having a hockey player around was not a solution to high society woes. Then her parents locked her out of the family fortune.

"We began to fight, she began to scream. We both drank way too much. I became a boozehound." I didn't have the heart to tell him now that he still drank way too much and easily.

"She had an attack. Her appendix. Afterward, she got an infection and nearly died. After James…I lit out, drinking from the moment I got up until the moment I passed out. She had moved into the Palmer Hotel by that time, unable to be in their home. She sent a car for me one day. She heard from mutual friends I was in a bad way, and she rescued me from her deathbed. Made me live there with her till I got back on my feet.

"Then hockey practices started and I left, moving into their old house. She was still a wreck, but I got what I needed yet one more time, and I left again. Don't you see? Are you really this stupid?" Jean-Paul got up and walked out of the train car, leaving me listening to the hum of the train wheels rolling along.

CHAPTER THIRTY-NINE

December 7, 1926

The Coliseum was rocking with chants and cheers long before the game started. Unfortunately, they weren't screaming for us to come out. They were showing their excitement for the players of the mighty Ottawa team taking the ice for warm-ups. We had been stacking up a pretty impressive season. Our home ice attendance had been going up slightly with each game, but so many people traveled with the team from Ottawa that the stadium was almost filled.

It had only been a few nights since he had told me to steer clear of him for my own sake, but he kept racing through my mind anyway. I was torn. I wanted him so badly, but I was mad at him at the same time. For what, I wasn't exactly sure. He had mistreated Margret something awful. But she had used him as well, so was anyone really the bad guy here? It was all so confusing. My heart filled with longing every time I looked across the ice at him.

Out on the ice, keeping my focus became second nature and was never really all that hard. I wanted to talk to him, but I knew it'd have to wait. When the puck dropped, I found myself far too busy chasing around the high-speed Ottawa boys. They were whizzes on their skates and deathly dangerous with the biscuit. They had won the Cup three times in the last six years. And everyone, including some of our own boys, thought they were the front-runners. We certainly talked before the game about setting the tone early, making sure they knew we were the ones to beat.

The P, B, and J line had come up with a big goose egg with their number of successful hits in the first period. We had fallen behind two to nothing by the end of the second. It was frustrating as hell. I couldn't seem to get anything going. I normally don't lack for confidence on the ice, but this had gotten ridiculous. We didn't seem capable of gaining entry into their zone to save our lives.

We took the ice hard at the beginning of the third period. I was bound and determined to carry my team to a come-from-behind victory. I caught an ugly pass from Mickey, busted across the blue line, and headed straight for the net. I confused the guy trying to stand me up in the middle by a quick deke to the left before bursting right. I felt the magic enter me and knew what was coming next. It was my first goal of the game and first ever against Ottawa.

Their main defenseman was named King Clancy. He was a sharp veteran who was no stranger to the penalty box from an honest scrap. He had come across the ice from the left, unbeknownst to me, and clobbered me hard across the side. It was a good clean hit that sent me sprawling to the ice. I wanted to score so badly that I forgot to keep my head moving. My head bounced off the ice when I fell. Everything went black, faded brighter to grey, and then I felt like upchucking. I swallowed hard as I tried to get to my skates. I was wobbly and must have looked like a goony bird taking flight as I limped back to the bench and flopped onto it.

Babe managed to score a goal while I was off the ice. Inside my head, I heard a high-pitched, shrill shrieking as my teammates cheered him on. I vaguely sensed someone leaning over, talking to me. I pulled myself together with all my willpower and convinced Dick I was fine to play. He didn't look like he believed me, but he had often said we each have to hold ourselves accountable. He let me play.

On my next shift, I skated around in a daze, not really helping out the team in any discernable way. I was able to feel my legs again a little bit after the next shift or two. Jean-Paul practically stood on his head to keep the puck out of our net. We were not playing these guys very well as a whole. Jean-Paul blocked a hard shot with his left pad, kicking it out to the middle where I was waiting. I scooped it up as I took off to the opposite end. I was in all alone against their goalie, who happened to be one of the best in the league. But this kind of thing, scoring in high pressure situations, had become my bread and butter.

I dragged the puck behind me under the blade of my stick so he couldn't get a good look at where I was going with it. I jerked my shoulders and head to the left before taking a half a step to the right to pull the trigger. The goaltender believed my fake and slid over to block me. My actual shot looked as if it would sail easily past him on the right. At the last second, his hand shot up and snatched the puck out of midair. I took a whack at his glove with my stick, but he had the puck locked up tight. For my efforts, I got a stiff crosscheck across the back that sent me tumbling into the boards.

The rest of the game went like that, and we lost four to three despite Babe and Mickey's goals. The stands erupted in some severe pro-Ottawa sentiment. Some would call it anti-Chicago sentiment. We heard that some fights broke out in the crowd. It was dangerous to go to another team's arena to cheer for your team. It was more dangerous to do so after your team beat our team.

The steam from the shower felt good blasting the back of my neck and dripping down my aching back. My head had throbbed since the hit from Clancy at the beginning of the third period. I probably should have left the ice for the rest of the game, but hockey players are kind of stupid that way. We don't leave when the game is on the line. Well, we don't leave if it isn't. We play on, so that's what I did. Now, cascading waves of nausea kept swirling in on me. I bent forward to let go at one point in my shower, but nothing came up.

Jean-Paul leaned in close to me. "Are you going to be all right?"

His concern was exactly what I needed after the horrible way he had left things on the train. I wondered if he had basically told me to go spit. I guess in his way he had, but it felt good to know that he still cared whether I lived or died. At least maybe I had a chance. The thought of him watching me vomit on my own feet helped me choke it back.

"I don't know. I think so."

Margret was waiting for me outside the Coliseum. We didn't have any plans I could remember. With my head throbbing the way it was, a bunch of things might have gotten knocked out of it for all I knew. She waved at me excitedly. A couple of the fellas started whacking me on the back and whistling at her.

"Who's the pretty filly, Brett?" Mickey asked me. "Is that the dame you been spending all your time on?"

As we approached her, Margret put out her arms to go in for a big hug. When I tried to hug her, she leaned her face into me and planted a long, deep kiss right on my lips. She made a loud moaning noise. All the boys started whooping it up around us. I liked the idea of them seeing me kiss her, so I tilted her head back, dipped her and deepened our kiss.

Mickey hollered. "If that's what you get when you lose, I can't wait to see when we win!" Laughter followed.

I let her up with a hug. Behind her head, I saw Jean-Paul get into his car and drive away. He must have seen the whole display. I wondered if he was mad at me for it. He knew the score, so that was doubtful. We walked toward the Bugatti she had parked behind the Coliseum. Some young boys were gathered at the roped-off area to the side of the doors. They usually gathered there to get autographs of Babe or Dick.

"Brett!"

"Mr. Bennet! Mr. Bennet!"

"Over here!"

"Can I get your autograph, sir?"

It was amazing to see the group of young boys waving to get an autograph. My autograph. None of them had ever said my name before. Why they wanted my signature eluded me. I looked to Margret, who just winked at me. "You're famous." She looked giddy with joy for me.

I walked to the boys to start signing whatever they had in their hands for me. I noticed that I was signing little strips of paper, and that only one of the boys had a ticket from tonight's game for me to sign. Could they not afford the fifteen cents admission? It was a lot to spare for most folks, I guess.

"Hey, boys. Thanks for coming out today."

"Gee thanks, mister," one boy said. "I listened to your game the other day on the radio. You're amazing."

"Did you not get to see me play, son?" I asked, knowing full well he hadn't. I was also enjoying the odd sensation that came with being called sir, at eighteen years of age. Not much older than these kids.

"No, sir," they all said in unison, save for the boy who was holding up tonight's game ticket. He looked like he was about to say something before I cut him off to keep him from making a stupid mistake.

"Margret, dear?" I asked her.

She had been hanging back behind us staying out of the limelight. She stepped up closer to me. "Yes?"

One of the boys was wide-eyed. "You're a doll. Er, I mean—sorry, ma'am." Margret snickered at him.

"That's quite all right, young man. I'll take every compliment I get."

"Do you have tickets for the next game?" I asked her.

She pretended to look in her coat before telling us that she didn't have any. The boys looked sad and defeated. I reached into my coat pocket and pulled out four tickets for our upcoming game against New York, handing them to the first four boys I could.

"Thanks, Brett, sir!" one of the kids said. They all agreed it was the greatest thing that had ever happened. Then they scampered off, waving the tickets in front of the faces of the boys not close enough to have gotten one.

"Come back next game, and we'll see if I have more," I said to the remaining kids before they ran off after the others.

"Are you going to give away all your free tickets?" Margret asked me.

I shrugged my shoulders. "What else am I going to do with them? You won't come to the games."

She entwined her arm in mine as we walked toward the car. "I don't think I'd have trouble getting tickets to your game, if I wanted to go, that is."

"Oh, low blow, miss," I said in an imitation of one of the young boys as I bumped her with my shoulder. "At least this way maybe I'll build up a loyal fan base. I may need it if I keep playing like tonight."

"Did you not win?" she asked.

I stared at her. "Really, you have to start paying more attention."

Chapter Forty

S o my friend has invited me over to one of his swanky private parties, and I want you to come," she stated.

"I don't know, Margret," I said. "I'm kind of sleepy after the game today. I could use some rest. My head's still hurting something awful." I didn't want to let her down, but I was feeling woozy. My vision had been fading to blurry and back since the hard check that knocked me on my head.

"You could use a stiff drink or two and some time thinking about something other than that barbaric sport and, frankly, Jean-Paul."

I reluctantly admitted some time away from everything might do some good, so I agreed to go. "Get in the car," I said, exasperated. We were already by the left door, so I swung it open for her before heading to the right side to get behind the driver's wheel.

In the car we talked some to catch up. I couldn't wait to fill her in on what was going on with Jean-Paul and me. "I'm kind of scared, Margret. I mean, it was fantastic, but then he acted so cold, trying to get me to leave him alone."

Margret sat quietly for a long time before interjecting. "Maybe that's what he really wants." This shocked me. After all, wasn't she the one who had told me all about Jean-Paul's game playing and how he often wanted the exact opposite of what he said?

"Wait, I thought you said—"

"No, right. I don't know. Brett, you deserve to be loved by someone. I mean wholly."

I didn't want to say what I said next, but felt I had to. I regretted it the second the words left my mouth. "He told me that he's just a user. That he used James. He told me about your money situation."

She sat rigidly. "What did he tell you?"

"That your parents cut you off, and that you two schemed to get it all back." We sat like that, listening to the sound of the road underneath and between us.

"And you don't lie to your parents? Haven't held the truth from them for your whole life?" Now she seemed to be getting angry with me. She had me dead to rights there.

"I guess I understand that."

"You understand? You can't understand what it meant to be cut off. Not financially, not to be controlled like that. And Jean-Paul wasn't just some fella I ran into. He needed me to be that for him too."

I glanced over at her as I took the next turn. "What do you mean he needed you too?" But I already knew. He already told me.

"His teammates were getting suspicious of him. He wasn't always the cool loner he is now. He developed that over time, playing hockey, playing the boys. The guys, well, you know, they like to go around together all the time. Drinking. Slumming for women. A man that doesn't do that looks awful queer to them after a while. He said they were questioning him, and he was getting uncomfortable."

"So you think I was using him? He asked me to play the moll. So I did. And it worked like a charm. Just like it's working for you, I might add. Well, my family bought it and so did his cronies." Tears ran down her cheek. I felt bad for her with all she must have gone through. Yet, why did she kiss me tonight? Was she helping me or using me? I loved her and felt close to her, until right then. I didn't know how I felt about all this lying. But what she said about me being a liar was true. It was all so confusing, maybe because the pounding in my head made it hard to think straight. "Believe me, he got as much out of it and fared better than I did." Those last words hit me like a ton of bricks.

I knew she was crying about her lost love, and probably so much more that I didn't know about or she didn't have the heart to mention. So I held out my hand to her. After a few long seconds, she put hers in mine, and we squeezed each other tight until I had to shift gears. The Torpedo whirled down the street, and at last we arrived at our destination. How we hadn't careened into parked cars or lampposts along the way was a minor miracle, my head being so swimmy.

Her friends lived in a luxurious mansion on the far north side of the city. I hated to admit it, but I was getting used to all the nice big houses I had been in over the last few months, from Margret's lush apartment with the indoor swimming pool to the Allerton hotel in the sky. With all this wealth surrounding me, I found staying grounded harder and harder. All I needed to do to remind myself of my proper station in life was to pull out my pocketbook. Maybe what Margret was saying had some truth to it, and money and privilege had made it easier to lie to people. The unfathomable possibility of it all fading away chilled me to the bone.

The three-story house Margret pointed at towered over the other mansions on the block. It had a magnificent peaked roof and turret sides with two chimneys. I couldn't remember seeing a home with more than one fireplace. It was as wide as two normal-sized houses. "What do these people do for a living?" I inquired.

Margret gave me a cross-eyed look. "They sell bootleg liquor." She laughed, which made me wonder if she was telling the truth. A butler answered the door and showed us to the main hall after taking our coats. Twenty or so people milled about the room, engaged in conversations. I noticed right away that most of them were men of the variety called "nancy boys." Although I had been coming more to terms with some people around me knowing about that side of my life, it still made me a little uncomfortable. I also knew being caught here would get me billy-clubbed, jailed, or worse.

The clubs that we had been going to around Tower Town were like this on the inside, full of homosexuals and Bohemians. They were just darker. Being in the full light of the room, without a show or being drowned out by music, made it all seem more real to me somehow. I wasn't sure if my feelings about these people were good to have, since I was basically judging myself. That fact wasn't lost on me. I was having the hardest time accepting things. I was an athlete, not some sissy.

Over at the makeshift bar, some men wore makeup. Others had on extremely tight shirts. My nerves started to kick in. I began counting down the moments to when I'd have a problem. Margret didn't know about my little nerve issues yet. She knew I had flaws. The idea of her finding out this one scared me. I reached into my pocket to retrieve one of the little nerve pills. I discreetly popped it into my mouth and swallowed it hard without water.

"What was that, honey?" Margret asked, having seen my fast swallow.

"Nothing. Headache."

Anybody who said Prohibition made getting alcohol harder hadn't been in my company for the last few months. Everyone had hooch in their hand. I thought better of drinking the vodka handed to me as we walked the room. In about twenty minutes, when the pill kicked in, I was going to calm down so much I might pass out if I mixed it with alcohol.

I was relaxing a little when we ran into some of Margret's friends. Steven was about Jean-Paul's age. His friend, Jeremy, was a little older, maybe thirty. They were both dressed to the nines in suits and cravats. Both of them were in good physical shape. Neither seemed to fit in with the rest of the decidedly older crowd. They looked impeccable. They had obviously put on their nicer clothes, but they were not too extravagant.

"Brett," Jeremy said, "have we had the pleasure of meeting you before, maybe? You look very familiar."

"I-I don't think so—that is…" I stumbled, very nervous about the possibility I might be recognized. I was worried one of these people would expose me. If that were to occur, I couldn't imagine what might happen. My hockey career would be over in a second. These thoughts were causing me to hyperventilate a little. When would the pill really start to kick in?

"Ease up on the boy, love," Steven said, interrupting the inquisition. "I don't think Brett is ready for all of…you." He turned his attentions back to me, looking very consoling. "You look a little peaked. Are you all right? Do you need to sit down?" I decided that despite the condescending language he had used, I was going to like Steven. Jeremy wasn't a bad guy, either. As a matter of fact, both of them looked very normal.

"No, I'm fine. I'm fine. Just a little tired is all."

"He took a whack to the head earlier tonight. Since then he's been acting funny, saying all sorts of odd things," Margret said, both informing them and taking a shot at me at the same time.

I turned on Margret in surprise. "Margret!"

She giggled. "Boys, you'll have to excuse my friend. He's worried you guys will tell tales outside of school." I couldn't believe she was being so crass and so forward about me to these strangers. Well, they weren't strangers to her, but they were to me. I took a snort from the drink in my hand out of instinct.

To his credit, Jeremy stepped forward and took me gently by the elbow, which actually helped steady me. "We are so excited to meet one of Margret's friends," he said. "She is a good judge of character and only surrounds herself with the best people, mostly." It didn't sound as stuck-up coming from him as it might have from someone else. "Hopefully, after tonight, you can count us as friends."

"I'd like that," I replied, meaning it. The pill kicked in at just about that moment. My head felt light and my eyelids heavy. "I'd like that. I mean I'd, you know, like that a lot." I wasn't sure of it, but I believe I started to repeat myself a little bit.

Steven told a story about some copper that had hassled them the other night when they went to the Dreamland Café. I jumped in, sounding a little drunk already, and shouted, "Clara!" They all kind of looked at me like I had slobbered on myself.

"You know Miss Clara?" Steven asked.

I steadied myself. "Oh yes. Nice lady. My pal Mickey almost clobbered one of her friends, er, band members. Well, I guess truth be told, he probably would have been the one getting clobbered. He was quite drunk and there were a bunch of them. I mean, by them, I mean not blacks, but just that there were several…several…"

Jeremy tried to fill in the gaps. "Gentlemen?"

I pointed at him with an expression of absolute glee. "Yes!"

"What's wrong with you?" Margret whispered in my ear. "Are you drunk already?" She leaned back to look into my face. Instead of being angry, she looked worried.

"I'm sorry, Steven. I'm sorry, Jeremy. I have had a lot happen today. Sometimes when you get your bell rung, it's real hard to clear your head for a few days."

Steven looked interested. "How did you say you hurt your head? What is it you do?"

All my worries had either melted away because I was as high as a kite from the Nervine pill and the alcohol, or it was because these guys seemed like nice people? "I play hockey."

"Hockey?" Jeremy exclaimed excitedly. "I've had the hots for a few hockey players." Steven slapped him on the shoulder in mock anger.

"Oh yes," Margret said. "You aren't the only one, right, honey?" I wasn't quite ready to talk to these boys about that.

"Well, we do excercise all the time," I answered, which brought on fits of laughter from them, which made me happy.

"I bet you do. Look at you!" Jeremy said.

I pulled my shirttails out of my pants and lifted them up high enough for them to see as I patted my stomach. He did look me up and down then. Margret grabbed my arms, forcing me to put my shirt down.

When the laughter died down, Jeremy spoke. "You boys skate up and down the ice a hundred times a day, I'll bet."

"We do. Well, most of us. The goalie doesn't. He just kind of stands there." They laughed again. This made me wish that Jean-Paul was there with us. I didn't know what I was talking about anymore. I needed to switch the topic. I had been wondering what other homosexuals did for a living, so I asked them what they did.

"I'm a clerk at a law firm," Steven said. "I basically do the lawyer's entire job without getting nearly enough money for it. Jeremy is an art dealer of sorts."

"Art dealer?"

He looked at me as if I had said something stupid. "Yes, I help private collectors purchase art from other private collectors, mostly. I do a little museum work as well." I couldn't imagine what it took to get into that kind of work.

"Wow, I bet you never get too dirty doing that."

"Well, it isn't easy work," he said in a quick huff. It seemed as if I had offended him without meaning to.

"I'm…whoa…I'm sorry. I was just trying to say that I hate how filthy I am at the end of a day at work. I mean, don't get me wrong, I wouldn't want to do anything else. It's just a dirty job. Not the ice so much, but the sweat." I wasn't helping myself, so I stopped talking and knocked back more vodka, feeling pretty owled.

Steven stepped over the big hole in the floor I had just dug. "The only time Jeremy gets dirty is when he has to get on his knees and kiss those old rich ladies right on the—"

"Steven!" Jeremy cut him off, obviously angered.

We all stood in silence a moment before Margret jumped in. "Ha! We're practically old friends already." We joined her in some laughter as another couple of men came over to us. One of them was about mid-fifties and dressed in a snappy suit. The man hanging on his arm was much younger, probably mid-twenties, wearing some loose-fitting silk shirt and slacks. I wondered at first if he was a prostitute. I concentrated so hard on not asking him if he was that I lost my balance a little and stumbled forward.

The elderly man caught my arm and steadied me. "Whoa, easy there, handsome." He turned to Margret. "Margret, dear. Who is your friend?"

CHAPTER FORTY-ONE

She introduced me to him. His name was Sylvio, and he was one of those rare art collectors that Jeremy sold art to. She never did say what he did to make all that money. I frankly didn't care enough to ask at the time, although I probably would have been more interested if my head wasn't swimming so much.

Sylvio held me by the arm the whole time. "Brett, this is Mark, my lover." I'm not sure what I felt inside when he said those words, but my body was in revolt. The pill, the drink, the insane life I had stumbled into all in the hopes of being with Jean-Paul.

"Excuse me. I need some air," I said as I stumbled toward the balcony doors. I pushed people out of the way as I headed outside. They must have noticed I was in trouble because no one made a fuss over it. I grasped the wood of the railing as tight as I could and I leaned over to retch, but nothing came.

I felt strong, steady hands hold my back and shoulders. Steven had come to check up on me.

"I guess I am not making a very good impression on you," I said meekly.

Steven smiled. "Actually, we both like you very much. You seem interesting and nice." He paused for a moment to see if I was going to be all right. When I leaned back against the railing, took a few deep breaths and settled myself, he continued. "The truth is, Jeremy and I don't really like these soirées very much. They are either stuffy or they fall into sordid affairs. I'd like to think people like us could just get together to enjoy each other's company without all the drugs and sex."

I noticed my mouth was agape and had to consciously close it. I felt the same way about most of the clubs we had been to. Until he said that, I was wondering what he wanted from me. I wondered if he was hitting on me like Sylvio had been. And right in front of his…lover, no less.

"Really?"

"Well, no. I'm being overdramatic, but sometimes it seems like it. There really are lots of us." Steven paused until he saw me staring blankly at him. "Yes, honey, there are lots of us around. You just have to know where to look. But I meant those of us in…what would I call it? Marriages? After how many years does one stop being referred to as your boyfriend?"

I was in shock now. I had never heard anyone talk about my feelings, the life I wanted, in such plain terms. It might have been the pill, the booze, the moment, but I wiped a tear away from my eye. "I want what you have for us. You know? I do."

"That's great. Who is it?"

I looked down at my feet for a moment, finding the courage to go on. "I met someone at work, if you can believe it. We became instant friends. And the attraction was fast for me. Him too, I think." Steven looked puzzled, clearly confused about something I had said. Wasn't I making perfect sense? Still, Steven was all smiles when he gently touched my arm.

"Sounds great. Well?" He was prodding me to go on, and I found myself wanting to, even though I didn't know this man at all.

"I think I'm in love. No, I know it. I love Jean-Paul."

Steven spat vodka over his glass and onto my coat. "Oh shit, Brett. I'm sorry. Jean-Paul. Really? Wow. You have got it bad."

"Do you know him?"

"Yes. Unfortunately, we all know him, honey. I hope you don't get your heart broken."

I was getting mad now, although the effects of the pill probably made it look more like grogginess. "No, you don't know him. We are in love. We made love!"

"I'm sure it feels that way, but Jean-Paul is bad news."

"No. He's wonderful, and I am going to be with him." I pushed away from the railing and headed back into the house. My head felt clearer now even with all the movement, and I saw Margret coming toward me. Suddenly, I felt filled with rage.

"Are you—"

"Why? Why did you bring me here? Huh? Was this some sort of setup to condemn my love?" I was shouting too loudly for the room we were in, and everyone around us turned to gawk.

"Brett, you are making a scene." Jeremy tried to calm me, but I kept on.

"Was that part of the plan? Did he put you up to this?"

"What are you talking about?" Margret asked, looking as confused as Steven and Jeremy. Sylvio and his kept boy stood off to the side watching the show.

"Did you bring me here to show me that I could have some normal life, some better life without him? Well?" She stood there in stunned silence. "We are in love! I love him! And we will be together."

"Oh, Brett, my darling. Jean-Paul doesn't love you. I mean, I don't know if he knows what that is anymore." When she said Jean-Paul's name, several people in the background snickered, which brought me to a boiling point. I felt like striking someone. "The life you're talking about is what Steven and Jeremy have, Brett. It's what I want for you. Jean-Paul doesn't believe in that. Believe me, I know."

"Don't speak for him. I know what you've done. The last thing I need is some spoiled, little rich girl telling me anything about my life." Her face flushed red, and she cracked me across my face as hard as any hockey player. I tasted the copper twinge of blood in my mouth.

"How dare you? After all I've…"

"What? Say it. Done for me? You mean loaning me some car? And that kiss, why did you kiss me in front of all those guys? Are you trying to trap me like you trapped him?" Before the full weight of my idiocy hit me, I turned and ran. Behind me, the room was silent.

Chapter Forty-two

December 25, 1926

I headed into downtown to meet Jean-Paul at a cozy little breakfast place he claimed catered to our kind of people, whatever that was. He promised they would be open on Christmas, and there he was sitting in the window of the restaurant, holding his coffee cup between both hands, warming them while slowly sipping. It was so comfortable and adorable. It would be a nice morning before the game later today. The previous night we had gone out with Margret for dinner and exchanged some gifts. She seemed to have shrugged off my mistreatment of her, chalking it up to pressure and vodka, so the expensive coat I bought her seemed unnecessary but made me feel a tad better.

"Such a high-profile table for a change," I commented from behind as I had walked up to surprise him.

I sat down in a creaky old wooden chair, draping my coat across the back. I rubbed my eyes while ordering a much needed cup of coffee from the waitress. She was a young, perky, flapper girl with short blond hair who bopped along her merry way, leaving us to ourselves. The city seemed mostly deserted, being Christmas Day. Not many people had to work.

"Yes. Boy, I could really use something stiffer than coffee." At this, he pulled out a flask from his inside jacket pocket and waved it in the air toward me. I couldn't help but laugh while holding up my hand to deny it. Of course, his coffee smelled like it already had a few draughts of vodka.

"I am glad to be spending my Christmas with you."

"Mmm," he replied through his mug.

"Mmm? That's all you have to say? Palooka." I eyeballed him a second and could see some sadness in him. "Is it hard without family today?" I admit I was poking him.

"No. You know why." He was referring to the fact that his parents had basically written him off completely.

"So yours have never even come to see you play?" I asked, unbelieving.

He had taken another long, slow sip of the hot concoction. "Not even my sister, who I sometimes got on with well enough. No, I don't really have a family anymore."

"Me neither," I replied. My heart filled with sadness for him, and I wanted to lean into him and never let him go. But even in this place where I probably could have done it, I refrained.

"Jean-Paul, I am incredibly grateful that you have been taking care of me."

"And for last night, *mon petit*?" he joked.

I swatted his arm. "Come off it. And Margret. I thought she'd hate me, but you were right. She's been great, although I feel awful."

"Yes, she's really good when she wants to be. But don't get me wrong. She really does love you, or she wouldn't have done it in the first place, much less put up with your tirade."

"Hey, I was out of my mind."

"Nothing new there." I swatted him playfully. He swished his coffee in his mouth for a few seconds before adding, "I would say that you need to be careful with that one. With both of us. I've told you this."

"How do you mean?" I asked, wondering what he could be referring to.

"Margret is a complicated woman. I think I might know that most of all. And well, now you know some of it too. She is a terrible free spirit, but some of that is not truthful."

I was confused now. "How do you mean?"

Jean-Paul took another a long swig of his drink before answering. "She gets around a lot. You know what I mean, no? She will go off and kiss many men a night at the clubs."

"I've never seen her with anyone." My response sounded a little defensive. I couldn't think of any times when she had left us to be with someone else, but everywhere we went people seemed to know her. I wondered what kind of private life she had when we weren't around.

"That's because she makes sure that you are the center of the room for her."

"Do you mean she has a...for me? Even with how she knows about...us?"

"No, not in the way you think. I do not think she has been with another man since James passed away. Which is my point. She sends out those signals all over town and lets men think things about her, and then she withdraws if it gets too...physical. Now men that don't really want her that way, like you, well, that's a different story. She can be more open with you."

Now my head was spinning. How screwy was Margret? Was I causing her any type of pain? I cared deeply for her and couldn't dream of causing her any more pain than had already happened. But having her fall in any kind of love with me just wouldn't work. And what was that crack about being more careful with him all about? *He plays so hard to get all the time, but then invites me out to breakfast when he knows I need it the most. What is that about?*

"I don't know what to think about that. I do love her. I know that much. I don't know what I'd do without her support and friendship. Yours as well, Jean-Paul. No, wait. I know you think you're some island that doesn't need love but here you are, with the man that you know is head over heels in love with you."

"Why do you have to make things into something that they're not? Can't we just have breakfast? Can't we just get together when each of us wants to? You really have to learn to just have fun."

He was being untruthful with himself. The things he had done for me and with me were not the same as those he had done for the ones he met, bedded, and left. I was going to be damned if I let him write me out of his real life to allow him to feel more independent. "Why can't you just admit that you love me?" I said with a grin.

Jean-Paul stuffed some pancakes into his mouth. His jaw had tensed up, and not just because he was chewing. He was getting frustrated with me, but this seemed like the moment I had been waiting for. He'd asked me out after having spent the night with me. That meant something.

"This morning I was so worried that Moira would see you sneaking out and wonder about who you are, why you stayed in my room. But deep down I wasn't really all that concerned about it because if she found out and kicked me out of her home, I could move in with you. So why don't we just do that now?"

He stopped eating and looked up, his face contorted with the beginning stages of anger. "Are you out of your fucking mind? Huh?

You think I love you? Do you? I love no one. I go out and I have sex. Every night. With you. With a lot of men. Yes, I like being with you—"

"See? I knew it."

He took a quick breath. "Let me finish. I do like being with you—"

"See?" I pushed it a little, trying to lighten the mood.

"And no, not just for sex. But in the end, that's all it can be. I've told you. People like me, like us, we can't have what they have." Just then he jutted his chin out at a man and woman walking across the front window. They weren't holding hands or anything. The woman looked like she could win a bare knuckle boxing match with anyone, but I got his point.

"We are meant to live hard, sleep with whomever we want, no strings attached, and fly away into the night. Maybe it's time you understood that." Before he finished saying his last line, he had gotten up from the table.

"Where are you going?" I asked.

"Doing what I told you I'd do. Leaving."

I sat in stunned silence as he left the restaurant and walked off down the street. It took a full minute before the tears came. A slender waiter came over to clear the table and noticed my tears. He put a hand on my shoulder. "I know, honey. That one's a real heartbreaker."

My head must have jerked around a bit too fast, my eyes looking at the waiter with the type of death-glare gazelles must recognize on instinct. His face turned from consolation to fear. He turned away from me quick enough to drop food off the plate he had been carrying. I was no threat to him, having turned back to the window to be alone with my sorrow, wondering if I had been wrong all this time, if people were right, that Jean-Paul was a bastard.

CHAPTER FORTY-THREE

January 23, 1927

For a month, the only joy in life had been Margret's constant needling me to snap out of it and start living again. She had gotten over my ridiculous outburst at her friend's house without so much as a conversation. I said that I was sorry and that was all it took. She also promised to get back at me for it and had not paid that debt as yet. Maybe she was above that type of thing.

She had been there with me every night since Jean-Paul walked out on me. She comforted me. She put up with my pining. She never told me to give up on him either, which meant more to me than any of the other things.

Margret had also been there for me through the drought I had been in since the infamous breakfast. In eight games, some at home, some on the road, I had not managed a single tally. Not one goal. Not an assist. Not even a blocked shot to show my contribution to the team effort. Zero.

Being on the ice had always been my solace, my place of perfection. No matter what occurred in life, I always had hockey. But for some reason, my problems with Jean-Paul permeated my play. Maybe he meant so much more to me than anything else. And to make matters worse, I couldn't forget him. Every time I went to work, he was there. Mercifully, he mostly made efforts to avoid me.

I'd try to talk to him, and he'd walk away. I'd go stand near him, and he'd skate over to the skate sharpener to have a reason to get away. He wouldn't talk to me, either. Not more than a grunt in response. It was like we'd broken up because I cared too much about him and made the grave mistake of letting him know. It ruined my life but had also ruined my game, which was on the verge of utter collapse.

The other boys tried to get me to go out once they realized I was upset about something. Mickey kept asking me to go out with him to the Dreamland, where he had taken a liking to one of the singers. But it just sounded exhausting. I'd spend my nights counting the tiles on the ceiling while Margret swam alone at her hotel pool. Even when she managed to get me into the water, I'd just stand there, caught in another of my—by now—common counting, nerve pill moments.

"Tell me what happened today, honey," Margret said in a calm, soothing tone after handing me a cup of hot tea.

"The coach called me into his office today after practice. You know we played a game yesterday?"

"Yes."

"Well, I stunk up the place. Again. So coach, he calls me into his office after practice and reamed me out something awful. I'm worried about getting benched, or worse, kicked off the team." I put my head into my hands and felt the water works starting to switch on.

"It's going to be all right, Brett."

I snapped my head up to lock eyes with her. "No, you don't understand. You can't. Not really. Playing is the most important thing in my whole life."

While I was speaking, Margret came over to sit next to me on the chaise lounge. "I don't think that it is. At least not right now."

"Does he ask about me?" I said, desperate to know if he even cared.

"You know I have tried to stay out of it, but honey, how do you think I knew to come get you tonight?"

"What?" Did she just say that Jean-Paul had told her about my run in with the coach? What did that mean? Did he still care?

"I told you that to play the game with a pro like Jean-Paul would take a lot of skill. And you'd have to put up with a lot of his bullshit, to be able to wade through it all to get to the real person inside."

I was staring at her through water-filled, swollen eyes, in amazement. "Why on earth did you not tell me before that he talks about me? Oh God, Margret, have I hurt you that badly?"

She rubbed her hand along my back. "Oh darling, I forgave you for that long ago. No, I just didn't really know what he was thinking until just the other day."

"The other day?"

"Well, I didn't think you were ready."

"Tell me what you mean," I interrupted, impatiently.

"I did try to tell you that it wasn't over, that there was still hope. But, Brett, you've been popping so many of those damned pills lately. And you've been mixing them with far too much booze. You weren't listening. Or you weren't ready to listen."

I didn't know what to think. He meant everything to me, but his rejection led to the worst month of my entire life. Should I try again? Did I even have a choice to live without him?

"I'm listening now," I declared as I handed her my nearly empty bottle of nerve pills. "I won't be needing these. Thanks to you." We sat for several minutes in the building hope that seemed to be spreading around me. "And Margret, I wish I could help you realize that you are worthy of real love too."

Her eyes filled with tears. She said nothing more but continued to sit on the chaise holding my hand in hers. My mind was racing with plans and plots on how to get Jean-Paul back. I was not going to let him block me out anymore. And I was going to get my game back in line if it was the last thing I did. The coach told me that I needed to do a lot better by Pittsburgh, and I aimed to do just that.

CHAPTER FORTY-FOUR

January 27, 1927

The Duquesne Gardens in Pittsburgh had a streetcar line that ran right in front of the arena. When a streetcar roared by, it made such an enormously fantastic racket you could hear the noise inside. I couldn't tell the arenas apart anymore, seeing one every few days, only staying inside a few hours, and then getting back on a train. So this place was pretty memorable only for the cacophony of the streetcar until now. Now it would be remarkable to me because it would be where I got back in my proper groove.

Dick tried to encourage me before some of the last few games. He had grown worried about me, not just whether I'd do well. He was now concerned that whatever "it" I had within me was now gone. Each night he'd look into the dead eyes of loss I'd been carrying with me, say his words of encouragement, then walk away with a pained shake of his head. But after a few minutes of looking at my fiery gaze tonight, there was no need. I was bound and determined to get it all back. My game and my Jean-Paul.

The second the puck dropped to the ice, I was all over it. My legs pumped hard against the slush to get to the action before anyone else. I slammed myself and anyone in my way against the cages as hard as I could. The problem was that my rhythm was all off. A drought is hard to break because the not-doing, the not-scoring becomes your new rhythm.

One of their players, Lionel, one of the bruiser types, clipped me in the side of the head and had sent me sprawling. It was my own fault for reaching way out from my center of balance for a puck, trying desperately to make something happen. Percy skated up close to me.

"That's the spirit, kid. Now get up and let's get it."

Zooming to the corners, I had gotten in a scrum with Lionel and Babe for a loose puck. We battled for what seemed like an eternity to get the thing onto one of our sticks. Babe pushed me out of the way. "If you're not going to be any use out here, why don't you go sit down?" he shouted at me.

The fire was well-lit and burning out of control now. Babe came away from the corner with the puck and was heading toward the middle to take his shot. Before I could even think about what I was about to do, I slipped my stick in between Babe's and the rubber disc, and I stole it away from him.

Before he could protest, I cut straight across the goalmouth, dipped my shoulder, and ripped a hard wrister past their goalie, old Roy Worters. Score! The drought had ended.

"Ahhhh!!!"

I screamed to the rafters. Until my teammates skated to me, all I could hear were the hearty boos from the crowd. They sounded special. Everyone patted me on the backside or the head in celebration. They all knew I had been struggling hard. Everyone that is, except Babe. He was pissed and had every right to be.

The rest of the night went just like that for me. I flipped passes with the greatest of ease. Standing in front of our goal, one of their forwards took a mean ice level shot at Jean-Paul. I kicked my skate out quickly and caught the puck square, redirecting it to the corners.

"What are you trying to do?" Jean-Paul shouted as I skated away. "Take my job away from me?" It was very funny and made me feel ten feet tall inside. His admiration for my skill felt so good. I was back. At last.

We no sooner had closed the door behind us in the locker room than the Babe grabbed me by the sweater, shoving upward so that his clenched fists jabbed my throat. He pushed me against some boiling steam pipes that came out of the ceiling before curving back into the wall. I could feel them burning through the back of my sweater, the sweat from my back turning to steam.

"What the hell, Babe?" I shouted in pain. I tried to push back, but he was more muscular, stronger than I was. He just kept drilling me against the pipes.

"Who do you think you are, punk?" There was that word again. He went right for the jugular every time. "You steal from me again, boy, I end you."

He pushed harder, and the heat was becoming unbearable. A couple of the boys came up and had placed their hands on his shoulders so he didn't go too far, but they were not pulling him away. They were waiting to see what would happen. I looked around the room for Jean-Paul but didn't see him.

"Your boyfriend isn't here to save you this time, punk." He let me go with a final shove before saying through a cold dead stare. "I'll end you."

I slumped down away from the heat of the pipe and rubbed my throat. Dick sat on his bench right across from where the scene had played out, taking off his uniform. I glared at him. "Why didn't you stop him?"

Dick stopped unlacing his skates to look up at me. "I reckon you had that one coming." I stared, dumbfounded. Then I took a deep breath and remembered I probably *did* have that one coming for stealing his puck. When I started to storm away, Dick said from behind me, "But Brett, nice job. Good to see you playing again."

My pride had taken a roller coaster ride in the last few minutes. But he was right. I was playing again. And the intention was to keep on playing hard in all arenas. In the personal one, I made sure to sit next to Jean-Paul on the train to Toronto and planned to keep just as close as he'd let me, whether he liked it or not.

"Thanks for the help," I said accusingly to him after we settled into our seats.

"Eh, not my job." He sounded cold at first, but his body settled into his chair. He relaxed his legs and slowly eased one of them over to rest against mine. It was far too controlled to have been anything other than intentional. It felt good. He gently nudged my ribs with his elbow. "And Dick's right. Had that coming, *mon petit*."

CHAPTER FORTY-FIVE

February 5, 1927

The road trip ended in Ottawa after five games away and over a week of hauling our bags and tired butts through one train station and arena after another. We didn't win them all, of course, but I was on fire again. I'd scored a goal or had an assist in each game and two goals in Montreal, which was real nice. But Ottawa was where I wanted to be. Ever since King Clancy had rung my bell, I'd wanted to score on him. Maybe even get a little payback. But since I couldn't hurt him myself, I thought scoring several goals to beat them would do the trick.

I was a little too eager in the first period, and it got the best of me a few times. I took a run at Clancy when I thought his attention was directed down at the puck. It wasn't, and he stiffened his shoulder up and laid me down nice and easy. Near the end of the first period, I was overzealous again. I tried to make a run from end to end and had the puck stripped away from me when I reached too far ahead with it. They took it back down the ice and scored. It was embarrassing.

In the locker room, Percy and Bob sat down on either side of me. Did that make me the jelly in their sandwich? Bob spoke first. "Look, kid. You're still new to this thing. We know you want some payback. Take it easy and let things happen as they will."

I wasn't sure what kind of cryptic thing he was on about when Percy piped up. "You focus on scoring and getting us well ahead of this thing, and leave the heavy lifting to us."

Bob closed it out. "Deal?"

"Deal," I agreed, looking at each of these massive men. My zeal had put us down on the score sheet. A debt I needed to set right.

In the second period, I stripped the puck from Finnigan, who by all reports was tearing up the score sheets this year. My stick bobbed and weaved down the ice, flipping the puck on its end and then back down flat again. I deked out of the way of the defense and put the puck on edge before smacking it across the top, making it fly forward in a spin. It hit the ice hard during a rotation and began to wobble, which made it a faint, ghostly image of odd shapes. This confused the goalie, who stared at it with a stupid, vacant grin as it spun in past him.

Percy slapped me on the butt with his stick as he passed me by. "There you go, killer."

In the middle of the third, we were up four to one. Dick passed the puck back to me to take it up the ice. I looked down ice only to see Clancy patiently waiting. Bob and Percy were on either side of me as we all shifted into gear together. I lost sight of them as I crossed the blue line. I cut across the ice to keep the goalie moving so he couldn't plant himself. Right before I reached the area near the front of the goal, Clancy skated into view with his shoulder tensed. He was going for my body, not for the puck.

I prepared to duck out of his way when out of the blue, Bob and Percy crunched him between their two giant bodies, sending old King Clancy slumping to the ice. I skated past him with a gleaming sense of glee spreading across my face. When the goaltender started to move his feet again to the left, I flipped the puck across his right side and into the net.

With my hands raised in victory, I saw Clancy on his back looking up at both Bob and Percy standing right over him giving him the evil eye. It was fantastic. Both teams angrily came together over Clancy and lots of pushing and shoving occurred. No major fights happened, but the tension had grown exponentially. It felt great.

I was on a high after the game, having paid back Clancy by not only handing him defeat, but by my teammates coming to my rescue. But the high I was feeling couldn't hold a candle to how I felt when a grinning Jean-Paul asked me to go with him to a little bar downtown that he knew about. Margret had reminded me to keep pressing forward, and she was right again.

The wine bar was the type where you could get liquor without worry of the coppers. It was also our kind of place, where big drag queens wore bright lipstick with lots of rouge. During one of the torch songs, I slowly reached my hand across the table and slipped my fingers into his. He surprised me by not pulling his hand back.

It felt amazing to be there with him, or to be anywhere with him again. After the club closed down at two in the morning, we caught a cab back to the hotel. I didn't want the night to end. As we got to my room, which I was sharing with Mickey, Jean-Paul touched me discreetly on the hand, shivers running up my arm. As he pulled away to head off to bed, I knew I couldn't go to bed without kissing him good night.

He turned his head to watch me as he walked down the hall, but I followed him. "What are you doing, *mon petit*? Are you crazy?" he said, a smile spreading across his face. I knew he always had his own room on away trips. It adjoined another teammate's, but I didn't care. I wanted to be with him.

We walked down to his room and slipped quickly in. Before the door was even closed, I planted kisses all over his face and neck. In the morning, I walked down to the communal shower, got ready, and slipped into the room I shared with Mickey, ready to tell him a lie. It was unnecessary because he was still sawing logs. From the smell of his clothes, he had an alcohol-drenched night and probably wouldn't remember much anyway. Thankfully.

Sleeping in Jean-Paul's room was reckless.

But it was worth it.

Chapter Forty-six

The team had a free day in Ottawa to do whatever we wanted. Our train was going to ship out to Chicago at ten. The night before I had convinced Jean-Paul to go with me to the circus in town. It wasn't hard to do after all the talk about how I had grown up around the circus, and how I had run away to join the circus once. He was intrigued, to say the least.

The Duquense Gardens had been converted from ice hockey to a grand circus overnight. It cost us ten cents apiece to get in, a fee that Jean-Paul laughed at when I insisted on paying. The crowd was large, despite the brisk cold of the day. "I didn't know there was a circus in the winter time," Jean-Paul commented.

"There never used to be, but a few outfits travel even in the winter now that they have these arenas big enough for the whole thing to be inside. This one used to camp back home in Del—"

"I know where you are from."

"So, I might even know some of the people." It had been some years, but someone might even recognize me. It was as exciting a prospect as it was scary. But my heart wanted to see it, and as I was learning, the heart wants what it wants.

We took our seats, and it wasn't two minutes before some kids recognized us. One of them pointed and shouted. "You're those guys, right?"

"Man, great goal last night. Can I have your autograph?" another added.

We signed a few circus entrance tickets with whatever pencils they thrust in our faces. The area started to turn into a mob scene when some ushers came over and escorted us out of the stands. We smiled and waved at the crowd as we exited.

"Do you think they know we don't actually play for Ottawa?" I asked.

The usher laughed. "Yes, sir. People take their hockey very seriously around here, and you, well, you both, are quite famous." We chuckled.

"Hear that?" I said to Jean-Paul. "I'm famous." I was grinning ear to ear. Having kids waiting for me after games back home was the cat's meow, but being sought after in a foreign country was amazing.

"We," Jean-Paul corrected me quickly. "Um, he said *we* are quite famous. Not just you. We." To accentuate his point, he jabbed me in the ribs.

"I heard the man. But now we are gonna miss the circus," I whined, rubbing my side.

"You sound...*enfantin*, like, eh, a little kid," Jean-Paul commented, struggling to find the right words in English.

The usher laughed as well before he clarified what was happening. "No, sirs. I've been instructed to take you to the owner's box."

"The owner's box?" Now Jean-Paul looked like a little kid.

We were escorted to our seats. Jean-Paul tipped the usher with the smooth, sleight-of-hand manner he reserved for doormen and waiters. We barely sat down before we were introduced to the owner of the Gardens, a rough-looking businessman type, and to Frank Ahearn, the president of the Ottawa hockey club. My first thought was that Mr. Ahearn couldn't have been too happy with us after last night's game.

"Pleased to meet you, sir," I said, extending my hand. He shook it gruffly.

"Bennet," he said, looking me dead in the eye, "I do believe I'm going to have to acquire your contract, if for no other reason than to keep you out of my net." This brought a good round of laughter from the crowd. "I've got a great net minder, Jean-Paul, but watch me. I might just get yours to be safe."

The owner of the building introduced us to a man who had just walked in. "Boys, this here is Mr. Fox, the general manager of the Fox Family's Flying Circus." Mr. Fox was a tall, slender man with a bright red coat and hat as if he were meant to be the ringmaster.

"Pleasure to meet you, sir," I offered. He vigorously shook my hand and seemed to be a pleasant fellow.

Jean-Paul shook his hand. "Mr. Fox, gentlemen, did you know that we are lucky to have Brett here as a hockey monkey, as he once tried to run away to join the circus." This elicited great laughter and chortling. My face turned bright red.

"Is that so? Well, if the hockey thing doesn't work out for you, Brett, we can always use some help. What can you do?" This was met with much more laughter.

Once he learned where I was from, he grew cheery. "Ah, Delavan, Wisconsin, our old home away from home. Gentlemen, Brett must surely know of our circus and of a great many others. I'd be pleased if you'd come back to our train after the show and join some of us for dinner. Your friend too, of course. I'd love to hear how people are doing back home."

"Well, I don't know too much about what's been happening back home, sir, but we would still love to have dinner with you all, if it's still okay?"

"Of course, of course. Always room for another monkey," he jibed, setting off another round of laughter at my expense. Accepting it graciously and liking it are two completely different things.

We watched the woman ride the elephant before leading it through some scary, risky tricks. Then the lion tamer flashed his whip all over the arena before the big act. The highflying trapeze artists entered the arena and deftly scaled the high ropes. The Vicenzi family of flyers was the star act of the show. I remembered them from childhood. We were often chastised for sneaking into their tent to watch them practice. They were amazing, doing the most frightening tricks.

"Sir," I asked Mr. Fox, "I've heard that one of your flyers can do a triple somersault. Is that true?"

"Surely not," Ahearn said in protest.

A broad smile grew across Fox's face. "Antonin can do the death-defying triple. In fact, he is the only flyer in the world who regularly achieves this maneuver." The triple was one of those magical tricks that often ended with the flyer missing the outstretched hands of his partner. It involved twisting too many times in midair than makes sense. Scientists had actually declared it impossible at one point, saying the human body would fail under such stress. "I tried to stop him, of course, but Antonin is bored of the double twist."

The Vicenzis had come out in their bright red and yellow capes and tights. Now high above the crowd, they waved confidently. They started swinging and getting into their rhythm, and soon they were twisting and leaping through midair. Each time they'd leap, the two performers would seem to grasp each other's wrists at the last possible second.

Then the younger Vicenzi, Antonin, a tall, muscular vision, waved to the crowd, his hand going up and down to get them riled. Then he waved away the net, and it fell slack against the ground. He leapt from his perch and made a beautiful arc, flying through the air. He sped up his swinging, his catching partner matching his movements. He made a single twist jump, followed by a double and then a double twist, and then he went for it. The triple.

His shoulder muscles looked as if they would pop right out of their sockets as he propelled himself off the last swing of the bar. His body was a blur. His long, slender frame curled up and flipped through three consecutive rolls like lighting. I think we all collectively wondered if he could sight the hands of his partner, or if he'd plummet to his death in front of us. He arched his back and stretched his arms out at the last possible minute. The crowd let out an enormous sigh of relief followed by outrageous cheering when the flyers' arms connected, and Antonin swung safely to the platform.

He raised his hands high in the air in victory. The crowd went wild with appreciation and awe. At some point in this madness, I had started to clasp Jean-Paul's hand in mine and he had not pushed it away. As the crowd came to its feet, I thought better of it and let go of his hand.

"Marvelous. Simply a marvel, Mr. Fox," Ahearn exclaimed.

CHAPTER FORTY-SEVEN

We'd better make sure to hotfoot it down to the other end of the station by ten, or we'll miss the team train," I warned.

Jean-Paul did not seem to care one bit about what time it was. He was too busy gawking. With all his worldly attitudes and his grown-up lifestyle, I sometimes forgot Jean-Paul was barely twenty-five himself. In some respects, that made him still a kid in most people's eyes. Catching a glimpse of this level of innocent wonder from him was pretty rare. I let him bask in it, making a mental note to check my watch so we wouldn't miss the train.

We passed the lion car and heard the giant beast pacing and growling behind the thin metal walls of the long train. It was cold outside. With lions being from Africa, they must be in a constant state of unease, wondering why it's so damn cold. A man waited at the front car holding up a lantern, showing us the way to the private dining car.

Jean-Paul insisted we return to the hotel to change into better clothes before heading to dinner. We dressed in nice suits due to his need for style. Despite saying how circus folk didn't stand on fashion, we ended up outfitted for a night of fine dining, with only our thinner, dressy overcoats bracing us from the cold night. We had then sent our bags with one of the trainers, knowing timing would be close.

Once we climbed aboard, we saw that all the people on board the dining car were finely dressed. Usually I felt underdressed, and had it not been for Jean-Paul's insistence on changing, I would have been. For a circus train, I had expected more dirt, grime, and unwashed people. Instead, Mr. Fox had assembled the nicest, cleanest group of circus folk to ever board a train. Mr. Fox greeted us with outstretched hands.

"Brett, Jean-Paul, so good of you to make it. I know you have your own train to catch, so we will make sure not to keep you too long.

Unless, Brett, you still intend on joining our circus?" The table broke into hilarity unbecoming a group of such finely dressed men. Fox must have told them what we talked about in the owner's box. Great.

"That is exactly why we are here, sir. My friend here," I said pointing to Jean-Paul, "doesn't have too many talents, but in his line of work he stands still while people throw things at him at ninety miles per hour. Do you have something like that?" This brought the house down.

Fox slapped Jean-Paul on the back. "I think you might find our little job a tad boring, my friend. Although that level of nerve would be good in a big cat man." Some people chortled.

"Big cats?" Jean-Paul asked.

"You know, lions, tigers, leopards. You stick your head in their mouths. The rubes love it," said a heavyset man from the table while he pantomimed opening the mouth of something and sticking his head in, drawing even more laughter.

We sat down. Introductions were made. Saying I remembered them all would be a lie. They were all men. Apparently none of the female performers attended these dinners. We were all sniffing brandies before dinner and telling stories about accidents that almost happened, rubes that had done stupid things. None of them talked about the skills and the art of the circus itself. We really wanted to hear about that, but those things probably felt mundane to them.

After a few minutes of idle chitchat, the door opened, letting in a cacophony of noises from the workers who were packing up the train. In the doorway stood a beautiful woman of about thirty-five or so, with long blond hair and a lean but athletic build. She was stunning in a little black evening dress that clung to her curves, showing off her slender waist, ample bosom, and wide hips.

"Is this an all boys' club or can anyone join?" she quipped.

The men shifted so she could sit down at the table. Fox introduced her, but we already knew from the show she was Angela Vicenzi, leader of the high flyer troupe. "It's a pleasure to meet you boys," she said after shaking our hands with a firm grip. "What brings you to our train?"

"The boys were at the circus today, causing a stir in the crowd. They are famous hockey players, you know."

She looked us up and down. "'Zat so?" Her words had a certain swagger to them, the same way her body did when she entered the room. It was commanding and demanding, but feminine all the while.

Jean-Paul spoke up. "Yes, we saw your act. The triple was fantastic."

Angela laughed. "Yes, Antonin likes to show off, doesn't he?"

"I bet he gets all the girls in every town with an act like that!" I posited. My question was met with silence and some uncomfortable looks shot between the men. Some of them turned their gazes to the floor.

"Let's just say he is consumed by his work. That is his passion," Angela declared. Both Jean-Paul and I knew what she meant, and what all of the looks and silence was for after I mentioned girls fawning over him. Angela broke the unease at the table. "Who does a girl have to sleep with to get a drink around here?" All of the men save Jean-Paul and Mr. Fox practically threw themselves over the table with a drink in their hand to offer her. She took one and swigged it back.

"How does one become a trapeze artist?" Jean-Paul asked Angela.

"How does one become a professional hockey player? Or most anything, I suppose? Family. Expectations. You fall into it. It falls on you." She took a swig and wiped her chin with her sleeve. She eyed us both with a suspicious gaze for a while before returning to her meal.

After dinner of lamb shank and mashed potatoes, my watch showed half past nine, and it was time to make our exit. If we missed the team train, we'd be fined fifty dollars and who knows what else. "Thank you so much for your hospitality tonight. No, we really must be leaving."

"You boys come see us again on the house, both of you," Mr. Fox proclaimed.

"Thank you so much. We get around a lot, so maybe we will."

"I bet you two do," Angela said, making me feel terribly uncomfortable.

We were going to be late for the train if we didn't run, so we picked up the pace as we ran down the length of the circus train. After we had gotten off, they started moving on down the track, heading to their next town. Half way down the train, Jean-Paul stopped and grabbed my sleeve. "To hell with this. What say we jump back aboard?"

"Are you crazy?" But it was too late. He found an open doorway and had already thrown himself up onto the boxcar floor. He stuck his hand out to me to help me up. I had frozen, watching him slowly glide away.

"Now you wanna actually join the circus?"

His rakish grin returned. "No, I heard one of the guys at dinner say that they were heading to Iowa next, and they have to go through Chicago, so we get a ride from them. It'll be a lot more fun."

I planted my feet firmly on the platform. "No, Jean-Paul, that's crazy. And what about the fine?"

"To hell with the fine. I'll pay it. Hurry now, get on board before someone sees us hitching." More worried about being separated from him than wanting to hitch the circus train, I turned on my heels and ran the short distance he had traveled. I climbed on board, and we walked through the car's back door to a storage car.

"This is crazy. You don't know carnies. They can be a little—"

"Stop worrying. We look like important men in these duds. Just do what I do," he said as he pulled the handle and opened the door to the next car. I wasn't stupid, here. By the way he frantically searched through the cars, I figured he was looking for someone. And after that slip up about Antonin, it was safe to assume he was the reason for the train hopping in the first place.

"Brett? As I live and breathe. Little Brett Bennet." Standing in the doorway was the man I recognized from the gatehouse at Jacob's farm from when I was a kid. He was now in his mid-forties and had put on quite a few pounds. He looked weathered and worn.

"How...how are you, sir? It's real good to see you."

"I haven't seen you since..."

He meant Jacob and the night his parents banned me from their farm. "How is he these days? Jacob."

The large frame shrunk a few feet into the seat. "Oh, I'm sorry to tell you, but he passed on."

He must have meant Jacob's father. "Passed?"

He sighed deeply before beginning the tale he probably thought to never have to tell. "He got married at seventeen to some pretty girl from the popcorn stand. Story went that they had troubles, you know, marital troubles. She caught him with someone else." At this, he closed his eyes for a second to regroup. "Took his own life. Very sad."

Jean-Paul leaned in close behind me so that the ruffles of his suit jacket were touching my sleeve, and I could feel him pressing in closer. "He killed himself," I stated as more of a truth than as a question.

"After that they closed up their act and moved on, the family. Needless to say, I needed me a job and here I am."

"I'm...I'm glad you're doing good." My head gained a hundred pounds of sadness as I shuffled past the man and his cronies and into the next car. Jean-Paul had put his hand on my shoulder as we walked.

"Killed himself? Oh, God. I didn't even ask how." I had turned as if to go back but Jean-Paul gently pushed me forward away from the door.

"Are you all right?" he asked. I stopped still in the middle of the train car in shock, holding back tears. Tears for the life of a boy I used to know. Tears for the life that he should have led if only…

A few minutes passed, and we walked through the next car where people were eating. We sat down. Out the window a train pulled parallel with us on the next track. Jean-Paul grabbed me by the collar and pulled me down in the seat on top of him.

"What the hell?" I exclaimed.

"It's our train. They left without us."

"Oh. Great." Out of the corners of our eyes, we could see some of the boys settling into their seats through the passing windows.

"Do you two need a minute?" a voice said in a thick Italian accent from somewhere over our table. We popped back up to see the tall, slender Antonin the flyer, grinning back down to us. He was a beautiful man, maybe in his late twenties, and he had a dashing athletic build.

Jean-Paul invited him to sit with us, despite the fact that my face looked like a raw radish, straining to hold back the tears from the shock I had just received. And now it was filled with anger at him for asking this other man to sit with us. This other man whom I guessed to be like us. The real reason we were on the train.

"The hockey players from Chicago. My sister has told me about you two. She did not do you justice," he said, looking at Jean-Paul. I could have been invisible, which was fine with me right then.

"We were quite impressed today. Your…display was splendid," Jean-Paul flirted.

Antonin leaned back and looked down his long, slim nose at him, as if he was displeased with the comment. But he wasn't. It was his game. "This fan talk is beneath you."

Jean-Paul leaned forward a bit on his elbows and flashed that boyish, rakish smile. "Ha ha. Not your quadruple twist thing," he said, obviously throwing the wrong name for his flip in there to put Antonin off his pedestal, and it visibly worked, "I meant your tights. Quite… revealing."

Antonin was intrigued by Jean-Paul's aggressiveness. "This

conversation is quite revealing as well, my friend." He leaned forward until he was almost touching Jean-Paul's nose with his. "Let me show you my private chambers." He had said this as if I wasn't even there.

"Just so you know, the men in the front car are wise to you." I had meant it to cut, but it did not.

"Boy, I am the star of the show. I could wear a diaper and sleep with everyone on this train for all they'd care." He stood up and motioned Jean-Paul to go with him. I stared at Jean-Paul, waiting for him to say that he was flattered but had to pass. He didn't. He got up and started away with Antonin. "Oh, and you'd better be careful the bulls don't find you on our train. They do not take kindly to strangers."

Jean-Paul looked back at my brokenness, sitting alone in the booth. He started to grin but turned sad on seeing my face. I knew he wasn't a one-man guy. I always knew he slept with other men.

They went off down the aisle and out the door. Together. I was left alone on a strange train, in trouble with my team, in a foreign country, and my lover had just left me for some flyer with a goofy Italian accent. If it even looked like I was interested in someone else he cut in, but he could pursue whomever he wanted? I got up to confront them, but once I entered the next train car, all I found was madness. Circus people crowded around, throwing things, juggling, flipping knives. It was like a show going on while the train bobbed and swayed on the tracks.

Surprisingly, nobody paid any attention to me as I made my way through the crowd to the back door. Once inside the next car, I saw it had been structured as a row of sleeping compartments. As I passed one of the little rooms, someone called out to me from behind. "Hey, handsome." It was a woman's voice.

I turned to see the enormous body of the bearded lady filling the cabin and my field of vision. She was smoking something from a long tube, like the Indians do over in India or somewhere.

"You're not from the circus, but you are not taken back by it neither," she said, eyeing me up and down as if deciding what to do with me.

"So, you're the bearded fortune teller?" It was rude, but I felt rude and crude.

"So, who hurt *you*, love? Come sit and tell Mama Bertha all about it."

"Today just can't get any damned worse." I slumped down in a chair.

"Well, thank you."

"I'm sorry," I said.

"As far as I can tell, things are looking up, handsome. What's your worry? Some girl done you wrong? So you jumped on the next circus train? Wouldn't be the first."

I was sitting silently, holding back the tears, fighting the building nerve outbreak I was about to have for the first time in weeks. Until this moment, it hadn't even dawned on me I hadn't taken a pill or had a problem in that long. Now it was all I could feel. It was coming.

"It's not some stupid girl."

A look of understanding flashed across Bertha's face. "I see. So you jumped the train to chase down the trapeze boy? Honey, everyone does." I couldn't tell if Bertha was a man or a woman. Her voice wavered from feminine to manly like a drag queen at a club down by the Water Tower. The bad ones anyway. Her beard was thick, but she had enormous breasts. I guess she could have gotten them on account of being so obese. It was confusing, and I had enough going on, so I stopped thinking about it.

"Not exactly. Jean-Paul was supposed to be falling in love with me." She reached out and gently put her hand on my knee. This caring act made me feel at ease and supported. I told this strange woman the story of my romance with another man. Outside of Margret, she was the only person I had told. It felt good to get it off my chest. And I would never have to see her again.

After wiping my face, I looked up at her and could see that she had been really listening, really caring. "Better now, honey?" In fact, it did feel better now, even though Jean-Paul was still off having sex with some stranger. I knew deep down he loved me in his way. The bearded lady leaned forward and grasped my hand. "Now I've helped you, you want to…"

"Um, huh?"

She pulled my hand closer to her chest. "Come to Mama." She tugged me toward her, planted her lips on mine and kissed me roughly.

CHAPTER FORTY-EIGHT

G et away from me!"
        Shock cleared my head enough, and I pushed her away from me. She tumbled from her seat and nicked her head on the side of the table. I could see the gash I'd caused.

"What? I'm not good enough for you?" she said while holding her now bleeding head.

I backed away, turned, and ran. I could hear her behind me as the train door closed on her screams.

I went through four or five cars until I came across one with hay stacked in every corner for feeding the animals. The car was cold, the wind coming in through the open sliding door. I sat by the edge, the Canadian February air gushing over me, chilling me to the bone.

Then the counting came back to me as if we had never taken a break from one another. My eyes tried to hold the passing trees still, and when they couldn't, they found another tree to try to hold fast to. It was a never-ending battle with no way to win, no way to stop. I couldn't close my eyes.

Fear didn't even pull me free when I heard the door open to the car from the direction I had come from.

"*Mon ami*, I'm so glad I found you." It was Jean-Paul. He had come looking for me, but even this was not enough to stop my nervousness and counting. "Brett, you're doing it again. Snap out of it." He shook me by the shoulder, but still I counted trees. His voice grew more and more distant as he faded away, the counting growing louder in my head. The water from my eyes had leaked onto my cheeks and felt frozen there. "I'm sorry."

That was when he did it. He must have grabbed me by both shoulders, spun me to him, and kissed me deeply. I struggled to get out of his arms to be able to see the trees. I was frustrated by his interference when I should have been happy. What the hell was wrong with me?

He kept kissing me as he slid the door closed, cutting me off from the outside world, turning my focus inward, in to him. Had he come to save me? "What the hell do you want with me?" I choked out through my tears.

He jerked his head back, a little shocked by my rage as if I had slapped him. "Brett, *mon petit garcon amoureux.*"

I started to become more grounded in our reality again. "Where is he? Did he kick you out? Or were you done that fast? Damn you."

Jean-Paul put his hands on my shoulders again. "You stupid, beautiful boy, you. I came back for you."

"Wh-what? You didn't…"

He smiled softly into my face. "No. He took me to his cabin and ripped off his clothes in record time, and—"

"And?"

He looked away before looking back into my eyes. "He wasn't you, okay?"

"You came back to find…me?" I shivered from the cold in the car, and he scooted closer to me to put his arms around me.

"Of course," he said and kissed me on the top of the head. "Have you been sitting here this whole time?"

"No."

"Are you—?"

"The bearded lady wanted to, wanted to have sex."

"The—ha ha ha!" His laughter felt infectious, but I was far too damaged to join.

"I am dead serious, Jean-Paul. Her name is Bertha."

He had fallen back against the ground and started rolling, blurting out laughter. "A fat lady named Bertha? That's *magnifique*…brilliant."

"I think I hurt her."

"Well, I don't think the man of the flying trapeze is too keen on me right now either."

The door to the hay car burst open. The first person I saw was Bertha, holding a blood-soaked rag to her head and pointing at me. We were already on our feet when a midget carrying a long pipe over his head came toward us. My first instinct was to laugh, and I'm not sure why. Behind him were three large men and Antonin the high flyer, wearing a terrible scowl. They all yelled to each other, but I was too busy getting the shit kicked out of me by the midget to notice what was being said.

The little man swung the pipe at my legs so fast I couldn't block it. The force knocked me to my knees, and he head-butted me repeatedly. Bob and Percy could never find out about this. The other men had knocked Jean-Paul on his back and were kicking him. Antonin opened the sliding train car door all the way open.

"Out." The mob of people had hold of us, about to throw us from the speeding train.

"Wait!" A feminine voice broke through the mêlée. It was Antonin's sister, Angela. She was in charge of their act. Would she save us from this death sentence? That was not the carnie way, to side with outsiders.

Bertha showed her the bloody rag. "I was just listening to the little one's sad story of his homosexual love for this Frenchie when he hit me."

Antonin shouted against the wind. "It's our way, Angela. They are stowaways, stowaways that attacked us. They get tossed." I knew this. Why did I agree to get on this train? Jean-Paul, that's why.

"Don't deal well with disappointment?" Jean-Paul quipped.

Angela glared at her brother and backed away from the door. "Out."

CHAPTER FORTY-NINE

Before the shock of hearing her agreeing to kill us could set in, they gave us the bum's rush and we were flying through the crisp, cold air. A half second into the flight, we slammed into a high snowbank. I plowed right through the top of the snowdrift and sailed over the edge of an embankment down a rolling hill, ass over teakettle. Branches smacked me in the face on the way down, leaving little red marks or droplets of blood.

During the rolling, I heard Jean-Paul screaming out, so I knew he had to be close. I shouted for him to no avail. Once I came to rest in the deep snow, I assessed my limbs. I didn't think I had broken anything, but I was standing knee deep in snow in trousers and my overcoat, probably already on my way to freezing to death. When I finished climbing up the embankment, I looked out across the field.

"Hey! Jean-Paul! Can. You. Hear. Me?" I shouted.

"*Oui*. Over here!"

"Are you hurt?" By the time I reached him, he was on his feet brushing himself off.

"Yes, my pride. And my ass is killing me." He laughed.

I didn't join him. "We're really behind the eight ball now."

"Huh?"

"You are aware that we are now in the middle of Canada? In February? Alone? Lost? Probably miles from anything?"

"Come this way."

"What?"

"When we were sitting on the train, I noticed a few houses back that way." He pointed from where we had come.

I gave him a quizzical look as if to ask how he could have seen them in the dark moving so fast.

He shrugged his shoulders. "Goalie eyes."

We walked for about thirty minutes. My legs were icicles, and I was shaking apart. "Goalie eyes?"

He grabbed my lapel and pulled me forward. "It's this way. Let's keep moving. It's there. I promise."

"How are you not freezing to death?"

"Trust me, I am," he said.

After a few more minutes of walking, we crested a small hill and came upon a stream. It was mostly frozen over but had small patches of rushing water. "Oh no, I'm not crossing that."

Jean-Paul again grabbed my shoulder and pushed me forward. The ice was thin across the stream. Closer up, it wasn't gushing but was a very slow-moving stream almost ready to freeze over. "Don't fall in."

"No shit," I said.

Halfway across, the ice started to crack, the fast pace of everything crashing to a halt. Nothing mattered anymore save growing light as a feather to cross the abyss of spiderwebbing ice.

"Jean-Paul!" He stopped and turned back toward me, his face a funhouse mirror version of itself stretched impossibly in horror when I fell straight through. The water freezing, explosions of unbelievable pain ripped across my entire body. Under the icy water, my body tumbled weightless. For an eternity, the darkness was overwhelming. Something light slowly filled my peripheral vision. My body twisted toward it, instinct more than mind driving forward. My head banged against the ice that had formed on the top of the stream. I was trapped.

Someone's, a stranger's hands, not mine, scraped and clawed against the ice on my side, desperate to break through. I didn't feel any of it. A shadow appeared overhead, blocking out what little light I saw. The hands that had been scratching away to no avail, gave in. Letting go of the ice shield of the upside down world, drifing weightless, pointlessly, the stream pulled me downstream. I died, I lived, I rushed to something. Something was chasing me. My head burst upward through a hole in the ice, but it was way too cold to let out a scream, a call for help, or anything other than a pained gasp.

The stream was only about five feet deep. I could touch the bottom, but the flowing water was strong enough to keep me bobbing up and down as it again pulled me downstream. The current was sending me right to a frozen section. An angel filling the edges of my vision when my head crested the water, Jean-Paul deftly sprang from each iced-over area until he was in front of me, leaning over with his arms outstretched.

Exhaustion sucked me down, my arms folding inward. His blue eyes were ablaze, willing my hands to stretch forth to him.

We grasped each other at the wrists like trapeze artists, but my hands were so cold, I couldn't close them. He squeezed mine with all his might as he hoisted me up out of the current and onto the ice where we lay. My head lolled, half-dead eyes on him, the shivering threatening to crack my ribs. After an eternity, we regained our breath and he stood over me, trying to pick me up.

"No. No, I can't. I can't. I'm going to die out here."

Over his shoulders, the sky erupted into green walls and pink swirls, like a rainbow that couldn't hold its shape. I exhaled against my will and my head felt like it was sinking deeper into the snow-covered ground. The dazzling light show in the sky continued to grow in size and shape. I must have let out some sound of amazement as the peace and contentment washed over every inch of me.

My shoulder ached from where he jerked me from the ice to the other shore. He ripped off my wet coat and put his over me, forcing my arms into the sleeves. "Come on. We need to go."

"It's a wonder," I whispered.

"Forget the damn Northern Lights. We're going."

"No coat, then you'll die too."

"No one is dying out here. Let's go." He shoved me up the embankment. Once we were at the top, I saw salvation against the waviness of the aurora-filled sky, a dark outline of a house in a field way off in the impossible distance.

CHAPTER FIFTY

The house had been locked up tight for the winter. It was probably a summer getaway for some rich family from Chicago or Detroit or some place far from here. Jean-Paul sat me down on one of the benches on the porch while he searched for a key. He looked under rocks and above doorways until he found one under the leg of an old table on the porch.

"Holy shit. There was a key out here."

"Dying. Hurry," I squeaked out.

Inside, Jean-Paul stripped me naked and wrapped me in blankets he found hanging across the old couch in front of the fireplace. I had stopped shivering and talking. This was what it was like to slip off into the void, to die.

Jean-Paul ran outside to grab firewood and start a fire. He found a lamp, lit it and turned it up to cast some light on the situation. I heard him chopping wood outside, probably to make some kindling.

"Stop worrying after that. I don't even feel anything. I'm fine."

"Oh, God. Hang on." I had no clue what he was talking about.

After a while, a fire slowly grew in the fireplace. Jean-Paul had stripped off his wet clothes as well now and was squatting in front of the hearth, using the bellows to stoke the flames.

"Come on. Come on, God damn it, already."

"I'm...not even cold."

Once the fire had grown to a sustained height, he unwrapped my blankets and climbed in with me on the couch. After a few minutes, I could feel his warmth. It felt amazing, but it woke my body up to the fact that it was blue with cold, and I started shivering again.

"Oh my God, your lips. They're blue." He kissed me, rubbing his face and lips against mine, loaning me his warmth, and when he pulled away, I heard him crying. "No, baby, don't die, *mon petit*, my love," he sobbed. I forced my frozen arms to encircle Jean-Paul, pulling him closer to me. He arched his back from the cold of my skin, but he leaned in closer, and we fell asleep in front of the fire.

I couldn't tell what time it was when I woke up, as our watches had become waterlogged or broken during the journey. It was still dark outside. The Northern Lights must have stopped their dance across the sky because the room was no longer shadowed in reds and greens. Dawn was only a few hours away. Jean-Paul stirred next to me, and I could feel that I was fully erect against his side, and he was as stiff as me.

"Baby, are you awake?" I asked, grabbing hold of him. The fire had burned low, the room grown cold. I kissed him several times. He held my face in his hands.

He stopped kissing me and leaned back to get a good look at my face. "*Mon petit*, how are you feeling?" His concerned expression was touching. Nothing could take back those moments before sleep took us in its grasp.

"Put a few logs on the fire and get back under here, and I'll show you."

"*Non.* You need to rest."

He was worried about me. I felt warm head to toe from this feeling that swept over me. No sickness would stop me from savoring this victory. It's not the most romantic way to think about it, being a victory, but this dance had gone on forever.

"I'll rest up after."

His look of concern didn't fade, but he complied. The logs from outside had been wet from the snow and had smoked on the fire earlier. Sitting next to the fireplace all night, their moisture had been steamed out, and they caught fire almost right away. The heat filled the room over the next few minutes. When we threw back the blankets, the heat felt comforting, lifesaving against my back. All of this was lifesaving. As I rubbed my hands against his chest, I felt the warmth of the fire and his passion for me.

His back arched as I entered him while kissing his nipple. He wrapped his arms around my back and rocked back and forth slowly. It was the greatest moment of my life. We collapsed in exhaustion a few minutes later, our chests matching large breaths one after another until our bodies relaxed again. I wanted to make love again and again, but he had been right saying I should probably rest. Seconds later, under the glow through the windows from the rising sun, I fell asleep.

"What on earth did you find?" The smell of coffee and some kind of meat cooking woke me up.

Jean-Paul was wearing his trousers with someone else's sweater. The sweater must have belonged to the owner of the house, who was much bigger judging how it hung off him. And who could come back at any time and shoot us for trespassing. And we needed to get back to Chicago to play our next game in a few days. And we had to face the music for missing the train. With some effort, I pushed those thoughts from my head and decided to just enjoy living here for however long we could.

"I found bacon cured outside in a storage shed. A bit salty but good. And biscuits. Sort of. There's preserves too. And beans, which I did not cook for breakfast."

"Smells good. What time do you figure it is? What day?" Deep down I did care about getting back in time.

"It tastes pretty decent too. I figure it's mid-afternoon. Maybe three."

"Do you have a plan to get out of here?" I asked.

He smiled back at me and winked. "Yes, while you were sleeping. You snore, by the way. I—"

I interrupted him to defend my honor. "I most certainly do not snore! Liar." I knew it was true, though. My brother Michael had told me back when we shared a room.

"Anyway, I found a map in a desk drawer over there," he commented as he pointed to the desk. "Going by the position of the train tracks and creek from here, it seems we are a mile away from town and the train station."

He sat back, impressed with himself and his bit of map making. It was a lie, and I knew it. "Going by the position of the train and the creek, huh?" I stared at him until he cracked.

"And while I was outside, I heard a train whistle. They usually only blow the train whistles in towns or when they are departing." He was so full of himself. I continued to stare, challenging him to tell me more. "I also found some mail to this place. It was on the map."

I rolled back over on the couch and chuckled loudly. We were saved, and he was being so funny about it. And it was so damned adorable. I loved him this way. As we sat at the kitchen table, wrapped only in a blanket, we ate the meal he'd cooked over the fireplace. The biscuits and preserves were excellent, but the bacon was like eating a salt lick. We drank coffee made with snow water. I slid my hand across the table and took his in mine.

"Thank you."

I looked into his eyes before he could protest or ask what I was thanking him for. He just squeezed back. My heart was swollen, and I wanted to tell him I loved him and wanted to spend the rest of my life with him. But I had learned many things about how to act with him. I settled for the look and the hand squeeze, and the knowledge that he had gone to extraordinary lengths to save me last night. After our meal, we cleaned up as best we could. We lay down to get some sleep so we could head out early in the morning to try and catch the train.

To prepare for the journey into town, we put on some heavy clothes and coats. Jean-Paul handed me a pair of clunky boots, holding out a bag for me to put my shoes and things in. "I took their address. When we get back, I'll send them a note with some money for the use of their things."

"I think that'll be all right." We locked the door and hid the key before heading into the snowdrifts toward town. It was pretty easy going in the daytime without being soaking wet. The man working the train station eyeballed us all the way onto the platform from where we exited the fields. It probably wasn't every day someone came out of nowhere to catch the train. Jean-Paul still had his wallet and paid for two tickets to Chicago. The train departed in two hours. Luckily no one bothered us while we sat inside the little station waiting for our salvation.

CHAPTER FIFTY-ONE

February 7, 1927

"What kind of horseshit show are you running?" Pete Muldoon shouted at Dick, who was standing between Pete and I. "I oughta sack the both of you."

"What's the fine, Pete? We can get this boy paid up and back to work. He's really turned it around lately. Let's not sack him yet." Dick was calm.

Pete was not. "Fine? The major told me he heard Ahearn met with the kid after the game. Are you trying to get traded? Huh? Are you? 'Cuz that ain't gonna happen. I'll sue you for breach of contract. You'll be all washed up." The vein in his head was throbbing as he yelled.

"So, fifty dollars should teach this kid a lesson, Pete." Dick went about the business of saving my neck. Pete agreed to fine us both fifty and bench me one game. Not Jean-Paul, though. You can't really bench the goalie. I was to dress and sit on the bench as a form of punishment. He was right. That hurt far worse than the fifty dollars, especially because Jean-Paul swore he'd pay my fine. Although it might be a good thing to put a few weeks between me and old King Clancy.

Outside the office, I tried to thank Dick for his help. He cut me off and told me if I wanted to pay him back, it'd be by having dinner at his house with his wife that night. I had no other option than to accept. It meant a night of stern looks and uncomfortable questions I couldn't answer if my life depended on it. And it did depend on it.

His house was small. Modest. Many of the guys lived beyond their meager salaries with the team, so their captain should be living high on the hog. But he wasn't. It was a small, white A-frame home snuggled in the middle of a sleepy, tree-lined block. The bell rang with a Westminster chime, which set off some commotion behind the door.

When the door opened, I saw the noise had come from Dick's two children, who had been fighting to see who got to open it.

In their haste to open the door, they forgot to invite me in. A brunette in a kitchen apron and a plain yellow dress tugged their shoulders. She stood aside and said, "Won't one of my rude children welcome our guest?"

The children, Dick Jr. and Sarah, turned out to be well-behaved for the rest of the night. They gave me a tour of their home, pointing out things their father was in the middle of fixing, which I assumed his job kept him from getting around to. Dick saved me from having to squat on the floor to play dollhouse with Sarah when he told the children to go get ready for supper. I figured playing on the floor with children was going to be preferable to the awkward meal that was sure to follow.

The pot roast and potatoes were quite good. I got lots of tidbits of information about Dick during supper that deepened my opinion of him. His kids idolized him, hanging on his every word. They seemed to want to spend every moment getting him to do something with them, which explained the many unfinished repair projects.

"You see, Brett, my husband is either gone to another country or faraway city for most of the year. Or when he is in town, he's at that Coliseum with his other children." She then corrected herself. "Oh, I don't mean to offend anyone, you see. My husband works so hard to take care of all of you, it's like you are his as well." Her simple beauty and charm were infectious. Her natural smiles came easily. She was still very much in love with him and maybe a little jealous of me for getting to spend so much time with him.

"Honey, I'll help clean up later. I want to show Brett the basement." We were excused from the table, making our way down into a small basement that had storage boxes stacked neatly around a wooden desk and a couple of chairs. The desk was covered with hockey plays and notes on the team. He obviously spent time down here planning. As Dick never drank liquor, our purpose for being down there was quite narrow, and I braced myself for it.

"You have a very nice home and family here," I said.

"Thank you. Frankly, I don't know why they put up with me. Sometimes I wonder if they even remember who I am come June."

"Dick, I don't think you have any worries about them forgetting you. Those people worship the ground you walk on." It was said with reverence and not a hint of sarcasm, so he did not take offense.

"Well, Brett, it took a lot of hard work to get what I have. I don't just mean being the captain of the team, but I mean the whole thing. Life. It's happening all around you at full speed. It doesn't seem to matter what a man says he wants, either. It's the choices one makes that matters."

This was starting to feel like it was turning on me, but it didn't seem mean-spirited or judgmental at all. "I hope you know that I am giving it my all out there on the ice, trying to—"

"Yes, of course," he said, cutting me off. "Hockey, playing hockey, isn't about all these X's and O's on my game boards over here. Brett, tell me something. What do you want out of life?"

"Out of life?" I had been staring at all of his hockey plays to see if I could catch sight of a new one before any one else when he sideswiped me with that question. "I've lived my whole life to be the best hockey player." By the look on his face, that answer was not what he thought.

"Yes, but what do you want out of life? Is there anyone out there you'd like to settle down with, make your wife? Do you want a home with kids to come home to?" I sat in silence looking down at the table while his words hung there in the staleness of the dark basement office. "Your personal life is yours to live, just like all the boys, but the happier a guy is with his home life, the better player he becomes. All the partying around and whatnot takes its toll after a while."

"You do seem to have a wonderful life here," I said. What I wanted to tell him was there was someone I wanted to settle down and be a family with. *You know him too, and he makes me so incredibly happy. If we could only be together.* But I couldn't say that to him. I could never say that out loud to anyone on the team.

"You know you've had a good year so far, but lately I'm worrying about you."

He must have been referring to the train incident. I tried to reassure him. "I swear something like that'll never happen again."

Dick looked me right in the eye with his piercing blue beams. "At first I thought it was great that someone finally got Jean-Paul to open up a little and join the rest of the team. I don't know if you knew this, but I knew Jean-Paul before this year."

I couldn't tell if he was asking a question or not, but I answered him anyway. "I didn't know that."

"Yeah, as big as our little world may seem, it really is just a small patch. I'd heard about him as a player, but I'd also heard some rumors." He floated that for a few seconds. I wanted so badly to ask what rumors he meant, but I was afraid he knew about us already. "Now, he's done right by the team, so I guess it's only fair to a man to let him live on the way he wants. I just want to make sure you really know what you want in life."

My head was on fire, spinning with a hurricane of questions. Did he know about Jean-Paul, about me, about us? What was he talking about? What rumors? Did people know that Jean-Paul was a homosexual? Did that mean they knew that I was? Why hadn't they confronted us with it already?

The panic in my face must have showed, because Dick reached over and laid his hand on my shoulder. "Son, there's only so much protecting I can do for you." After a long dramatic pause that raised my tension level to unknown heights, my brain itched with the old familiar urges to count. I fought back with everything I had because the last thing I needed was for him to think even less of me.

"Cutting back on the carousing and boozing would do all of you a world of good, really." He laughed, cutting the tension. He slapped me on the back, and we headed back upstairs, but my legs were shaky, and I felt weak in the knees. It just didn't seem like he was talking about my late-night parties. I made a decision right then and there on the stairs to be more careful about letting my personal life affect my work life, and to make sure that nobody suspected us.

"I thought you two would never be able to pull yourselves away from all that hockey talk," his wife said when we returned to the kitchen. She handed me a piece of pie with a wink. "Now, Brett. Have some pie, and let's talk about a special girl down at our church we want you to meet."

Oh boy.

CHAPTER FIFTY-TWO

March 25, 1927

Montreal had been on fire for the last few games, but so had we. We finished the regular season with a last second win on a Babe goal that he received as a pass from me. Not a bad way to end the season. The boys popped open beer bottles in our Montreal locker room to celebrate. We were going to the playoffs, and it was only our first year in the league.

I took Dick's words of warning to heart and kept my personal life off the ice. Jean-Paul made it easy considering we spent all our free time together or with Margret now. He hadn't pushed me away in a long while, and I had been careful not to push him too hard in return. Frankly, I hadn't felt the need.

"Let's go celebrate tonight. The train doesn't leave until tomorrow," Jean-Paul said. I knew he meant for us to slip off to the men's club we frequented on St. Catherine's east end. Before we could get changed and get out of there, Mickey threw his arm around my shoulders.

"All right, Brett. You're going to come celebrate with us tonight, or I'll kick your skinny ass all the way back to your farm!" I shot Jean-Paul a desperate look, but all he did was nod. Lately, he had been saying I should also spend some time with the boys.

"Okay, you big lug. Let's go." On the way out, with Mickey's meat hooks around me, I managed to grab Jean-Paul by the collar.

"And just where do you think you're going?" I said as we dragged him with.

Most of the fellas went just a few blocks from the stadium to a little dive bar and took it over. The frosty air filled our lungs, so I was glad we weren't walking far. We must have looked quite the sight trudging through the snow in our street shoes.

Mickey bought me a beer. As the festivities continued, he kept pouring shots of moonshine down everyone's throats. I mixed that with some of the red wine they passed from player to player in a jug. It became an expectation to drink, and to drink hard, all night.

"See what you've been missing?" Mickey shouted at me with a breath so hot and foul with drink that if I weren't already spifflicated, I would've been on that alone.

Shortly after one of the fellas crash-landed on the edge of a billiards table, Jean-Paul and I evaded Mickey's watchful eye to head out of the place. We caught a cab down the block and told them to take us to St. Catherine's. He shot us a judgmental look and then took off. "Whatever you say, boys." It was the way he said "boys" to us that struck a nerve.

"Wait," I said through about a mile of mushy brain. "What does that mean? No, what are you trying to say?" I must have sounded pretty aggressive.

"Whoa. Don't get 'em in a twist. I was only joshing ya." The cabbie looked a little scared of me, which for whatever reason made me even angrier.

"Take it easy," Jean-Paul said, to no effect.

"I...I don't give a shit what you think. Everybody keeps telling me...telling me what I'm supposed to do. You know what...," I spat, swaying from drink. "Drive the fucking cab." Jean-Paul squeezed my arm pretty hard.

The cab pulled over in front of the club. It was one we had been to before. I stumbled out, and Jean-Paul paid the driver. I was halfway into the club when Jean-Paul caught up with me and put his arm under mine to steady me. "Mmm, that feels good," I said. His back thudded against the wall where I had pushed him, pressing my body against his. Our kiss was deep but sloppy.

"What was that for?" he asked.

"Just a deposit. I'll collect later," I replied, pulling him onto the dance floor. After a few faster-paced songs, the band played a nice slow jazz tune. Jean-Paul leaned in close. I put my head on his shoulder and hugged him to me.

"That feels nice."

"Yes, it does," I agreed.

"Are you feeling a little better?" I didn't want him to worry, but it felt good to have him show concern for me. He still held back during any of our more tender, emotional moments.

"I am now."

After the song was over, we sat down and got a couple of drinks. "Are you sure you need another?" he asked.

"Are you asking *me* if I need another drink?" He grimaced. I was being a total asshole and was wound up about the things Dick had put in my head. I couldn't stop myself.

"Sorry."

"No, baby, I'm sorry," I said, kissing him gently on the lips. "I am acting like a soused fool tonight. All I wanted to do all night was to be with you, sitting right here, holding your hand. You holding mine." He squeezed my hand. "It's just I…you know how I feel about you. So much."

"Come on, doll, let's get out of here." He stood up with me and we walked out into the street hand in hand.

The cabbies in this area of town did not bat an eyelash at two men holding hands, and it was easy to get a cab back to our hotel. It was late and most of the hotel lights were out. The restaurant next to the hotel had a late-night party going on. The lights were blazing in there. We could see people dancing and swinging around.

I felt so romantic watching the people, the couples, hand in hand, arm in arm. I grabbed Jean-Paul by the lapels of his coat, pulled him into a dark, shady area on the side of the hotel awning and laid a big kiss on him. He kissed back a second, and then pulled away.

"*Mon petit*, we better—"

"Better what, hide? But I want the whole world to know that I…" He was looking into my eyes. The moment overcame me, and I threw caution to the wind. "That I love you. With all my heart I love you."

Jean-Paul kept on looking into my eyes, and he must have seen the pain in them, the longing for him to return my love. After he kissed me, he spun us around so that I was up against the wall. He held my face in both hands, took a deep breath, and said, "You fool, you stupid fool."

His face was contorted as if in pain, and he started to back away. I held him tightly. If he were to walk away from me now, I would die. He all but stopped trying to back away before he leaned in close to my face. "Don't you know that I do?" He paused, breathing deeply, and then he continued. "Don't you know by now that I love you?"

Tears sprang to my cheeks like a leaky faucet and ran across his fingers. He tried to wipe them away with his thumbs, but they were coming too fast. We hugged there in the darkness on the side of our hotel.

"Let's go up to my room." When I agreed, he leaned one last time into my body, both of us against the brick wall, lost in our kisses.

"What the fuck is this?" a stern man's voice slurred from behind us, sounding angry and spiflicated. We had been seen kissing! My legs trembled, and Jean-Paul spun around.

"Mind your own—" but then he stopped dead in his tracks as he had turned to stare directly into the face of Bennie, Montreal's goaltender. They knew each other. Bennie's face turned up in disgust.

"Holy shit, Jean-fucking-Paul Moreau. A fucking faggot. And who's this?" He looked around Jean-Paul to the side of my head as I tried to avoid him. "I know you too. You're that new kid."

Bennie started to walk off down the street, but Jean-Paul chased after him, grabbing him. I was paralyzed with fear. My whole life was over in the blink of an eye. Twenty seconds ago, I was on top of the world. Now this man was about to ruin everything.

Jean-Paul pushed Bennie up against the wall. "You aren't going to do anything about this, understand?"

Bennie pushed Jean-Paul off him, turned, and walked away down the street. My legs decided that if they weren't going to be used to run that they would just stop working all together, and I fell down. I slammed against the concrete, but I couldn't feel it. My stomach churned, my head jolted to the side, and I upchucked all over the sidewalk.

Jean-Paul picked me up, carried me up to his room, cleaned me off, and put me in the bed. I was blubbering and crying, asking what we were to do now that my life was over. Jean-Paul just reassured me that it was going to be all right, that he'd handle it. I passed out.

CHAPTER FIFTY-THREE

The next day the world started out normal. It did not fold in on itself until I stepped back into our hotel room. Mickey sat on the end of the bed, fully dressed, waiting for me. His serious appearance startled me.

"Where exactly did you get off to last night? You just left," he accused me.

"Lay off, da'," I tried, doing my best Scottish accent to make him laugh and forget whatever he had prepared to say to me.

"Right. I wish I were your da'. Then I could…I don't know."

"Are you still soused, Mick?" He looked pretty sober and serious.

"Brett. You're my pal. Until lately, even my best mate."

"I thought we were brothers?"

"Yeah," Mickey replied. "We were, are, I don't know." He paused a bit before looking me square in the eyes. "I think I know what you've been up to with that, that…"

"That what?" I challenged him, desperate for it to be out in the open once and for all, yet terrified that he would actually say it.

"I don't like what people are whispering about. I'm afraid it's going to turn into more than that, lickity-split." Mickey got up off the bed and approached me. All I could think about was how this man, once he knew about me, really *knew*, could hold me down while the other boys tied the noose around my neck.

"Saying what about me?"

"Brett. I'm not stupid. I know. The Bible says it's wrong. Evil, even. This man is taking advantage of you. It needs to stop." Mickey held me by the shoulder, softly, all his caring resting between his hand and my body.

I brushed it aside. "Listen, Mickey. You don't know what you're talking about. I don't know what you're talking about. But if you want to talk about sin, look right there in that damn mirror!" I shouted, pointing to his reflection in the dressing table's glass.

He clenched his fists, and my heart immediately began pounding twice as fast. I closed my eyes for a second, having visions of the Wee Scott pummeling me into submission. He took a step toward me before stopping and relaxing his powerful hands.

"I care what happens. We're a team, Brett. And you are hurting the team with this." I could have burned a hole through his skull with my eyes at the idea that my relationship mattered one bit to him or the team, knowing full well it would. I turned to storm out of the room.

"Leave me alone from now on," I said through clenched teeth.

He rushed up to me faster than I could react, grabbing hold of my arms and pinning them to my sides. "I can't leave you alone, Brett. You are a brother to me, but I wish I was your dad, so I could've beat some sense into your head a long time ago."

I turned my head in the cramped inches between our bodies pressed against the doorway to face him. My hot breath was making his eyes blink. "It's too late for that. He tried that long ago." Mickey released his grip on me, took a step back, and allowed me to open the door. I paused, catching my breath, but it was him that spoke first.

"He's no good," he breathed.

I used all the inner strength I had to calm myself. "If we were brothers at all, you'd keep your mouth shut." I hurried out of the room and down the hall, heading to the train.

The train ride was quiet. I made sure to sit next to Bob, who was nursing a serious hangover and was in no mood to talk. That worked great for me, because all I wanted was to have Jean-Paul hold me and keep telling me how everything was going to be all right. I wanted to run. The last thing I was capable of at that point was holding some meaningless conversation. I watched for Mickey to board, waiting to see what would happen.

Back in Chicago, we set a practice schedule with the team and were released until tomorrow. Jean-Paul jumped in his car and headed out after telling me he'd meet me later at Margret's. We had to get her help in sorting this out. I cruised straight to the hotel to see her in the Torpedo, which had been sitting behind the Coliseum for the last few days. I found solace in knowing we had made it all the way back and through a meeting without being called to the offices. Had Mickey and

Bennie both decided not to ruin our lives, or was something else at play here?

When I walked into Margret's place, I heard a radio on and some commotion in the bedroom. Instinct should have told me to turn and run for the exit, but instead I grabbed the knob and opened the door. Margret was on top of some man in her bed, riding him like he was a rodeo bull.

"Oh my God, I am so sorry."

"Jesus, Brett. What are you doing here?" She pulled the sheets up over her breasts as if they were some new secret that I had never seen before. The man who had been lying under her stood at the edge of the bed wearing nothing but the fear in his face.

"Who is this?" he asked hoarsely.

"Oh. Brett, William. William, Brett." The man stuck his hand out nervously, his stiff pecker standing between us. Realizing his hand had just been covering his privates, he put his hand back on himself. The innocence flowed from him, casting a wonderful aura.

"Excuse me."

When Margret got close to me, I leaned in to her ear. "Um, who's this? This seems more than kissing." Normally, Margret played with men as if they were toys to be spun around the dance floor, kissed, and abandoned. Anything more seemed like cheating. Even if the person she would be cheating on had long been cold in the ground.

She blushed. "I don't…you know, I don't know. He's…different."

"I better go," I offered on my way to the door. "Sorry to barge in," I threw back at William.

"Oh, no problem," he said as some sort of instant reply.

"Don't be silly." She stopped me by the chaise lounge. "Are you going to tell me why you had to rush here straight from the train?"

Making her dismiss her new beau was the wrong thing to do, but I had no one else to confide in, no one else to tell any of this to. After he was dressed and gone, Margret poured a couple of stiff vodkas and sat down next to me in her skimpy negligee.

The whole thing flooded out of me as if a dam had broken. She didn't stop me until I told her what Jean-Paul had said.

"Love? Really? Applesauce."

"Margret, let me finish."

"Wait. That's not the story? There's more than that? What could possibly be more than that part, honey? You've been working on getting him to…" She fell silent the moment she could see the strain in my face, probably a little surprised I wasn't crying like a little girl as usual. She couldn't know that I was cried out.

"We were a little ossified. Well, more than a little. And it was all my fault. We were going into the hotel, and I just had to have one more kiss. On the street! How stupid. And what are the damned odds that the person to walk by and catch us would be—"

"What do you mean, catch you?" she said, it being her turn to interrupt me.

My head held low and steady a long time. "That's what I have been trying to tell you this whole time. We were caught. He's a hockey player from another team we both know. And there's more."

"More?" she asked in a high-pitched squeal.

"Mickey suspects too. He more than suspects. I'm pretty sure he knows. He warned me to stay away from Jean-Paul."

"Oh my God. What the hell?" She stared into the couch for the longest time before continuing. "Wait, this happened last night? And no one knows yet? Well, honey, if they didn't go straight to everyone and tell them what they know, maybe they won't. At least Mickey."

"No."

"Maybe the other guy was as zozzled as you were and slept it off."

"Do you think?"

"Darling, I have no idea. But why would he wait?" She was right, but it didn't make me less worried about what the rest of my life would look like. I was going to lose Jean-Paul for sure. He hadn't shown up at Margret's like he said he would. Margret tried to reassure me it was just Jean-Paul being himself. I wasn't sure. This was as good a reason as any to hightail it out.

After dinner and a glass of wine, I fell sound asleep on the chaise lounge and didn't wake up until dark. Someone had pulled a quilt over me and had taken my shoes and socks off while I was asleep. Standing in the doorway between the living room and the entryway to the bedroom with a quilt draped over my shoulders, I heard Jean-Paul.

Before I could call out to him, I heard him sniffle. He was crying. He was crying to Margret all because of me. It made me feel awful inside. Still no tears came. I was dried up.

"You really are, aren't you, Jean-Paul? In love?" She hadn't sounded accusatory, more in awe. "I didn't think it possible."

I turned away from the doorway, wanting to stop eavesdropping, but my desire to hear this was too great. I stayed as still, as silent as possible, straining to hear everything they said without getting caught.

"That is not the point. He is innocent and shouldn't have to—"

"Damn it, honey. Just admit it. Tell him, or you're hurting him worse than this blackmailer or anyone you're afraid of on the team."

Jean-Paul leaned in close to her, making it difficult to see clearly in the dark, but it seemed like he put his head on her chest and began to cry. My knees went weak, and my dried up tear ducts swelled over.

He sighed deeply before speaking so quietly it was barely audible. "Yes, *cher*, I did tell him I love him. I'm terrified for him." She shushed him as she rocked him back and forth, saying that it would be all right. I slipped back to the couch as quietly as I could and lay down when I heard her tell him that everything would be all right.

My heart was broken for him.

CHAPTER FIFTY-FOUR

March 29, 1927

The next few days went by uneventfully, as far as the impending ruination of everything I held dear was concerned. Bennie had not told anyone. This was certain, because our careers would have been finished if he had. Instead we were seconds away from entering the ice in the packed Coliseum to face off against Boston in our first playoff game.

Getting back into the game was a welcome distraction. I needed to do it. It might be my last game. Every practice could have been my last time holding a hockey stick, hitting a puck, scoring a goal. I had treated the last few days as the last of my life. But there I was, waiting for the whistle to blow and the puck to drop on my first professional playoff game. I was scared. But I felt something much more than that.

I was hungry.

When the rubber hit the hard ice, I did what I was trained to do. What I loved to do. I caught the first pass from Babe, who had put his need to win above his rivalry with me for the moment. I skated toward their goal. One of the most skilled players that year, Eddie Shore, stopped me from getting to the net a few times, but after about five minutes, I caught another pass and shot up the ice. Eddie tried one of his fancy spin moves to get me off the puck, but it didn't fool me a second time. I popped the puck between his legs and dipped around his spinning body to pick up the puck on the other side.

Without deking, I sent a fast wrist shot past their goalie, Winkler, and saw the netting snap up behind him. When the horn blew, I raised my hands in the air, and the team surrounded me in cheers. These two games against Boston were different than regular season games. To win, we had to score more goals over both games, not just win each game. They called it a "total goals wins" contest instead of a "best of" series. We were going to play twice and needed to score a bunch to make it to the next round of the playoffs. I skated back to the center of the ice and slapped my stick down on the ice, letting everyone know that I was ready for the next face-off.

By the time we had gotten to the locker room after the first period, we were up three to nothing, two of which were mine. I was on a mission like it was the last game of my life. Jean-Paul looked shaky at his half of the ice. Bob and Percy had to slide block several shots. They only do that sort of dangerous stuff when they feel a goalie is having a tough game. He was acting nervous, off a little bit.

It was tradition to leave the goalie alone in the locker room during the breaks unless he approached you. It was more like a superstition, which goaltenders had no shortage of. I chose to break that tradition.

"Jean-Paul, what is going on with you tonight?"

"I'm fine."

"Babe," I whispered to him, "you are not fine. You bobbled some easy stops already. It's not like you."

"I said I'm fine."

"Okay, just, you know." He looked up, and I could see the fire in his eyes. He wasn't fully lit yet, but he was getting there. How could I be so steady when I had done nothing for days but practice and worry my life would be over at any minute? Planning your doom was exhausting, and I had to give it up. I was taking a note from Jean-Paul's usual calm and cool self. He could lean on my calm for a change.

"Score more goals," he said before standing up and walking off to a trainer to work on his straps.

I burned up the zones out there. In the second period, I scored another goal and had an assist. Their star Eddie got so mad, he punched me in the mouth. It hurt like hell but meant I was getting to them. Well, to him at least, and that was good enough as a start.

Jean-Paul let in two goals but was looking steadier. When all was said and done, we stopped every shot in the third period, and I scored two more goals. We won the game by a score of six to two and were in good position to head to Boston. After the game, I went to Jean-Paul hoping we could spent some time together, to comfort each other while we waited for…what could come.

"No. I am going home," he said coldly.

"Don't do that. Don't pull away from me now."

He sighed. "I'm not pulling away from you. Don't you think I've learned you wouldn't give up? I'd lock the door and you'd climb the chimney." He flashed a partial rakish grin at me. "It's just probably a good idea to lay low and finish out the year."

"Okay, then, I guess I'll see you later. Maybe I'll climb the chimney."

"You were amazing tonight," he said as I walked away from him, heading back to my place. My heart soared. Jean-Paul very rarely commented on my play. I don't recall if he'd ever complimented on it like that.

CHAPTER FIFTY-FIVE

March 31, 1927

Boston was just as cold as Chicago, and our reception at the train station was less than hospitable. We had to walk across a snow-filled field with all of our gear to catch an ice-cold bus. After we found out it wouldn't start, we had to unload our gear and hike to another bus. By the time we got to the hotel, it was late, and we were all exhausted. Which I guessed was their plan the whole time.

Jean-Paul and I had been lying low for days now. I had grown terribly restless, wanting to see him. Really see him. It had been about a week since the incident in Montreal, and I was easing out of my fear a little bit. I couldn't describe it to Margret. She sort of knew about what we went through, having to lie to everyone to stay safe, to have a career. She knew the pain of not proclaiming our relationship to the world. As supportive as she was, she could not fathom the breath catching and bloodcurdling fear of being found out. I was a walking, ticking time bomb trying to live my life. Sometimes I wanted to walk into the locker room and just get it over with, to tell everyone, to proclaim my love to the world and be damned.

Those feelings passed quickly.

Mostly it was just horrible, crushing fear.

But I was going to be with him tonight if it killed me.

Boston had other plans for me that night on the ice. Eddie and the other boys targeted me almost exclusively. It worked to keep me away from the net, but that left the Babe and Dick to slam in four goals. That also didn't stop them from knocking Jean-Paul over into the hard steel of his net at every opportunity.

The score quickly shifted from our dominance to our fear that they would overcome their huge deficit. They scored four goals in a matter of minutes, which filled us with the fear they would be able to not just tie the game, but they could even make up the goals from last night. This total goals match up depended on momentum, which we were clearly in danger of losing. Jean-Paul had never been beaten that hard throughout the whole year.

With ten minutes to go, the team quickly met on the ice and decided to shift to all defense to keep them away from our net. I took an elbow to the ribs but held my ground to keep one goal out of the net. Sully got chopped across the teeth, losing one to keep big Eddie away from Jean-Paul. The referees had decided, regardless of what Dick or Pete shouted at them, to let the boys play as hard as they could, rules be damned.

With a minute to go, our whole team battered and bruised, Boston could not catch up. We were going to the next round of the playoffs. That's when it happened. One of their defensemen clobbered Percy over the head with his stick. That started a mêlée of hockey sticks in the air, gloves flying over the cages into the crowd and a fight that cleared the benches. Even the referees and coaches couldn't stop it. The timekeeper kept the clock running until the horn announced the end of the game.

The crowd started booing at the tops of their lungs well before the horn sounded. By the noise, it sounded like none of the Boston faithful left their seats. If we stayed a few more seconds, there might have been a massacre. Dick was a wise man, seeing the futility of the fight. He grabbed Babe and me by the elbows and headed for the bench door. The boys saw it too and followed suit. The Boston players let us leave for the most part, being tired and hurt just as much as we were.

Jean-Paul exited the rink holding his gloved hand up to his bloody lip. The sight of his blood, of his hurt, sent me into a blind rage. If it hadn't been for Cully and Mickey holding me back, prodding me along the walkway, I would have climbed back out there for some more. It was insanity. We were drenched with warm soda and buckets of stale popcorn by angry fans as we left the ice.

We had won our first playoff match, bringing us one step closer to the championship. Pete took a call on the phone in the locker room. The whooping and hollering slowly came to a halt, the older players knowing what the call meant. Soon, Pete announced the score of the other game of the night. We already knew we were going to play against New York since they had gotten a bye to the next round on account of their record. They were rested and waiting for us.

What we didn't know was who was going to go play against the mighty Ottawa team next. If whoever played Ottawa won, we might be playing them. I had different motivation to pay attention. I closed my eyes, holding my breath, silently praying that Montreal would not advance to the next round, ending my fears of seeing Bennie again.

"It's Montreal."

The very real possibility of having to play Bennie's team, to face him again, landed on my head like a ton of bricks.

CHAPTER FIFTY-SIX

April 2, 1927

Over the next three days, all I could do was keep my head down and focus on the games at hand. We were playing New York at home. That team was not to be taken lightly. It would take our focus to be able to win the two-game-most-goals-wins competition in order to go all the way to the Stanley Cup.

Jean-Paul had been playing his emotions too close to the vest. There had been no talk about what he had said to Margret that night when he thought I was sound asleep. He hadn't exactly pushed me away, but he'd become driven somehow. Much like me, he had pushed all of his fears and worries into his competitive nature. After the jitters in Boston, he had laid it all aside, lighting him up like a Christmas tree. He had the same fire now that he usually had on the ice.

We hadn't really talked about Bennie and what all of this might mean. We were bound and determined to go all the way. But I might be shooting against a man that knew our secret and had kept it to himself all this time. We had no logical solution, no real explanation. All we could do was to play on and play hard. To do that a person needed drive, and we had no lack of that.

Draped on my arm, Margret waved to Jean-Paul and Alistaire, who had just gotten out of his Imperial in the back of the Coliseum. I hadn't seen her in several months. Several of the players were coming into the building with their wives or girlfriends hanging on them. This was a big deal. When we left practice two hours ago, coach said the press area just inside the doors was to be filled with reporters and photographers before the game. They were sure to be blinding us with their flashbulbs, bombarding us before the big game today. All the boys had been complaining how their gals had been hollering at them to let them enter the back door so as to get their picture in the paper.

Jean-Paul suggested Margret should come with me and make a big, smooch-laden deal about it in front of all the fellas. He said if I could get my picture with Margret together as a couple, it would protect us. What he didn't account for was Margret taking his idea a step farther by eliciting help from Alistaire. She has never been his biggest fan, not for a long time anyway, but apparently she relished the idea of making Jean-Paul as uncomfortable as possible in public. Alistaire must have had some experience acting on stage, because she handled her part like a pro. She lavished Jean-Paul with wet kisses while she called him sugar and daddy. He returned her affections, even kissing her, but anyone that knew him could tell it caused him great pains to do.

At least he'd better not have been enjoying it.

I wasn't crazy about using Margret like this. She had been used enough in her life. She had been used enough by us. Now that she had met William, she was finally breaking through her blockage about moving on to real love after James's death. It was just like her to stick her emotional neck out to save us, regardless of what it might mean to her own love life. She had simply snorted and said William was fine with it, meaning she had him wrapped around her pinky finger like the rest of us. However, that meant she had told William all about the precarious situation we found ourselves in, which did not inspire me with confidence. I was sad to have been so wrapped up in my life not to notice her getting so close to him. He made her happy, when all we brought was trouble.

When I stepped into the back door of the Coliseum, at least fifty flashes blew up in my face, blinding me temporarily. I shielded my eyes with my hands while they tried to get the perfect photograph for the papers. Someone grabbed me roughly around the shoulders and led me into the room. I couldn't tell who it was until the major whispered into my ear. "Win, beat, championship, teamwork, determined. Go."

Giving me those enigmatic instructions, he pushed me in front of the newspapermen, where I stood dumbfounded, rubbing my eyes. "Gentlemen of the press and honored guests," he said, "let me introduce you to the young man you have all been asking about. The speedster with more goals than any other player, the terror on the ice, soon to be the star of the Stanley Cup, the Blond Bomber, Brett Bennet!"

A cacophony ensued. Journalists threw questions at me from left and right. Margret had managed to get close to me, but the major had a death grip on her arm, keeping her away from the spotlight. Her steady hand on my back would have made all the difference, but any photos of me, I'm pretty sure, would show her as well. Then they would write about her. That was the whole point. I hoped so anyway.

As the blinding white light of the bulbs died down, it dawned on me that the major had just given me a nickname. The Blond Bomber. It sounded ridiculous, and I cringed thinking about the ribbing coming to me from the locker room. They were probably making signs for me right now so I would never live it down. The press ate it up too, calling out to me using that horrible moniker.

"Say, how does the Blond Bomber feel about tonight's game?"

I took a deep breath. My mind had gone blank. Should I introduce Margret? Then the major's words came to me. "Our team has worked hard, and we are determined to win tonight! I think we have the skill to beat them. We've done it before. Then it's just one more game to the championship." It came out wooden and stilted, but the little voice in my head thanked the major right about then.

"Bomber, how many goals are you going to score?"

"A lot—" The room erupted in laughter that drowned out the rest of my sentence, which included the words, "I hope." Players are never supposed to disrespect the other team or say things that make it seem like they are already beaten. It tends to enrage them and motivate them. We always stay away from that kind of talk, so as soon as those words fell off my lips, I just knew they'd come back to haunt me.

"Good job, dumb ass," Cully said when I'd stepped into the locker room. Some of the boys laughed at it, but some held me in a death glare. Most hockey players were pretty superstitious. I was in the latter camp. It was a mistake. I should have kept my big yap shut.

When the game started an hour later, I realized I had given New York the spark they needed. They came at us hard. Every time one of them skated by me they said things like, "How many is that, bomber?" and "Good job, Blondie Bomber." They also made it their life's mission to smash me at every turn. Most of the time when a team tries that strategy, we can shift around and have other guys carry the puck more. We were having the hardest time figuring out their patterns.

The score was three-zero at the outset of the third period. We had to get those goals back and then some if we were going to win the games. During the break, we kicked around several ideas to combat New York's strategy. Some of them might have worked, but some were so asinine, they got shot down immediately.

We finally came up with an idea. When the puck was thrown down, I slipped back behind everyone and switched positions with Percy on defense. We were playing man to man, so the player who was supposed to cover Percy got confused and bumped into my player. That allowed Percy to skate into the zone and almost up to the goal before he wound one up and knocked it in.

Our little ploy wasn't going to fool them again. We had talked about it in the locker room, deciding I would switch positions with a different player at each face-off. It worked like a charm several times. Sometimes it didn't, and I got hammered. The confusion this caused resulted in several good plays for our team but angered the other team. They started gunning for me. The good thing that came out of it was that Babe scored twice, eventually tying the game. It brought his recent anger with me down to a slow boil.

When the Cook brothers pulled their now famous and oft-copied drop pass and shoot move that I had used many times now, they scored. The game ended five to four in New York's favor. But we felt pretty good that we caught on to their plans and countered them at every turn. We put a cap on the leak, but we needed to catch up in the next game.

We had two days to come up with a better plan to win. I wondered if the plan should just be to bench me completely and see how they reacted. Then the coach could shift people to the best places before putting me back out there. As people debated strategy, the coach decided we would go back to our regular game. He felt they had tried their new tactic, and it hadn't worked enough for them to keep it up. But he was wrong. It clearly worked. That was the problem. I was worried. About a lot more than game plans.

CHAPTER FIFTY-SEVEN

April 3, 1927

The train to New York was a welcome break from the madness home had become. The list of people that constantly swarmed us was growing. There were newspapermen, radio broadcasters, and fans. The film the major had made was now playing in every theater. Most of the year, we had been left alone to be the team who struggled to break even. Now that we had been given home ice advantage and had done pretty well, the city embraced us. It meant they also wanted to know about us. Each of us. Thankfully, Margret made it into many of the pictures.

Jean-Paul and I sat next to each other on the train as usual. It felt so good to just sit, talk, and be with him. We both thought that Alistaire had been over the top in the role of loving girlfriend.

"Jean-Paul, she practically never let you go for two days before we left."

"What can I say? You jealous?"

"Come on now. Jealous? I know what you like, remember?"

We laughed a lot, even when things weren't that funny. We were making up for the fact that everything was on edge and could turn absolutely horrible at any moment. We had come to believe we had taken all the right precautions, done the right things, and everything would hopefully be fine. Some of the boys plopped down with us.

Everyone was tense now, so no one bothered to ask why a guy looked like something was troubling him. We were all troubled. That made it strangely refreshing not to have to hide. It certainly felt good to let loose with all this anxiety.

"This time they better be double-teaming me! I'm the Babe!" Babe said as he turned around from several seats in front of us. Long seconds passed without anything between all of us except the sound of the railroad ties smacking the wheels, until Dick broke the silence.

"Cecil, you get off your duff and score a couple of goals, and we'll call you the big babe bomber or any old name you want." This brought the train to a roar and the Babe to a red huff.

The train rolled into the station in the middle of the metropolis of New York City once again. Each time we traveled there, you could count on one of the boys gawking at the big buildings and flashing lights from the train windows. No matter where we went, this place always seemed different, powerful, on fire. Some of the guys had been trying to brace everyone for what was to come next. The busing would surely be screwed up accidentally on purpose, and we'd have to walk a mile in the snow. That tactic was tried and true. You always do best what you practice most.

When we headed out of the station with our bags in tow, grunting about the weather and already complaining about the coming screwups, we saw a row of big buses waiting for us. Plastered on the side were signs announcing that they were the property of McLaughlin Coffee. The boys practically rolled onto the streets with laughter.

"It's about damned time someone brought me some coffee," Gordie shouted to much applause. The guys jumped into the buses, and we headed off to the hotel. When we got there, however, the concierge told us he didn't seem to have a reservation on file for our rooms.

"The hell you don't," Mickey shouted.

Cully laughed over the crowd. "Maybe the major has some old coffee sacks for us to use as sleeping bags." The boys seemed to think that was funny. During all the commotion, Dick had stepped up to the front desk. I leaned in to hear what he was saying.

"I understand that you want your town to win tomorrow. I get it. But if your town beats a bunch of punch-drunk, tired, useless men, how much will that trophy really weigh?"

The concierge seemed to think about this for a minute or so. He looked pained by what he was about to do. "I'm sorry," he said. "We do not have enough room." It was a valiant effort, but at that point Babe walked behind the counter.

"Sir, you can't come back—" Babe bumped into him as he twisted behind the man to reach into the wooden cubbies with room numbers on the huge wall behind the counter. He grabbed handfuls of keys, and he started throwing them out to each of us, calling out room numbers. This brought down the house for sure.

When the keys were given out, Babe grabbed a key to the suite. "And if I have to call my friends at the *Times*, I will talk about your rotten, bedbug-infested flophouse until the entire five boroughs refuses to stay here. Clear?" The concierge swallowed once and nodded agreement. It was one of the grandest displays I had ever seen. By the way he'd been treating us all, and mostly me, I would never have expected Babe to do anything for the team.

Living dangerously, I snuck down the hallway and rapped gently on Jean-Paul's door. As often as I bunked with Mickey on road trips, sometimes I was paired up with Cully or Gord. Bob and Percy always shared a room, and sometimes one of us was able to wangle a single room like Jean-Paul always had. With everything going on between Mickey and me, it was lucky I was assigned to room with big Duke, who could fall asleep while skating across the ice. Once he was out cold, I could start my adventure.

Jean-Paul answered before I finished knocking. He pulled me in and started to rip off my clothes in a mad frenzy. All thoughts of whatever I was going to talk about drained away. All that was left was the passionate clawing at each other. Keeping quiet while we were carrying on was a different kind of challenge, one in which we did not always succeed. It was amazing to be able to hold him in the dark, listening to his breathing as he slept, with nothing on my mind but how he felt against me, how he made me feel. There in the night in our shanghaied room, we had a peace that we might not know in a lifetime.

In the locker room, our nerves were exposed and raw. Some of the boys snapped at each other over the smallest things. Jean-Paul could not find his new, clean socks and was tearing through his equipment and the lockers of the guys next to him looking for a pair. When the dam was about to burst, I reached into my bag and retrieved the pair I always kept for him. I tossed them at him, and they hit him in the back of the head. He was so focused on finding socks, he even said thanks when he picked them up and started to put them on.

A fight seemed to be brewing, and maybe that's what the boys needed to let it out. But of all the people in the room you'd count on for leadership at a time like this, Babe Dye stood up in front of his bench, pulled his sweater over his head, and spoke as calm and steady as I'd ever heard him. "Listen up, gentlemen. We are down goals. Tonight, I am going to play the greatest game I have ever played in my entire life. All I need you to do is follow me to the Cup. Just follow me."

You could have heard a proverbial pin drop. He smacked his gloves together, grabbed his stick, and walked out of the room. Many men would have taken that as arrogance, but at that moment, each of the men in that room heard a man promise to do what it took to get us to the championship. We owed it to that man to do the same. Each of us did just that. One at a time, each man slapped his gloves together, grabbed his stick and headed out.

Dick smiled as he passed me. What he had said to Babe about contributing had really struck pay dirt. The old dog knew just how to motivate each of us. As good as he was as a player, and he *was* good, he was wasting his time. He should have been our coach.

Babe took the first face-off. He won it and sent the puck dancing back to Mickey before he dashed across to the left and knocked Bill Cook on his backside on his way by. Mickey slid the puck across to me, and it slapped against my stick with a solid crack. After a few feet of skating forward, I dropped it back to Babe, who came from behind me as fast as a man could skate. The goalie fell on his butt when he leapt backward to stop Babe's shot. He was too slow, letting us score and tying the total goals contest at five.

Babe was as good as his word. He was getting older, but he had moves that I copied, speed that I envied, and brawn that rivaled Percy. Babe crashed through men twice his size, delivering buttery passes across enemies that landed flat and true on our sticks. And when he got the puck close to their net, he scored. He was on fire. With ten minutes to go in the game, we were ahead five to nothing, which meant we were up nine to five overall in the two-games-most-goals contest. Jean-Paul was perfect in the net. His calm, controlled demeanor had returned, and nothing got close to going by him.

All the lead in the world would not allow Babe to break his promise. For the next ten minutes, he was on every inch of the ice surface. He skated harder, faster, and deeper than any man out there. He knocked Frank Boucher down a couple of times before Bill Cook slid over to him and dropped his gloves, signaling him to fight.

They squared up. Babe was not much of a scrapper. Most of us goal-scoring showboat types weren't. Most were afraid to hurt their hands. Some detested the unnecessary violence. But in that minute, Babe turned into a bruiser like Bob or Percy and punched old Bill so many times about the head and face that the referee had to put a stop to it. He went over to them, pulled Babe off, and stood over the sprawling, bloodied New Yorker, directing Babe out of the arena.

Getting ejected was never good. Until that moment. This time, every Chicago player banged their sticks on the ice or against the boards and cages to make an uproarious furor as Babe skated off the ice. He was a man of his word. He had secured us a warm bed last night. Today he had almost single-handedly delivered us a spot in the finals. The crowd booed mercilessly. They wanted their championship. They wanted our blood.

At the edge of the ice, Babe shouted back to us. I couldn't hear exactly what he said, but it sounded a lot like, "You tell him. Tell that man I am coming for his Cup!" Before any of us had time to figure it out, a seat bottom slammed into my side and knocked me down. A fan had ripped up his seat and had thrown it over the cage at me. With thirty seconds left on the clock, the crowd threw so much detritus on the ice that the referees let the last twelve seconds run out as everyone left the ice, letting it fill with debris.

We hit the locker room, grabbed our clothes and gear, and headed straight to the buses. People slapped Babe on the back and thanked him in their own ways as we all headed out of town before we lost our lives. The buses were on, warm, and in gear when we loaded up. Mickey dove across the seats into the laps of some of the guys, comically yelling, "Go, go, go!"

We were still looking over our shoulders with apprehension while waiting for the train to be ready. The boys nervously boarded, settling in for our long ride home. When the train pulled out of the station without any of us getting attacked or anything, we breathed a sigh of relief. That's when the doors between cars slid open, revealing the major pushing a trolley full of champagne in ice buckets. Trailing behind him, his wife Irene stole the show with her ravishing beauty.

"Nothing but the best, boys. Enjoy," Irene said.

"Yes, drink up. Let's go get that trophy!" the major shouted to many cheers and shouts in return.

I eased into the booth next to Jean-Paul and handed him a glass of champagne. I looked around before pulling in close as I dared. "You played the greatest game tonight, baby. A shut out in the playoffs."

He swallowed the entire glass in one swallow. "It was good, was it not, *mon petit*?"

"I don't know what that means," Cully said as he dropped down across the seat so that he was laying across Jean-Paul's lap, "but it was a damned great game tonight, Jean-Paul. A shutout!" He screamed back to the majority of the players, who whooped and hollered. Cully straightened himself out and threw his arm around me. "Now, you need to step it up a little, young man." He almost spit up on himself from laughing so hard before he got up and stumbled away, unable to hold his liquor.

Jean-Paul saw the terror in my eyes and almost imperceptibly shook his head a few times to settle me down. Cully had heard Jean-Paul calling me his pet name. It's only part of a phrase and doesn't even mean anything. He couldn't know what it meant, even if Cully knew French, which I doubted. It literally means "my little." What could he guess from something so small and so disconnected? My little what? He got up, walked down the train, and sat down by himself.

"Have a drink and settle down a little, Brett. But not too much," Jean-Paul said. I didn't relax until Cully slumped over in his seat asleep from the liquor. How could we be so careless?

Several hours later, the train pulled into the Chicago station. Despite the late hour, a crowd had gathered. Most of the boys had drunk themselves to sleep and awoke looking disheveled and lost. Dick got everyone up and told us newspapermen were outside and to keep our drunken mouths shut.

Most of the boys were already afraid of saying the wrong thing. After the nightmare I had caused with my press gaffe, most of them wouldn't even talk to the newspapers. It was a command they could follow for a change. We waved to the crowd of well-wishers and reporters alike. In the jostling crowd, it was easy to lose your footing and stumble into a group of them. When I tripped into one, he bombarded me with a question.

"Boy Bomber, what do you have to say about your next opponent?" My blank stare must have made him think I was drunk, refusing to answer, or that I didn't yet know who we were playing. I was also a little flustered by having my stupid nickname changed from blond bomber to boy bomber. It's a crap nickname already, but he could at least get it right. Focusing on who the next opponent would be was too much right then. I had barely registered that we beat New York. I hadn't really believed we were going to the finals even. He saw the confused look on my face. "What do you have to say to the guys out in Montreal?"

My face had become one from a Greek statue, my fear and horror forever frozen in the timelessness of photos rather than plaster or stone. Montreal had beaten Ottawa. We had to play Bennie, the man that now had every reason to ruin my life.

Our life.

CHAPTER FIFTY-EIGHT

April 7, 1927

Practice had been grueling as we prepared to head into the finals. Everyone was tired. Jean-Paul and I were no different. We had barely been able to talk about the upcoming championship game, Bennie, our relationship, anything. Whenever we were alone, we were consumed mostly with a great sense of foreboding. The silence between us spoke volumes, knowing nothing we could say mattered. We were now on borrowed time. Whatever had prompted Bennie to keep our secret wouldn't stand up under the pressure of the finals.

Being with Jean-Paul was all that mattered now.

The newspapermen had become relentless. After every practice, someone was there begging for a quote, a picture, or our time. Time was the one thing we didn't have much of. I didn't have time to give quotes, either. A swarm of reporters and their accompanying photographers had even set up shop inside the locker room after practice.

We had been hitting the ice three times a day since the last game. We were doing early morning runs, followed by after lunch scrimmages. Then to make it the best day ever, Pete added after-supper trainings. Those were mostly fun drills, like two-on-ones and breakaways. Both were chances to try new moves on our goalies, which I was normally overjoyed at. It would have been fun too, if we weren't so exhausted.

"Blond Bomber, Blond Bomber, come on, Brett, tell us something. What'cha gonna do to those boys from Canada?"

"Come on now, fellas," I jibed. "You know I'm not gonna give you anything printable. We're determined, they're a great team, we are gonna work hard to bring that Cup home to Chicago for the first time." When I was just about to step away from them, Margret spun me around, planted a smacker dead on my lips, and held it there for far too long. Flashes went off, so I closed my eyes for the photos. Margret was laying it on thick.

"Bomber, tell us—"

"Who's the real bombshell?"

"When are you gonna propose?"

"The only jewelry I want from my man is a big silver cup, boys," Margret said. This sent them all into a tizzy. It also secured at least one photo of us on page six. Behind this scene, Jean-Paul had his arm around Alistaire, her squirming in his grasp, not quite as enthralled as Margret was. There's no telling why, since he's such a hunk and such a good kisser. They have history.

The girls jumped on the bus with us before the team pulled away and headed for the train to Montreal for our first two games. The final series was a best-of-three-games series. Most of the boys hated the league's playoff format. Why we had two rounds of total goal games and then ended with having to simply beat the other guys twice was strange. Most of us wanted winners to be based on who won the games, not goals. For instance, if a player has a hot night or a goalie has a bad night, those goals can decide the whole series. Whereas if the same thing happens in a best of three series, a team can shrug off a bad night, win by one goal two times, and win the championship.

We had to say good-bye to the girls at the train. They weren't allowed on it. Some of the wives would be catching another train or driving up to see their men play later. Our girls booked a luxury car to drive them up. As much as Margret liked to drive, she could have taken the Torpedo, but with the snow and ice, especially up in Canada, it was much safer to go by rail.

Margret insisted on going to the games in Montreal so we could all be seen on the town at night. She was still convinced we would be fine if we just stuck to the plan. Truth be told, I wasn't sure I didn't want to get it over with. The suspense was killing me. Jean-Paul was way too eager to pretend he was in love with Alistaire, and knowing for a fact he had made love to her before made it all the more nerve-wracking. Or made me jealous, to tell the truth.

There were no hijinks from the good people of Montreal, Quebec, as there had been in the other cities during the playoffs. It seemed that the finals were treated with a different level of respect and awe. In Canada, they took every hockey game seriously, to the shame of the people back home. Chicagoans had become involved in hockey recently, but nothing like Montreal's fans. It would be nice to see that level of involvement when we got home as well.

CHAPTER FIFTY-NINE

The Forum, somehow home to both of the professional hockey teams from Montreal, could seat ten thousand people. A porter told us as we entered the back door that all the seats had sold out, and they were still selling standing room tickets at the gates to lines of people. That amounted to a lot of people screaming for your heads out on the ice. It motivated me to think up ways of making all those people mad. We wanted that kind of madness in Chicago, but had yet to draw a full house. Hopefully game three at home would be sold out.

"Gentlemen—and I say that with all the sarcasm that I can muster—tonight is the night," Dick said, the boys chuckling at his attempt at humor. "Tonight, most of us Portland folk who traveled all the way to Chicago from the Pacific Northwest, well, we have a chance to finally win that championship. To prove that we are the best. I am not going to top Cecil's speech from the other night. All I want to say to you tonight is that I am proud of what our little team has been able to do.

"We have made Chicago our home. We have made each other family. Win, lose, or draw, we still have that. But that being said, I expect each of you to grab your sticks and dig deep. We have two games to win, two games right here. I don't want to get back on that train having to beat them at home. I want to get on the train with a bunch of drunk and disorderly bums carrying some new hardware. Now, let's do it. Play hard. Be smarter." It wasn't the best speech in the world, but we needed very little. This was the championship of all sports.

Some of us were going back to other jobs during the off season, wondering if we'd ever be hired on to play again. Some were probably done this year. Babe and Dick were getting older. Some of the guys worked construction and others in factories. But you can best believe that if they went back as winners, they'd never have to buy a beer all year. I just wanted to get out of this thing alive.

The crowd drowned out the sounds of even my breathing the second I stepped foot on their ice. They let each of us know with all their hearts that they wanted us to die in horrible ways. Not a single word affected me, though. I always lived to get my feet on the cold slab, and I held tightly to my blade. The game.

I watched for the opponents to make their way to the ice, but found out I had been wasting my time. The second the Maroons' first player's head became visible, the crowd lost their minds. So did I. I was watching for the goalie to come out, for him to look around at our team, for him to make eye contact with me. Would I even be able to start, let alone finish this game?

The big man, Punch Broadbent, skated out onto the ice with a swagger and a pure brutish grin that sent a shiver up my spine. Each time we played them, Punch made sure to cross the ice to smack me as hard as an ice truck. Behind him, Nels, the real threat, zipped past and skated fast circles around their half of the ice. He had scored seventeen goals this year. Just behind him came the man they called the magician, Merlyn Phillips. The man scored a couple less than Nels but spent a whole lot more time outside the penalty box than in. That put him in position to score more often, and I didn't like that. They also had their own version of the Babe, who actually happened to be named Babe for real. He spent much of his game trying to find ways to knock me on my ass as much as our Babe probably wanted to.

Bennie came out last, slowly padded through the slush to his crease, and stood there. He didn't do the slue footing back and forth, the ice packing, or any of the other things goalies did. He just stood there. His head was even down a little, dropping as if he were tired. I made sure to keep facing away from his line of sight as much as I could until the first whistle blew. I caught Jean-Paul giving me the shrugged shoulders once or twice, I guess telling me to relax. There was just no telling as to why nothing had happened to us yet.

The nerves were there at first. Not just about Bennie and what he had the power to start, but about playing. That went away when the puck slapped against my stick. That sound struck a deep nerve way down in my bones. Each player was charged up, shouting at each other to pass, shoot, or skate hard. There was a lot of swearing going on too. Some of it was downright funny to hear. Made-up words or groupings of actual words that shouldn't go together. "Get that puck, you fuckass." "Skate, shitbird." Ridiculous things like that.

"What's going on with this ref? He blind?" I asked Percy after the referee called a penalty on Dick that had struck me as outrageous.

"You can thank the major for that shit," Percy said, leaning forward between pants. "He forgets with all his American flag waving that the league is mostly full of Canadians, including the refs."

"You mean they're cheating?" I asked a little too loudly.

Dick shot a sharp, reproachful look at the pair of us, which had its desired effect on us both.

When I finally got the opportunity to take a one-on-one run at the goalie, I only had a minute left in the first period. The game was tied at zero, both teams trying to work out the kinks. There had already been too many silly mistakes, both sides working through the nerves of playing in such a high-stakes game. I dipped to the left, then skated right to cross the goalmouth and hopefully get the goaltender to move a bit too much. Bennie just stood there. He didn't skate from left to right like every other goalie would have. He didn't twitch or flinch. He just...stood. I popped a wrister at him that he snapped up in his glove with embarrassing efficiency. He had barely moved.

When I skated by him, he exhaled. A puff of whiskey or some sweet, foul-smelling liquor pervaded the air in front of him. He was soused. Worse. He was soused and had just made me look like a junior player. As the referee got set for the next puck drop, I made a beeline to Jean-Paul.

"He's a stone drunk!"

"He's drunk?"

I answered while shaking my head and forming a big smile. "Yes. He's *a* drunk. He doesn't remember me." I was too far for Jean-Paul to say anything else, as I had to zip over to my line before the referee got mad at me for being out of position for a face-off. Tension melted away from me in perceptible waves. Giddy laughter emanated from my chest, even though I tried to stop it.

"What's gotten into you?" Mickey asked, obviously noting my glee. I put a cork in it and went back to what I loved most in the world...hockey. Joy filled my heart, knowing we were all but free and clear now.

For the rest of the game, nothing kept me from going at their goalie full tilt. Nothing other than the body checks from their Babe and Punch, that is. I drop passed to Babe, I slammed shots from Dick, and I deked my way right to Bennie. I even faked him out so well he went down to the ice on both knees and slid away from me. As soon as the biscuit left my stick, I knew he was a beaten man. But at the last possible second, Bennie easily twisted around and flopped over on the puck, leaving the game tied at zero. We had gone through the second ten-minute overtime without scoring a single goal. There were so many close calls, no fan could say they got a boring game just because there was no score. It was evenly met.

The fans booed when the referee, with instructions from the owner's box ferried down to him by a porter, called the game a tie after the fourth scoreless overtime. Our best-of-three series was now a big question mark in everyone's mind. Would we go to four games now? What if we tied again? None of that mattered to me the way it was stressing everyone else. I knew we had a great chance of winning the Cup. And with Jean-Paul throwing me that rakish grin of his, I knew we both felt the same thing. Our troubles with Bennie were over, making me as happy as a clam.

CHAPTER SIXTY

April 9, 1927

"What the hell does that mean?" Babe shouted across the locker room.

"Yeah, who does he think he is?" Cully said.

"I hate to tell you mooks, but he's in charge of the whole league. Whatever Calder says, goes," Pete said.

"I don't understand," Duke said.

Pete explained it again. "He said that since the first game went to overtime and ended in a tie, we can't keep going on like that. They want a winner."

"We're gonna win it," someone shouted out and interrupted him. "They know that." The boys handled their apprehension by engaging in a round of cheering, shouting, and banging on the locker doors.

"Settle down," Dick said, loud at first, growing soft enough at the end that all the guys quieted down to hear him.

Pete shot Dick an unfriendly look. "Anyway, it's now basically like starting over, best of the next three games—"

"Like the last one didn't count?"

"The first team to win two games wins the Cup," Dick finished, ignoring the outburst. "The kicker is that we can only have one overtime period per game. If no one wins after four games, we share the championship."

The tone in the room was frustration mixed with anger. There were grumbles about the league rules, and how the last league the team was in out west would have handled it better. Percy finally broke the tension. "I guess it's simple. We go out there right now and make sure there's a winner." This fired up the team.

Nothing was getting in the way. And when the puck got dropped, flames shot out of my eyes. Dick had a great game. He was getting older and walked a little different than the younger guys, but he skated like a kid.

In the middle of the second-period scoreless stretch none of us were comfortable with, Dick stole the puck away from their top offensive men. He led the team across the blue line into enemy territory. I followed him. We all did. And when he got close to the net, two players blocked him. He barreled his whole body into them, pushing them back, and with his left skate, kicked the puck back out to where I was rushing in behind him.

I caught his kick pass with my stick, lifted the puck off the ground, and sailed it into the net between an obviously drunk Bennie's pads. The net made a gentle whoosh sound as the twine was stretched by the speed of the shot I had taken. I was able to assist Percy with a thirty-footer, but they kept on fighting back until they took the game three goals to two.

They sent us home on the verge of losing the Cup.

CHAPTER SIXTY-ONE

The rhythmic thump-clack of the train was a familiar sound. Unfortunately, being able to hear it usually meant we lost, and there was no joviality on the train to mask the sounds. The sound still comforted me. Margret had taken an early train and was going to meet us at the Coliseum with Alistaire. Jean-Paul told her that we didn't need to worry about being exposed anymore, since the man who knew our secret had been so soused he couldn't even remember us. She insisted on being there anyway.

It was a good thing since Jean-Paul was taking the loss pretty hard. Even when I slid in next to him in his booth and touched his knee under the table, he didn't seem to relax at all. He didn't pull away from me, which let me believe that being with him was helping. But he was in a state.

He stared out the window and didn't register when I spoke at first. "It was a tough game, Jean-Paul. They were crowding the net, and we should have done more to shake them off of you. It wasn't your fault. Next game'll be better, I promise." I wasn't sure why I was promising. I really couldn't do anything but score as much as possible. I tried to do that every night. What more could I do?

"Not my fault? Ah, *mon dieu*. It is…I tell you now, *mon petit*." He turned so he was facing the rest of the team and continued, much louder. "I will not let another goal in for those bastards. This whole thing has been…trying. I am done. No more." I had never seen him so public with his emotions. It wasn't a rally cry or a heartfelt speech, but it was better. It was something the team needed at just the right time.

The train came alive. The men got out of their seats and came to our booth and slapped Jean-Paul on the back, or started exchanging strategy with one another. Babe came over and slapped me on the shoulder. I was astounded by it. We had no idea before that moment how much influence Jean-Paul had on this team. The sense of power and responsibility resting on the shoulders of a goaltender is enormous. The entire game, for better or worse, could be decided by whether he is having a good or bad day.

Back at the Coliseum, Margret and Alistaire waited among the late-night news crowd, who were anxious for a statement. Not one of the boys stopped to talk to them. Not even Pete. We silently walked to our cars. Some had wives waiting for them, some had parents giving them rides, some left with each other. Let them write what they wanted. Margret gave them a kiss photo if that was what they wanted, but it was quick and nowhere near as passionate as the others we'd been giving them.

"Where are you going?" Jean-Paul asked from over the aisle. When we reached the automobiles, I started to walk to the Torpedo with Margret. "Aren't you coming with me?" Over the hood of his Imperial, his blue eyes sparkled against the backdrop of snow-covered crates and fences. He batted his dark eyelashes with each blink, looking like an expectant puppy. I almost ran over and hugged him in front of everybody. Instead, I locked the door of the Bugatti back up, and all four of us climbed in with Jean-Paul. Our little group drove away together.

After we dropped the girls off, we went back to his house on the north side. It had been several days since anyone had been in there, so it was cold as a tomb. We did our best to warm it up, Jean-Paul's eyes on mine, our fingers locked, as he slowly thrust himself inside me until we exhausted ourselves. After we made love, Jean-Paul held me close until he fell asleep. His heartbeat was invigorating, the strong and steady thump-thump lying there under his warm skin, filling my heart with love. The stress of the last few weeks drained away with each beat. This was how it was always supposed to be.

CHAPTER SIXTY-TWO

April 11, 1927

Chicago came alive in the madness of the championship series taking place in the giant Coliseum on the near south side. Last year had started without a major hockey team, followed by months of apathy regardless of wins and losses. Now that we were at the precipice of victory, the city's royalty all came out to play.

In the stands, the grandest and richest of the city were in attendance in all of their glorious, outlandish clothes. The entire Field family attended in force. Margret sat with Marsh in one of the bigwigs boxes. The Allertons, Robert and his lover J.W., were in the box next to the Fields. It was a tad nerve-wracking to have friends who knew my deepest, darkest secrets so close to the owners of the Coliseum, the major, and his wife. At any moment, that spiteful J.W. could slip out some damaging bit of information about us, but Margret was there to make sure that didn't happen.

A haggard-looking Mayor Dever was also in the box. Several gruff-looking men in dark suits surrounded him. They were not looking toward the ice at all. They were busy surveying the crowd for possible danger to the mayor. The papers said he had been targeted by the mobs because of his harsh anti-liquor law enforcement policies. Some pressure helped the mob out, forcing people to go to the speakeasies they owned to buy their booze, but too much pressure cost them money. The mayor was smart to have security there.

About forty feet away from him, sitting in the front two rows, Al Capone and his henchmen staked out their area. It was awful close to Margret. If gunfire did erupt, she would be caught right in the crossfire. Those thoughts swirled in my head, but I pushed them down so I could focus on the game. If trouble did break out, what good would I be from down on the ice anyway?

Doing the warm-up skate before the game gave me time to size up the crowd as well as shake away any nerves. I was about to play in the biggest do-or-die game in my admittedly short career. Winning the championship in the big time in your first year was unheard of. Jean-Paul had told me it might even be a curse to win so big so soon. He thought it could mean spending the rest of your life trying to get something you've already won, maybe fruitlessly. That made some sense, but was one of the many harmful thoughts I needed to skate out of my brain.

Jean-Paul took his spot in the net, conserving his energy. His face was set with a powerful look of determination. For those of us that knew him, he looked happy to get the chance to live out his promise not to let in a single goal. I was determined to do my best to make that happen for him. For us. I knew he knew that.

On the other end of the ice, Bennie stood still as always. He didn't rememeber what happened, but I worried about him, boozehound or not. Both teams had a bundle of nerves to work through at the start of the game. We were all rushing in sticks first and mostly ended up taking wild shots or making bad passes. But not Jean-Paul. Every time their Babe, Nels, or the magician got close, Jean-Paul practically stood on his head and stonewalled them.

In the locker room after the first period, Jean-Paul was off in the corner fiddling with his pads, which were sopping wet. I had gotten up and taken a step toward him when Percy put his hand on my chest from his bench. "Let him alone, kid. He's playing the best game of his life." I had only wanted to cheer him on, to tell him how proud I was. But Percy was right, so I left him alone.

The second period proved to be the real start of the game. We all settled down into our roles and started getting real chances. So did they. Dick passed the puck across the ice to our Babe and was intercepted by Merlyn, who took it straight across the blue line. It didn't take long before his team had crossed over as well. Merlyn spun around Bob and ducked under one of Percy's big boy, crunching checks, tripping him and sending Percy to the floor.

I couldn't let him close to Jean-Paul. There was no way I was letting anyone ruin his promise to the team if it could be helped. Right in front of the goalmouth, I threw my body down toward the puck, hoping to smother it up underneath me. Merlyn saw it coming and flipped the puck up toward Jean-Paul's stick side high. Twisting myself to slide on my back, I caught sight of Jean-Paul's lightning-fast reaction. The puck popped off his goalie stick and back toward the front of the net where I was sliding. Over my shoulder, I saw Punch barreling at me with his stick in mid-swing. He was going to take my head off as he took his rebound shot at the net.

Going hand over hand, I slid my stick up my sprawling body and slapped at the puck as it crossed over my head. I made contact with the edge of the rubber and sent it flying safely into one of the corners, away from our goal. Ice chips from the puck broke off and landed right in my eye. I became less than useless out there, making a blind stab at getting back to the bench so someone could replace me.

While I sat on the bench with a trainer holding a towel over my right eye, Mickey knocked one past a staggered Bennie in their goal, breaking the tie. The boys on the bench were alive with talk of the other goalie, who might be a little drunk. We all knew he was one of the best in the game; we just didn't know he was able to do it while embalmed. We all hoped a few hours without booze might give us the upper hand. During the last game, that was not true. He got stronger as the night went on, but we were clinging to hope.

Tonight, it was true. Although I was too busy spending my time on our end of the ice, sliding in front of shots meant for Jean-Paul, throwing my body into players as they tried to cross the blue line, Bennie was getting knocked around by our Babe, Mickey, and Cully.

With a minute to go, the game was all but decided. Five to zero was impossible for them to come back from in under a minute. Dick instructed all of us to play heavy defense and get Jean-Paul the shutout, without actually saying those words. All hockey players know better than to jinx a goalie that way. We were also gearing up for the fight that was about to break out. When a big game like this one gets lopsided, the bruisers on the other team, like Punch, Nels, and their Babe, were sure to be looking for a little payback blood. It sent a message for the next game.

Bennie seemed to have sobered up some and was making some good saves. Here in the last minute, after being given instructions to protect Jean-Paul and to do nothing to provoke a fight, I stole the puck and made a beeline for their goal, for as much a I could see it with my eye blurry. Sometimes my own drive to be the best takes over the part of my brain that thinks.

I evaded the big checks, and my team formed up with me, although they were shouting at me to fall back. Avoiding a closed gloved fist from Punch of all people, I made my way right across the goalmouth. I pulled my stick back a few inches to take the swing and held there in the anticipation that Bennie would make his move to stop me. Like most of his kind, he took it, moving to the left. He had proved he was too good to fool with a shot back across him to the right. I went with the grain and flipped the puck at his left side.

He might have willed the puck to blow up in midair or caught it in his teeth for all I knew, as Punch had caught up with me and knocked me down to the ice into the netting. My body knocked Bennie off his feet, and he collapsed on top of me. I wriggled and jerked to try to shake the man and his waterlogged pads off me to no avail. Punch grabbed my legs and tried to pull me out of the net, but Bennie's full weight held me down. The referee had blown his whistle.

"No goal."

The horn went off, signaling the end of the game. Still Bennie held me under him, looking me dead in the face for the first time. His eyes, which earlier had been glassed over with drink or remnants of drinks past, were now awake and aware.

"I know you. Wait, you're one of those—"

I struggled harder to get away.

"Oh my God! You're—" He was thankfully interrupted by Punch pulling me out from underneath him to smack me repeatedly in the face and head with his gloved fists. A full-scale brawl had broken out around the goal. Their team wanted to protect their goaltender, mine to protect the foolish boy who took an unneeded and foolish shot.

Run! My mind screamed louder than the game horn could blow. It screamed at me to get away far louder than the thousands of jubilant hometown fans. I got pounded by several fists before I made it to the bench. Behind me my teammates were fighting my fight. I didn't care. I needed out of there.

CHAPTER SIXTY-THREE

A while later, Jean-Paul found me in the shower room, leaning against the back wall with the water running over me, counting the drops of moisture on the walls. My skin had pruned, and all of the hot water had been used up some time ago. I didn't care about the cold. My mind was far away from that place anyway. It had wandered away as the sound of each joyful player packed up and left the locker room to go celebrate our victory. It left me out on the ice, laid flat inside the opposing goal.

"*Mon petit*, you must be frozen!" Jean-Paul reached up and turned off the faucet, which left me naked and cold. I slid down, miserable on the tile floor. He picked me up off the tiles, and I fell limp into him, letting him do it. He dried me off and dressed me in street clothes. "There now, relax. It'll be all right."

My body calmed down despite the fact that my life was now over. His touch soothed the damaged beast within. He finally got me to a place where I could speak, at least enough to answer him. I could only get out one thing.

"He remembers."

That was really all that he needed to hear. He knew what this meant for us, for him. He rubbed my back to keep me calm as we walked down the empty corridor toward the cars. By now the party had moved out of the building. The newspapermen and photographers had given up wondering about where we were and left. As far as they knew, we had slipped out a different exit.

"Where are you ladies going so fast?" someone said from out of the shadows. Immediately I knew who it was.

Jean-Paul quickly slipped his arm off of my back. "Wh-what do you want?" He was uncharacteristically shaken.

Bennie stepped out of the shadows and let us see his full face. He wasn't the angry, disgusted drunk he had been that night not so long ago on the street. Now he was clear-eyed and calm.

"Oh, I am sure that you both know what I want."

"Please." The word came out of my mouth before I knew what I was saying.

"Don't. Don't you dare think that you can ask me for anything." My plea seemed to enrage Bennie beyond words for a second. "You both make me sick to my stomach."

Jean-Paul rushed forward with me in tow, pushing Bennie against the corridor wall. The three of us stood there, two bodies taut in expectation of a fight, mine limp and beaten.

Bennie calmed down quickly, much quicker than Jean-Paul, whose chest heaved so hard that all three of us moved back and forth with the weight of it.

"Whenever you're done with this bullshit, step back and get your faggot hands off me."

There it was, without a doubt. We were done for.

"What is it you want?"

Bennie straightened up his suit and took his time before answering. "You two...boys...have a decision to make." I held my breath. "The both of you need to have the worst games of your lives two days from now, or I'm going to ruin you. Ruin!"

My mind reeled. He wasn't going to tell people? He wanted us to do what? Did he say we had to throw the game? Jean-Paul took a deep breath. "You must be crazy, *mon ami*. Who is going to believe you, a fall-down drunk?"

"You don't think people already know about you, Jean-Paul?" Bennie said, not rattled. "It took me all of five minutes tonight to find out that a lot of guys think you are a bit light in the loafers. And that spicy redhead you've been clinging to." He looked at me. "Everyone knows that she was with Jean-Paul, and now she's with you and you all go out together. That ain't normal, and it ain't real. So yes, they are going to believe it, since it's true. And shame on you, Jean-Paul. It isn't enough to be a degenerate, but with a child at that? How old are you, anyway?"

"I'm eighteen, you asshole!" I interjected, getting angry. I lunged at him, but Jean-Paul held me back with one arm.

Bennie was all smirk and judgment. "Tonight is a night of revelation for all of us. You know, right after the game, the coach came over to me and told me I'd better not be drinking before the next game. You wanna know what I told him?" He paused for the longest time. "I told him that I've never been more sober in my life."

Bennie sauntered down the corridor away from us. I had been shaking from head to toe in rage, fear and anticipation throughout the entire conversation. As he was walking away, my knees gave in to the pressure, and I crumpled into Jean-Paul again, in shock. Before turning out of sight, Bennie added his requirements in case we missed the point. "Throw the game. Throw it as far as you can."

CHAPTER SIXTY-FOUR

April 12, 1927

The morning light beamed through the curtains of Jean-Paul's bedroom, blinding me as I awoke the next morning. I didn't remember going to Jean-Paul's house or getting into bed. I didn't cry all night worrying about my future in hockey. I wasn't upset about the idea that our own teammates might do us harm. Those things certainly caused me grief. But something else jumped to the top of my heaping pile of problems.

I was not going to win the Cup. Not this year. Maybe never.

Who was to say Bennie would keep his word if I threw the game? He thought we were below human. Why would he allow us to continue, playing against him as soon as next fall? Would he tell people about us no matter what?

Jean-Paul was dressed and ready to take us to practice at the Coliseum. I dreaded going back to that building, to all those potential threats, but we had to go prepare for the biggest game of our lives. Whoever won the next game won the championship. We got in the car, he drove us to work, and we got out on the ice, all without doing more than holding each other's hands for a moment during the ride in. We had not spoken about whether or not he was going to give in to Bennie.

Was I? Was there really a choice for either of us?

Coach rode us pretty hard that morning, me in particular. "Are you tired, son? Is that it? If you don't really want to play, let me know and you can relax for a while with a nice soda. On the bench! Now get your ass out there and play!" He apparently noticed I was dragging.

"What are you doing out there?" Jean-Paul asked me when I skated near him.

"What do you mean?"

"You are not seriously throwing the game."

"What?" Other players skated by, ending our conversation.

Dick yelled as we left the last practice of the day. The whole team had caught what was in my head, but they would shake it off. For me, it was deeper than that. I was about to lose the most important things in my life. *If I do what I have trained, lived, and breathed for all my life, I lose the man that makes me feel more alive than all the hockey in the world. And if I choose him and win...*

"We need to talk." Jean-Paul looked more serious than he ever had before. He was frying bacon over his stove while we sat in his house after the day of practice. I knew we were going to have to talk today. We needed to make a plan about the game and what we were going to do. How did you even throw a game?

"Jean-Paul—"

Ding-dong. Someone at the door halted our conversation. Jean-Paul motioned at the skillet as an excuse for not going to see who was there, so I answered the door. Margret, dressed in red with her beau, William, in tow, was not in a good mood. But William's face showed he was happy to be with her doing whatever it was she was doing.

When everyone had settled into chairs in the kitchen, Jean-Paul destroyed the uncomfortable pall that had been growing. "It did not work, eh?"

"What didn't work?" I asked, swiveling my head between them, even looking at William for some information.

"Jean-Paul, I told you to tell him." Margret sighed as she sipped from the coffee we had been chugging for the last half hour before she showed up. When he said nothing, Margret filled me in on their secret plan. "I went to this man, Bennie, and I offered him money."

"How much money, Margret?" I asked with a little too much bitterness dripping from my tongue. The whole thing had left a terrible acid in my throat.

"Too much for him to pass up on, I thought."

"He did, though, right? Of course he passed on the money. That's how my life works. And what is wrong with the two of you? Why didn't you tell me what you were up to?"

Jean-Paul turned from the stove for the first time. "It was my idea. I wanted to be able to tell you tonight that it was all over with."

"But it isn't all over with." He looked so passionate and sincere in his desire to make me feel better, but the emotions of the moment had become too much to handle. "And now because of my stupid, drunken…how goddamned stupid was I to think I could kiss you out on the street? Why didn't you stop me?" I shouted directly at him. I regretted it the moment the words came out. Jean-Paul's face twisted with pain. My face dropped in sadness.

"Baby, I'm sorry. I didn't mean it," I offered. Out of the corner of my eye, I saw William tense and wince a little when I called Jean-Paul baby. I wanted to turn my anger at William.

"What are you guys going to do tomorrow? That's the real issue," William said.

We each stated our opinions again until we circled back on ourselves before I noticed Margret was crying.

"Margret?"

"Darling, why are you crying?" Jean-Paul asked.

William stood up and placed his hand on Margret's shoulder. "Do you even know what she is doing right now?"

We all looked at Margret in her bright, beautiful red dress and shoes. She looked amazing. But behind her eyes was a pain and sadness we had been too self-absorbed to notice. We still sat there in silence looking at her, wondering what William had meant.

"What is it, Margret?" I asked sympathetically.

"Oh, Margret," Jean-Paul whispered. "James. You haven't stepped foot in this house since he died and I moved into it. You said you'd never come back here."

"This is more important than that," she said.

Jean-Paul pulled her up from the chair and held her tight against his chest in a heartfelt hug. "No, *mon cher*, it is not."

"Margret, I am so sorry," I said, the words barely a whisper falling across my lips. How did I not know this and William did? He had been with her such a short time and knew all of this information about us. He had accepted who we were, more or less. At least he was here with us instead of trying to scam his own money from her. While Jean-Paul had Margret in his arms, I laid a hand on William's forearm.

"Thank you."

Margret, after accepting a moment of love, moved us all on to the business at hand. "Now what do you do?"

"Throw the game," I said.

Jean-Paul slowly and deliberately raised his head from Margret's shoulder to glare at me. "What?"

"What? There is no choice here. We go out there and throw the game so that—"

"So that the two of you can be together, Jean-Paul," Margret said, finishing my thought.

"It seems the only reasonable thing to do now," William added. "Besides, it's just a game." This comment was met with looks of death from Jean-Paul and me. He shrank back in his chair, recoiling as if he had been punched in the head.

"Jean-Paul—"

"I just can't let you give up on your dream. This is so important to you."

"How can we even be talking about this? What other option do we really have?"

The four of us took up space in the kitchen listening to Jean-Paul's bacon sizzling in the frying pan. Margret got up and took the pan from the stove and served everyone pieces of burnt bacon along with some toast and more coffee. "You know this is breakfast food, right?"

"We need to keep the weight up since practices have been intense," I informed her. Talking about hockey and what we did for the game took my mind off the crisis at hand for about one minute, and then I was back to it.

"So walking away isn't an option?" Margret asked.

I ignored her.

"If we win he will tell everyone, the coach, our friends, maybe the newspapers. Those bastards hawk around begging for a story. That'd be it. We might be killed in the locker room before we even have to answer one question. If not, we surely would be kicked off the team, chased out of the game, and then tracked down and killed. If we throw the game, Jean-Paul, it is our secret again," I pleaded.

"And then he tells everyone anyway. Tomorrow, next season, whenever he gets drunk enough. And what does this tell about us? That we throw this important, once-in-a-lifetime game, for what?"

"For our lives. My life is with you. I can't have that if we win the game."

"If I go out there and lay down for this man, it means that I fear him more than I…" He dropped his head down and stopped talking.

"More than you what?" I asked.

"Love you," Margret said to me for him. "Jean-Paul, you think that if you win, you will be showing Brett that you love him? I hate to say this to you, honey, but he already knows."

"Maybe he is right," I agreed halfheartedly.

"What do you really want, Brett?" Jean-Paul asked me.

"You."

"Well, you can't just have me. We have to live in the real world. We can't be together. Not in the way that you want."

"I would do almost anything to make our time together last, to hold on to this forever. But I love you too much to be so self-serving. I want you to be around a long time. But if you decide you foolishly need to destroy our lives for it, then by all means, go out there and win. I can't throw the game by myself, but you can. I don't want to lose you to this, Jean-Paul."

Jean-Paul put his hand on mine and walked me to the living room. He sat me down on the couch. "I hope you understand what I am saying, what we are all saying."

"I understand completely."

"I don't know that you do," he said.

"All I need to know is that I love you with all of my heart, and nothing, no one can take that away." Tears welled up in the edges of my eyelids and started to trickle over the edges, threatening to drop down my face. "I think we should run away together. I don't care anymore. I just want to be with you forever."

"This is not like running away to the circus like a child, *mon petit*. This is something completely different. Playing hockey isn't just what you and I do. It is who we are. The way you can play is special. We can't just leave it. I do not pretend to be an expert on this, but love does not mean being a coward to a bully, and it certainly doesn't mean letting the person you love ruin his life for you."

"Love means doing anything on this earth to make that person happy, to protect them, no matter what you need to sacrifice to make it happen."

Jean-Paul leaned forward and kissed me full on the lips for the longest time. I felt my watery face brush up against his and leave it wet. When we had finished kissing, he stood up. "We should get some rest tonight for the big game tomorrow. Margret, would you and William be so kind as to please take Brett home so we can all get some rest? We can think more clearly on it in the morning. The game is not for many hours yet."

Margret and William drove me home in his Ford, and we meandered our way through the desolate streets. The weather had not broken from the grip of winter. The season had been relatively mild, but cold still clung to the buildings and roads like lovers embracing before departing for a long trip. Even in the unbearable heat of summer, Chicagoans knew it was only a matter of time.

"Help me here. I don't understand his reasoning. Why won't he just throw the damned game?" I begged for an answer.

"What I don't get is how you have done what you've done," Margret said.

"What do you mean?"

"Jean-Paul has never believed in love. Never even said the word as far as I know. Not that I'm a prime example of that myself," she said as she slipped her hand across the seats to place it in William's.

I knew what she said was true. I spent the entire season doing everything in my power, even going so far as to manipulate and practically stalk him so he would see me the same way I saw him. His bravado and lifestyle wasn't who he really was. When I met him, he didn't believe people like us were even capable or deserved love. We were meant to burn bright and die young.

"I don't know if I've done anything. He is a few hours away from ruining my life," I said, knowing full well how I sounded.

"Oh, honey. You are so young. I'm sorry. I don't mean to sound condescending. I just mean to say that you just don't understand."

We sat in silence for the rest of the ride. They dropped me off at Moira's. Before I opened the front door, I wondered if she had given away my room by now. I hadn't spent the night here in some time. I gathered my things, which by now amounted to a lot more than I had brought with me. I had acquired clothes mostly, and hats, and a few small knickknacks. I gathered them together so I could put them all in the Torpedo in the morning on the way to practice, in case tonight was my last night in Chicago.

CHAPTER SIXTY-FIVE

April 13, 1927

The locker room was a mass of bodies dressing and taping sticks, but not talking. Nerves were high. Each player knew the importance of the game. Most players could and would live their entire lives without winning the championship. Being here was a gift. An amazing gift. They were all quietly preparing, going over strategies and practicing their moves in their heads while we waited for the go ahead to take the ice. Little did they know what was about to happen.

One of us could betray everything the team had fought so hard to achieve. Either Jean-Paul or I could make sure we didn't win. Last night, I was absolutely sure it would be me. I was ready and willing to throw the game in order to be able to be with Jean-Paul forever. I didn't have any idea where his head was at before the game because we didn't share more than a few pained looks across the room.

Last night he had gone batty with the idea that he was going to win the game for us. Today, I didn't know. I was sure after some time away from me, he'd wake up and change. But now that I'd had some time away from him, I wasn't sure what I thought either. What would it mean if I let them win today? Was this worth dying for?

"All right, boys." Dick had stood up and commanded our attention. "Tonight is the night. Your entire life in one game. Ain't it exciting?" The boys cheered and banged the lockers with their sticks. "We've been through a lot together. We've fought. We've lost together, and we've won together. We're a family now. And I'm depending on my family to go out there tonight and scrape the ice, taste the blood, and lay everything on the line for each other. That's what family does. Now lets bring that dented silver trophy home to Chicago!"

The noise in the locker room grew to a deafening level. My blood started to boil under the heat of his moving speech. We had become like a family. Mickey had blossomed with his new friends, and Bob and Percy had become two overprotective brothers to me. They didn't even realize that having them in my life filled a crevice I had forgotten existed, but they had done it. And Dick, our leader, our captain, had been the father I never wanted but never knew I needed.

How could I go out there and utterly destroy them? I started shaking from my knees up through my waist and couldn't get it under control. The thought of getting into the game, my usual solace, was now the source of everything that was wrong in the world. I couldn't do it.

Jean-Paul was the last to leave the locker room as always. Since I was frozen in fear, I was there when he reached the door. His eyes were red and swollen, as if he'd been crying. But in a year he had cried exactly one time. He just didn't. He was too strong.

"I don't know what I'm going to do anymore," I exclaimed to him under my breath in a forced whisper, all my nerves tingling on their ends.

He looked at me, if only for a few seconds or so. "Oh, *mon petit garcon amoureux*," he whispered back to me, "I do not know what I am going to do anymore." And then he tried to walk past me, but I reached out and grabbed his arm.

"Wait, what do you mean? What should I do?" I begged him for guidance.

He just stared into my eyes, searching for the answer. "I don't know."

CHAPTER SIXTY-SIX

B ennie kept glaring at me while I skated circles on our half of the ice during warm-up. I tried my best to look away, to look anywhere else, but his presence drew me, out of fear and loathing. I detested that man and the way he had put me in this position, in this place. And most of all, I hated myself for my dalliance that night in Montreal, kissing Jean-Paul on the street like a schoolboy unable to control his emotions. He nodded to me, but I did not nod back. What would I be nodding for?

The referee skated to center ice and blew his whistle. We all crowded around in our usual formations, and he let it tumble to the ice. Dick swatted at it but Nels, their star center man, pulled it back to his team so they could begin their charge up the ice. Instincts took over. I had stolen the puck before I could think about what I was going to do with it.

Fortunately for me, Punch knocked me off my skates before I even got to the red centerline, so I didn't have to make a decision. But sooner or later, probably sooner, I would have to make one.

It took all of two minutes before Montreal had capitalized on a breakdown of our defense and taken a wild shot on Jean-Paul's goal. He easily swatted it away to the corners. Was that his decision or was the shot too easy and too obvious for him to let it go in? His face had set into the usual determined look. Mine must have looked like a jumble of raw confusion.

"What's wrong, kid? Get your head in the game now," Percy encouraged as we skated behind the puck that Babe carried up the ice.

"I'm fine," I said stiffly, wondering what Percy would say if he found out about us tonight, and I skated away from him.

I hadn't made a conscious choice yet, but my body, alive with instincts, continued to send the puck to my teammates to make the big plays. But Bennie was on fire. When I skated by him in goalmouth traffic, he didn't smell like a distillery anymore. He looked determined. It scared me. Late in the second, Dick passed the puck to me, and I had my first good chance. I skated up the middle, leaned into it, and flipped the rubber into a tiny hole on the right side that looked open. I didn't think. I didn't worry. Instincts drove me forward. Quicker than before, Bennie snatched my goal away. It had gone on like this for two scoreless periods. Something had to change.

In the end of the third period, we were still tied at zero when the horn blew. Once again we were going into overtime in the final series. If we tied this game, Calder had said there would be no fifth game. We would share the championship. Bennie surely would not let that slide.

Babe blasted up the ice just a few seconds after the overtime period began. He was determined to score quickly and get this season over with. Dick and I raced up the ice with him like we always did. Babe passed it to Dick, who quickly passed it back to Babe, ignoring me. They knew I wasn't firing on all cylinders and must have talked about it during the break. I was surprised I was still out on the ice at all.

Babe passed the puck back to Dick and broke for the goal. I raced just as hard. When Dick threw the puck off his stick toward the center mass of players where Babe and I were waiting, I reached out my stick for it. The puck bounced up, and in an awkward attempt to corral it, I ended up tripping myself forward into Babe's back. My stick knocked the puck clear of the goal, and my body sent Babe sprawling harmlessly away.

"That's more like it," Bennie said under his breath as I got up and collected myself.

"What? I didn't…"

"Bennet. Here. Now!" yelled a red-faced Coach Muldoon.

When I reached the bench, he started yelling at me. "What on God's green earth was that shit? Sit down. You're done. I don't know what the hell's wrong with you—"

"You stupid son of a bitch." Before he could finish his tirade, Babe had slid up behind me and punched me hard in the back. "What the hell were you thinking? Are you trying to lose this game?"

My throat tightened around the anger there. I wasn't trying to lose. I had done nothing but try all game and nothing had gone… *There it is.* I was too busy thinking while having a rotten game. I need to stop thinking.

I needed back in the game.

When I looked up, Punch and Merlyn were putting on a passing and spinning clinic, giving our guys a run for their money. I knew that if I was out there, I could have anticipated the spins and stripped them of the puck, but I was on the bench, maybe for good. The sound of the wood against the frozen rubber cracked across the stadium on their way to our net. It was the only thing anyone could hear in the vacuum of the Coliseum.

All six thousand plus fans, Margret and her family, the mayor, Big Al, the usual elite, all stood on their feet collectively in hopes that they somehow could help Jean-Paul fend off the attack. I should be out there.

Merlyn slipped the rubber between his own legs and caused Jean-Paul to overcommit to the right. Punch waited on the left for the pass that didn't come. Merlyn took his shot at getting the puck by Jean-Paul's right side. He whacked the puck at the net. Jean-Paul swatted it down with his glove hand. The puck bounced, and Merlyn went down to one knee to get his own rebound.

The tip of his stick caught the edge of the puck and sent it spinning just out of Jean-Paul's reach. He threw himself sideways onto the ice, which sent his legs in front of the oncoming shot to block it. The force of Jean-Paul's padded legs smacking into it sent the puck out toward the spot on the ice in front of the net that Punch had claimed as his own. Punch slapped his stick on the ice and scraped a shower of snow and ice into the air, along with the biscuit that was tumbling end over end toward our net.

Jean-Paul, who was now on his side on the ice, pushed his body in a circle, bringing his legs into the air. He hit the puck square with his legs high above his body before they both flopped back down to the ice. The black disc seemed to hover in the air for an eternity until gravity took control and dropped it straight down into Jean-Paul's waiting glove, just outside the line. My heart for him swelled to bursting. Our team had finally caught up and leveled Punch and Merlyn.

The referee made the motion for "no goal," but it was unnecessary because the roar and thunder from the capacity crowd let everyone all the way in Montreal know that our goalie had saved this game. The whistle blew and the referee waved, but the crowd continued to stomp their feet, clap and cheer. I thought I had seen Jean-Paul perform the greatest saves in the history of the game, but now, in the final contest of the biggest championship in sports, I had finally seen the true beauty of the game. Of him.

I leapt over the bench to the ice, Muldoon screaming at me from behind. I had to win this for him, for us. Dick waved him back, smiling. "Let's do this, kid."

Dick won the face-off and dropped the puck back to me. I slipped past the first defender, the second, and Percy smashed their forward into the boards and out of my path. Mickey was slapping the ice with his stick, calling for the pass. Right then, I saw it. A tiny movement of Bennie's jaw. His eyes bored a hole into me full of threat and malice. Maybe he thought I would pass, too afraid of the consequences to take the shot myself, or miss on purpose like he wanted. After Jean-Paul's declaration a moment ago, he was wrong. Dead wrong.

Two more strides, and I turned my head to Mickey as my stick swung over the puck, pretending I was passing. Bennie bit and started to move, maybe realizing I would not lie down. It didn't matter. He wouldn't avoid this. My head swung back and I locked eyes with Bennie, daring him to stop me, daring him to try. With all the chasing and dreaming of love, this man, this drunk, would not take from me one more second, and now he knew it. He became small in the net. I chopped the biscuit back and forth so quickly it became a blur, reached back, and snapped the puck toward the net.

The crowd drowned out Bennie's gasp of disbelief as he fell to the ice. They were on their feet, streamers in the air, the band's song accompanying the chanting in a crescendo of joy. My team swooped me away in their arms leaving defeat and hate in their goalie's eyes.

CHAPTER SIXTY-SEVEN

The locker room exploded in joyous celebration. The shiny, wobbly championship trophy was placed on a small table, its bowl filled with champagne the players took turns lapping up like crazed hounds. Every hug and slap on the backside drove home the point that soon, Bennie was going to ruin our lives for good. I should have been delirious with joy, drinking from the Stanley Cup. But instead I was wracked with fear.

With each passing moment, with every new person invading our locker room to join the party, my mind started spinning and driving me to once again lose myself in meaningless counting. In this madness, that would have been an easy out and a welcome distraction, but it was not to be.

The door burst open once again, but this time, standing in the doorway, covered in sweat, wearing the maroon and white of the opponents we had just laid low, was Bennie. His face was contorted in crazed rage as he wobbled across the room as fast as his pads would let him move when off the ice.

"What the Sam Hill are you doing in here?" someone shouted.

The boys circled up around Bennie just as Jean-Paul appeared from behind a steam pipe and clobbered him across the face with a wild haymaker. Bennie fell back against Percy, who pushed him violently back toward the circle of angry, half-drunken men. It occurred to me that Bennie might be the one to not make it out of this room alive.

"Quiet!" Dick raised both hands and stopped any further attack. "You better tell us what you're doing in here, right now. Speak!"

The blood pooled under his chin from the cut that Jean-Paul's haymaker had opened up on him. It dripped down and landed on the floor around our feet, making a pattern that looked like a crimson question mark.

Bennie spit some blood out on the floor. He grinned and showed his red-stained teeth. "I just wondered if you all knew that you had two sick, degenerate faggots in your midst."

Jean-Paul lunged forward again to strike, but Cully held him back on Dick's orders. The crowd had grown uneasy after Bennie's accusations.

When I looked at Mickey, his chest heaving under the stress of this horrible moment, I saw a lifetime of worry in his eyes. If he could speak to me through the din of the room, what would he say? Would he tell me that he warned me? Would he tell me how he is sickened? I wanted them, needed them to be on my side, after all this time.

"I know you're mad as a man can be right now, but that doesn't give you the—"

Bennie interrupted Dick by pointing at Jean-Paul. "No, you had no idea that you had this fairy among you all this time. But I've seen him doing disgusting things. With him." He shifted to point directly at me.

"You goddamned liar!" Mickey roared, leaping forward to strike Bennie down. He had chosen to be my brother after all. His arms held back, as powerful and dangerous as the rushing tide, he changed nothing.

Dick told the boys to kick Bennie out of the locker room, but some of the boys paused, looking from Jean-Paul to me. Dick finally judged the situation to be bigger than he could handle by just removing Bennie. "Fine. Stop. Bennie, I've known you for several years, and I've never known you to be a liar before. But you better have some proof."

Bennie laughed. "I don't need any. Ask them yourself."

Dick eyed us up and down. "What do you have to say to this, Jean-Paul?"

Jean-Paul shook Cully off and stood up straight. He looked to me first before he said anything. "My life is mine to live, and this sorry bastard has no right to ask me to answer for it one way or the other." He looked at Bennie. "You're a sore loser."

The men in the room were audibly confused by his answer. He hadn't denied it. He didn't admit to it, either, but in his own way he had admitted to it without doing as much. The boys looked at him, some in shock, some in confusion. and others in disgust and disbelief.

Dick turned to me, his face downcast and hurt. He had spent so much time with me, helping me, getting me through the tough times. Now he must have been thinking it was all for nothing.

"Brett?"

My mouth moved faster than my brain. I would say anything to protect us from this. "What? I don't know what disgusting shit is going on in his twisted, sick brain, but I'm no faggot. The thought makes me sick."

"You heard him, boys, get this piece of garbage out of our house," Dick said. They grabbed Bennie, carried him to the door and threw him out on his ass, him yelling obscenities about Jean-Paul and me the whole time. His voice faded to a dull, distant cry after the door was slammed. The boys slowly returned to their celebration, avoiding Jean-Paul and me completely.

Jean-Paul stood by his bench getting dressed without saying a word to anyone. I got dressed as quickly as I could, but saw him wiping away tears several times. I wanted so badly to go to him, to hold him through this. But I couldn't. *He thinks I betrayed him.*

As I made my way down the corridor, I saw Margret, Alistaire, and William waiting for me by the door to the back parking lot.

"Where is he?" I asked.

Margret slapped me full across the face as hard as she could.

"You bastard!"

"Margret," I said, my eyes screaming for forgiveness, but I realized he had told her.

I had betrayed more than the team, more than my friends and my new family. I had betrayed the heart, the beautifully opened heart of the man who held my love in his hands. The tears sprang from my eyes, knowing what I had done. My chest clenched, tortured with the terrible knowledge. I had ruined him. And I knew without hearing it, that I, maybe we, would never see him again.

Margret held her hand over her mouth, desperately trying not to say what she said next.

"He's gone."

CHAPTER SIXTY-EIGHT

I burst out into the parking lot, scanning the few remaining automobiles for any sight of him. The thick metal door clanged off the railing, sending vibrations and a boom into the emptiness. Dim lights from the few electric lamps scattered along the back row of the staff entrance of the Coliseum cast a pall across everything. In the greyness, smoke billowed up from the back end of a Chrysler Imperial, his Imperial, at the edge of the lot. It encircled the car, casting strange shadows as it crossed the beams of the headlights.

I ran to the car as fast as I could. Jean-Paul sat behind the wheel, gripping it with both white-knuckled hands. His face was a wet mess, his black hair having fallen in his eyes.

I stopped in front of him, caught in his headlights. I looked at him through more pain, sorrow, and agony than my heart could stand. I had been broken. Now I stood in front of him.

Somehow, with my focus on the man sitting in the car, I heard Mickey call out from the corner of the lot. "Hey, Brett. No."

I turned to face Mickey and his judgment, the scorn surely to come. "You...you don't understand, Mick." My voice came out as a silent whisper of a plea. A plea for support. For understanding.

With the quickest movement I had ever witnessed from him, Mickey crushed the sore muscles of my arm under his iron-fisted grasp. He pulled me toward him, close enough to taste the foul champagne on his breath.

"You can't. You. Can't. Do. This!"

"Please, Mickey. Please," I begged through eyes filled with tears.

"Brett," he said, pausing to look over his shoulder, back toward the doors. "Please, let this go. As your friend, let it go."

I turned my head back to the Imperial. "I have to, Mickey. Don't you understand? I...I love him."

Mickey loosened his grip on my arm, which dropped back to my side. I felt him step back away from me. With a sudden jump in my chest, my eyes locked on Jean-Paul, waiting. Waiting for a sign. Nothing else mattered. Not being discovered, losing hockey, my father's hate, my mother's indifference. None of it. All that mattered was that I had hurt him, failed him. I needed him to forgive me. To love me again.

Jean-Paul stared back, looking into me. Our gaze went on forever. We faced off, two lonely gunslingers in a dusty Old West town, waiting for the other to move a muscle. I couldn't force it. It had to be him. Then, almost imperceptibly, he relaxed his death grip on the wheel.

I ran to his door in three strides, flinging it open. I pulled him out of the car and held his shoulders in both hands so he had to look at me.

"I'm so sorry."

We stood there like that for what seemed an eternity. "I love you, Jean-Paul Moreau. Nothing else matters. I never should have…never should have denied it. I love you! I want everyone to know. I don't care about anything else."

I encircled him, hugging him to me, our bodies rocking back and forth. I squeezed him with all my strength, willing him to hug me back. It was as if by doing this, we would become one again. He stood limp against me, his tears streaking across my face, arms drooping at his side.

Somewhere behind me, I heard the metal bang of the door, people coming outside. I didn't care who saw.

"Please, just say you love me back. Please. Just say something. Forgive me. Love me."

He slid his arms slowly across my back, his hands pressing into me.

"*Mon petit.*"

A Note from the Author

A great deal of historical research went into writing *The Long Season*. Although there is no real connection to actual people, places, or events, I thought it might be interesting to know some of the amazing history of Chicago and its people, some version of which enter these pages. Some things are so remarkable that they would pale when turned to fiction anyway. It all started with a picture. I had this idea that came to me when someone gave me a copy of the *20th Century Hockey Chronicle* by Stan and Shirley Fischler and I first saw the team photo of the Kenora Thistles from 1907. The players are draped around the Stanley Cup, but also around each other, legs crossed over themselves, touching. It kind of seemed like one of them was not looking at the camera, but instead at another player. So I wondered, what if one of them were gay? That started me down the road to mix my interests in hockey, gay rights, Chicago, history, and the larger-than-life Roaring Twenties people like Al Capone, who makes a cameo, into a story. That picture shows up in a scene as well. So what did I learn about history, and what was used?

The 1920s, a vibrant decade fresh from the horrors of world war where Brett's fictional brother Michael served and died. Prohibition was the law of the land, which bred illegal speakeasies run by flashy but deadly gangsters. Chicago was home to a system of underground tunnels like the ones in the story, used to run hooch and help patrons escape raids that connected the real Aragon Ballroom, Green Mill, and Riviera Theatre in the Uptown area. The Green Mill was owned by a Capone man. Al sat in the same stool I placed him in so he could see both entrances at all times. The speakeasies were allowed to remain open due to well-placed bribery and payoffs. Mayor Dever, in real life as in my novel, tried to drum out booze trafficking to moderate success.

He was also able to straighten the Chicago River and build Wacker Drive.

Chicago had the first skyscraper. There was unprecedented growth, much of which went upward. A horrible train wreck rocked the city the day Brett arrived to town. This actually happened; a train carrying tourists rear-ended another coach and five people died and fifty were seriously injured. Cars like the Bugatti Torpedo Brett drives and Jean-Paul's Chrysler Imperial had grown in number and filled the streets, many of which did not have traffic control, and still had to compete with horses in some areas. As much as there's an appearance from the women of the Christian Temperance Union campaigning against the drink, there were suffragists fighting for equal voting rights. Many women, like Margret, cut their hair and dresses short and danced free as flappers. The male flappers were called Flaming Youth, and many of their archetypes make an appearance as well. Many people of the era were superstitious. The nation enjoyed fortune telling, Ouija boards, and séances. Harry Houdini spent a good deal of his time debunking clairvoyants like his real-life assistant Frank Kukol fictitiously does at a party Halloween night. Houdini died that day after a punch to the stomach he'd suffered days earlier, which we hear news of in the book. Much advance was being made in medicine, but Brett's nervous disorder, OCD, had yet to be explored. Many people with mental health issues were treated with drugs like the real life Nervine pills Brett used.

The '20s was a time of jazz. Real clubs like the Dreamland Café where Louis Armstrong played, and the Rainbo Room, which had a revolving stage so bands could be ready to swing into place to play so the music would never stop, were popular nightclubs. Since segregation was enforced, white bands entertained white customers. Sometimes black band members were allowed to perform, but black customers could not enter. The city's south side clubs grew in popularity in a section called The Stroll, where those same bands who played at the all white Uptown clubs and the performers from other ethnicities came together to play late into the night.

Something I discovered digging into the past was that gay clubs populated the Water Tower area of Chicago, which then was a Bohemian neighborhood known as Towertown. Real gay-friendly clubs, referred to as "Pansy Parlors," often hosted by drag performers, were well attended. The Dil Pickle club with its orange door and single green entry light actually had a sign that read *Step High, Stoop Low, Leave Your Dignity Outside*. The Bally Hoo Café on Halsted had female impersonation acts and cross-dressing clientele. An estimated thirty-five such clubs dotted the near north side. Other cities the players travel to in the novel had gay clubs as well. One factual popular performer named Gladys Bentley makes an appearance. She dressed in male drag in tuxedos and performed with backup dancers in drag at the Clam House. Due to laws and social mores against homosexuality, much political activity happened in private parties. The real Henry Gerber created the nation's earliest gay rights organization, named the Society for Human Rights, from Chicago in 1924. It was quickly disbanded due to open discrimination and poor treatment of any culture besides the mainstream. Political correctness, gay rights, and equal military and marriage access would be many decades away.

The game of hockey had changed much since the Roaring Twenties. I borrowed from history with the players Brett encounters, but their actions are pure fantasy. Team owner Major McLaughlin and his wife, model Irene Castle, were larger-than-life characters on the Chicago scene. A coffee empire allowed him extravagances like owning a hockey team. Her accomplishments as a dancer led to her being a fashion trendsetter. This, along with being married to the team owner, allowed her to design one of the most famous and beloved hockey jerseys of all time. Coach Pete Muldoon led the team to a dismal first season, unlike the one in my story, and when chastised by McLaughlin, famously "Irish" cursed the team to never win first place in the league, a position that eluded them for forty years. Captain Dick Irvin became one of the winningest coaches in hockey history in Montreal, leading great players like Maurice "The Rocket" Richard. The rest of the team, like Mickey MacKay, may have been nice people or may not have, but their personalities in the story are complete fiction, as is everything about them save the great tradition of hockey nicknames like Babe and The Wee Scotsman. Those, I'm afraid, actually happened.

The goalies in the book depict the real-life insanity of those athletes who faced frozen pucks without masks, wore thin pads, and had the same rattan-stuffed gloves the other players wore. Players also faced the dangers of high sticking, which was legal, and getting smashed into the chain link cages that circled the back of the net instead of the flexing glass of today. The players often stayed on the ice for the entire game instead of the fast line changes we see now. I have more line changes in the story than would actually have happened. Many hockey plays did not exist back then, like the slap shot and drop pass, which were invented by Bun and Bill Cook, as shown in the book. Nowadays everyone wants to drive a Zamboni. Back then, men with buckets of water and long brooms were the ice sweepers making the uneven surface. 1926–27 was the first time the Cup was solely contested by the NHL. A gift from Lord Stanley, it is considered today to be the most difficult trophy to win in all sports.

The Coliseum, its grand look and history, felt like a major character to me. Once a Civil War prison, it became the home of many teams, including hockey's Black Hawks, Cardinals, and Americans, as well as NBA basketball. It housed political events such as Republican National Conventions, and when alderman and "Boss" "Hinky Dink" Kenna staged parties there to raise money for the Democratic Party, it grew so large he called it a "lollapalooza," a term destined to be connected with the city. The Coliseum became a famous concert venue for acts like Jimi Hendrix and was the site of a riot caused by technical difficulties before a live closed circuit broadcast of a Muhammad Ali–Joe Frazier fight. Nothing remains except its namesake on a park across the street.

There are actual famous people in the novel like Marshall Field III, a publisher and heir to the Field fortune, who did not have a sister named Margret. Millionaire Robert Allerton, who met his alleged younger lover John Wyatt Gregg and adopted him in order to circumvent laws against same-sex marriage and inheritence, allegedly lent his name to the Allerton Hotel, although it might have no real connection. The hotel was the first building built with the newly designed setback to aid in stability. It also housed a known gay hangout in the forties on the top floor named the Tip Top Tap.

Brett's hometown of Delavan, Wisconsin, was a circus town to as many as twenty-six circuses during the mid to late 1800s, often used as a winter colony due to its pure water and open pastures, so important to supporting circus animals. P.T. Barnum Circus was founded there. In 1894, the last major troupe folded its tent, thus ending the era, leaving only a smattering of small outfits. This history is so rich, I had to extend it a few years so it could be backstory for Brett. I hope the giant clown and elephant statue in the center of town can forgive me.

Another major entertainment connection is found in Riverview Park and its many roller coasters like The Bobs, The Comet, and The Silver Flash. Brett also comes across Cubs Park, which was renamed prior to the 1927 season to the more famous chewing gum company name Wrigley Field. He also hears about a football team that played there, and it is true that the Bears played there for forty-nine years before moving to Soldier Field.

Chicago is steeped in rich history, architecture, famous people, inventors, World's Fairs, Ferris wheels, beautiful lakefront beaches, sports superstars, and political machines that I encourage you to read about. We claim hometown heroes Michael Jordan, Walter Payton, and Jonathan Toews. Sears/Willis and Hancock Towers provide goal posts to one of the most recognizable skylines in the world. Is there a better place about which to write a book? No. But I'm from here, so forget about it.

Thank you,

Michael Vance Gurley

About the Author

Michael Vance Gurley was born in a Chicago hospital that was quickly condemned and torn down. He grew up and worked in the shadow of Capone's house in a union hall, where he first discovered a love of gangsters and the Roaring Twenties. Being an avid hockey fan led him to kissing the Stanley Cup, and as an ardent traveler, he kissed the Blarney Stone, both of which are unsanitary and from which he's lucky to only have received the gift of gab. Michael has many literary interests and aspirations. He self-published *One Angry Koala*, a well-received comic book. His poetry has been printed in the Southern Illinois University newspaper, which was a real big deal back then.

Michael has worked with special needs children for nearly twenty years. His work with young adults led to a love of YA books, but he was raised with classic horror, beat poetry, and comics. As winner of a "Pitchapalooza" author event, Michael received some helpful guidance for his first novel, *The Long Season*, from literary agent/authors Arielle Eckstut and David Henry Sterry, and editor Jerry Wheeler. Michael still lives in the Chicagoland area, and despite it being clichéd, gets asked about gangsters whenever traveling abroad.

Books Available From Bold Strokes Books

Crimson Souls by William Holden. A scorned shadow demon brings a centuries-old vendetta to a bloody end as he assembles the last of the descendants of Harvard's Secret Court. (978-1-62639-628-9)

The Long Season by Michael Vance Gurley. When Brett Bennett enters the professional hockey world of 1926 Chicago, will he meet his match in either handsome goalie Jean-Paul or in the man who may destroy everything? (978-1-62639-655-5)

Triad Blood by 'Nathan Burgoine. Cheating tradition, Luc, Anders, and Curtis—vampire, demon, and wizard—form a bond to gain their freedom, but will surviving those they cheated be beyond their combined power? (978-1-62639-587-9)

Death Comes Darkly by David S. Pederson. Can dashing detective Heath Barrington solve the murder of an eccentric millionaire and find love with policeman Alan Keyes, who, despite his lust, harbors feelings of guilt and shame? (978-1-62639-625-8)

Men in Love: M/M Romance, edited by Jerry L. Wheeler. Love stories between men, from first blush to wedding bells and beyond. (978-1-62639-7361)

Slaves of Greenworld by David Holly. On the planet Greenworld, the amnesiac Dove must cope with intrigues, alien monsters, and a growing slave revolt, while reveling in homoerotic sexual intimacy with his own slave Raret. (978-1-62639-623-4)

Final Departure by Steve Pickens. What do you do when an unexpected body interrupts the worst day of your life? (978-1-62639-536-7)

Love on the Jersey Shore by Richard Natale. Two working-class cousins help one another navigate the choppy waters of sexual chemistry and true love. (978-1-62639-550-3)

Night Sweats by Tom Cardamone. These stories are as gripping as the hand on your throat. (978-1-62639-572-5)

Soul's Blood by Stephen Graham King. After receiving a summons from a love long past, Keene and his associates, Lexa-Blue and the sentient ship Maverick Heart, are plunged into turmoil on a planet poised for war. (978-1-62639-508-4)

Corpus Calvin by David Swatling. Cloverkist Inn may be haunted, but a ghost materializes from Jason Dekker's past, and Calvin's canine instinct kicks in to protect a young boy from mortal danger. (978-1-62639-428-5)

Brothers by Ralph Josiah Bardsley. Blood is thicker than water, but you can drown in either. Jamus Cork and Sean Malloy struggle against tradition to find love in the Irish enclave of South Boston. (978-1-62639-538-1)

Every Unworthy Thing by Jon Wilson. Gang wars, racial tensions, a kidnapped girl, and a lone PI! What could go wrong? (978-1-62639-514-5)

Puppet Boy by Christian Baines. Budding filmmaker Eric can't stop thinking about the handsome young actor that's transferred to his class. Could Julien be his muse? Even his first boyfriend? Or something far more sinister? (978-1-62639-510-7)

The Prophecy by Jerry Rabushka. Religion and revolution threaten to bring an ancient civilization to its knees...unless love does it first. (978-1-62639-440-7)

Lethal Elements by Joel Gomez-Dossi. When geologist Tom Burrell is hired to perform mineral studies in the Adirondack Mountains, he finds himself lost in the wilderness and being chased by a hired gun. (978-1-62639-368-4)

The Heart's Eternal Desire by David Holly. Sinister conspiracies threaten Seaton French and his lover, Dusty Marley, and only by tracking the source of the conspiracy can Seaton and Dusty hold true to the heart's eternal desire. (978-1-62639-412-4)

The Orion Mask by Greg Herren. After his father's death, Heath comes to Louisiana to meet his mother's family and learn the truth about her death—but some secrets can prove deadly. (978-1-62639-355-4)